Celestia
Origins Mark of the Prodigy

by
Noah Smith

Copyrights

Paperback ISBN: 978-1-964551-97-5

Contents

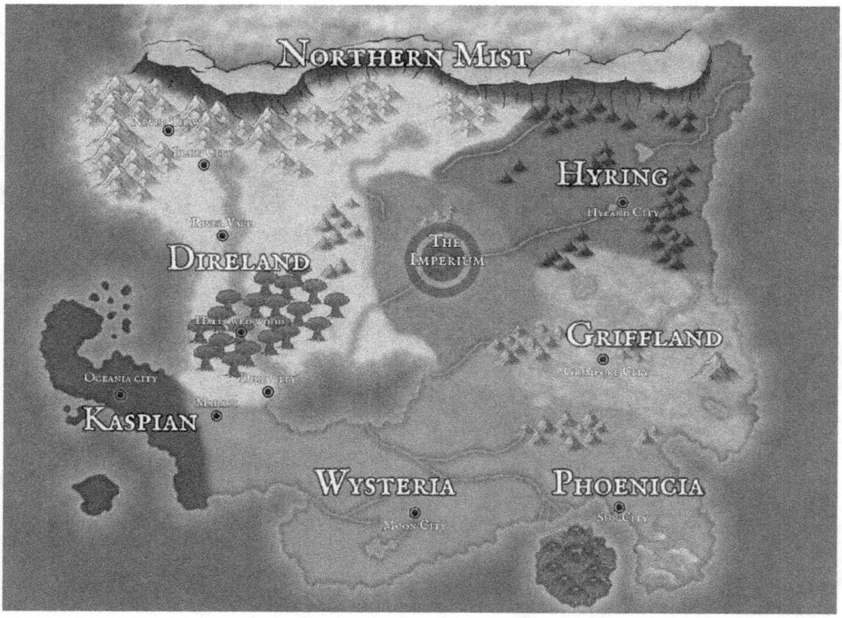

Northern Mist
Hyring
Hyland City
The Imperium
Direland
Griffland
Oceania city
Kaspian
Wysteria
Moon City
Phoenicia
Sun City

Wyrm

Kraken

Griffin

Hydra

Dire Bear

Phoenix

Chapter 1

In the beginning, before the creation of our world, before the creation of the heavens, before there was life and death, all of existence began with a simple seed. Eons passed, and little by little, this seed began to grow until eventually, it bloomed. And from this blossom arose a powerful and great being: the First Celestial.

Upon awakening, the Celestial looked about and saw that he was alone and became distraught. He did not want to be alone. So, he went and took the plant from which he had risen, and with it, he created many more seeds. Diligently and carefully, he nurtured these seeds, and in time, they all began to blossom. It was from these blossoms that the Celestials arose. Surrounded by his new brothers and sisters, the First Celestial rejoiced, for he was no longer alone.

But as time wore on, his joy began to fade away. For an endless void surrounded them. This emptiness distraught the First Celestial. So, he gathered together his brothers and his sisters and instructed them to go and help him fill this void with all manner of creations. And so they went and did as they were instructed, and they filled the void. They created the heavens, and within these heavens, they placed innumerable worlds and countless stars.

When they finished creating the heavens and, the worlds, and the stars, the Celestials returned to the First Celestial. The First Celestial then created another world, the greatest of all worlds—a world for them to dwell upon. Together, they descended down upon this world and they called it the Core.

As they lived out their lives here on this world, the Celestials soon began to seek a leader and a ruler who could lead and guide them. And the one they chose to become a leader and ruler over them was the First Celestial. Thus, the First Celestial became the Crowned Celestial. Together, on their new world with their new leader, the Celestials rejoiced; they lived happily.

But once again, as time wore on, the Crowned Celestial became distraught. For the world they dwelled upon was barren, as were the many other worlds. So again, the Crowned Celestial gathered together his brothers and his sisters and instructed them to go and fill the worlds with all manner of life and vegetation. And so the Celestials went and they filled the worlds with all manner of vegetation and waters. Then they created beasts and, fowls and, fishes, and all manner of life to inhabit these lands.

When they completed their work, the Celestials returned to the Core and together with the Crowned Celestial, they once again rejoiced and lived happily. Yet again, as time wore on, the Crowned Celestial became distraught. There was something missing. He wanted something more, but he didn't know what that something was.

For a long time, the Crowned Celestial sat and pondered on how to fill this void within his heart. At last, he found a solution. He gathered together all of the Celestials once more and again, he instructed them. He instructed them to go and to create a new form of life—an intelligent form of life modeled after themselves. And they called this new life humanity, and the Celestials went and scattered humanity across many of the worlds and gave them civilizations.

After all this, many of the Celestials returned home to the Core. But there were also many Celestials who stayed behind to rule over and guide the humanity they had created. And at last, the Crowned Celestial was able to live happily and content, for everything was perfect. Now, this creation of the heavens and, the worlds and, the stars, and everything therein would come to be known as Celestia.

Lily Alaric closed the book she was reading from. Her three small children lay asleep in bed together. She gently set a hand on her belly, where a fourth was on the way. As she watched her children sleep, she thought about the future of her family. They all lived together on a humble farm, and they were happy there. But something bothered her. Her eldest son, Adonai, was born with a sacred mark only heard of in legends. He was born with the mark of the prodigy. She was afraid that, because of their poor origins, her son would never reach his full potential. She watched her sweet babies a little longer, then left the room, gingerly closing the door behind her.

Later that night, Adonai was awakened by a strange light. Above the foot of his bed, a bright yellow shard hovered in the air. He looked to his younger siblings, but they remained fast asleep. He rubbed his eyes. For a while, he did nothing; he just watched the shard curiously. The light emanating from it had a warm glow that filled his entire body, making him feel safe and at ease.

As he continued to watch, the shard gradually grew brighter and brighter until it shone as if the sun itself was in the room. Yet, despite its brightness, it did not hurt the eyes to look at this shard. Adonai glanced again at his siblings; they were still fast asleep. Suddenly, overcome with the urge to touch the shard, he crawled to the end of the bed and reached out for it. But as he reached out, the shard vanished, leaving him there in the dark.

For a while, he sat in the dark, confused. He did not understand what the light had been. Though the light was gone, the warmth and the comfort that filled his body remained, as if the shard had never left. Through all of this, his siblings stayed fast asleep, and his parents remained unaware.

Still confused, Adonai climbed out of bed and searched the room for the shard, but he couldn't find anything. After his search proved fruitless, he tiredly crawled back into bed next to his brothers. He convinced himself it was probably just a dream. Closing his eyes, he fell back asleep.

Chapter 2

A man in a black cloak dashed through the Purple Swamp at a blistering pace. The Purple Swamp gets its name from the abundance of purple flowers, wisteria, that grew there. And it wasn't just the swamp filled with these purple flowers—it was like this across the entire nation, hence the nation's name, Wysteria. It was a new moon tonight, leaving everything in deep darkness. This had been planned, of course. They had waited for the darkest night of the month before finally making their move.

Though it was dark, the darkness didn't hinder the man as he traveled. He continued moving swiftly without losing his footing or stumbling once. He muttered curses as he went. He was running late. Being late was never a good thing, especially now. This was an important mission. The man cursed himself. Though he was able to move quickly through the marsh, it was taking longer than he had anticipated.

Finally, he arrived at the meeting place—the outskirts of a small village. There were four others, each dressed in the same attire as him: covered in complete black along with black masks to hide their faces. All of them except for one. The only difference between this person and the others was that his mask had a red numeral of five displayed across the face, marking him as the Fifth Descendant.

Though all five of these men were part of the same organization, none of them actually knew each other. Secrecy was of utmost importance. They never revealed their faces, nor their names, nor their voices, nor anything else that might hint at their true identities. Everything they wore was infused with mana. The masks changed their voices, the cloaks hid their smell and slightly adjusted their body figures, and the boots left no tracks.

"Greetings, Fifth Descendant," the man said upon his arrival.

"Brother . . . you are late," the Fifth said coldly.

"My sincerest apologies," the man replied.

The Fifth Descendant looked the man up and down as if deciding what to do with him. Then he spoke, "You . . . are forgiven."

The man bowed slightly. "Thank you—"

Suddenly, the world began to spin. The world spun round and round. The man, oddly, found himself falling. He hit the ground with a thud and found himself looking up at the night sky. The stars were beautiful tonight . . . but how had he found himself staring at them?

Something hit the ground beside him; he tried to look over to see what it was, but he couldn't turn his head. He tried to get up, but his body wasn't responding. A thick, warm liquid began to pool around his head, and a sharp pain throbbed in his neck. What was going on? He tried to speak but could form no words. That was when the man realized what had happened. His head had been removed from his body. He had been decapitated. He was dying.

The Fifth Descendant's sword had materialized in his hand, and he had cut off the man's head with a single strike faster than the blink of an eye. That was the penalty for being late. Only perfection must be allowed—nothing less. He wiped the blood from his blade. The others watched him clean his blade in silence. They felt only indifference. The death of their brother meant nothing to them.

"Our brother has been cleansed," the Fifth Descendant told the others. "May his spirit find rest with Inuuk and the Celestials." Then he turned away from the corpse and gave the order, "Let us begin."

The four cloaked men left the cover of the swamp and ran toward the small village. Two guards armed with spears patrolling the village took notice of them. One of the guards stepped forward and began to shout . . . but no sound left his mouth. He was dead in an instant, cut in half by a swift blade. The other guard suffered the same fate.

The Fifth Descendant snapped his fingers, and a raging ring of fire erupted around the entire village, forming a barrier that stopped anyone from escaping.

"How do we find him?" one of the cloaked men asked.

"Just cleanse the village," the Fifth Descendant instructed. "He'll come."

And so they began. One of the cloaked men channeled his mana; he reached up into the air as if to grab something and then pulled it down. With this motion, he created a sinkhole that swallowed a nearby house along with everyone in it.

Another cloaked man flew up into the air; the wind before him swirled violently until it formed a tornado. He unleashed this tornado, and it began to leave a path of destruction.

The third cloaked man reached down, then thrust his arms upwards, creating giant wooden tendrils that exploded up from the ground, tearing apart buildings and throwing debris.

The Fifth Descendant continued toward the center of town. With every wave of his hand, another building burst into flames. The ground shook, the wind raged, and the night was filled with the screams of those being cleansed.

A few villagers managed to escape the chaos and tried to flee, only to find themselves at the edge of the fire barrier. A few attempted to run through the wall of fire, but their bodies were instantly burned to a crisp.

More than half the village was destroyed before he finally emerged from hiding. An older man with graying hair confronted the Fifth Descendant in the center of the village. Despite his age, his body remained strong. The three cloaked men quickly arrived by the Fifth Descendant's side.

The Fifth waved them off and said, "Go finish the cleansing."

The three men in black darted away, and the Fifth Descendant turned his attention to the man before him.

"You're a hard man to find, Yir'on," the Fifth Descendant said.

"Apparently not hard enough," Yir'on grumbled.

"I hope you understand that our offer still stands. We value men like you. It's never too late to join hands."

"I'd rather die a thousand deaths before joining your vile cult," Yir'on spat.

The Fifth Descendant shrugged. "A pity, but oh, well. I can't say I'm disappointed. It's been a long time since I last fought a strong opponent. You're not going to disappoint me, are you?"

Yir'on's sword materialized in his hand. "I'm happy to fight you, but why don't we take this fight elsewhere? These are innocent people here—good people. There's no reason to kill them. Call your men off and leave the innocent alone."

"Innocence?" the Fifth Descendant laughed. "Such things don't matter. The only thing that matters in this world is strength. That is why we cleanse the weak."

Yir'on cursed him. Mana swelled within his body, and he began to emanate a bright green aura. The Fifth Descendant followed suit and emanated a red aura even brighter than Yir'on's. He raised his hand and shot a blazing fireball. Yir'on caught the fireball with his free hand. The speed and force pushed him back, but he remained firm in his stance. He threw the fireball back at the Fifth Descendant, who swatted it aside, sending it crashing into an already burning building.

The Fifth Descendant took a deep breath, trying to contain his joy. Then he and Yir'on dashed toward each other. Their movements were lightning-fast, swords clanging against each other in a violent frenzy. Yir'on jumped back and created a large wooden tendril that burst from the ground, landing on it. He raised his hand, and more wooden arms erupted from the earth around the Fifth Descendant, threatening to crush him.

The Fifth Descendant jumped up and gracefully landed atop one of the wooden tendrils, launching a fireball. Two of the wooden arms rushed to Yir'on's side and blocked the fireball. Four other wooden tendrils shot toward the Fifth Descendant. With a single strike, the Fifth Descendant cut down the wooden tendrils.

But Yir'on didn't stop his attack. Giant tendrils continued to burst from the ground, chasing the enemy as they attempted to squash him. The Fifth Descendant danced around, avoiding the attacks while cutting and burning the tendrils. They battled fiercely. By now, Yir'on had created dozens of giant wooden tendrils in an attempt to kill the Fifth Descendant.

The battlefield had turned into a complete mess. Then the Fifth Descendant jumped into the air and unleashed a massive wave of fire. The fire washed over and engulfed the entirety of the village, consuming everything and everyone.

Yir'on looked out at the desolation, and rage overtook him. He cursed sharply. "You dare! You dare to do such a thing!"

He charged wildly at the Fifth Descendant. Every strike of his blade shook the ground, forcing the Fifth Descendant to retreat. But then the other three black cloaks, who had been carrying out the cleansing, returned. They attacked Yir'on together, halting his assault on the Fifth Descendant.

A bolt of streamlined wind shot through Yir'on's shoulder. Then another wind bullet pierced his chest, followed by one through his leg. But Yir'on kept fighting, ignoring the wounds. He fought back against the four black cloaks, but there was only so much he could do alone. One of the men in black stabbed Yir'on in the back, but he still kept fighting. Then one of his arms was cut off. Still, he kept fighting. He lost an eye, a foot, his ribs were shattered, and his body burned to the bone. Yet, so long as his heart beat, Yir'on fought.

He finally struck down one of the black cloaks and then cut down another. Their blood stained his sword. A dozen giant wooden tendrils burst up from the ground and thrashed violently, but each of them was destroyed. Yir'on's body was beginning to fail him. He was tired, exhausted. He swung his sword one last time at the Fifth Descendant before collapsing to the ground, his aura fading.

Yir'on attempted to climb back to his feet and raise his sword once more, but the Fifth Descendant smote off his remaining arm. Yir'on fell back to the ground. He tried to curse him, but he couldn't even speak.

"A fitting end for scum like you," the Fifth Descendant spat. "You could have been a part of something greater, something glorious! But no! You had to go and side with the weak like a fool!"

The Fifth Descendant sighed. "But, I suppose there is no need to lament, for on this night, I shall cleanse you here."

He raised his sword and cut off Yir'on's head.

Chapter 3

The air was thin and cold this high up, and the rising sun had only just begun to peek over the horizon. A thick layer of snow covered the ground and trees, crunching beneath Adonai's feet as he climbed the mountain. The Dire Mountain range was filled with towering peaks that reached far above the clouds. Though Adonai spent a lot of time exploring the range, he had yet to summit any of these peaks. Even when he strengthened his body with as much mana as he could muster, he couldn't reach the mighty peaks. Every time he tried, the air would grow far too thin for him to breathe.

After climbing to the top of a cliff, he stuck his spear into the ground and took off his pack, setting it down. The top of the cliff he had just climbed put him above the clouds. He stood on the edge and looked out over the white sea that lay before him. In the distance, several other peaks broke past the clouds and continued on higher and higher. The Dire Mountains really were an amazing place. Even though he had seen this view many times before, it still amazed him.

Adonai sat down; it was time to do what he had come here to do. He crossed his legs and closed his eyes. He slowed his breathing until he was breathing only once every few minutes. In turn, his heartbeat also slowed. Mana condensed around him as he drew it in. He began to shift his focus, going deeper and deeper within himself until he felt his spirit.

Mana naturally flowed through and around everything—it was the basis of all life. The mana within the spirit specifically was incredibly dense and served as the foundation for those who pursued power. As Adonai concentrated on his spirit, he disrupted the natural flow of the mana and began to gather it within his spirit. The more mana he gathered, the more strenuous it became on his body and mind.

He continued to gather and condense the mana until his spirit was practically bursting. It was as if little tears were forming in the spirit. But as he continued to focus on his spirit, it began to stabilize. And as it stabilized, the little tears seemed to repair themselves, leaving the spirit stronger than before. This would happen again and again. Growing the spirit was like growing a muscle.

From there, he began to shift his focus from the spirit to the body. He gathered mana into himself. As he did, a sensation of power began to flow through his veins and circulate throughout his body. This was the body-strengthening stage, the most fundamental form of mana application. It was something he had already spent a great deal of time learning. By applying mana throughout the body, a person could exponentially increase their strength, motor skills, and cognitive abilities.

When Adonai had been climbing the mountain that morning, he had been circulating mana throughout his body the entire time, allowing him to climb and run much faster. He pulled in and circulated as much mana as he could muster. The influx of mana created a burning sensation throughout his entire body. The more he pulled in, the more the mana became chaotic. He continued to gather and gather the mana until he couldn't gather anymore. Then he held on, held on to the mana as tightly as he could, focusing on it, stabilizing it, controlling the chaotic mana. Gradually, it began to stabilize.

Once the mana consolidated within the spirit and body, he could move on to the next and final step: the formation of aura. By reaching out past the body to the mana that flowed through the air and gathering it around the body, the mana would manifest as a light that enveloped the body. The greater the control exerted over the mana, the brighter the aura would become, and the greater the quantity of mana gathered, the larger the aura would grow.

As of now, Adonai's aura was very faint, nothing more than a slight white glow. He continued to gather more and more mana and condense it around his body. But it was still too much for him. It burned. It hurt. Finally, he lost his concentration. The mana dispersed, and the faint white aura vanished.

Adonai took a deep breath; he was sweating profusely. When he opened his eyes, the sun was already setting. He had spent the entire day meditating, something that happened rather often. It was always hard to keep track of time when he meditated. He climbed to his feet, grabbed his spear and pack, and descended the mountain.

Never Thaw was a small village in Glacier Valley, deep in the Dire Mountain Range. Buildings were neatly arranged in a circle at the bottom of the valley. In the center of the circle stood a temple dedicated to the Celestials—a place for prayer and worship.

Adonai loved and was fascinated by the Celestials, and he often went to the temple to pray to them and worship. There were three heads of worship. The first and highest was the Crowned Celestial, the greatest of all living beings who stood above all else. Below the Crowned Celestial was Inuuk, the Celestial responsible for the creation of this world and its overseer. And below him were all the other Celestials.

The temple stood out among the small village; it was the largest building, and its white marble walls seemed to shine. Compared to it, the rest of the village looked old and run-down. This place had been Adonai's home all his life, and the nearby mountains were the furthest he had ever gone from the village. His family lived on a farm on the outskirts. It was near the end of winter, yet a thick blanket of snow still covered the ground and buildings. There was always snow here—after all, the town was called Never Thaw.

Adonai arrived back home just after dark.

"Adonai!" Maybel cried out when he walked through the door. She ran to him, jumped up, and hugged him.

Maybel was Adonai's youngest sibling at six years old. Unlike the rest of the family, she was blond.

"I missed you; you've been gone for this long." She jumped down and held out her arms, extending them as far apart as she could. "This long!" she repeated.

Adonai smiled and ruffled her hair. "Sorry, May May, I got distracted."

"That's what you say every time," she pouted.

"Because that's what happens every time," Adonai said with a smile.

Adin and Laor came over to greet him as well. Adin was eleven this year, and Laor was nine. Adonai and his brothers all shared the same dark-brown hair and hazel eyes.

"Did ya bring anything back?" Laor asked eagerly.

"Yeah! Yeah! What'd ya bring? What'd ya bring?" Maybel beamed.

"I brought back . . ." Adonai paused for effect. "Nothing."

Maybel frowned. "You're lying. You always bring something back."

Adonai laughed. "I can never get anything past you, can I? Here." He reached into his pack and took out a pouch.

Maybel snatched it and looked inside to see it filled with berries. "WE GOT HUCKLEBERRIES!" she cheered.

She and her two brothers all began helping themselves to the berries. Their mother, Lily, was sitting at the table knitting something, and their father, Adon, was by the hearth adding wood to the fire. Alaric was their family name, a name that had been passed down for generations.

"How was your trip this time?" Lily asked.

"It went well. Nothing much happened," Adonai told her as he put away his spear and pack. Then he suddenly remembered. "The festival is tonight, ain't it? Weren't you all gonna go?"

"Of course we're going; we were just waiting for you," Adon told him.

"Let's go, let's go!" Maybel cheered with a mouth full of berries.

They all left the farm together and walked over to town. Adonai's brothers joked around as they walked, and Adonai laughed with them.

Every year, a caravan arrived in Never Thaw near the end of winter. And every year, on the night before the caravan left, a festival was held. This year, when the caravan left, Adonai would be leaving with it. This was something every youth did after they turned fourteen. They would leave their home and go to the nation's capital, where the pantheon stood—a glorious temple. And once there, they would undergo their bonding rituals. Adonai was very excited for his ritual; it was something every youth looked forward to.

Most kids would travel to the capital with their parents. But there were a few who didn't have that luxury, like Adonai and his friends, so they traveled with the caravan instead.

The village was lively when Adonai and his family arrived. Stalls and booths lined the streets, musicians played music, and lanterns lit up the town. After spending some time walking around with his family, Adonai told his parents he was off to find his friends.

He went to the town's only inn, run by the Rolfes. The Rolfes' inn was probably the most popular spot in Never Thaw since there weren't many places to gather. The common room was filled with people drinking and chatting when Adonai arrived. A large fire crackled in a pit in the center of the room. A large green tapestry with the Dire Bear insignia hung on the wall to the right. Normally, the Rolfes children would be running around the common room playing, but tonight they were out enjoying the festival.

Adonai's three friends, Chaver Rolfe, Dahlia Greenfield, and Asher Smith, were seated at their usual table in the far corner.

Chaver was a little short, a bit chubby, and loved to talk. He often got himself in trouble for running his mouth more than he ought to. He was the oldest child in the Rolfe family and worked with his parents at the inn serving guests and sometimes helped with the finances.

Dahlia was a bit of a timid, quiet girl. She didn't interact with others often, but when she did, she was always very kind. She was incredibly pretty and was very close to Chaver—the two of them had a sort of unspoken relationship. Her family, the Greenfields, were herbologists, so she spent a lot of her time studying and experimenting with plants. When she wasn't working, she would often pass the time at the inn talking with Chaver—or rather, listening to him. Chaver talked a lot . . . a whole lot.

Asher was tall and well-built. His family ran the local blacksmith shop. He had been helping his father around the smithy ever since he was little. Just a couple of years ago, he became an official apprentice blacksmith working alongside his dad. His dream was to become a renowned blacksmith known across the entire world.

"Adonai! 'Bout time ya showed up!" Chaver shouted when he saw him.

"Sorry, Maybel just kept on begging me to stay," Adonai said as he sat down with them.

Asher and Dahlia were drinking a light beer, and Chaver was drinking ale as he usually did. Gabi, Chaver's mother, brought a glass of water over for Adonai.

"It's always a pleasure to have ya here," she said to him with a warm smile. The smile disappeared when she looked over at Chaver.

"And you . . . Don't you go makin' a fool of yourself tonight, punk."

Chaver raised his hands halfway. "Hey, come on, I never make a fool of myself."

Gabi stared daggers at him.

Chaver gave in to the pressure. "Okay, okay, I'll be good, I promise."

Her smile returned. "Good. You kids have a wonderful night." She turned and walked away to tend to her other guests.

Chaver grumbled something incoherent, then quickly looked around to make sure his mother didn't hear. Then he spoke to Adonai, "When are you gonna actually drink somethin' real rather than gettin' water all the time, ya poltroon?"

Adonai shrugged. "I prefer to stay sober," he said, taking a sip.

"You're crazy," Chaver said, shaking his head before taking a long swig from his mug.

A group of people wandered into the bar, talking loudly.

". . . I haven't seen a thief in years," one of the town's guards was saying. "It's so quiet here that sometimes I find myself wishin' for some punk to stir up trouble."

"Speaking of thieves," one of the traders, a big plump man dressed in thick wool, began, "I've heard that in the eastern territory, thieves and bandits have been running rampant these days."

"I've been hearing the same. It's quite bad over there," another trader added.

"Really? What about them military fellas? Shouldn't they be doin' somethin' 'bout it?" one of the men asked.

The plump trader shrugged. "They should, but for whatever reason, the control over the eastern territory seems to have fallen apart. They're havin' trouble keepin' everything in order."

"I've heard it's because the Pillar in charge of the eastern territory went missin'. What was his name again? Gabriel?" one of the female traders suggested.

"No, Gabriel is the southern territory's Pillar. Yir'on is the eastern territory's Pillar," a tall, thin man with a bushy mustache corrected. "I've also heard he went missing several months ago."

"Really? Nobody knows where he is?" the guard asked.

The tall trader nodded. "Nobody. And ever since his disappearance, the eastern territory has been in turmoil while the other Pillars scramble to cover for his absence."

"You think he's dead?" the plump man asked.

"Nonsense. Those Pillars are powerful men who live for hundreds of years; there's no way he'd die so easily," a townsfolk insisted.

Many nodded and muttered in agreement.

"No, there is a way . . ." the tall trader began. "I think this is the work of the Telestials."

That got mixed responses from everyone in the room, some in agreement and others in disagreement. At this point, everyone in the room had become fixated on the conversation. The topic of Telestials was a sensitive one.

"What exactly are you suggesting?" a trader who looked like the personification of average asked.

"What do you mean what am I suggesting? Everyone knows there is a deep hatred between the Telestials and us normal mortals," the tall trader asserted.

"True, but to go as far as killing a Pillar? There's just no way. The Keystone would never allow that. Even though he's a Telestial, he's very adamant about equality between mortals and Telestials," the female trader explained.

"Even so, there are many who hate and seek to destroy this equality. It's not as if the Keystone is all-powerful; surely there are situations he can't control," the plump trader insisted.

"But for them to kill a Pillar . . . I find it hard to believe. There's just no way," one of the townsfolk said.

Again, there was more muttering of agreement and disagreement as everyone was drawn into the conversation.

"If this is the work of the Telestials, doesn't that mean there's somethin' else goin' on? Somethin' bigger? Why would they go as far as killing a Pillar?" another person asked.

"Perhaps they're finally acting to overthrow the government," the tall trader suggested.

"Rubbish," the average trader asserted. "This is all nothin' more than rumors and speculations. There ain't nothin' deep goin' on. You're all just paranoid."

The tall trader shook his head. "It's the Telestials, I'm sure of it. If not them, then how could a Pillar go missing?"

The argument over Yir'on's disappearance continued as Adonai and his friends left the inn.

"What do y'all make of all that?" Chaver asked, answering himself before anyone else could. "I think it's true. All those Telestials are bad people. They think they're so much better than us just because they're part Celestial."

"Chaver, you've never even met a Telestial. What would you know?" Dahlia scolded him.

Chaver shrugged. "It's true, ain't it? None of you like the Telestials either."

"There are some bad Telestials, just like there are some bad mortals. Of course not all of 'em are good," Asher insisted.

"Yeah, whatever," Chaver said, dismissing the argument.

They didn't talk much about the Telestials or Yir'on's disappearance after that. After all, it had nothing to do with them. Instead, they walked through the streets, enjoying the festival and eating all kinds of treats.

When the night grew late, they went to the edge of town, where Harold, the storyteller, was getting ready to tell a story. In past years, his stories had always been one of the best parts of the festival, and many people would come to listen. Harold was old, probably the oldest person Adonai had ever seen. Nobody knew for sure just how old he was. Some speculated he was hundreds of years old, maybe even a thousand.

When Adonai and his friends reached the edge of town, a large group of people had already gathered in the field. Harold was standing beside a raging bonfire. Adonai and his friends pushed their way through the crowd to the front, where they sat down on the ground with the other kids.

After a short while, Harold motioned for everyone to quiet down, and they quickly did. Then he cleared his throat and began his story.

"Tonight, I will tell the tale of Ohad, the heir, and Yacova, the vile. Thousands of years ago, when the Celestial Inuuk still dwelt on our world, he had many children with mortal women, giving birth to the Telestials. And of his children, the two firstborn were twins, Ohad and Yacova.

Ohad and Yacova were both greatly favored by Inuuk; he truly loved them. He named them his heirs. They were to rule the world when he would eventually, inevitably, leave. When the day of Inuuk's departure came, the two brothers ruled together, and our world thrived. But Yacova . . . he envisioned something . . . different.

He envisioned a world—a perfect world. A world inhabited only by those he deemed worthy, a world of only Telestials and the chosen. So Yacova abandoned his position as co-ruler. Ohad begged him to stay, begged him not to go down this path of thorns. But Yacova would not listen. And just like that, he disappeared.

For a hundred years, there was no sign, no word, nor any manner of hint to Yacova's whereabouts. Some thought him dead, others believed he was alive and thriving, but no one knew for sure. And just when everyone began to forget about him, that was when they came.

They called themselves the Kin of Inuuk—an entire army consisting purely of Telestials with Yacova at their helm. They adopted the strong mortals into their ranks as the chosen, but those who did not submit, and those who were deemed weak . . . they were slaughtered. Hundreds . . . thousands . . . millions died.

Finally, Ohad led his people against the Kin of Inuuk in what would become the most dreadful battle. Mountains were upturned, valleys were buried, lightning fell like rain, and fire swept across the plains like an ocean. Many were wounded, many were killed—far too many to count. But in the end, Ohad rose victorious. The Kin of Inuuk were exterminated.

After the battle, both Ohad and Yacova suffered grievous injuries, injuries that Ohad would eventually succumb to. And as for Yacova . . . he disappeared without a trace.

After the war, the world was divided into six nations that dwelt in peace, and after hundreds and hundreds of years, the great Imperium was created—the fruit of all six nations. The first Keystone, the ruler of the Imperium and leader of the six nations, Urhad, the grandson of Ohad, was appointed.

Ever since, we have lived in peace. But there are rumors . . . rumors that Yacova lives. Rumors that he is hiding in the shadows, reviving the Kin of Inuuk, waiting for the day when he will finally return and create his perfect world.

But those are just rumors. Yacova is dead, and the Kin of Inuuk have long been forgotten, erased from history, only remembered by a few old geezers like me."

Harold clasped his hands as he finished his story with a big smile. "That's all," he told everyone.

With the story over, the crowd began to disperse.

"That's the first time I've heard that story," Chaver said as they left.

"First for me as well," Adonai added.

"How old do you think Harold is to know things like that?" Asher asked.

"Who knows? That guy's gotta be at least hundreds of years old," Chaver said.

"I've heard he's well over a thousand years old," Dahlia told them.

"You guys even think that story was real?" Asher asked the group.

"I don't know," Adonai said. "I've never heard of a Telestial named Yacova, nor the Kin of Inuuk. I have heard of Ohad, but there isn't much information about him. After all, he died thousands of years ago. In the end, it's just a story. It's all made up."

"Well, I think it's real," Chaver announced. "And I bet that those Kin of Inuuk will come crawling out from the shadows any day now and slaughter us all."

Dahlia elbowed him. "Don't go sayin' stupid stuff, you."

He just laughed. They walked around the festival a while longer before returning to their homes.

Chapter 4

The morning was cold. It was always cold. Though it was early, most of the town had gathered at the southern entrance, where the caravan was preparing to leave. Travelers made their last-minute preparations, and traders checked and double-checked to ensure all their goods were accounted for.

"Goodbye, Adonai. We love you," Lily said, giving him a big hug. "Stay safe out there," Adon added.

Maybel tugged at Adonai's coat sleeve with one hand and tiredly rubbed her eyes with the other. "You're leaving?" she asked innocently.

"Yeah, I'll be gone for a while."

"How long?"

Adonai held out his hands a moderate distance apart and said, "This long."

"That's too long," Maybel said sadly.

Adonai ruffled her hair, as he often did. "Don't be sad. You'll have Adin and Laor to play with."

"Yeah, you still got us," Adin repeated.

"All right, I gotta be going," Adonai said to his family.

They went through one more quick round of hugs before he left. He tossed his spear and pack into one of the wagons. Chaver, Asher, and Dahlia were huddled together near a different wagon, having already said goodbye to their families. Adonai went over and joined them.

"Nice of you to join us." Chaver yawned.

Even when he was tired, he still liked to run his mouth. He continued talking, "You guys excited? I am. I've never left the valley before. I guess none of us have. I can't wait to see what the rest of Direland looks like. I heard the Dire Woods is a forest with trees as tall as mountains. I'm also excited to finally get my bond. What about you guys? What do you think your bond will be? I think I'm going to get the Dire bear—"

"Chaver . . ." Dahlia interrupted him, covering his mouth with her hand. "We've talked about this before. When you have a conversation, you have to let other people speak as well. Besides, we're all too tired to deal with your yappin'."

Chaver grinned and spoke with her hand still over his mouth, "Right, my bad."

Emilio walked up to their group and threw his arms around Asher's and Adonai's shoulders. "Hey, hey. How are you all doing on this wonderful morning?"

"Good," Chaver said quickly. He was about to go on another rant, but then he stopped himself.

Emilio was tall, with broad shoulders and blond hair. He was one of the few guards of Never Thaw. He wore a green cloak with the Dire bear insignia, a uniform used throughout the nation of Direland. He was going to accompany the four of them to the capital and back, ensuring they returned safely.

"You guys excited to get your bonds?" Emilio asked.

"Heck yeah," Chaver said enthusiastically.

"What was it like when you received your bond?" Asher asked.

"It was great. It's like a whole new world opens up to you. You'll be able to sense and use mana on a whole other level, and you'll even gain an affinity for one of the elements, if not more. I grew a lot when I received my bond."

"What bond did you get?" Chaver asked.

"The Dire bear. With our heritage, you all will probably receive the Dire bear as well. Except for you, Adonai. Knowing you, you'll probably get two, maybe even three bonds. I'm excited to see how your ritual turns out," Emilio told him.

"I'm completely fine with just a Dire bear bond," Adonai admitted.

The caravan leader began to shout, "All set! All set! Let's get a move on!"

"Seems it's time for us to go," Emilio said.

21

They waved goodbye to their friends and families as the caravan set off.

After a day of traveling, they made it to the end of the valley. Now what lay before them were the Dire Plains—an ocean of grass as far as the eye could see. The ground was flat here, something unfamiliar to Adonai. Without the aid of trees or mountains, the wind was harsh. Only patches of snow dotted the ground rather than coating it entirely. Herds of bison and elk grazed across the fields. They had been traveling for several hours, with everything going smoothly.

Adonai had found the plains exciting when they first arrived, but he quickly grew tired of the monotonous landscape. Suddenly, a high-pitched screech sounded throughout the plains—a screech that made the blood run cold and hairs stand on end. It was the screech of a Dire hawk.

Adonai looked up into the sky, searching for the massive bird. He spotted it almost immediately. It was circling not far from the caravan. It was hunting.

In the past, he would sometimes hear the screech of a Dire hawk in the distance while in the mountains. But this time, he heard the screech so closely and clearly. It was one of the scariest things he had ever heard.

Most of those traveling in the caravan began to panic. Some dove onto the ground to try to hide in the grass, while others huddled close to the wagons. Adonai remained where he was and watched the Dire hawk.

"Adonai! What are you doing! Get down!" Chaver yelled at him from a few meters away, where he, Dahlia, and Asher were crouching down, trying to be as small as possible.

"What are you so worried about?" Adonai asked.

Chaver was baffled. "What are we so worried about? Have you lost your freaking mind? Did you not hear the screech? Of course, you heard it—heck, you're staring right at the bird this instant! Get down, ya shmuck!"

Adonai just waved him off. "There's nothin' to be afraid of. That Dire hawk ain't here for us—it's here for them."

He pointed to where a herd of bison had been grazing just moments ago. However, now they were running in every direction. "Why would a Dire hawk choose to eat one of us when there's much better prey right over there?"

Chaver seemed to relax a little after hearing that. He stood up and walked over to where Adonai was standing to watch the bird circle above; Dahlia and Asher also joined them. Some of the other travelers noticed them watching and seemed to relax a little as they understood the situation. The Dire hawk wasn't there for them; it was there for the bison.

Dire hawks lived high on the peaks of the Dire Mountain range, but they all came to the plains to hunt—a place with plenty of prey and no trees or obstacles to obscure the view, an easy hunting ground.

One of the panicked bison was running directly toward the caravan. There was another screech, and the Dire hawk shot toward the ground in a downward dive. It traveled so fast that there was a loud boom as it broke the sound barrier. With its talons raised, it slammed into the bison. Adonai could hear the loud crunching and snapping of bones all the way from where he stood. Blood sprayed from the bison, going as far as splashing against the wagons and people. Then, with a powerful flap of its wings, the Dire hawk launched back up into the air. And just like that, it was gone, carcass in tow.

The whole thing had happened in just a few seconds. Adonai had never seen anything like it.

Chaver muttered a curse.

Emilio came running over to the four of them shortly after the Dire hawk left.

"Are you all alright?" he asked worriedly.

"Yeah, we're good," Chaver said.

Emilio let out a sigh. "Good. That was crazy. I've never seen a Dire hawk before, much less seen one obliterating a bison like that."

"It was huge," Chaver added.

After everyone recovered from the fright, the caravan resumed moving forward. Everyone was either shaken up or excited from the experience.

"I've heard that some nobles keep Dire hawks as pets," Emilio said as they walked.

"Really? Do they ride them?" Chaver asked.

Emilio shook his head. "Sometimes, but they're usually far too wild to be used as mounts. It takes a great deal of time, money, and effort to train them into serving as a mount. So instead, they're mostly kept in cages as nothing more than eye candy. Kind of sad, really."

"That is sad," Dahlia agreed.

After the Dire hawk attack, nothing interesting happened as they crossed the Dire Plains, and the caravan made quick progress.

Chapter 5

William Hart stood in the midst of a field of ashes. The black dust swirled around his feet as the wind blew. Apparently, there had once been a town here. But looking at it now, no one would ever suspect that this place was once inhabited.

William was a tall and handsome young man. He wore a green uniform with the insignia of the Dire bear. A badge on his shoulder marked him as a Pillar. He was young for a Pillar, one of the youngest ever. He had risen quickly through the ranks, and by the time he was sixty, he had already earned the position of Pillar.

He nudged at some of the ash with his foot, as if doing so might unveil some kind of clue or message. Under normal circumstances, he would never even be here. He was in charge of the northern territory of the Direland nation. Where he was now was a small village surrounded by a swamp, located in the northwestern corner of the Wysteria nation, just below the Direland border. Apparently, the name of the small village was Madaul or something like that. There was nothing special about this small village, yet for some reason, in a single night, it was reduced to ashes.

The only reason William was there now was because of a rumor about a man who had supposedly been living there. The Imperial army had already conducted an investigation of the incident. It was concluded to be an accident—a stupid conclusion. That made William especially angry. Just one look and you could tell this was no accident, which led him to think that one of the higher-ups was covering up something important. However, the investigation did manage to turn up just a little bit of useful information. The only thing out of the ordinary in Madaul was the presence of an unknown stranger. The man stuck out like a sore thumb in the small village. He had the face and accent of someone who was from Direland.

It was the people from nearby villages who suggested that the stranger had something to do with Madaul's destruction. They noticed him when they came to the village to trade. They said there was an immense pressure around him. He was a big, old man who always hid his face with the hood of a cloak. The stranger had been determined to be in the village at the time of the incident and was pronounced dead.

However, this stranger, though the description was lacking, matched up with one of William's friends, his fellow Pillar, Yir'on. Several months ago, without a word, Yir'on had suddenly disappeared. William had been a little concerned about it but hadn't given it much thought. So when he heard these rumors about a man who resembled Yir'on in a small town in the middle of nowhere, he immediately looked into the case. After finding nothing useful, he decided to go to Madaul himself. That's how he ended up here now.

Looking around at the field of ash, William somewhat understood why the case was abandoned. There were no leads of any sort, no clues, nothing. He mumbled a few curses, then walked over to where his captain, Henry Allard, was sifting through the ash.

Henry was his second-in-command and his closest friend, so naturally, he had been brought along for the investigation.

"Found anything?" William asked.

"No. You?"

"Nothin'."

"Are you sure that the man was Yir'on?" Henry asked.

William shook his head. "I can't say I'm completely sure. But I want to look into it anyway. I just have a feeling . . . and if that really was Yir'on . . . then we may have stumbled upon something serious."

"You think the Telestials have something to do with this, don't you?" Henry asked.

William nodded. He was always very wary of the Telestials, always suspecting them of colluding against mortals like himself. It was only a matter of time until a war broke out.

Finally, William sighed. "I'm going to have to ask you to take this investigation upon yourself, Henry. I have duties as a Pillar that I can't stray away from, even more so with Yir'on's disappearance."

"I'll handle it," Henry told him confidently. "Do you have any thoughts about how I should proceed?"

"A little. Though Yir'on is only missing, I want you to treat this investigation as if he really was the strange man who had been sighted here. Turn over every stone, every twig; do whatever it takes. Find the truth. If it turns out he really wasn't the stranger residing in Madaul, then just drop the case and forget about it. But if it does turn out to be Yir'on . . . things will change."

Henry scratched at his chin. "We've probably gotten ourselves into something we shouldn't be meddling with, haven't we?"

William nodded. "This is probably a conspiracy that runs deeper than we could possibly imagine. And if they've taken action against Yir'on, a Pillar, it probably won't be long before they begin to take more drastic measures. Well then, I'm going to be off. I must return to Dire City. Good luck."

Henry watched as William rode away on his horse. He kicked at the ash some more, then mounted his own horse and left. First, he would visit the surrounding villages and inquire with the locals about the stranger to try to confirm whether or not it really was Yir'on who had been in Madaul.

Chapter 6

Plain City was the largest city in Direland's northern territory. However, the northern territory was mostly empty, so despite Plain City being the largest, it was still a relatively small city. But even though the city was small, its commerce was not. There was a huge harbor filled with giant trading vessels—glorious ships, some of them with as many as three masts and seven sails. The roads were worn from the constant coming and going of wagons, carts, and people.

The Dire Plains offered few resources, so there was a constant demand for all sorts of goods. And though most resources were lacking, that didn't mean that the Dire Plains were completely worthless. On the contrary, the plains were actually very valuable. Large deposits of direite could be found all over the plains—a precious metal capable of circulating and even amplifying mana, second only to adamantium. In addition to all of this, Plain City was built along the shores of Dire Lake, which connected to the Dire River. The Dire River was the largest river in all of Oalm Catantan. It ran down nearly the entirety of the Direland nation, starting at Dire Lake and going south, where it fed into the Dire Sea. And from the Dire Sea, three more rivers branched out: the Eastern Celestial River, which ran northeast across the continent, passing through the Imperium and ending in Celestial Lake in the nation of Hyring; the Southern River of Inuuk, which ran southeast through Wysteria and emptied into the ocean; and the third river, which ran east into the Western Griffland Mountain range. The constant need for supplies, the large deposits of direite, and the extensive river access all made Plain City a merchant's paradise.

The caravan arrived at the city after a week and a half of traveling; this was their first stop on the way to the capital.

"I'm going to an inn. I'm hungry," Chaver announced after they passed through the city gate.

Dahlia and Asher both agreed that it was a good idea.

"You guys go on ahead. I'm going to stop by the temple," Adonai told them.

"Really?" Chaver replied, somewhat surprised.

"Yeah, I want to take some time to pray."

Chaver shook his head. "Alright, whatever. I guess we'll see ya later then."

Chaver turned and began to look for a suitable place to eat; Dahlia and Asher followed him.

Adonai walked down the crowded streets toward the center of town, where a beautiful temple was erected in the middle of a large square. It was bigger than the one in Never Thaw, the workmanship was far better, and it was ornamented with direite. The silvery metal glistened in the sunlight and made the white building stand out even more.

Adonai walked up to the temple's entrance and pushed open one of the large doors. The noise of the town square faded as the door shut behind him, leaving him inside the silent hall. Sunlight streamed through stained windows and splashed across the floor, and candles cast a soft glow through the room. Incense burned, filling the main hall with a pleasing fragrance. There were several rows of pews with a few people scattered between them. At the front of the room was an altar made entirely of pure direite. Only a few townspeople sat in the pews, along with a few monks. Adonai walked up to the altar, knelt before it, and offered up a brief prayer to the Celestials. After that, he got up and left. Though he didn't spend long, he was satisfied with his visit to the temple; he felt it important to regularly offer up thanks to the Celestials, and it made him happy to do so.

When he left the temple, there was a large crowd gathered along the edge of the square. They were gathered around a wagon. Intrigued, Adonai joined the crowd to see what was going on. In the center of the crowd around the wagon were people dressed in white robes with the Imperial insignia displayed over their chests. They were helping old, sick, and injured people into the wagon.

"What is all this?" Adonai asked, talking to no one in particular.

A middle-aged man dressed in ragged clothes turned to look at him as if he were an idiot. Adonai just looked back at him with a puzzled expression. Then it seemed as if something clicked in the old man's head.

"Ah, you came from up north with the caravan, didn't ya?"

Adonai nodded, and the old man continued, "That explains why ya don't know. You northern folk never know anything. Those folks there, dressed in white, they're the Imperial Saints. They come around every so often and pick up the sick and afflicted and whatnot. Then they take 'em back to the Imperium, where they're given treatment and offered a better life."

"That's nice."

"Yes, it's very nice. Everyone loves the Imperial Saints. They do a lot to help us common folk out," the old man finished.

Adonai watched as more people in need were brought forward and helped into the wagon. The people were being crammed in really tight, leaving no spare room.

Finally, one of the Saints stepped forward and began to wave everyone off. "That's it! We're all full! Make way! Make way!"

The crowd slowly parted, and the wagon started off. Adonai's stomach grumbled as he watched it leave. It was time he went and found his friends—he was hungry. He made his way back through the streets to the northern side of town.

When he found his friends, he saw they were outside an inn. Chaver was having a shouting match with some blond kid who looked to be a little older than them. They were both furious.

"I'll hit ya so hard, snot will fly out your rear!" Chaver yelled.

The other kid yelled right back, "Then do it! Do it! I dare ya, you short clod!"

"You son of a—"

Adonai interrupted them. "What's goin' on?"

"This punk was tryin' to get handsy with Dahlia—"

The other boy slugged Chaver across the face while he was in the middle of talking. Adonai went to step in, but Chaver stopped him.

"No, no, no. Lemme handle this," Chaver said, wiping blood from his lip.

He lunged forward, throwing a heavy fist at the blond boy, hitting him across the face. Then Chaver began to bob and weave as the other boy threw punches at him. He hit the other boy with a heavy right, followed by a left hook, knocking the blond boy to the ground. Chaver spat on the back of his head. "Stay down, ya shmuck."

The blond boy spun around and screamed, "I'll kill you!"

He shot up, charged, and tackled Chaver. They crashed into the ground and rolled around trading blows. Finally, Chaver got the boy off him and scrambled back to his feet. The other kid scrambled back to his feet as well, muttering curses. They were both beaten up pretty good. The blond boy wiped some blood from his nose and spat on the ground. Then he pulled out a knife. He lunged for Chaver. But before he could close the distance, Adonai was between them. He grabbed the boy's wrist and twisted it, making him drop his knife.

"Peter!" an angry woman shouted and then stormed over to where they were all standing.

Peter's eyes filled with fear.

"Boy, you're really gonna get it this time. How many times have I got to tell ya to stop starting fights?" She grabbed Peter's arm and began to pull him away. "I'm sorry for any trouble my boy's caused," the woman said to Adonai's group. "Brat's bigger'n the other kids 'round here and thinks he can do whatever he wants. Come on, Peter, we're gonna go have a talk with your father about that knife you pulled today."

"I'm sorry, Mom. I'm sorry—"

The angry lady stormed off, pulling Peter along. Chaver smiled, watching them leave. "Serves that punk right. I hope he gets a real good whuppin'."

With the situation resolved, Adonai made his way into the inn.

"I'm hungry. I want food," he said as he walked past his friends. They followed him inside.

A few days later, it was early in the morning when the field just outside the south gate was filled with the noise of wagons being loaded. A few men stood in the midst of all the chaos shouting orders to the others as preparations were made.

It had been a few days now since the caravan first arrived at Plain City; now it was time to leave. Lots of new people were joining the caravan, while others were leaving.

Adonai and his friends were huddled next to a wagon as they waited for departure. As they stood there, two smaller boys, around the same age as them, approached.

"We heard one of you beat up Peter," one of the boys said.

Chaver smiled real big and declared proudly, "Yeah, that was me. Why? You friends of Peter? Ya lookin' for a fight?"

The two boys were grinning. "Absolutely not. We hate Peter. He's always pickin' on us and the other kids just because he's a little older and bigger than us. We couldn't be happier that he got beat up. My name's Roi, and this is my best friend, Ari," Roi said, gesturing to the other boy.

"Are you guys also going to the capital for your bonding rituals?" Ari asked.

"Yeah, we are," Chaver told them.

An older man dressed in the same guard's uniform as the ones from Never Thaw followed Roi and Ari over. Unlike the guards from Never Thaw, he had a sword at his hip rather than a spear.

"You boys doing alright?" the man asked.

"Yeah, we just made some new friends," Roi said.

That made the old man smile. "Good." He introduced himself to Adonai's group. "My name's Kadan. I'm the guard accompanying these boys to the capital. I hope they don't cause you too much trouble."

Chaver smiled. "Naw, they're fine. We look forward to traveling with y'all."

They continued chatting as preparations were made. After another hour or so, the caravan was finally ready, and they departed from Plain City. They traveled along the Dire Road going south. When night came, the caravan pulled off the road and formed a circle to set up camp. Chaver was telling some wild tale, making grand gestures while they sat around a fire and ate stew.

"Blind Bucky was the man's name," Chaver began. "He was more than two meters tall and could chop a tree down with a single swing of his axe. Like his name implies, he was blind, couldn't see a thing. Now, there was one day when he was walkin' through the woods, drinking a beer like he always did, when suddenly a Dire bear leapt out from the bushes and attacked him! Now, Blind Bucky might not be able to see, but that didn't stop him. That Dire bear had no idea what he'd gotten himself into. Blind Bucky strangled and mangled that bear with a single hand, all while he drank his beer with the other. And now they say that after that day, every time the name Blind Bucky is mentioned, a Dire bear somewhere falls over and croaks right there on the spot."

Chaver finished his story, and Asher shook his head. "You really do come up with the dumbest stuff, don't ya?"

Chaver was taken aback. "Dumb stuff? Lemme tell ya, that tale is one hundred and ten percent true. I seen it with my own eyes."

"Sure," Asher rolled his eyes.

Adonai finished his food and set down his bowl. "I'm gonna go out for a bit," he said, standing up.

"Go out? Go out to where?" Ari asked.

Chaver waved him off. "Don't bother, that guy just likes to go wander off on his own. He's a weirdo."

Ari still looked confused, but he let the matter go.

Adonai walked out into the dark, away from the camp, until it was quiet. Then he sat down and began to meditate. It had been a long time since he last meditated, and he was starting to feel like a divide was growing between him and the mana that flowed through the world.

This time, he didn't go through all the stages; instead, he focused entirely on strengthening his spirit. The spirit served as a foundation of sorts when working with mana. If one didn't have a strong spirit, it would be more difficult to use the mana within their body and far more difficult to use the mana that flowed outside the body.

Before long, the night faded away into morning. Adonai woke up from his meditation when the sunlight from the rising sun hit his eyes. Even though he had been up all night meditating, he didn't feel tired; instead, he felt rejuvenated—the effects from focusing on the spirit. If he had been gathering the mana within his body or the mana outside his body, he would be exhausted right now.

Adonai got up and rejoined his group to have breakfast. After that, the camp was broken down, and the caravan set off again.

Chapter 7

Henry walked through the streets of Dire City. It was the middle of the night. There weren't many people around at this time. He had only just returned. He had spent the past week going through all the villages near where Madaul had once stood, questioning nearly every person he came across. Most knew nothing, a few knew something, but even that something was practically nothing. The only thing worth mentioning was that he had managed to confirm the presence of a man who resembled Yir'on.

Henry cursed under his breath. This whole situation was so . . . troublesome. It could end up turning out that there was nothing of importance regarding this situation, and it was all a big waste of time and energy. But on the other hand, it could turn out to be something that would shake the foundation of the whole world. He prayed that it was the former, but his gut was telling him it was the latter. And so he carried on with this painstaking investigation.

Henry soon arrived at Yir'on's compound. Two men stood guard at the gate. He approached and greeted them, "Gentlemen."

"Captain Allard," the guards greeted him back.

"What brings you here at this late hour?" one of the guards asked.

"I need to enter."

"We can't allow that. Sir Yir'on is currently away and therefore not receiving guests."

"I know that, but—"

"No," the guard asserted.

Henry sighed and walked away. That went about how he expected it to go, but it was still disappointing. Yir'on's death hadn't been confirmed, nor was he officially declared missing. He should have been declared missing a long time ago at this point. But the Cornerstone Ramiah refused to acknowledge that Yir'on was missing, which was strange. So instead, Yir'on's status remained as absent, and the standard for the compound in such a situation was to deny entry unless authorized. And since Yir'on was missing, or more than likely dead, there was no way to receive authorization. Still, Henry had asked in the hope that they might let him in, but of course, he was denied. Now he was left with one option; all he could do was sneak in.

After he was out of the guards' sight, he slipped into an alley and scaled the building. He then leapt from roof to roof until he had circled around to the other side of the compound, away from the guards. From where he stood, he could see over the five-meter-high wall that surrounded Yir'on's compound. There was a good distance from Henry's roof to the compound wall. Most people wouldn't be able to make such a jump, but for Henry, this was a simple matter. He circulated mana through his legs and launched off the roof and over the wall, landing on the ground with a soft thud.

The inside of the compound was deserted. Normally, there would be more guards and servants. Instead, the compound was abandoned. He made his way to the front door of the mansion and pushed on it. It was unlocked and swung open. There was a layer of dust covering everything inside the house. Henry climbed the stairs and walked the halls until he found Yir'on's office. Again, the door was unlocked. When he opened the door and went inside, he found the room completely trashed. Shelves and cabinets were destroyed, and papers littered the ground. Someone had already come here—a bad sign.

Henry still searched through everything, but in the end, he found nothing. He muttered a curse. The possibility of something sinister being in the works just became real. The fact that the office had been searched already meant that Yir'on had likely discovered something he shouldn't have. And after that discovery, he went into hiding and then eventually died because of it.

Henry sat down, and for a while, he just stayed there in the room, trying to wrap his head around everything, trying to think of what to do next. He had no clue. There was clearly something going on— something that warranted the death of a Pillar. Henry got up and went through everything a second time and then a third. Still, he found nothing. Finally, he gave up and left. He needed to get some sleep; maybe that would help him figure something out.

The following morning, Henry was walking through the streets, trying to think through things: Yir'on going missing. A village reduced to ashes. Yir'on's home being ransacked. Ramiah refusing to declare him missing, preventing anyone from entering his compound. That was scary, to think that even Ramiah was somehow involved in all of this.

As Henry walked, he came across the Imperial Saints. He stopped and watched them load sick and afflicted people into the wagon. And then he remembered something—something that had completely slipped his mind. Yir'on never said where he was going nor what he was doing before he disappeared. However, what Henry just remembered was that Yir'on had a strange obsession with the Imperial Saints.

He approached the wagon to talk with the Saints. "Morning," he said.

"Good morning, sir. Is there something we can help you with?" one of the Saints asked.

"I was just watching you, and I was wondering if there was something I could do to help."

The Saint shook his head. "We thank you for the kind gesture, but we'll handle everything here. That is our duty."

Henry pressed further. "I understand that, but you see, I was just really interested in what you guys do. Perhaps I could accompany you on your journey back to the Imperium."

The Saint shook his head again. "I apologize, but we do not allow the interference of outsiders."

Henry nodded. "Okay, I understand."

He stepped back and then continued to watch them as they helped more people into the wagon until it was full and they rode off. He saw nothing wrong with the Saints—nothing suspicious nor strange. But he had no other leads, and he couldn't just give up. So he decided to do the only thing he could think to do, and that was to go directly to the church of the Imperial Saints in the Imperium.

Chapter 8

The sky was clear when the caravan arrived at River Vale. This city was bigger than Plain City. River Vale was home to the Twin Bridges. The Twin Bridges made up two of the three bridges that crossed the Dire River. The reason for the lack of bridges was that the river, like everything else in Direland, was massive. Normally, it was free to cross the bridges; however, because of Yir'on's absence, the Telestials had taken control of the city and begun charging a hefty toll to anyone who wanted to cross.

Adonai followed Emilio and Kadan into an inn along with his friends. Emilio arranged a few rooms for their group, and then they sat down to eat.

"You guys stay safe," Emilio was telling them. "This city is in the eastern territory. It's dangerous here."

After eating, Emilio and Kadan went to their room to settle down.

As soon as they were gone, Chaver said, "We should go to the river."

"Didn't Emilio just say it was dangerous out there?" Ari said timidly.

"Eh, we'll be fine. We got Adonai with us. He can protect us, ain't that right, Adonai?"

Adonai shrugged. "Sure."

Chaver jumped to his feet. "Then it's settled. Let's go." He began to leave. Adonai and everyone else, aside from Ari, also got up to follow.

"Wait, are you all really gonna leave just like that?"

Asher turned around and said, "That's just the way Chaver is. Besides, he's right. As long as we have Adonai with us, we'll be fine."

Ari hesitated but then followed the rest of the group. They left the inn and began to make their way to the Twin Bridges. There weren't many people out and about. There weren't even any guards. Everyone seemed to be staying inside, probably because of the increase in crime.

As Adonai walked, he saw two men arguing with each other. One of them was bald, and the other had long, flowing hair and an equally long beard. They were screaming in each other's faces when the bald man punched the hairy man, knocking him down. The hairy man quickly got back on his feet and drew his sword. At this point, Adonai and his friends had stopped to watch. The bald man drew his sword as well, and the two of them clashed, their swords clanging with every swing and strike.

"Should we do something?" Dahlia asked.

"Do something? What are we supposed to do?" Chaver said.

At this point, a few other people had also stopped to watch the fight. Nobody made a move to break it up. Then the hairy man drove his sword through the bald man's heart. He pulled it out, and the corpse slumped to the ground. The hairy man wiped his blade and then went on his way. With that, everyone else also went on their way, leaving the bloody body in the middle of the road. Nobody seemed to care that a person had just died. It made Adonai sick. That was his first time watching someone die. Everyone else in his group also seemed shaken up by the fight.

"Maybe we should just go back to the inn," Chaver said.

The others agreed; nobody really seemed to care about seeing a couple of bridges anymore. They walked back without talking much.

Along the way, a man in a brown cloak slipped out of an alley, blocked their path, and pulled out a dagger. The man had a twisted smile. Adonai went to the front of the group, putting himself between the man and his friends. Ari and Roi were terrified; everyone else seemed unfazed.

"You lot will fetch a nice price," the man snarled, licking his lips. "Just be good little kiddies, and I might let ya live."

This man wasn't particularly strong; Adonai could sense his mana—it was weak. He began circulating his own mana, and a faint white aura formed around his body. The man was taken aback. He had never expected any of them to be capable of forming an aura. But because they were just kids, he took courage.

"You might have an aura, boy, but you're still just that—a boy.

Stand down, and I might let you live."

Adonai didn't stand down; instead, he said, "Just leave us alone. We don't want any trouble."

The old man frowned. He was pissed. "As if I'd let a brat tell me what to do."

He jabbed with his dagger. Adonai caught the blade and ripped it from the man's grip. Then he struck him in the chest with the heel of his palm, knocking him to the ground.

"Yeah, get him!" Chaver cheered.

Adonai remained where he stood and watched as the man scrambled to his feet and disappeared back into the alley.

"You better run, ya punk!" Chaver shouted after him.

"Yeah, you better run!" Ari repeated.

"Come on, guys, let's get to the inn," Adonai said.

When they reached the inn, there was a crowd nearby surrounding a wagon. It was the Imperial Saints. Adonai was surprised to see them again so soon. Their wagon, just like last time, was crammed full of people.

"What's with the crowd?" Asher asked as they approached the inn.

"They're the Imperial Saints," Adonai explained. "They take people in need and bring them to the Imperium."

Chaver gave Adonai a confused look. "How do you know that?"

"I ran into them back at Plain City, and someone told me about 'em. Ari and Roi probably know about 'em as well."

Ari nodded. "Yeah, they show up every now and then to help people. Have you guys not seen them before?"

"No, we've never seen 'em in Never Thaw, probably because it's such a small town," Adonai told them.

"It's a surprise that you got to see them both in Plain City and here in River Vale; they don't come 'round that often," Roi said.

They watched the Imperial Saints for a minute before going inside the inn. Emilio was sitting at a table with Kadan.

"There you guys are," Emilio said when he saw them walk in.

"Where have you been?" Kadan asked. He seemed a bit worried, unlike Emilio, who was laid-back.

"We were gonna go to the river," Adonai told the two guards.

"Yeah, but then we watched somebody die along the way, so we decided to turn back," Chaver said nonchalantly.

"You watched somebody die?" Kadan repeated.

Chaver nodded. "Yeah, and then some other guy tried to kidnap us. Adonai beat him up, though."

Kadan was dumbfounded; he looked back at Emilio, who was laughing.

"How can you be laughing about this? They could have been hurt," Kadan demanded.

"Because you don't understand," Emilio told him.

"Don't understand? What don't I understand?"

Emilio smiled. "That Adonai is stronger than both you and me."

Kadan looked at Adonai, then back at Emilio. "But he hasn't even received his bond yet."

"I know, it's ridiculous. The kid is famous back in Never Thaw; everyone there knows about him. He's a prodigy."

Kadan looked back at Adonai. "You're really that strong?"

Adonai shrugged. "Yeah, I suppose."

Kadan ran a hand through his hair. "Alright, but next time, tell us when you're gonna wander off like that."

It was getting late, so everyone went up to their rooms. Adonai, Chaver, Asher, Ari, and Roi were all staying together in the same room.

"There are only two beds," Roi said when they walked in.

Chaver grinned. "Guess that means we'll fight for it—" He trailed off and looked over at Adonai.

"I'm fine sleeping on the floor," Adonai told them.

"Then we fight for 'em!" Chaver shouted.

Asher tackled Chaver as he ran for the bed, and then Ari and Roi dove on top of them. Adonai watched them fight for a while, then hopped in himself. At some point, the other four boys ended up teaming up and coming at him together. He still won in the end. Asher and Roi got the beds, and the rest of them slept on the floor. It was a good time. Adonai was glad to be here with his friends.

When morning came, the caravan was already preparing to leave. Unlike Plain City, River Vale was loosely controlled, and most of everyone was anxious to leave.

Adonai stood outside watching as the wagons were loaded. It was much warmer here than it was in Never Thaw. While it was pleasant, he found himself missing the cold, as well as the solitude he felt when up in the mountains. He missed home. But he was excited for his bonding ritual—so much that it made his homesickness a little more bearable.

After several minutes of watching the wagons being loaded, his friends arrived. Two new kids were with them.

"There you are!" Chaver exclaimed when he saw Adonai. "What are you doing over here all alone?"

Adonai shrugged. "Being alone . . ."

"Oh . . . okay. Can't argue with that. Anyway, this here is Daniel and Ariel." He gestured to the two new kids.

Daniel had a strong build; he wore nicer clothes than everyone else and had a sword at his hip. Ariel had long red hair and a fairly cute face, and she clung to Daniel's side.

"Daniel's training to be a knight," Asher said.

Daniel and Adonai shook hands. "Like Chaver said, my name's Adonai—Adonai Alaric."

"It's nice to meet ya. I'm Daniel Ortal. I'm the heir of the Ortal family, one of the few noble families without Telestial heritage," Daniel said proudly, then continued, "I hear you're quite strong. You and I will have to duel at some point."

"Sure, but I don't have a sword. I fight with a spear."

"That's fine. Your spear against my sword—it will be a good

fight."

Adonai smiled. "I look forward to it."

Daniel walked back next to Ariel and held her hand.

"You two seem close," Chaver said.

"We're engaged, actually," Ariel said with a smile.

"No way, already?" Chaver turned and looked at Dahlia with a big grin.

"No," she said bluntly.

Chaver frowned and then shrugged. "Had to try."

After a while longer, the caravan left.

Chapter 9

Direland was known for having excessively large landmarks. The Dire Mountains rose high above the clouds, the Dire River was so wide it was more like an elongated sea, the Dire Plains were vast, the Dire Sea was seemingly endless, and the Dire Woods were no exception.

When the woods first came into view, Adonai had thought they were a distant mountain range. They were not. The enormous hardwood trees stretched up and up. Their giant roots rose and fell from the ground, turning the forest floor into a labyrinth. The largest trees could reach up to fifty meters in width and were hundreds of meters tall. The wood was as strong as steel, making it a valuable commodity.

The road to the Dire Woods had been enjoyable. Just as Daniel had suggested, he and Adonai sparred during the nights when the caravan stopped to set up camp.

"I hope you can put up a good fight," Daniel had said before their first sparring session. "I've been training to become a knight my whole life, and one day, I'll rise through the ranks and become a Pillar," he gloated. "Don't worry, though. I'll be sure to go easy on ya so it's a fair fight."

Adonai grinned. "Thanks, but I don't think you'll need to go easy on me."

He wasn't really one for showing off, but it was still fun to do so every now and then. Lots of people were watching—not just their friends, but many other members of the caravan had become interested in the fight as well. Bets were made on who would win, with most people putting their money on Daniel. After all, Daniel was bigger than Adonai and had received formal training.

There was lots of noise as everyone placed their bets, but Chaver could be heard above it all: "Don't beat him too quick; make it entertaining!"

The crowd assumed Chaver was shouting to Daniel, but Dahlia and Asher both knew who he was really shouting to.

Daniel drew his sword and took up a fighting stance. "I'll let you make the first attack. I'm curious to see just how strong you really are."

Adonai still had a big grin on his face. "Fine by me."

He readied his spear, his eyes locked on Daniel. And then, he charged forward, making a half-hearted thrust, which Daniel easily blocked and then knocked Adonai back with his other hand.

"Ha! Don't tell me that's the best you've got! If so, I'd have to say I'm greatly disappointed!"

Adonai swung his spear, which was once again blocked. Daniel leapt forward, thrusting his sword, which Adonai dodged with minimal movement. But Daniel didn't stop there. He planted his foot and continued his attack by slashing at Adonai. Adonai blocked the attack, but then Daniel kicked him, knocking him back. He quickly regained his footing and tightened his grip on his spear.

"Come on! Give me more! Or is this the best you can offer? Please tell me you can do better!" Daniel jeered before striking again with a downward slash.

Adonai sidestepped it and whacked him in the head with the shaft of his spear, staggering him.

"You shouldn't talk so much," Adonai smirked.

Daniel quickly recovered and grinned. "That's more like it."

The two of them dashed at each other. Their weapons collided, and for a moment, they remained locked against each other. Both of them were smiling, thinking they had the other within their grasp. Adonai disengaged and then quickly reengaged, swinging and jabbing with his spear. Daniel blocked and dodged the attacks and then began to throw in some attacks of his own. The two clashed again and again. Each of their movements was swift and precise. The air rang with the clashing of steel, and sparks cast a faint glow across the two boys. They seemed to be evenly matched. But then, Adonai began to gradually increase the speed and strength of his attacks. He began to drive Daniel back. Finally, he whacked Daniel across the head with his spear. The strike hurt him. In an attempt to recover, Daniel immediately pivoted and swung his sword in a wild arc. Adonai ducked beneath it and then swiped Daniel's feet off the ground with a low spinning kick. Daniel lost his sword and crashed into the ground. Before he could recover, the tip of Adonai's spear stopped just before his neck.

Daniel smiled and let himself fall back, sprawling across the ground. "You bested me. It was a good fight."

Adonai lowered his spear. "Yeah, it was alright."

A few of the spectators cheered loudly, but most of the crowd groaned and complained when the fight was over. A lot of people lost their money, while the ones who won the bet could be heard gloating about their winnings.

Daniel climbed to his feet and picked up his sword. "Rematch?" he asked.

Adonai shrugged. "Sure, if you want to lose again."

"Ha! As if I'd lose to you twice in a row. This time, I'll bring ya to your knees."

Adonai smiled. "Bring me to my knees? My knees don't know the feeling of the ground."

Daniel smirked. "Then they'll come to learn that feeling."

The two fought again. Adonai's spear clashed against Daniel's sword. Again Daniel lost. And then he lost again and again. They fought late into the night. Many of the merchants and travelers from the caravan watched and cheered them on. The crowd's bets shifted from betting on who would win to whether or not Daniel could even land a blow. He couldn't.

After Daniel lost so many times, Gev, the guard who had accompanied Daniel and Ariel from River Vale, stepped forward.

"Why don't you let me give it a go? Surely you're not afraid of fighting a full-fledged soldier, are you?"

Adonai smiled. "Of course I'm not. But on the other hand, are you sure about fighting? I wouldn't want you to feel embarrassed after losing to a kid."

"Embarrassed? Ha! You have a lot of courage, boy. Don't think I'll be holding back, because I'm not. You might have been able to best Daniel, but you should know that me and him are on completely different levels."

Adonai twirled his spear in his hand. "Good. Then I won't have to hold back either."

Gev drew his sword and took a fighting stance, and then his aura ignited. A deep green aura enshrouded his body and cast a faint light across the small clearing they were in. The crowd marveled at his aura. Then Adonai did the same and ignited his aura as well. The pure white aura sparked surprise from everyone there. Most of all, Daniel was surprised as he learned just how far the gap between them was. Even among Telestials, being capable of forming an aura at such a young age was unheard of.

"Impressive," Gev complimented him. "Seems I underestimated you. But don't think you can win just because you can form an aura; decades of experience separate the two of us. I'll be sure to show you just what a difference that makes."

Adonai smiled as they held eye contact. Then he made the first move. All he did was dash past Gev. However, it happened so fast that Gev wasn't even able to react. He spun around, slashing his sword at nothing but air. He had assumed that Adonai was going to attack him from behind. Instead, Adonai stood back and watched with a grin as Gev frantically attempted to defend himself against an attack that never came. He didn't want to end the fight with a single attack. Instead, what he really wanted to do was send a message. And that message was heard loud and clear. Beads of sweat began to form on Gev's brow.

The crowd had fallen silent. Everyone was shocked by the stunning display of pure speed Adonai had presented to them. Gev tightened his grip on his sword and gulped. He couldn't allow a mere brat to humiliate him. He dashed forward and attacked. Their weapons clashed, and they both fought vigorously. Attack after attack. Gradually, Adonai gained the upper hand until finally he knocked Gev to the ground. His spear stopped just a short distance away from his neck, just like with Daniel. Then Adonai reached out a hand and helped Gev up. Both of them were out of breath.

"Never did I ever think I'd lose a fight to a boy who had yet to even receive his bond," Gev panted.

"It was a good fight," Adonai told him with a smile.

"It was," Gev agreed.

That was it for the fighting that night. Afterward, everyone went to bed to get some rest before continuing their journey on the morrow.

The road through the Dire Woods was surprisingly smooth. A path had been carved through the giant roots and trees long ago, creating a straight route through the woods. There was little light as they passed through; the massive Dire trees created a thick canopy that almost entirely blocked out the sun. All along the road, the ground was littered with the Dire nuts native to this land. Thick brush and foliage filled the gaps between the large Dire trees, making for a deep and luscious forest.

Hollowed Wood, also known as the city in the trees, was a city built deep in the Dire Woods along the Dire River and was the caravan's third stop. This city was unlike any place Adonai had ever seen. It wasn't like a traditional city. Most of it was carved directly into the giant Dire wood trees. High above, dozens of rope bridges ran back and forth from tree to tree. All sorts of buildings were built up in the branches, with giant nets sprawled beneath them. Floating lanterns hovered in the air everywhere you looked, illuminating the city. Dire hummers, birds that resembled giant hummingbirds, darted back and forth with people riding their backs. This city was deceptively large because not only did it spread outward, but it extended upward as well, adding multiple layers to the city.

In the center of the city was the stump of the first Dire tree to have ever fallen. It was said that the tree was chopped down by the Celestial Inuuk himself with nothing more than a wave of his hand. A glorious wooden temple was built atop this stump, and sunlight streamed down all around it through the opening the fallen tree had left.

Chaver muttered a curse and said, "This place is amazing."

Dahlia punched him on the shoulder. "Watch your language, punk," she said, though she was just as amazed by the city as he was.

"I'll go arrange a place for us at an inn. You guys can go and explore; just stay out of trouble. Come nightfall, go to the temple where we'll meet up," Emilio told them before wandering off.

Hollowed Wood was a safer city than River Vale, and the kids' group had grown larger with the addition of Daniel and Ariel. With

Adonai among them, Emilio wasn't concerned at all about them going off on their own.

"Where should we go first?" Asher asked.

"What do ya mean where do we go first? We go up," Chaver said, pointing to the branches.

Some of the trees had spiral staircases that wrapped around them and went up into the branches. They excitedly ran up the nearest staircase all the way to the top. Everything a normal city had could be found here in the branches. They explored the market and nibbled on pastries as they wandered. There was such an abundance of Dire nuts that the nuts were left all over the city for people to pick and eat as they pleased. Adonai lifted one up; it was the size of his head and quite hefty.

Daniel cracked one open. "Here, we can all eat some of this one," he said as he passed the contents around.

The nuts had a mild flavor. They weren't amazing, but when prepared properly, they made for delicious food.

"Hey, what's that place over there?" Adonai asked, pointing to a tree with a large castle that had arenas and fields built around it.

"That's Hollowed Academy," Daniel told him. "It's one of the seven grand academies."

"Huh . . . the seven grand academies?" Adonai said, confused.

"Yeah, each nation has a grand academy, as well as the Imperium. You didn't know that?"

"I'm from some tiny village way up north, deep in the mountains, that everybody forgets about. Of course I don't know about this stuff," Adonai said plainly.

Daniel laughed. "Alright, well, like I said, there are seven grand academies. Hollowed Academy is the grand academy of Direland. Wysteria has Moon Academy. Kaspian has Oceania Academy. Phoenicia has Sun Academy. Griffland has Grimlore Academy. Hyring has Hyland Academy. And lastly, the Imperium has the Imperial Academy. Then, of course, there are other smaller schools, but those pale in comparison to the grand academies."

"That's a lot," Chaver said.

"What do they do at the academies?" Asher asked.

"They teach all kinds of stuff, but their main purpose is to train soldiers—super soldiers."

Again, Adonai was confused. "Why train so many soldiers? I thought the world was at peace."

Daniel nodded. "It is, but it's a delicate peace. Each nation is constantly striving to increase its power to keep the others in check. And then, there's the difference between us mortals and the Telestials. I've overheard my dad talk about it a little. There's a sort of silent war waging between the Telestials and mortals. I don't know how much of that is true, though."

"It can't be that serious," Ariel said. "After all, the Keystone is a Telestial, and he keeps the peace."

"Yeah," Roi agreed.

Daniel shrugged. "That's just what I've heard."

They continued walking, with Chaver rambling on and on as they went. Eventually, it was beginning to get late, so they left for the temple to meet up with Emilio, Kadan, and Gev.

"Do you think you'll go to an academy?" Daniel asked Adonai as they descended one of the trees.

Adonai shook his head. "No, I don't think so. I'd rather just stay at my home in Never Thaw."

"That's too bad. But then again, I suppose someone like you doesn't really need an academy. You're already stupid strong," Daniel told Adonai, which made him grin.

"What about you? Do you plan to attend an academy?" Chaver asked.

"Yeah. I want to attend the Imperial Academy—the best of the best. I'm not sure if I can make it, though."

"I hope you can make it," Chaver told him.

Daniel smiled. "Me too."

They arrived at the temple, where they found their guards waiting for their arrival. Since they were at the temple, they all decided to offer up a quick prayer to the Celestials before leaving for the inn.

The night before the caravan left, a festival was held in Hollowed Wood, just like in Never Thaw. And again, like in Never Thaw, a large crowd gathered around a bonfire to hear Harold tell a story. The old man stood before the raging fire, waiting patiently as people arrived and settled down. After a while, he motioned for everyone to quiet down. A hush quickly fell over the crowd, and he began.

"Tonight, I will be telling a story. A story that I myself personally experienced. Tonight, I tell you the story of the Etzion expedition." He smiled to himself as he watched the reaction from those in the crowd.

"It seems many of you have heard of this expedition before. To those of you who haven't, allow me to enlighten you. The Etzion expedition was a mission to explore the treacherous Northern Mist. I'm sure many of you have heard rumors about the Northern Mist— sick, twisted, cruel rumors. I'm telling you, those rumors are true.

"This expedition would be both the first and the last. Etzion, the leader of the expedition, was a young, ambitious man of pure Telestial heritage. The team he assembled consisted of the rising generation's elite—all of them Telestials.

"Now I know what you're thinking: How could I have witnessed this tale personally? Well, I'll tell ya. You see, the team also needed someone to carry supplies—a porter. With a Telestial's pride, they would never stoop so low as to serve as a porter, so they hired mortals. Mortals like me.

"There were twenty of us in all—sixteen Telestials and four ordinary mortals, including me. We were in high spirits, filled with confidence and brimming with courage. We were proud; after all, we were doing what no man had done before.

"We entered the Northern Mist by the Western Hyring Strait. At first, the Mist seemed harmless. Though it was thick and made it hard to see, that was it and nothing more. We marched through without hesitation. We had no fear.

"The land we crossed was barren—no creatures in sight, nor a single plant. Things were going well, but then, at some point, when we were already deep within the Mist, it . . . changed.

"It did things to our minds. We became disoriented, losing our sense of direction; our minds became foggy to the point that it was nearly impossible to concentrate or focus. It threw our sanity into disarray. One man took his sword and killed himself on the spot. Some vomited; others curled up and cried. A couple ran off further into the Mist like madmen. Those men were never seen again.

"For what felt like days, we remained where we were, trying to get a grip. Eventually, our senses returned to some degree—enough for us to get a grip and try to figure out what to do next. At this point, there were only seventeen of us left. We tried to think of a solution, any solution. We argued over which direction to go.

"But what we had to do was inevitable. And that was to march. We didn't know if we were going in the right direction, but we had to do something, and so we marched. We marched and marched for who knows how long. It could have been a day, it could have been a week.

"Finally, we arrived at the edge of a forest. We were going in the wrong direction. We didn't know much, but what we did know was that there was no forest near the entrance. We should have turned back. We should have left. But Etzion . . . he had become determined not to return empty-handed. He had gone mad.

"He wanted us to enter the forest and press forward. One man objected. Etzion killed him. And so we entered the forest. It was teeming with life—incredible, magnificent life. Giant fireflies, bigger than your head, buzzed around. Elk with glowing antlers grazed, and all sorts of little critters scurried about. There were berries, fruits, and moss that glowed. It was fascinating.

"For a while, the forest seemed like a wonderful place . . . but it did not remain that way.

"One man went to pick one of the glowing fruits. What he grabbed instead was the bulb on the end of an antenna attached to an enormous toad. The toad opened its wide mouth and swallowed him whole. That made sixteen of us left.

"After a few more days—or hours, or who knows how long—of wandering the forest, the clicking began. Distant clicks. Click . . . click . . . click. It grew louder. Click, click. It grew faster. CLICK, CLICK, CLICK, CLICK. It began to come from every direction, still growing

faster   and   louder.   CLICK,   CLICK,   CLICK,
CLICKCLICKCLICKCLICK!

"A terrifying beast the size of a horse leapt out from the Mist, its claws as long as daggers. With a single swipe, a man who had once been whole now lay in two. Fifteen of us left. Another beast leapt out from the Mist—fourteen. Then another, and another. Ten. Seven.

"We were hopeless. Men were dying left and right. I fell to the ground and prayed to the Celestials with all my might. I begged Inuuk to spare my life.

"And then my prayer was answered.

"A blood-curdling roar ripped through the air. It made my blood run cold, it made me freeze in fear, it made me experience a terror unlike anything I had ever felt before. But I was not alone. The beasts that had been attacking us fled.

"I lay there on the ground, unable to bring myself to move. There were only two others left. The three of us were surrounded by blood and severed body parts. I don't know how long we lay there, but it was a long time.

"At last, we calmed a little, and the three of us got up. We had no clue where we were. We had no clue where to go.

"One of the survivors took up a sword and ended his life. That made two of us left. Me and the other man—I didn't know his name; he didn't know mine. We looked at each other with empty eyes. Then he turned around and wandered away. That man may have seemed alive, but he was already dead on the inside.

"Me, I still had some hope; after all, my prayer had been answered. I was alive.

"And so I set off on my own. I don't know how long I wandered. But by some miracle, I found my way out.

"I had escaped. I had survived the Northern Mist," Harold finished his story.

His eyes were glazed over and distant. He really looked as if he experienced those things. Who knows, maybe he did.

"The Northern Mist is scary," Ari said as they walked away from the fire.

"Eh, Harold's a storyteller. It's just a bunch of exaggerations and lies," Chaver said.

"I don't know, did you see his face? Seemed fairly real to me," Asher argued.

"That's just 'cause he's a good storyteller," Chaver insisted.

"What do you think, Adonai?" Dahlia asked.

He thought about it for a minute and then said, "I don't know."

"It's probably fake," Daniel said. "There are no records of anyone ever returning from the Northern Mist alive."

When they returned to the inn, the boys had another wrestling match to decide who got to sleep in the beds.

Once morning came, Adonai and his friends waited by the wagons as the caravan prepared to leave. Chaver was ranting about something. He had changed the subject like four times; Adonai wasn't even sure what he was talking about anymore.

Three new kids approached their group.

One of them called out, "Hey!"

Chaver stopped his rambling to turn his attention to her. "Hey, are you guys also going south for your bonding rituals?" Chaver asked.

"Yup. My name's KT. This here is Rachel, and this is Hyrum. We're triplets," KT proclaimed.

"Wow, I feel sorry for your parents," Chaver muttered.

"Huh—" KT began.

"Anyways," Chaver cut her off and changed the subject. "Were y'all there last night for Harold's story?"

"Yeah," KT started. "It was a good one. I've never heard that story before."

"Is there anyone else joining the caravan?" Dahlia asked.

"Nah, it's just us," Hyrum said. "Everyone else has already left for the capital."

"That's probably for the best. If there were a whole bunch of us, there'd end up being fights," Chaver said.

"Yeah, because of you," Dahlia added.

After a while longer, the caravan left. The next stop would be the last. The next stop was Dire City.

Chapter 10

The Imperium was a vast city. Buildings stretched out as far as the eye could see, and still, they went on even further. A great wall surrounded it all, and many more walls divided the city within. It was divided primarily into three sections.

The outer section was for the poor—it was where the commoners lived. Most of the outer section was covered in farmland, while the rest was filled with incredibly dense housing districts. The buildings were crammed together; some streets were so narrow that two people could hardly squeeze past each other. Tens of millions lived within the outer wall.

It wasn't all cramped, though. Walled compounds dotted the outer city, creating little bubbles that seemed like paradise compared to the surrounding city. These compounds were home to the barracks of lower-ranked soldiers, merchants, governors, judges, landlords, and anyone else who possessed high status.

The middle section held a far higher standard of living than the outer section. The streets were neither crowded nor filthy. Buildings were larger and more spread apart. Fortresses and watchtowers were spread throughout the middle section. The soldiers in the outer section only wore chain mail and carried steel-tipped spears, but the soldiers in the middle section wore half plate and were armed with swords. Expansive markets offered just about anything a person could want. As in the outer section, compounds dotted the middle section, where glorious mansions were built.

Last was the inner-most section. This part of the city was filled with castles, estates, citadels, manors, and villas. The soldiers here all wore full plate armor and wielded weapons of their choice. The inner section was home to the Keystone and the six Pillars of the Imperium, as well as other influential people and families, mostly Telestials. Only a few thousand lived in the inner section, unlike the millions in the other two sections.

At the center of the inner section was Celestial Lake. In the center of Celestial Lake, there was a small island where the grand pantheon stood. The Western Celestial River fed into the lake, and the Eastern

Celestial River flowed out. Thousands of canals branched from the rivers and lake, running throughout the three sections of the Imperium.

The construction of the Imperium began over a thousand years ago under the rule of the first Keystone, Urhad. All six nations—Phoenicia, Griffland, Hyring, Wysteria, Direland, and Kaspian—occupied the Imperium together in peace.

Henry found himself in the middle section of the Imperium. The Imperial Saints operated between four churches, one built in each cardinal direction. Henry was near the southern church, which was built within a compound, walled off from the rest of the city.

He had been questioning the locals about the Saints, but there was very little information known about them. It was said that to join the Saints, you didn't go to them; rather, they would come to you. Over the past few days, Henry had been lingering around the Saints' southern compound. Every time he saw one of the Imperial Saints, he raced to ask for permission to enter their church. He was turned down every time.

He questioned the guards around the compound, he questioned the locals—he did everything he could to obtain information about the Imperial Saints, but it availed him nothing.

After another day of tirelessly inquiring about the Saints, he retired to one of the local inns. He fell back on his bed, exhausted. This whole investigation was stressing him out. Perhaps this was the wrong direction. Perhaps the Imperial Saints had nothing to do with Yir'on, and all he was doing was wasting time. Perhaps the man thought to be Yir'on wasn't even Yir'on. Henry found himself questioning everything.

Down below him, he could hear the chatter and laughter of those in the inn's common room, drinking and gambling. When this was all over, he would love nothing more than to sit down and enjoy a drink.

While he was lying in bed, thinking things over, the noise from below died down. It wasn't until a few minutes passed that he noticed the silence. He looked out the window—even the street was empty. What was going on? Usually, this place was busy at all hours, but now there was no one.

A knock came at the door, and a chill ran down Henry's spine. He didn't know what was happening, but he had a bad feeling. A few seconds of silence passed. Then the door came flying in.

Two men dressed in black cloaks walked into the room, their faces covered by black masks. A pair of thugs? No, these men exuded a far more powerful presence than mere lowlife criminals.

"Who are you? What do you want?" Henry demanded.

He received no response. Swords materialized in the cloaked men's hands. Henry cursed and pulled his own sword from his interspatial ring, making it materialize in his hand. The two men in black began to emit black auras. A green aura ignited around Henry.

For a moment, the three stood facing each other. One of the men in black raised his hand, and a powerful blast of wind shot out of his palm. Henry tried to shield himself, but he was blown back against the wall. The other cloaked man dashed forward and crashed into Henry, breaking through the wall behind him and sending them tumbling to the ground.

In the fall, the two men dropped their swords. After hitting the ground, Henry pushed away and distanced himself from the cloaked man. His body was tense, his heart pounding. He looked around but saw no one else nearby; he was completely alone with these two strangers. The other cloaked man jumped down from the hole in the inn to join the others on the ground.

Henry tried speaking to them again. "Listen, I don't know who you guys are or what you want, but there's no need for us to fight. We can work something out."

Again, no response. One cloaked man picked up his sword, and together, the two began to approach Henry slowly.

They charged.

Henry conjured his mana, and wooden tentacles burst up from the ground. The tentacles lashed out at the approaching men, but they cut the wood down. More tentacles sprang up and wrapped around the cloaked men's ankles. One of them conjured his mana, and his body burst into flames. The wood withered away from the heat, and the flaming man attacked.

Henry weaved between the sword strikes. More elemental attacks ensued. Wooden tentacles continued to burst from the ground and thrash about. The flaming man launched fireballs, while the other cloaked man swung his sword, each slash sending a sharp blade of wind flying toward Henry.

As their battle raged, the surrounding city began to suffer. Buildings caught fire and crumbled, the ground tore apart. Henry, now without his sword, dodged what attacks he could and blocked others with his bare arms and hands. The three seemed to dance around each other.

Henry struck one of the cloaked men in the throat, crushing his windpipe. The other cloaked man, still encased in flames, struck with his sword. Henry caught the blade and ripped it from the man's grip. His hands and arms were bleeding; he was burnt and bruised, but he fought on.

The two men traded blows. The cloaked man on the ground gasped for air, his aura fading. Henry landed a heavy strike on the flaming man, then another, sending him stumbling to the ground. His fire went out, and his aura faded.

Henry stomped on the ground, and a wooden spike shot up through the man's abdomen, killing him. A second wooden spike impaled the other cloaked man, ending him as well.

Henry wiped some blood from his lip. The bodies of the cloaked men turned to ash, leaving nothing behind.

Throughout the whole ordeal, no guards had shown up. Everyone who had been in the immediate area had vanished before the fight began. None of it made sense. Henry cursed under his breath and slipped into the shadows.

Chapter 11

It was the beginning of summer when the caravan arrived at Dire City. It was far larger than any other city Adonai had seen so far. They passed through the north gate in the evening.

"Don't go making trouble, especially you, Chaver," Emilio told the kids when they arrived.

"C'mon, I never get into trouble," Chaver said with a smirk.

Emilio gave him a look, and his smirk disappeared. The main road that led to the middle of the city was wide and filled with all kinds of shops. Carriages and wagons went back and forth through the middle of the road, and lots of people walked along the edge. Every building had a green flag or banner with the insignia of the Dire bear hanging out front. Stalls and carts sat along the road selling practically every food imaginable, as well as other knick-knacks and such.

Adonai's group walked down the street to explore while Emilio and the other guards went to find an inn, just like they had in the other cities. With the addition of KT, Rachel, and Hyrum, the group now consisted of eleven.

"Look! They're sellin' strawberry tarts!" Rachel shouted excitedly, pointing to one of the stalls.

She ran up to the stall and pulled out some coppers to buy one. The store owner took the money and went to hand her one of the tarts.

"Here you are," he said with a smile.

But as the tart was being handed to her, a blond boy stepped forward and snatched it. "Thanks, cutie," he said while taking a bite and walking off.

Rachel was dumbfounded. Who did this punk think he was? "That was mine," she said angrily.

"Yeah, give us some coppers so we can buy a new one," Hyrum added.

The boy turned around and acted as if he thought it over for a second, then shook his head. "I don't know what you're talking about. I paid for this."

The blond boy reunited with two other boys who were snickering. The three of them looked about the same age as Adonai and the others. The three boys wore nice clothes, even nicer than what Daniel wore— and Daniel was a noble. That, and there was something else about them. Their presence felt different from other people. They were Telestials. Adonai was sure of it.

"Ha ha, very funny. Could you please just give us a few coppers?" KT asked, trying to keep her emotions in check.

"You all are best to just leave it be. Here, I'll even give you back your coppers," the stall owner told them.

Hyrum was starting to get angry. "No, he stole from us. It's him who owes us some coppers, not you——"

"Kid, that boy's a Telestial. You're better off lettin' it go." The stall owner was urging them to just let it go.

"Yeah, listen to him. He knows what he's talkin' about," the blond boy said smugly.

Chaver began to walk toward him with his fists clenched. "Give us——"

Hyrum stopped him. Then he marched forward himself and shoved the blond boy. "Give us back the tart, you clod."

The other two boys began to move forward, but the first stopped them. "If you want the tart so badly, then take it." He tossed it down at Hyrum's feet, where it splattered on the ground.

The three boys laughed as if it was the funniest thing they had ever seen. That was when Hyrum had enough. He slugged the blond boy across the face. The boy then immediately slugged him back much harder. Then one of the other boys shoved him to the ground. Chaver, Asher, and Daniel began to make a move, but Adonai stopped them.

"No, I'll handle this." He was pissed. Pissed that one of his friends had been hurt, pissed that one of his friends had been stolen from, pissed because of these snobs' lousy attitudes, who thought they were so high and mighty just because they were born as Telestials.

Adonai's friends didn't object when he said he would handle it himself. KT and Rachel helped Hyrum to his feet, then stepped back.

"I'll give you one last chance: give us the money you owe us," Adonai told them in a calm voice.

"You're bold for a mortal. I hate that. You mortals should remember your place. Get him," the blond boy snarled.

His two goons smiled and stepped forward. One of them reached out and grabbed Adonai by the shoulder. Then, in a lightning-fast motion, Adonai smacked the boy's arm away and struck him in the chest with an open palm, sending him sprawling backward. The other boy was startled, but he took courage. He charged at Adonai and attempted to tackle him. But as he threw his arms around him, Adonai didn't move a centimeter. It was like running into a brick wall. The goon fell backward after colliding with him. The blond boy was shocked, but his surprise turned to anger.

"You two are pathetic. Completely pathetic. I'll just handle this myself." The blond boy conjured a fireball. He had a wicked smile on his face, and then he threw it.

The fireball came speeding toward Adonai. Adonai caught it with one hand as if it were a pebble, then closed his fist and snuffed the fire out. Then he began walking toward the blond boy, stepping past the two goons who were recovering on the ground.

The boy began slowly backing away. "Stay—stay away from me. I'm warning you. I'm Ryn Ben Elram, the heir of the Elram family. If you harm me, then you'll regret it."

Ryn's two friends climbed to their feet and ran away. Ryn watched hopelessly as his goons left him. Then he turned back to Adonai. Adonai stopped and picked up the strawberry tart Ryn had thrown on the ground earlier. "If you wanted this so badly . . . you should have finished it."

He dashed forward and slammed the tart against Ryn's face, knocking him flat on his back. The boy gasped for air; tears welled up in his eyes. He climbed to his feet and ran away.

"Yeah! You run away, ya poltroon!" Chaver shouted after him. The others began hollering at him as well as he ran away.

The stall owner began laughing. "That was great. I've never seen a Telestial get humbled like that. That really was great. Here, have some tarts, all on me," the stall owner said with a big grin.

They all got a tart and ate them happily. Adonai and his friends walked around the city a little longer. After that, they went back and found the inn where the guards had arranged a place to stay. Chaver happily told Emilio and the other guards about the incident with Ryn.

Emilio just shook his head. "You guys really have a knack for gettin' into trouble, don't ya?"

"It's Chaver's fault," Asher said casually.

"Hey! What do ya mean it's my fault?"

"It is. It's always your fault." Adonai nodded in agreement; so did the others. Chaver looked to Dahlia for help, but she just shrugged.

"I'll have to have a talk with your parents when we return home," Emilio told Chaver. Chaver was baffled.

"That boy said he was an heir; do you think his family will try to do something to us?" Ari asked worriedly.

"Naw, it was just a fight between kids. Nothing will come of this," Andy assured them.

Andy was the guard who came with the triplets from Hollowed Wood. He was a bit small for a guard and had bright red hair.

"It's a shame," Hyrum started. "I would've liked to get a few more licks in," he complained.

"The only one getting beat woulda been you," KT said, making fun of him.

"Would not," Hyrum grumbled.

They continued talking for a while in the inn's common room. Later that night, the boys had their regular wrestling match to decide who got the beds. On the morrow, they would finally be undergoing their bonding rituals.

The bonding rituals. Sacred rituals that had been created and passed down by the Celestial Inuuk thousands of years ago. It was a practice that bound together the spirit of a human and a mana beast. Humans were naturally weak—born with nothing; it was only through sheer effort that anyone was able to develop significant power. On the other hand, there were creatures born with the innate ability to manipulate mana. These creatures were known as mana beasts. There were six mana beasts throughout the world, one native to each nation: Direland had the Dire bear, Phoenicia had the phoenix, Griffland the griffin, Hyring the hydra, Wysteria the wyrm, and Kaspian the kraken. Each mana beast also had an element they naturally aligned with: the Dire bear aligned with the wood element, the phoenix with fire, the griffin with air, the hydra with earth, the wyrm with metal, and the kraken with water.

The purpose of these bonding rituals was to bind together the spirits of a human and a mana beast. Through this ritual, a person's power could grow several times over. They gained a greater ability to detect and utilize mana, as well as an affinity for the corresponding element. Normally, a person only received a single bond. In rare cases, a person might receive two, and in very rare cases, they might receive three. However, just because a person could only have one bond didn't mean they couldn't use the other elements. Naturally, everyone had the potential to use every element, but without the aid of a bond, it was very difficult—nearly impossible for many. And, of course, there were other ways to utilize mana, the most common of which was enhancing the body, mind, and spirit.

Today, Adonai and his friends would be receiving their bonds. They rose early in the morning and made their way to the center of the city. A glorious temple known as a pantheon was built atop a hill and surrounded by a wall. A splendid garden circled it. Every capital had its own pantheon, and it was at these pantheons that the bonding rituals were held. These rituals could only be held in the pantheons. They were majestic buildings built under the rule of Inuuk and had been around far longer than the cities surrounding them.

Long ago, before Inuuk arrived, mana beasts dominated the world—countless mana beasts. So many that there was no room for humanity. Then Inuuk came. He slaughtered them. He killed the mana beasts in order to create a world where humanity could thrive. After he killed off most of the mana beasts, he created the pantheons. They became the holdfasts for the spirits of the mana beasts Inuuk had slaughtered. So now, countless spirits lay dormant within the pantheons, awaiting their destined humans to bond with.

Adonai and his friends arrived at the pantheon gates. Two soldiers dressed in full plate armor stood guard. Only one of them was allowed to enter at a time in order to maintain the quiet and sacred environment.

"Who should go first?" Chaver asked the group. Everyone was both excited and nervous.

"I'll go first," KT said at last. She walked through the gate, up the hill, and into the pantheon.

"What bond do you guys think she'll get?" Dahlia asked.

"Probably the Dire bear. Most of us will receive the Dire bear," Asher answered. People were more likely to receive the bond of their native land.

"What about you, Adonai? I bet you'll get more than one bond," Chaver said to him.

"I'm hoping to receive a couple," Adonai responded.

Chaver's expression turned sour. "Oi, look over there," he said, pointing across the courtyard. Ryn and his two friends from yesterday were walking toward the pantheon gate.

"Looks like they're here for their bonding rituals as well," Dahlia suggested.

Hyrum clenched his fists as he watched them approach. "Think they'll cause any trouble?" Ari asked.

The three boys walked with a haughty air about them. But when they got closer and saw Adonai, they seemed to shrink back. They stayed back, keeping their distance from the group while they waited for their turn to enter the pantheon.

"Ha! Look at those cowards! Walking like they're all high and mighty only to cower like babies!" Chaver exclaimed, loud enough for the Telestial boys to hear.

It was evident they were upset about it. One of them turned to say something, but Ryn stopped him. They wouldn't dare do anything with Adonai there. After a while longer, KT finally came back out and rejoined the group. She was very excited about receiving her bond.

"Which bond did you receive?" Rachel asked.

"Dire bear," KT said with a big grin.

After her went Ariel, then Rachel, Dahlia, Hyrum, Daniel, and so on. Among the eleven of them, Adonai went last. He walked up the stone path, admiring the garden around the pantheon. There were all sorts of flowers growing among cleanly shaped shrubs. The doors to the pantheon were massive and made of Dire wood. Adonai pushed open the heavy doors, which moved surprisingly smoothly.

The entrance opened up directly into the central chamber. He felt heavy; every step felt like a thousand; his mouth ran dry. He didn't think he would get this nervous. Sunlight streamed in from stained windows and splashed across the room. There was incense burning, which left a pleasant aroma that seemed to stir the mana within the body. In the center of the room was a giant statue of the Crowned Celestial. The statue held its hands out as if to receive those entering the pantheon. The statue was highly detailed, except for one piece. No one knew what the Crowned Celestial looked like, and it was deemed that no matter how hard they tried, they would never be able to create something worthy of the most high Celestial, so there was no face carved into the marble. Instead, it was left blank. Further back was another smaller statue of Celestial Inuuk. Several nameless statues lined the sides of the room, representing the countless other Celestials.

There were several monks in the central chamber, most of them bowing to the statues in meditation. One monk was waiting by the entrance; he was dressed in a simple brown robe.

"Come with me, young one," he said to Adonai as he entered.

The monk guided him across the chamber to a doorway at the back of the room and led him through a hallway until they stopped before two dark doors. The monk stepped to the side and gestured to the doors for Adonai to enter.

"May the Celestials look down upon you with favor," the monk told him.

Adonai pushed open the doors and walked into a dark room; the doors slammed shut behind him. Then a fire suddenly ignited and circled the perimeter of the room. In the center of the room was a shallow pool with water that rose up to his ankles. There were six statues built upon pedestals, each one modeled after one of the six mana beasts. The kraken, Dire bear, and wyrm were along the left side. The phoenix, griffin, and hydra were along the right. Each pedestal was engraved with the insignia of its respective mana beast. In the center of the pool, there were two more pedestals. Atop one was a small fountain that trickled down into the pool below; atop the other was a small dagger made of pure adamantium. At the back of the room was a statue of Inuuk with eyes that seemed to burn into Adonai's soul. Strangely, he knew what he was supposed to do, as if something were whispering in his ear, as if something were guiding him.

He walked to the center and picked up the dagger, then cut the palm of his hand. He held his hand over the fountain and let his blood drip into it. As he did so, the water from the fountain quickly turned a milk-white color, the same color as Adonai's aura. As the white water flowed down into the pool, the rest of the water also turned that milk-white color. Mana surged into the room. It was so intense that Adonai felt as if he were going to be crushed. Then everything went black, as if he had fallen into a void.

Darkness. Endless darkness. He was floating alone. Then seven figures appeared: the Dire bear, the kraken, the wyrm, the phoenix, the griffin, and the hydra—all six of the mana beasts stood before Adonai. But the seventh was strange. It didn't resemble any sort of creature; instead, it looked like some sort of shard. A soft yellow light emanated from it and filled Adonai's body with a pure warmth. It felt familiar, but he couldn't remember why.

The six mana beasts each lowered their heads and said in unison, "We pledge ourselves to you, young master." Then all seven figures disappeared, and Adonai was plunged back into the darkness alone. It felt as if he were falling into an abyss.

And then he heard another voice: "Prepare yourself, for you, and you alone, are the only one." And then it ended.

Adonai woke up lying down in the pool, staring up at the ceiling. The water was no longer milk-white but was clear instead, like it had originally been. He climbed to his feet. He felt . . . strange. He lifted his shirt and looked at his chest and abdomen. When a bond is received, the insignia of the corresponding mana beast is branded onto the chest over the heart. When he looked, he had eight.

The eight brands started at his heart and ran down the left side of his abdomen in a straight line. The first branding, the one that sat over his heart, was the mark of the prodigy—the branding he was born with. The next six brandings represented each of the six mana beasts. And then there was the last one, the eighth. He had no idea what the eighth insignia represented, but he could tell it was something important. It almost looked like a shard of sorts.

Adonai cursed under his breath. He had all six bonds and more.

When Adonai left the pantheon, there was a fight going on outside in the courtyard. Ryn and his two buddies were shouting at the boys from Adonai's group. But when Adonai joined their little circle, the yelling stopped. Hyrum had a bloody nose, and Chaver, Daniel, and Asher looked a little roughed up. The three Telestial boys were mostly fine, but it looked like someone had landed a pretty good hit because Ryn had a bloody lip.

"You guys are lucky this time," Ryn sneered, then turned and left for the pantheon gate, his two goons following.

"Yeah! You run away, ya bunch of poltroons!" Chaver yelled at them as they walked away.

"You guys alright?" Adonai asked.

"Yeah, we're fine. Those punks started spitting insults and getting up in our faces the moment you left," Chaver told him.

Asher threw an arm around Adonai's shoulder. "Enough about that; it was just a little squabble. Now, what bonds did you get?"

"Yeah, what'd you get?" KT repeated.

Adonai hesitated when he answered, "I—I got three," he lied.

"Three!" Chaver exclaimed. "Holy crap, you actually got three? You're not lying, are ya?"

"Of course not. I got three, I swear it."

Chaver cursed and then asked, "Which ones?"

"The wyrm, phoenix, and griffin," Adonai told them.

Everyone in the group was in admiration. They all had only received a single bond, most of which were the Dire bear bond, which was to be expected. The only one who received more than a Dire bear bond was Daniel, who received a Dire bear and a hydra bond.

"This calls for a celebration!" Chaver cheered.

They left the courtyard and returned to the inn, where they spent the rest of the day celebrating.

Chapter 12

Henry watched the Imperial Saints come and go from their compound from a nearby rooftop. He was wrapped in a tight cowl, hiding his face. It had been a couple of days since his encounter with those strange men in black. He still wasn't sure what to think of that situation. They came without warning and attacked for seemingly no reason. They even went as far as clearing the immediate area of any witnesses. They were dangerous. And when they died, their bodies turned to ash, leaving behind nothing, not even their clothing. There was no connection between those men in black and the Imperial Saints, but Henry couldn't shake the feeling that they were somehow connected. He could feel it deep in his gut.

There was also something strange Henry noticed as he watched the Saints come and go. He could have sworn he watched them bring in lots of sick and afflicted people; he was sure of it. But for some reason, he had no recollection of it. He couldn't remember how many people came in, and he couldn't remember if they left or not; it didn't really make sense. So finally, Henry came to the conclusion that he would sneak into the church. After making that conclusion, he sent a message to William with a mana note, telling him about the men in black cloaks who attacked him, his suspicions of them being connected to the Imperial Saints, and his plan to infiltrate the church.

Henry continued to watch the compound from the rooftop until nightfall. When the last of the sunlight faded behind the horizon, he acted. He leapt down from the roof and quickly scaled the compound wall. The church stood in the center of the courtyard; light could be seen flickering through many of the windows. The courtyard was empty. Henry dropped down from the wall and made his way over to the side of the church. He peeked through a window into an empty room. Quietly, he climbed inside. The room was mostly empty aside from a rack with a bunch of white robes hanging from it—the standard uniform of the Imperial Saints. He took off his cowl and put on one of the white robes, pulling the hood far over his head so that it hid his eyes.

The room led into a hallway. There was no one coming or going. Henry moved silently through the halls until he came upon the central chamber. It was a large room with high ceilings. There was a great big statue of Inuuk in the center of the room and several busts of Inuuk along the walls. There were a few other Saints scattered throughout the room, worshiping silently. None of them seemed to notice Henry, and if they did, they didn't acknowledge him, which meant that he was blending in.

He went across the room to the backside and entered another hallway, and from there, he descended down a spiral staircase. A long staircase. It just seemed to go deeper and deeper. Finally, he reached the bottom. A dimly lit hallway. He passed a thick metal door and tried to open it, but it was locked, so he continued further. He was about halfway down the hallway when two Saints came out of a door further down and began to walk toward him. Henry continued to casually walk through the hallway, trying to act as if he were a Saint as well and knew what he was doing.

The two Saints stopped and greeted him. "Brother? We weren't expecting another. Did you come here to assist in the ritual?"

In a panic, Henry responded with the first thing that came to mind. "Yes, I'm here to assist in the ritual."

"Very well. Even though we weren't expecting another, it's always helpful having an extra pair of hands; it's always bothersome when the scum struggle."

The two Saints continued walking in the direction of the staircase. As Henry followed them, he thought about what they said to him: *It was bothersome when the scum struggled?* What was that supposed to mean? They stopped before the thick metal door he had passed earlier. There was the clanking of metal as one of the Saints pulled out a set of keys and began sorting through it. He unlocked the door and opened it. As the door slowly creaked open, a smell so foul, so terrible, so horrifying struck Henry's nose. It was a smell of piss and crap and, most of all . . . death.

One of the Saints conjured a small flame to provide light and walked into the dark room. Cages—lines of big metal cages—filled the room. Cages filled with people. There was groaning and moaning. People begging for food, for water, for their families, for freedom . . . even for death.

"Shut it!" one of the Saints yelled. Immediately, a silence fell over the room. Except for one little girl.

"Water . . . please, I only want a bit of water," she begged. There were four people in that cage. Three of them sat against the far side of the cage; they already looked as if they were dying. The little girl was the only one by the cage door who looked somewhat alive. "Water . . ." she repeated.

The two Saints stopped, and Henry watched as they pulled the little girl out from the cage and threw her on the ground. They beat her and stomped on her. She screamed. They continued until the screaming stopped. Then they tossed the limp body back into the cage, locked the door, and continued. Henry couldn't even tell if the little girl was still alive.

"This one," one of the Saints said, pointing to an elderly man.

They opened up the cage and grabbed the man. The old man didn't put up a fight. He just let them take him, as if he had been waiting for this day. All the while, Henry watched on in horror. They left the cage room, locking the thick metal door behind them, and went further down the hallway. Henry continued to follow quietly. Then they entered another room. This room smelled terrible as well. There was a statue of Inuuk on the far wall and a pit in the center filled with ashes. The old man was tossed into the pit.

One of the Saints stood before the pit, raised his arms up, and began a chant. "Oh, may the great Inuuk hear our words! For on this day, we present thee with an offering! Oh, great Inuuk, we cleanse this man for thee! Let this man be cleansed of his sorry state and enter into thy care!"

The Saint threw down his arms, and the pit erupted into flames. Henry watched as the old man screamed and burned. What the heck did he just witness? And there was something else he noticed as well. There was something strange about the chant. It was more than just a meaningless phrase—it was like a spell. Whatever it was, it erased the old man's existence from the memory of those who knew him. Even Henry himself would have forgotten about the old man if he wasn't being burned alive right before him. It was cruel. Evil.

Finally, Henry couldn't hold back any longer. He was angry,

enraged. His sword materialized in his hand. The two Saints were taken aback.

"Brother, why do you have a sword?"

Henry didn't say anything as he raised his sword and cut down the closer of the two Saints. The other Saint looked on in horror.

"What . . . Why? Why did you do that? Who are you—"

Henry cut that man down as well. Then he tossed their corpses into the burning pit with the old man, who was already dead. As Henry left the room, his thoughts were racing. There were so many people here suffering. Is this what the Imperial Saints have been doing all along, killing the people they claimed to save? And they got away with it all by performing that chant. He had to help the people; he had to save them. But how? For now, that would have to wait. What he needed to do right now was contact William. William would know what to do.

Henry quickly ascended the spiral staircase and navigated his way through the church. He did his best to act natural, but he was in such a panic, it was hard to tell if he was doing a good job of that.

Thankfully, he was able to make it out of the church without any issue. But as he made his way across the courtyard, a man dropped from the sky and landed before him. A man dressed in a black cloak and black mask, just like those other two men from a few days ago. Only, this man's mask had the numeral three written in red across the face. Henry stopped and pulled out his sword again, and his green aura formed around him.

"Henry Allard, it's nice to meet you," the Third Descendant said.
"You . . . how do you know my name?"

"Oh, Henry . . . I know a lot more than just your name." The Third Descendant took a step closer. Henry tightened his grip on his sword.

"Come on now, Henry, just relax. There's no need for us to fight."

"Who are you, and why are you after me?" Henry demanded.

"I can't tell you who I am," the Third Descendant started. "As for why I'm after you . . . you should already know that. After all, you saw it, didn't you? But like I said, there's no need to fight. Rather than fight,

I want you to join us. You're powerful, and that makes you valuable."

"Join you?" Henry cursed. "I'll die before I join you."

"Tsk, tsk. Henry, Henry, Henry . . . you disappoint me. It's a shame, really. But, well . . . I'm sure we can work something out."

A sword materialized in the Third Descendant's hand, and a yellow aura formed around him. Henry charged, closing the distance between them in a fraction of a second. Sparks flew, and the sound of metal striking metal rang throughout the courtyard. Giant wooden spikes and tendrils shot up from the ground, attacking the Third Descendant. The Third Descendant flew upwards to avoid the attacks and then completely obliterated the wood with powerful blasts of wind, sending splinters flying.

Henry leapt into the air after him, and their swords clashed in a flurry of attacks. As the two fought, Henry noticed that there were several other men in identical black cloaks watching. The two separated; Henry fell back to the ground, breathing heavily, while the Third Descendant remained unfazed as he slowly lowered himself to the ground.

"The offer still stands. You can join us at any time," the Third Descendant told him again.

Henry spat a curse and dashed forward again, unleashing another flurry of attacks. Simultaneously, he kept trying to create wooden tentacles to aid in the attack, but every time, they were evaded or destroyed. He was simply outmatched. Suddenly, he was hit by a powerful gust of wind that knocked him off his feet, breaking several of his ribs.

The Third Descendant could have ended it there, but he didn't. Henry climbed back to his feet and coughed up some blood. He was angry. He mustered up as much mana as possible, and his aura flared. Giant wooden tentacles burst up from the ground, tearing apart the courtyard, and thrashed around. The Third Descendant flew up into the air, dodging the tentacles' attacks.

Another wooden tentacle formed under Henry, and he rode it up into the sky. The wooden tentacles continued to grow and chase the Third Descendant around, turning into a wicked tower of sorts. They continued their fight, their swords clashing against each other again and again as they also evaded elemental attacks. Henry was gradually inflicted with one wound after another while he himself failed to land a single blow.

Then the Third Descendant blinked forward and slashed off Henry's left arm. A blast of wind knocked Henry off the wooden tentacle he was riding, and he crashed into the ground. A powerful vortex created by the Third Descendant completely obliterated the wooden tower, sending chunks of wood flying in all directions.

Henry, barely conscious, summoned his Dire bear. The Dire bear's body materialized. It raised its head and roared as it prepared to attack. The Third Descendant instantly cut it down with a single stroke of his blade. Then he walked over to where Henry lay on the ground.

"Oh, Henry. You refused to join me, and now look at you—on death's door. It truly is a shame. But don't worry, you won't die here. There's actually something I've been wanting to experiment with."

Henry muttered a curse.

The Third Descendant laughed. "Curse me all you want; in the end, it means nothing." Then he stomped on Henry's head.

Chapter 13

A few days after completing their bonding rituals, Adonai and his group left the capital. There wasn't any reason for them to stick around any longer. And to be honest, everyone was eager to return home and see their friends and family to show off their bonds.

At the moment, they were hiking through the Dire Woods. Without the wagons of the caravan, they had to carry everything themselves, so Adonai walked with his pack and a spear in hand. Emilio and Kadan led the way, while Gev and Andy brought up the rear. Chaver was singing some sort of song that nobody paid any attention to.

"So, what do you guys plan to do after this? I mean, after returning home?" KT asked, trying to start up a conversation as they walked.

"I'm going to attend the Imperial Academy," Daniel proclaimed proudly.

"Really? No way!" KT exclaimed. "We were also planning on applying to the Imperial Academy."

"Why the Imperial Academy?" Chaver asked. "Why not go to the Hallowed Academy where you're from?"

"Because the Imperial Academy is for the best of the best. Of course we're going to aim for it rather than settle for something less," Rachel explained.

"What about you, Adonai? Are you also going to apply to an academy?" KT asked.

Adonai shook his head. "No, I'm going to stay in Never Thaw."

"What! But you have so much potential! Someone like you could easily rise to become a Pillar! How could you not go to an academy?" KT exclaimed.

Adonai shrugged. "I just want to stay in Never Thaw and live a quiet life."

KT shook her head. "You're an idiot."

Hyrum punched her on the shoulder. "Hey, come on now, don't

Celestia

go calling him an idiot. I'm sure he has a good reason for staying in Never Thaw," Hyrum said, then asked, "You do have a good reason to stay there, right?"

Adonai shrugged again. "Not really."

"Oh . . . so you are an idiot," Hyrum concluded, to which Adonai just smiled.

"What about everyone else?" KT asked.

"I'm going to become a blacksmith. The greatest blacksmith the world has ever seen," Asher declared.

"Pfft. Yeah right, someone with a Dire bear bond is going to become the greatest blacksmith ever. Be realistic; everyone knows that the best blacksmiths have a wyrm bond," Daniel said, making fun of Asher.

Asher just about punched him. "Just you wait and see, I'll show you."

"I'm also going to stay in Never Thaw," Chaver said.

"I as well," Dahlia added.

"So you're all just gonna stay in that little town up in the mountains?" KT asked.

"Yup, and we couldn't ask for more," Chaver said happily.

"We're also gonna stay in our hometown," Ari said, and Roi nodded in agreement.

"What about you, Ariel?" KT asked.

"I'm going to stay in River Vale and wait for Daniel to return from the Imperial Academy," she answered.

"Alright, let's set up camp here!" Emilio called out.

They pulled off the road into a small clearing and set camp. They all stayed up for a while, listening to Chaver tell some random story.

Later that night, as everyone was falling asleep, Adonai snuck away from the campsite. He didn't go far, just far enough that he felt a little more isolated. It had been a long time since he took the time to sit down and meditate, and he was excited to try it again now that he had received his bonds.

He sat down and began to draw mana in. He drew the mana in and in and in—it just kept on going. The amount of mana he could control and hold onto had grown exponentially. He filled his spirit until it was practically bursting. He let it recover and then filled it up with mana again, forcibly making it grow. He did this over and over until he couldn't bear it any longer. Then he repeated the process with his body. And it was incredible. He felt weightless, his senses became extraordinary, and his thinking became crystal clear—or rather, it was more than crystal clear.

He became more sensitive to the sounds and smells of the forest. And then he reached outward. He could feel the mana flowing all around him like it was a part of his own body. As he drew it in, he became enshrouded in a pure white aura that glowed several times brighter than it used to.

As he sat there meditating, it suddenly felt as if something within him had awakened.

"Hello?" a voice called out.

It came from within his own head.

"Hello?" Adonai repeated aloud, opening his eyes and looking around, only to see that he was alone.

"Master?" the voice questioned.

"Master? Who is this?"

"I—we are your bonds."

"My bonds? You mean the mana beasts from the bonding ritual?"

"Yes, that is us."

Adonai sat there quietly for a moment, trying to process the situation.

"How can you speak? I've never heard of bonds speaking before."

"That . . . is not something we can answer. We ourselves know very little." It was a different voice that spoke this time, probably one of the other bonds.

"So I can talk with all six of you?" Adonai asked.

"Yes."

Again, it was a different voice that answered this time.

Adonai had been speaking to them aloud this whole time; he wanted to try conversing with them through his mind as they were.

"Hello? Can you still hear me?" he asked.

"Yes, we can still hear you."

"Good, good. So I can talk with all six of you whenever I want. That's incredible. But what about that seventh thing? That strange orange shard that appeared during the bonding ritual—do you guys know what that is?" Adonai asked.

But his spirits didn't know anything either.

"We can sense it; it dwells within your spirit with the rest of us, but we don't know what it is. It seems to be dormant."

"Interesting . . . Well, I suppose, now that I can talk to all of you, I should give you all names, shouldn't I?"

"No. Don't give us names. That's a stupid idea," one of the voices said, which caught Adonai off guard.

"Oh . . . okay."

Then another voice spoke up. "Shut up, you stupid phoenix. Don't listen to him, Master, he's an idiot. We would love names."

That made him chuckle a little. He stopped talking through the mana link and began talking aloud again, as it felt more natural.

"Alright then. Starting with you, phoenix, your new name will be Arson. Then, Griffin, you will be Aeolian. Hydra will be Terra. Wyrm will be Ore. Dire bear will be Weald. And Kraken will be Brine. How's that?"

"Those are wonderful names. Thank you, Master," Aeolian told him.

Adonai stayed up the rest of the night talking with his bonds, telling them about his home, family, and friends. They listened to him curiously. Before long, sunlight began to stream through the forest canopy. With that, Adonai returned to camp. Nobody noticed he was gone that night. They ate breakfast and then continued their journey north.

The following night, Adonai sneaked away from camp while everyone else was asleep again. This time, he wanted to try manipulating the elements. He had never tried elemental control before and was curious to see what it would feel like.

He began with earth. He took up a firm stance. Manipulating the elements only required the mind, but incorporating certain movements helped provide greater power and control. It was like practicing a form of martial arts. Movements associated with earth, wood, and metal were generally firm and strong, while movements associated with water, fire, and air were generally more fluid and smooth but could also be sharp and rigid.

Adonai stomped on the ground, and a small boulder shot up from the earth near him. As the boulder reached its peak, he punched the air and sent it flying forward, where it crashed into a tree. He went through another series of movements and created more boulders, pillars, and spikes. The ground was fairly roughed up when he was finished.

Next, he moved on to the metal element. Manipulating metal, depending on the environment, could be more difficult than earth as it required a person to extract trace amounts of metal from the ground. Adonai went through another series of movements, and metal spikes shot up from the ground. Shards of metal floated into the air and darted back and forth.

After that, he manipulated wood. Large wooden tendrils and roots sprouted up from the ground and followed his movements. The wood could thrash around like a whip or shoot up from the ground in the form of solid spikes.

Fourth, he used water. He pulled moisture out from the ground and the atmosphere, accumulating large portions of it. He moved the water around, making it fly through the air in smooth motions, or froze it to launch sharp shards of ice or heavy chunks.

After that, he manipulated air. He created gusts of wind to move things around, including himself. Adonai attempted to muster up a gust of wind beneath himself. He slowly rose into the air before falling back to the ground. Flying was something he would have to work on. He compressed the wind to launch powerful blasts that left a heavy impact or altered its compression to make it flat like a blade. He launched one of these wind blades at a tree, cutting it in half.

Lastly, Adonai manipulated fire. But when he threw the first punch, launching a fireball, he noticed something strange. The fire he created was white. Normally, fire would be orange, yellow, or red. In some rare cases, there was blue fire. When a person was capable of creating blue fire, they were deemed a prodigy. But Adonai had just created white fire.

He conjured a flame in the palm of his hand and closely examined it. It was strange. He had never heard of white fire. He admired the white flame a little longer, unsure of what to think of it. He decided not to worry about it and practiced creating flames and unleashing blasts of fire.

Adonai continued cycling through the six elements for the rest of the night. When the sun began to rise, he returned to camp before anyone had awakened.

Chapter 14

After a few days, Adonai's group arrived at the southern end of Hallowed Wood. The city was even more amazing than Adonai remembered. He was fascinated by the fact that the city was carved directly into the trees. They stayed in the city for a couple of days, resting and recuperating. Then they parted ways with the triplets—KT, Rachel, and Hyrum—as well as their guard, Andy. It was kind of sad leaving them; they would probably never meet again. Then they continued their trek north. There was still a long way to go before they reached Never Thaw in Glacier Valley.

After traveling all day, Emilio stopped and called out, "Let's stop here!"

They pulled a short way off the road and set up camp in the nook of a large root. Everyone sat around a fire, eating.

"I'm gonna go take a leak," Kadan announced and then walked off.

"Don't go too far!" Emilio called after him. Kadan just waved him off and kept going.

"Idiot," Emilio muttered.

Gev laughed. "You worry too much, Emilio. He'll be fine."

"It's dangerous out here. There are monsters and bandits, and it's easy to get lost."

Gev laughed again and handed a cup of booze to Emilio. "You need to loosen up a bit. Have a drink or two; it'll take the edge off."

Emilio grumbled, but he still took the booze. Daniel finished his food, jumped up, and started stretching.

"Hey, Adonai, why don't you and I do a little bit of sparring? I've been itching to fight ever since we got our bonds."

Adonai swallowed a mouthful of food and said, "Sure. But try to go easy on me. I'm tired."

He began to get up, but then there was a scream, and the scream ended just as abruptly as it came. Emilio and Gev shot up and readied their weapons.

"That was Kadan . . ." Gev mouthed.

Emilio muttered a curse. "Everyone, gather your things together and stay close to the fire. Be ready to run."

Adonai grabbed his spear; Daniel grabbed his sword. A large silhouette appeared on the edge of the camp. A dire bear. It was massive. Blood dripped from its mouth, probably the blood of Kadan.

"Run!" Emilio shouted to the kids. "Get back to the road!"

Adonai jumped forward to confront the dire bear with the guards.

Emilio stopped him. "No! You get out of here! You have to make sure everyone gets out okay!"

"But I can help—"

"No! We'll handle this! You need to run!"

Adonai gritted his teeth. He didn't know if he could take the dire bear, but he did know he had a better shot at taking it down than anyone else. But he listened to Emilio.

"Come on! Get to the road!" Adonai shouted.

They ran away, and he brought up the rear, leaving Emilio and Gev alone with the beast. The dire bear reared back on its hind legs and roared. Adonai ran without looking back. As they ran away, he heard the screams of the two guards. Tears welled up in his eyes, and he muttered a curse. He cursed himself. He should have stayed. He could have helped. Why did he listen to Emilio and run? He should have been the one to stay and fight the mana beast; maybe then the two guards would still be alive. He wiped away tears as he ran. It was too late to regret his choice. All he could do now was make sure his friends survived. Everyone made it to the road, and they continued running north as fast as they could. Adonai remained at the rear to ensure that nobody was left behind.

"Do . . . do you guys think we're safe?" Chaver huffed. They had been running nearly all night.

"I think we're okay," Adonai told them.

Everyone let out a sigh of relief. Chaver sat down on the ground, and Dahlia sat down with him. They were all tired.

"Do you think they're okay, Emilio and Gev?" Ari fretted.

There was a long silence. A heavy silence.

"I . . . I don't think we'll be seeing them again," Adonai said quietly.

Most of them were either holding back tears or crying. They were all worried and afraid. Adonai tried to cheer them up, at least a little. "But they might make it," he said. "In fact, they probably will make it. They've probably already defeated the dire bear and are on their way here right now. We'll just wait here until they catch up."

And so they waited. They huddled together on the edge of the road and waited all through the night. Nobody slept; none of them even tried. They made camp and then waited for another day. During it all, they got little sleep and ate little food.

"We . . . we should continue north," Adonai said at last.

"But what about Emilio and Gev?" Ari whined.

". . . I don't think we're going to see them again."

"I'm scared," Roi muttered.

They didn't have anyone to guide them anymore. They were just a bunch of kids, all alone. Chaver hopped up to his feet and tried to cheer everyone up.

"Come on, guys, it's not all bad. This will be like an adventure!"

Nobody seemed to buy in.

"We should get moving; we have a long way to go," Adonai told them. He took the lead, and the others followed.

Later, further up the central road . . .

"Oi, guys, look," Natan said, nudging Yakir and pointing to a group walking down the road.

Liad rubbed his eyes and then looked again, and a twisted smile spread across his face. "It's just a bunch of kids. Easy pickings."

"How much you reckon they'll fetch on the market?" Agur asked.

"Oh, they'll fetch a fine price, especially that red-haired girl!" Natan said.

All four of the bandits were grinning from ear to ear because of their luck.

"Eh, one of 'em's got a sword, and another's got a spear. Reckon they'll be any trouble?" Yakir asked.

Liad laughed. "Naw, they'll be pissin' their pants at the sight of us."

The other bandits chuckled. They were hiding in some brush just off to the side of the road. They had been waiting for a vulnerable group to pass by for days now, and they finally found their opportunity. They continued watching the kids from the shadows.

"Closer . . . just a bit closer . . ." Natan muttered. "Now!" he shouted, giving the order, and the four of them leapt out onto the road, swords in hand.

Liad started shouting, "None of you brats move! You lot just listen here, and we'll make things easy for ya!"

"Make a move, and we'll make sure you regret it!" Agur added.

"Drop your weapons!" Natan shouted.

The boys with the spear and sword exchanged a glance and proceeded to hold on to their weapons.

"I said drop your weapons!" Natan repeated.

A few of the kids were clearly terrified, but most of them remained unfazed. Strange.

Then one of the kids stepped forward and shouted back at the bandits, "Drop our weapons? Drop our weapons! Ha! Instead, how about you drop your weapons! If you do, we'll let ya off easy! How 'bout that!"

The bandits exchanged glances. What the heck was this boy spewing?

"Keep talking like that, and I'll have your tongue, boy! Now drop your weapons and get on your knees!" Liad shouted.

"No!" the boy shouted back.

He wasn't even one of the bigger kids; in fact, he was on the smaller side, and he was unarmed, yet he had the audacity to step forward and shout back at them.

It pissed the bandits off.

"We'll give ya one last warning! On your knees, and we can still do this the easy way!"

The short boy took another step forward and shouted again, "If you keep shouting at us like that, we're gonna beat you up, ya bunch of clods! Get out of our way!"

Liad was fuming. "That's it!" He stormed toward the little prick, raising his sword. The little prick quickly backed away and hid behind the boy with the spear.

"Come here, ya brat! I'll have your tongue! We'll see how much you can talk after that!"

"I'd like to see you try!" the boy shouted from behind the other boy's back.

Liad continued to storm toward them; he was prepared to kill the little prick. Then the boy with the spear raised one of his hands. Wooden tendrils burst up from the ground and wrapped around Liad's legs, stopping him in his tracks. For a moment, the bandits were taken aback. This wasn't an ordinary boy. But then their anger returned. Natan, Agur, and Yakir all began marching forward to lay their hands on the children. Liad broke free of the wood that entangled him, and he charged. The boy with the spear didn't even use the spear. He dropped it. In one deft motion, he dashed forward and landed a crushing blow on Liad's ribs, sending him sprawling backward several meters.

The others stopped and looked back at their companion, who had just been sent flying. By the time they turned their heads back to their opponent, the boy was upon Natan. He had no time to react. A fist slammed into his chin, and Natan slumped over.

Yakir cursed, "Be ready, Agur! This ain't no normal boy! Don't go easy on him!"

The two took up defensive stances and gathered their mana, forming their auras. Liad and Natan had been caught off guard, but the fight from here on would be different. Agur and Yakir were ready. After the two bandits formed auras, the spear boy froze. They thought it was out of fear. But then the boy formed a pure white aura, brighter than their own. Both the bandits cursed under their breath.

All the while, the rest of the kids stood idly by, watching the fight as if it were some kind of show. None of them showed any sign of stepping in to help. The boy who had been shouting before was cheering loudly for his buddy as if this were some sort of game.

"Yeah! Get 'em, Adonai! Teach 'em a lesson!"

"It's just us and him, two on one," Agur said to Yakir. "We can win this."

For a moment longer, the three stood off, staring one another down. Then Agur cried out and threw an arm forward to manipulate wood while Yakir charged with his sword. Wooden tentacles sprung up from the ground, beginning to wrap around Adonai. But just as quickly as the wood sprang up, it froze and retracted. The boy had countered Agur's elemental attack both perfectly and instantly. Yakir swung his sword wildly. He was fast, yet he failed to land a single blow. Adonai countered every attack and then punched Yakir in the liver. Yakir slumped over.

Three of the bandits now lay on the ground, incapacitated. Agur was alone. Sweat dripped down his brow. He was trying to decide what to do. Should he run? Fight? If he fought, could he win? If he tried to run away, was he even capable of escaping? Adonai just remained where he was, standing and waiting for Agur to make a move.

Finally, Agur dropped his sword and said, "I surrender. I surrender." He got down on his knees.

"Kick him in the mouth!" the one boy who had been cheering this entire time shouted.

"I'm not gonna kick him in the mouth," Adonai said back to his friend.

"Then I'll kick him in the mouth," the boy shouted as he began to march forward. But then one of the girls punched the boy, and he finally shut up.

"Come on, guys, let's get outta here," Adonai said to his group.

Agur held his breath as he watched the group of kids walk past him and leave. They really just let him off. When they were finally gone, Agur fell back and lay on the ground. He muttered a string of curses. Who in the world was that boy? No, what in the world was that boy? There was no way he was human.

Agur got back up and looked around. His friends had all gotten hit pretty hard, but for the most part, they were fine. He looked back down the road one last time at the now distant group, then went and helped his friends.

Further down the road, the boys were jumping excitedly.

"Holy smokes, Adonai, that was awesome! You beat the crap outta those guys," Chaver exclaimed, laughing.

"Those bums really thought they could rob us. Boy, did we show 'em," Daniel added.

"We? What do you mean we? You didn't even do anything," Ariel said, making fun of him.

"That's just 'cause Adonai was too quick. I didn't have a chance to step in. If I did, I woulda had those guys beggin' for mercy," Daniel proclaimed.

"Yeah, sure you would," Ariel rolled her eyes.

For the first time since the dire bear incident, everyone was actually somewhat in good spirits. That is, everyone except for Adonai. He smiled and laughed along with his friends, but he couldn't stop thinking about the dire bear attack. He couldn't stop thinking about the guards. About how things might have turned out differently if he had just ignored Emilio and helped fight. He couldn't stop thinking about it. And it hurt.

Chapter 15

Henry woke up in a dark room. A single lantern offered a faint light. The walls were stone and cold, and the room was bare. He tried to move but couldn't. Straps held him down. He tried to break them but couldn't. They were reinforced with mana—a lot of mana. His interspatial ring was missing. What was going on? His left shoulder throbbed. He tried to move it, and that was when he realized his arm was gone. In its place was a bloody stump. And then he remembered.

He remembered the night he snuck into the Imperial Saints' church. He remembered everything . . . the cages . . . the people . . . his fight with the Third Descendant. He tried to break free again and again but failed. He looked around. The room was empty—just him strapped to a table with a smaller table next to him. For a long time, he lay there in the dark. It was hard to tell how long.

Finally, the door opened. A person dressed in the same black cloak and black mask as those from before walked in.

"Who are you? Where am I?" Henry demanded. No answer. He tried again. "Say something. Just tell me something." Still no answer. The person pulled out a syringe.

"What is that? What are you doing?" Still, they said nothing.

They stabbed Henry with the syringe and injected something into him. It made him feel weak—probably some sort of drug that inhibited his ability to use mana. After that, the person left, and Henry was alone again.

A lot of thoughts raced through his mind. Where was he, and how long had he been asleep? Who were these people in black cloaks, and what was their relation to the Imperial Saints? William. He needed to reach William. He had to inform him of what was going on.

The door opened again. This time, Henry recognized who it was. The Third Descendant entered. Henry pressed him with questions like he had with the last person.

"Where am I? Who are you? What is going on?"

This time, he actually received an answer.

"Henry, Henry, Henry, I can't answer those questions."

"Then why are you here?" Henry snapped.

"Why am I here? To see you, of course. Oh, how I've wanted to see you. It was a real pain waiting all these days for you to wake up."

"Days? How many days?" Henry asked.

"Oh, days . . . weeks . . . months, years. Who knows, really? It's so hard to tell."

Henry spat curses at the Third Descendant—the most vile words he could think of. It did nothing to relieve his anger.

"Henry, you hurt me. Why must you speak such profanity toward me?"

Henry spat another curse at him. The Third Descendant ignored it and continued, "I was going to try asking you again to join us, but judging from your warm welcome, I don't think that's likely."

"You're a maniac."

The Third Descendant laughed—a little too much. "Ah, a maniac. Ha . . . that's exactly what I am. And you are going to become my special little experiment. We're going to have a lot of fun together, you and I."

Henry cursed him again.

"Alright, that's enough chit-chat." The Third Descendant pulled out a syringe and injected something into Henry. Instantly, Henry became dizzy. His vision blurred, and he started seeing colors.

"This is a special concoction we've created. We've yet to use it, so that means you're the first. Isn't that exciting? I'm excited."

Henry tried to curse him again, but his speech came out slurred.

The Third Descendant continued, "What this special concoction will do is slowly eat away at your mind. Your memories will fade. Your personality, too. Everything that makes you you will be dissolved, leaving us with a completely blank canvas. And since your muscle memory and power will remain, all we need is a little bit of remolding, and you'll be turned into the perfect soldier—completely subservient to us. It's perfect! And in time, every worthy mortal will join you. You'll all get to serve us Telestials together!

"Whoops, I said too much. Got a little excited. Oh, well, that's okay. You'll forget all of this soon enough. I'll see you again when you wake up, my dear Henry."

The Third Descendant turned and left the room once again, leaving Henry all alone.

Chapter 16

"Hey, guys, how many fowl do you reckon I could eat in a single sitting?" Chaver asked, talking to no one in particular.

"Chaver . . . you've been talking all day! Could ya just shut up for five minutes?" Daniel snapped.

Chaver ignored him and continued, "I think I could probably eat six or seven right about now, maybe eight on a good day."

Daniel groaned. "Stop. Talking." He was sick of listening to Chaver. Every few hours, he would snap at him, but Chaver would just ignore him and continue talking. This cycle repeated itself countless times during their journey.

"You guys ever think it's weird how everything in this nation is called Dire this and Dire that?" Chaver started. "No, seriously. There's the Dire Mountains, Dire River, Dire Woods, Dire Sea, Dire City, Dire Plains, Dire Lake—Dire, Dire, Dire. It's all Dire. You'd think that whoever came up with all this would have been more creative. Honestly, it's a little disappointing. If ya ask me, this nation should be called Chaver's Nation with the Chaver Mountains and . . ." Chaver continued rambling; nobody really listened.

Finally, the walls of River Vale came into view. Daniel's face lit up at the sight of the city.

"Finally! I can rid myself of this stinkin' mongrel!" Daniel cheered, referring to Chaver, obviously.

When they arrived at the southern gates, a large crowd of people was gathered along the edges of the road, making room for a group to pass through. Adonai and his friends joined the other citizens along the side of the road and watched the approaching group as well. A man in shining armor rode atop a large warhorse. He wore the green cloak of the Direland military. His cloak was embroidered with the Pillar's insignia. Four others rode behind him in the same attire. One of them was marked as a captain, and the other three were lieutenants. These men were powerful. Very powerful. Adonai could sense it. They made no effort to conceal their presence, as Adonai had made a habit of doing. Instead, they displayed their mana for everyone watching to see as a demonstration of their power.

"Who are those guys?" Chaver asked aloud.

"That's William Hart," Daniel told him, wide-eyed and admiring the gallant soldiers.

"Ohh, William Hart . . . who's that?"

Daniel gave Chaver an annoyed look. "He's one of Direland's four Pillars, you idiot. Specifically, he's the Pillar of the North. He's famous for becoming one of the youngest Pillars ever appointed. And that's not all—despite his young age, he's also one of the strongest Pillars ever appointed. And what's most impressive is that he's one of the few mortal Pillars. Most high-ranking officials are Telestials," Daniel explained.

"So what's he doing here?" Ariel asked.

"He's probably finally doing something about the nobles overstepping their bounds here in River Vale. About time, honestly. The bridges might finally be free to pass through again. And it's not just the illegal tolls and taxes either. There's been lots of corruption, underhanded deals, and all sorts of other stuff going on in River Vale."

They watched as the Pillar and his soldiers rode past. When they were further down the road, everything returned to normal, and Adonai's group entered the city.

"You should all come over and stay at my place. Even you, Chaver," Daniel said as they walked into the city.

"Wait, why did you call me out specifically?" Chaver asked.

Daniel didn't answer him and instead led them through the city to the plot of land that his family owned. Ariel separated from them on the way there to reunite with her family. The Ortals were lower-ranked among high-class society, but their mansion was still incredibly nice.

They were greeted by Henderson, one of the family's butlers, when they arrived. "Sir Daniel, welcome home."

"It's nice to see you, Henderson. These are my friends," Daniel said, gesturing to the others. "Would you mind preparing rooms for them?"

"Of course." Henderson ushered them inside the mansion and then went off to prepare the rooms for the guests.

Chaver whistled as they walked in. "This place is nice."

Daniel had a big smile on his face; he was enjoying showing off to the others. They walked into a big room where Daniel's parents, Sasha and Dylan, were sitting at a table.

"Daniel, you're home!" his mother exclaimed when she saw her son walk into the room. She ran up to him and gave him a big hug.

"Who are all these wonderful-looking people?" Sasha asked.

"These are my friends. They were also traveling with the caravan to the capital for their bonding rituals."

"Oh, how wonderful," Sasha said with a warm smile. "You all should stay here while you're in River Vale."

"Thank you, we would love to," Chaver said politely.

"Where's Gev?" Dylan asked.

A grim mood set over the group as they all stood in silence for a moment.

"Gev . . . didn't make it," Daniel said at last.

His parents wore worried expressions. "What do you mean he didn't make it?" his father asked.

Daniel went on to explain how they were attacked by a Dire bear and how the guards had stayed behind to buy them time to escape.

"Adonai was the one to lead us all here," Daniel said and then added, "He even protected us against a band of bandits."

Sasha went and gave Adonai a big hug. "Thank you for getting our baby home safely. If there's anything you need or want, just tell us."

"You letting us stay here is already more than enough," Adonai told her.

After that, Dylan had a feast prepared for his guests, which was one of the best meals Adonai had ever had. That night, when everyone went to bed, he lay awake for a long time. He couldn't stop thinking about the encounter with the Dire bear. He still felt he had made the wrong choice, and he felt horrible for it. It was eating away at him.

They spent a few more days at the Ortals' home before setting off for Plain City. When they left, the Ortals gave them lots of fresh supplies for the remainder of their journey. Daniel and Ariel saw them off at the northern gate. And with that, they were on their way to Plain City.

Chapter 17

William's warhorse clopped down the road. He was accompanied by one of his captains, Benjamin, and three of his lieutenants: David, Seth, and Corban. They were currently passing through the Dire Woods. The massive trees towered all around them, and the thick forest pressed in. William had passed through here many times throughout his lifetime, and it never ceased to amaze him. He and his companions were returning to Dire City from River Vale.

The corruption in River Vale had become a serious problem—so much so that William had gone there to handle things personally. He was afraid that if he sent someone else, they would just get brushed off by the Telestial nobles or even bribed. The whole situation went over relatively smoothly: the nobles took down their tolls, their grip on the city was loosened, and all the nobles involved received a hefty fine. But that was it. All they got was a measly fine, nothing more than a slap on the wrist.

William would have liked to see them punished more severely. He would have liked to see them lose their status, and for whoever the ringleader was to be executed. But he could do none of that. Ramiah, the Cornerstone, wouldn't allow the Telestial nobles to be punished so harshly. It was frustrating, but that was the way of this world. The Telestials were always treated like higher beings.

William was also worried about Henry. It had been three weeks since he had last heard from him, and the last thing he had heard was concerning. Henry's last report mentioned an attack by mysterious men in black and his suspicions of their connection to the Imperial Saints.

William stopped. He raised a hand and said, "Halt." His companions stopped behind him.

"Do you guys sense that? We're being watched . . . Guys?"

William turned around and looked at his companions; they all wore grave expressions. They shared the same look in their eyes, as if they were staring down an enemy.

"Guys? What's going on?"

Men who had been watching from the trees stepped closer. Two men in black cloaks emerged from the brush and walked into the open, one on the right, one on the left. And then there was another presence—a very powerful presence that sent chills down William's spine. A third man in black walked out into the center of the road. His black mask bore the numeral two printed in red across the face: the Second Descendant.

William cursed, and his sword materialized in his hand. He turned back to his companions. Something was amiss; he could tell.

"What is all this? What's going on? Why aren't you saying anything—"

"We're sorry, William," Benjamin said. His eyes were cold as his sword materialized in his hand. The others also pulled their swords from their interspatial rings. Benjamin continued, "We had no choice, really. It was join or die. We had to join."

"What—"

"William!" the Second Descendant called out.

William spun around to face him.

"I've heard many things about you. It's a pleasure to finally meet you."

William looked around again, evaluating his situation. He was surrounded.

"Don't bother yourself," the Second Descendant told him. "There are two options here."

"What options?" William demanded.

"Join us. Join our great cause and become part of something bigger, something better, something glorious. Or . . . die."

"I'm not sure I understand. Who exactly are you?"

"Who am I? Well, I'm the Second Descendant. But I don't think that was what you were referring to. As for who we are . . . well, that's something you'll come to learn after joining us."

"And what is it that you want?"

"What we want?" William couldn't see his face, but he could tell the Second Descendant was grinning deviously.

"What we want is to make the world a better place. A world without suffering. A world without weakness."

"If that's what you want, why the shadiness? Why go about all of this secretly?"

"Because there are those who are foolish. Fools who resist the greater good. Fools who do not understand. If a perfect world is to be obtained . . . then a filthy world must first be cleansed."

William didn't need to press further. He understood. These were madmen seeking to slaughter the people of this world.

"So, will you join us?" the Second Descendant asked.

"I'll die a thousand deaths before I join your cult," William spat.

The Second Descendant shook his head. "Shame. Henry responded in the same way."

"Henry! What about Henry? What have you done with him?"

"Don't worry about Henry; he's still alive, and he's in good hands. I'd tell you to expect to see him again, but . . . you'll be dying here."

The Second Descendant extended his arm toward him. "But I'll ask you one last time. Will you join us?"

William gritted his teeth. "By the name of the Celestials, I will smite you down right here and now."

The Second Descendant sighed. "Very well then . . . Kill him."

William spun around to see his four subordinates charging toward him. All of them, including the Second Descendant, specialized in the wood element. Knowing this, the Second Descendant had brought along two men specializing in fire. Roots burst from the ground around William, threatening to entrap him. William quickly abandoned his horse, using his mana to make a giant root shoot up from the ground beneath him. He rode atop it, putting distance between himself and his attackers.

His four subordinates abandoned their horses and did the same. Now all five of them rode atop their wooden mounts, while the two men in black cast fireballs from the sidelines. William snaked back and forth, evading and exchanging blows. All the while, the Second Descendant watched in satisfaction, enjoying William's struggle.

The giant roots created a twisted tower in the middle of the road, but then the tower was set ablaze. The fire quickly climbed, and the wood began to snap and pop. As the structure collapsed, William leapt into the air, channeling as much mana as he could muster. He slashed downward with an attack that obliterated the remaining roots and sent shockwaves through the forest.

His subordinates were flung back by the blast; however, the black cloaks resisted it. William ducked as a fireball soared over his head. He stomped on the ground, and a wall of wood shot up behind him, blocking another fireball. His subordinates dashed back into the fight.

"You don't have to do this!" William shouted as he exchanged blows with Benjamin, their swords flying at an inhuman pace.

Benjamin ignored him.

William continued to block attacks from all four subordinates while the mysterious men in black waited for an opportunity to strike a fatal blow. Despite the odds, William still held the advantage. He cut down Corban, then Seth. In a few more blows, David was struck down, and William drove his sword through Benjamin's chest. All four of his subordinates were dead.

As William pulled his sword from Benjamin's body, the two men in black pounced. Their flaming swords danced as William summoned wooden tendrils and spikes from the ground. Though his enemies evaded the attacks, William finally managed to impale one of them. With his companion dead, the remaining man didn't last much longer, and William swiftly cut him in half.

Now, only William and the Second Descendant remained. He was tired, his mind racing. He had just killed six men, four of whom had been his friends. But he couldn't afford to lose focus.

The Second Descendant slowly approached, clapping his hands.

"Well done, William, well done! You truly are a brilliant warrior. To think you'd kill six men all on your own. You know, the offer still stands. It will always stand. We don't have to fight. All you have to do is don the black. Don the black, and all your worries will wash away, giving you the opportunity to aid His Highness in creating a greater world."

William didn't answer. Instead, he resumed his fighting stance. Blood seeped from cuts all over his body; his back had been burned, and some of his bones were definitely broken, but he was going to fight on. The Second Descendant sighed again, and his sword materialized in his hand.

"Seems you will have to die today. Well, maybe. I could leave you alive. After capturing you, we could potentially turn you over to our side . . . but where's the fun in that? I'd rather see the light fade from your eyes as you die upon my blade—"

William dashed forward, closing the distance between them in a fraction of a second. The Second Descendant blocked the attack. In a flurry of strikes, their swords clashed together—fast, faster, faster than William had ever fought before. Their movements were invisible to the naked eye.

William broke contact and leapt backward, his breathing heavy. The Second Descendant casually and slowly walked closer. "To think you still have this much fight left in you after taking on six powerful men—I commend your strength. It's too bad that strength will be lost here today."

William glared at him. "You talk too much."

Once again, a giant root burst up from the ground beneath William. He rode it like a mount and charged at the Descendant. The Second Descendant did the same. The two clashed as their wooden mounts snaked around each other, forming another twisted tower.

The Second Descendant slashed William across the chest, leaving a deep gash, and then struck again across his leg. Steadily, more and more power was infused into each attack, the strikes ringing throughout the woods. The two continued their fierce battle atop the giant wooden roots.

As they fought, the Second Descendant began to realize something: William was far stronger than anticipated. Gradually, William gained the edge in their fight. A powerful strike knocked the Descendant back, followed by another, and another. Finally, the Second Descendant was knocked from his wooden mount and fell to the ground.

Another attack from above brought him to his knees. Even on his knees, he continued to fend off William's strikes, but it didn't last long. Smaller roots burst from the ground, wrapping around the Descendant and restricting his movements. With a final blow, William smote off his head.

William dropped his sword and collapsed onto the ground, his chest heaving with exhaustion. His entire being throbbed with pain from the overuse of mana. He glanced over to see the Second Descendant's body disintegrate into dust, leaving nothing behind—not his weapon, not his clothes. The same had happened to the other two men in black.

That pissed him off. All of this fighting, and he had gained nothing from it—save for his life.

As he lay there on the ground, he began muttering to himself, "I'll kill them. I'll find out who these people are, and I'll kill every last one of them."

William climbed back to his feet, but as he did so, his vision blurred. He fell back to the ground as darkness overtook him.

Chapter 18

Two of Never Thaw's guardsmen stood at the southern entrance of the town. Though it was noon and the sun was beating down on the valley, it was still cold, and the ground was still covered in snow. That's how it always was in Glacier Valley; after all, Never Thaw wasn't called Never Thaw for no reason. One of the guards noticed a small group of people appearing on the road in the distance. As he strained his eyes to look at them, he began to excitedly point and shout.

"It's them! They're back! The kids are back! They're back!"

The other guard shared his enthusiasm. "I'll go spread the word! You stay here and await their arrival."

He quickly turned and ran into town, shouting for all to hear and making known the return of the group. By the time Adonai and his friends arrived at the town's entrance, a large group had already formed. Chaver's mom was the first one to run forward and give all four of them a big hug.

"I'm so happy to see you all again! Chaver . . . seems you've also returned."

"Mom, why do you sound disappointed?"

Chaver's younger siblings crowded around, quickly followed by the other families. Adonai's brothers and sister cried out in unison when they arrived.

"Adonai!" Maybel ran and jumped up into his arms. "I missed you, big brother."

He patted her head and smiled. "Yeah, I missed you guys too." The whole town was excited.

Then one of the guards noticed something was amiss and asked, "Hold on, where's Emilio?"

"Yeah, where is Emilio?" another person added.

A stiff silence settled over the air.

"Emilio . . . Emilio isn't going to be coming back," Chaver said quietly.

"He's not coming back? Why? What happened?"

The question seemed to hang in the air for what felt like an absurdly long time.

"We ran into a dire bear . . ." Chaver began. "Emilio, he . . . he fought against it to buy us time to escape."

The silence seemed to grow heavier as everyone processed what that meant.

"I should have stayed and helped him fight," Adonai whispered, tears welling up in his eyes. "Emilio's dead because of me."

Lily tried to soothe him. "No, it's not your fault."

"Yeah," Chaver added. "We were able to make it back home safely because of you."

Adonai just shook his head and trained his eyes on the ground; he didn't say anything else. A solemn mood fell over the town. Chaver explained in more detail about what happened when the dire bear attacked and also shared how Adonai protected them from bandits and led the way back home.

That night, the whole town gathered at the temple to hold a ceremony for Emilio's passing. A small shrine had been built to honor the deceased guard. The captain of the guard, Ander, gave a short tribute.

"As you all know, we are gathered here because of the passing of Emilio. Emilio . . . Emilio served as one of our town's faithful guards. I had the pleasure to work alongside him. I had the pleasure of calling him a friend. Emilio was like family, not just to me but to all of us. He was kind and diligent. Hardworking and sincere. An honorable man. He died protecting the young generation of this town. He died a hero. And he will be remembered as a hero. May his spirit rest in peace with the Celestials above."

A heavy weight seemed to rest upon Adonai's shoulders, a weight that felt especially heavy during the ceremony. He still couldn't shake the thought that things might have turned out differently if he ignored Emilio and helped fight the dire bear. The town had declared him a hero for bringing back everyone else safely. He declared himself a fraud. But he didn't show that. He didn't show the resentment he held toward himself. Showing it would only make him look ungrateful for Emilio's sacrifice. He couldn't do that to Emilio. So he sat there with his family in silence, holding back his tears while he paid his respects. That was how the night of their return ended.

In the following days, Adonai spent his time at home with his family and helping on the farm. It was peaceful. After a few days, he rose early in the morning, grabbed his pack, and went to leave. He longed for the mountains, for the isolation, and for the harsh embrace of the cold. Before he walked out the door, a sleepy Maybel called out to him.

"You're leaving?"

Adonai stopped and turned to face her. "Yeah, I'm leaving."

"But I don't want you to leave," she said, rubbing her eyes.

"It'll be alright. I won't be gone that long. And I'll bring back huckleberries, a whole lot of 'em."

Maybel's eyes lit up. "You promise?"

"I promise."

"Okay, I guess it's fine if you leave."

He hugged her and left the house. The sun was just beginning to peek over the mountains. The cold air was refreshing, and the sound of snow crunching beneath his feet helped him clear his head. Adonai made his way through Never Thaw to the base of Glacier Mountain, where he stopped and began to fill his pack with rocks.

"What are you doing?" his griffin bond, Aeolian, asked. His other bonds were intrigued as well.

"I'm training." That's all he said and then continued to fill his pack until it was completely full of heavy rocks. Then he slung the pack over his back. He looked up at the mountain. It was huge. It was a long way to go. He looked up at the mountain for a while, admiring its beauty. Then he took off. He started with a slow jog and then continued to speed up until he was running. And it wasn't like a run at a decent pace; it was a dead sprint. With every step, he drove into the ground with all his might, and he charged up the mountain. The air gradually grew thinner, his breathing became heavier and heavier, and his lungs burned. He ran until he grew lightheaded and couldn't bring himself to go any higher. Then he turned around and sprinted back down the mountain. When he reached the bottom, he set his pack down, took out one of the rocks, put his pack back on, and then sprinted back up the mountain. Again, he went as high as he could, as fast as he could, and then again, he turned around and sprinted back to the bottom, where he took out another rock. He continued to do this repeatedly until his pack was empty.

Not only did he end up running all day, but he ran all through the night as well. When he finally finished, he let himself fall to the ground, exhausted.

"You said this was for training, but what are you training for?" the dire bear spirit, Weald, asked.

"I don't know . . . nothing?"

"Ah, I see . . ." the phoenix spirit, Arson, started. "You're an idiot."

"Watch your tongue, you wretch!" Brine, the kraken spirit, hissed at Arson.

The phoenix and kraken began to bicker with each other, throwing insults and slurs back and forth. They didn't seem to get along well, which made sense; after all, they were fire and water, polar opposites. Adonai ignored them. He admitted it was weird that he trained so hard when he didn't really have a reason to. It was just . . . deep down, he had an inescapable desire for strength. He had to train. He didn't understand why; all he knew was that he had to. Perhaps it had something to do with the mark of the prodigy he had been born with. Perhaps it had something to do with that mysterious glowing shard that appeared during his bonding ritual. Or perhaps he was just crazy. It had always been this way; ever since he was young, he would come to the mountains to train his body in one way or another.

After resting for a while, Adonai climbed back to his feet and began to make his way home.

"Wait, what about the huckleberries?" Aeolian asked.

"Crap . . ." Adonai groaned. "I forgot about my promise to Maybel."

He sighed and turned around and hiked back up the mountain to gather some berries before returning home.

The next day, after sharing a meal with his family and getting a good night's rest, Adonai returned to the mountains. He hiked to Glacier Lake. Glacier Lake was a small lake located deep in the Dire Mountains. The water there was a brilliant blue, and with the mountain tops surrounding it, it was a gorgeous place. The water of the lake was extremely cold—so cold that it should have been frozen over completely. However, there was a large amount of mana concentrated in the water, giving it strange properties that kept it from freezing over.

Adonai dove into the freezing-cold water and swam back and forth across the lake. Because it was so cold, he had to constantly reinforce his body with mana to protect himself, which made for great training. He pushed his body as hard as he could. It wasn't until nightfall that he crawled out of the water and sprawled across the snow-covered ground. After catching his breath, he hiked back down the mountain and returned home.

Adonai spent the next day resting at home—well, sort of resting. Though he was supposedly resting, he was still very active. He helped out on the farm with his parents, played with Maybel, and wrestled with his brothers, Laor and Adin. They were all elated when he brought them berries. It was nice, this life. He loved just being able to spend time with his family; he really did.

After another good night's rest, he once again set out for the mountains. Adonai climbed high, high up into the mountains and sat down on the edge of a cliff. He was so high up that he was above the clouds, which now looked like a white sea laid out before him. Down below those clouds were Glacier Valley and his home, Never Thaw. He closed his eyes and began to meditate, feeling the mana that flowed through and around him.

"Master . . ." Terra, the hydra spirit, asked, interrupting him, "why do you stop here? Throughout all your training, you have yet to summit the peak of this mountain."

The other bonds agreed with her that it was strange.

Adonai sighed. "I've tried. It can't be done."

"It can't be done? It's strange to hear that from you," Aeolian commented.

"Like I said, I've tried—many times at that. The Dire Mountains are just too big, and the air grows far too thin. It's impossible."

"Excuses. To think you were this pathetic. Perhaps I made the wrong choice in choosing you as my master," Arson said, trying to get a rise out of Adonai.

It worked. "Piss off, ya overcooked chicken," he barked at Arson.

"I ain't a chicken. I'm a majestic and noble phoenix."

"Sure . . ."

"Why don't you try climbing to the peak again?" Brine asked. "You didn't have us before. Surely now that you're stronger, you can do it."

"Stronger or not, what am I supposed to do about the lack of air? What good does my strength do when I can't even breathe?"

"Just find a way to breathe," Aeolian told him.

Adonai laughed. "Yeah, right, find a way to breathe. As if it were that easy." He lay back and looked up into the bright blue sky.

Maybe . . . maybe there was a way. He lay there thinking it over, trying to figure out a solution that would allow him to reach the peak. And then an idea struck him. He had the ability to manipulate the air. What if he just used mana to carry the air with him? If he created a bubble and carried that with him, then he would be able to breathe.

He shot up to his feet, eager to test his new theory. Adonai closed his eyes and inhaled deeply, exhaled. Inhaled, exhaled. Focus. He reached out and began to gather oxygen around himself. As he gathered more and more, his aura also began to form and gradually grow brighter. This was it. He would make it this time. He opened his eyes, looked up at the peak that towered above him, and took the first step forward.

For the first time, Adonai stumbled up onto the top of the peak. He had done it. He smiled to himself, proud of what he had accomplished. And then he noticed it. There, straight across from him, was a Dire hawk sitting in its nest. He muttered a curse and froze in place. The hawk glared at him with its big, beady black eyes. For a while, neither of the two knew what to do. It was an unexpected encounter for both. Then the hawk screeched—a loud, deafening screech—and its wings flared up.

Adonai panicked; he didn't have his spear with him, and he was out in the open.

"What do I do?"

"Fight," Weald told him.

"Burn it with fire!" Arson exclaimed.

"No, I'm not gonna burn it."

At that moment, the Dire hawk began to flap its wings and fly up into the sky, and as it did, Adonai had an idea. What if he subjected it? Beat it into submission?

Adonai smiled to himself. Taming a Dire hawk—it was a temptation he couldn't resist.

The Dire hawk was now circling up in the air. It screeched one more time, and then, with a powerful flap of its wings, it shot into a downward dive. The hawk raised its talons; Adonai narrowly slipped past them. As the hawk went to shoot back up into the sky, he grabbed hold of its tail feathers and pulled himself onto its back, and together they flew up into the sky. Unsure of what to do, Adonai began to punch the bird in the back of the head. The hawk began to fly frantically in an attempt to shake him off, but that only made its situation worse. He continued to pummel it in the back of the head until the hawk fell into a downward spiral and crashed into the snowy peak.

Adonai fell off its back, immediately scrambled back to his feet, ran back to the hawk, and jumped on top of it again, putting it in a chokehold. After a minute of this, the hawk stopped struggling. He released his grip and sat down on the ground to catch his breath.

"That might have been a little excessive . . ." Brine commented.

"Eh . . ." Adonai shrugged.

"You know what would be funny . . . if we lit it on fire," Arson suggested. He was ignored.

Adonai sat with the Dire hawk until it began to regain consciousness. As it did, he took some meat out of his pack and gave it to the hawk. At first, the hawk was skeptical, but after a moment of hesitation, it snatched up the meat. Adonai fed it more and more until he was out of fresh meat.

Then he sat for a while longer, just observing the Dire hawk. It was strange; most Dire hawks were brown, but this one was white. It was a beautiful color. They sat together for a long time and gradually became more comfortable with each other.

Come nightfall, Adonai left and descended the mountain.

Chapter 19

William leaned back in his chair and let out a deep sigh. Then he sat back up and buried his face in his hands.

"What do I do?" he muttered to himself.

It hadn't been long since he returned to his estate in Dire City. At the moment, he sat alone in his office, unsure of what to do. His body still ached all over from his fight with the Second Descendant. The Second Descendant . . . those men clad in black . . . just who were they?

The more William thought about it, the heavier his burden became. There was so much going on with this situation: the betrayal of his comrades, Henry's silence, and these mysterious and powerful people. Their descriptions matched the men Henry had described in his mana note after he had been attacked at the Imperium. He would have liked to have examined the corpses of the Second Descendant and the other men, but the bodies and clothes had all turned to dust. So William was left knowing nothing.

The only possible lead he had was the Imperial Saints. Henry had expressed his concerns about the organization, and it was possible that Yir'on was also investigating the Saints before his disappearance. But what did the Saints have to do with some shady organization? It didn't make sense. And that made things even scarier.

William sighed again, stood up, and walked over to his office window. He looked out at the distant street filled with people coming and going. So many people, all of them completely unaware of this conspiracy that threatened their beloved peace.

There was a knock at the door.

"Come in," William called out.

A young lad, a guard who worked on the estate, entered.

"You have a letter, sir."

"A letter? From whom?"

"It doesn't say."

The guard handed William a rolled-up piece of paper with a mana seal, a seal that allowed only the intended recipient to open the object.

"Thank you. You're free to go."

William dismissed the young man, who left and closed the door behind him. Then he sat back down at his desk and turned the message over in his hands, examining it. The mana seal placed on it was a high-class one, and whoever sent this had made sure that the message left no traces. William had a bad feeling about this.

He broke the seal and opened the letter. His heart sank as he read it.

William,

We didn't expect you to survive. We had thought our brethren were capable of defeating you. It seems we thought wrong. But that's okay; we're not mad that our brother is dead. If anything, this just shows that he was too weak to deserve to live. We hope you understand that the offer still stands. The offer will always stand. We look forward to our meeting again. Until then, we'll be keeping a close eye on you. May the Celestials be with you.

William dropped the letter. He felt sick.

Just who exactly were these people? Yir'on's and Henry's disappearance, the ambush, this letter—it was all sinking in. The Telestials . . . they really were planning something. A conspiracy theory turned true. A nightmare.

He mumbled a bunch of curses to himself. What was he supposed to do? How could he fight an enemy when he didn't even know who the enemy was?

As William sat there at his desk, turning everything over in his mind, he came to a single conclusion.

He couldn't just sit and wait. He had to do something. He had to fight back in whatever way he could manage.

Chapter 20

"Your name?" the Third Descendant asked.

"My . . . name . . .?"

"Yes, what is your name?"

"My name . . . my name is . . . Henry?" Henry said, unsure of himself.

"Good, good. And what is your purpose, Henry?"

"My purpose . . . my purpose is . . . what is my purpose?"

"You know your purpose."

Henry thought hard. "My purpose . . . is to cleanse the weak . . . and to serve the strong."

The Third Descendant smiled behind his mask. "Good."

The two of them sat in a dimly lit stone room. There was nothing there aside from the wooden bench Henry sat on while the Third Descendant asked him questions. The Third Descendant had been coming every so often; Henry didn't know why. He didn't know much at all. He didn't know why he was confined to this single room or why these strange men in black cloaks would come and inject him with some sort of fluid that caused a searing pain. He had no concept of time, no memories; all he knew was that his sole purpose was to serve the Descendants.

"I brought something for you today," the Third Descendant told him.

Henry watched curiously as he took something out from behind his cloak: a little pouch. He opened it and handed Henry a small seed.

"What is this?" Henry asked, confused, looking down at the little seed sitting in his palm.

"That is an ironwood seed from the Hyring nation. It's infused with a special formula and mana."

Henry was still confused. "Why are you giving me this?"

The Third Descendant smiled behind his mask again. "This is for fixing your arm."

"Fixing my arm?" He was indeed missing an arm, though he couldn't remember what happened to it.

The Third Descendant held out his hand, gesturing for Henry to hand back the seed. "Here, I'll show you."

Thick bandages were tightly wrapped around the stump where Henry's arm had once been. Slowly, the bandages were unwrapped, exposing the wound. He watched as the Third Descendant pulled out a knife.

"What is that for?"

"You'll see."

He took hold of the stump and jabbed it with the knife, leaving a deep cut. Henry winced at the pain as blood began to trickle down his side. The Third Descendant chuckled at his reaction to the pain. Then he took the seed, pressed it into the incision, and used mana to heal the opening, sealing the seed beneath the skin. During all of this, Henry watched patiently.

The Third Descendant then poured mana into the seed and stepped back to watch. The effects came instantly. The seed began to take root, digging deep into Henry. He wailed out in pain. The roots spread from his shoulder to his chest, back, and face. They wrapped around his organs and broke through the surface of his skin. When the roots stopped growing, half of Henry's upper body was covered in ironwood. Then the seed sprouted. A new arm, made entirely of ironwood, grew from the sprout.

At this point, Henry was rolling on the ground in pain, and the Third Descendant watched gleefully. After a minute, the pain began to subside, and Henry's breathing was heavy and labored.

"Get up," the Third Descendant ordered.

Henry groaned as he climbed to his feet.

"What . . . What is this?"

"What do you mean? This is your new arm, of course. It's a special present we decided to give you. Do you like it?"

Henry turned his wooden arm over, examining it, still gritting his teeth from the pain radiating throughout his body. The ironwood had a black coloring. While it did resemble a regular arm, it was still very clear that it was made of wood. He could manipulate his hand and fingers just as well as he could with his other arm. It was a great prosthetic, really.

"Well, what do ya think?"

Henry opened and closed his hand. "I like it."

"Good. We put a lot of work into that seed. Now that we know it works, we can prepare more of them."

"What are you preparing them for?" Henry asked.

The Third Descendant smiled. "You'll see, eventually."

Then he turned and left the room, closing the door behind him and leaving Henry alone in the dark. Henry sat down on the hard bench. His body was still throbbing with pain. It was kind of the Third Descendant to give him a new arm, even if it did hurt a lot.

As Henry lay there, something gnawed at the back of his mind. He was forgetting something, something important. But what was it? No matter how hard he strained his mind, he couldn't think of what it was. He sat there, continuing to think deeply, trying to remember what it was that he had forgotten.

Then the door opened, and two of the grunts dressed in black entered. It was time for the regular session. Henry sat patiently as they took out a syringe and injected a fluid into him. A burning sensation spread throughout his body. Then the men in black left, and Henry was once again alone. Whatever he had been thinking about before the men in black arrived, he had completely forgotten. But that was fine; he wasn't concerned about it. He lay back down and went to sleep.

Chapter 21

Adonai tossed a piece of meat to the Dire hawk, which it happily snapped up. The two of them sat atop the peak of Glacier Mountain, looking out over the sea of clouds. It had been a month now since he first ascended the mountain. Since then, he had been revisiting the peak regularly to spend time with the Dire hawk. He had started calling her Ciela, a name befitting one who was one with the sky. The two of them had formed a sort of bond at this point. Adonai would bring food for Ciela, and in turn, Ciela wouldn't attempt to maim him with her talons.

He tossed another piece of meat to her and watched her gulp it down. She was a beautiful bird. She was covered with white feathers, making her almost invisible in the snow. And the feathers were huge—so huge that a few of them were a little longer than Adonai's forearm. Not only were the feathers large, but they were surprisingly resilient, with a strength that resembled scales more than feathers. She shed a feather every now and then, and when Adonai came across them, he collected them. He wasn't entirely sure what he was going to do with them yet. Dire hawk feathers were valuable and could be sold for a lot of money, but he never really cared for money—nobody in Never Thaw did. So, he would find another use for the feathers other than selling them.

Adonai tossed another piece of meat to the Dire hawk. "It's really peaceful here, isn't it, Ciela? No wonder you spend most of the year here."

When there was no response, just like always, Adonai sighed. "It's too bad you can't understand me—"

As he said those last few words, an idea struck him. What if he formed a mana link with her? The idea made him excited. He had formed mana links with his spirit bonds, allowing them to communicate, so shouldn't he be able to do the same with Ciela? Though he didn't really know how he created the mana link with his bonds, it was something that just kind of happened.

"Hey, guys, do you know anything about mana links?" Adonai asked his bonds.

"No, why do you ask?" Aeolian asked.

"I want to try to create a mana link with Ciela."

"Hmmm, that's an interesting idea," Ore said.

"It is indeed," Weald agreed. "Unfortunately, our knowledge is limited, so we can't offer much assistance."

Adonai tossed another piece of meat to Ciela and thought hard about it. He didn't know much about mana links. His knowledge of mana was limited to the few books he had managed to get his hands on throughout the town and his own personal experience. Because of the mark of the prodigy, he was born with an innate ability to utilize mana, similar to a mana beast, so he had a whole lifetime of firsthand experience with mana—though so far, that was a short lifetime.

As Adonai sat there thinking, Arson made a suggestion. "We should go burn something to help clear your mind." He was ignored.

As Adonai tossed a piece of meat to Ciela, he finally made up his mind. He cautiously approached her, gently raised a hand, and then gently pressed his hand against her beak. At first, she pulled away from his touch, which made Adonai hesitate, but when he reached out again, she allowed him to touch her and nuzzled his hand. He wasn't entirely sure what he was doing; he was just acting on a mixture of instinct and hope that he would somehow figure it out. He started by circulating his mana through his body, channeling it into his hand and out through his palm into Ciela. As the mana circulated between the both of them, he experimented by probing the mana in various ways. Thankfully, the effect of the mana seemed to soothe Ciela, so she remained still during the process. A long time passed. All the while, the two remained motionless as Adonai dived deeper and deeper into the depths of the mana that flowed between them. And then, it was as if something clicked. As if a connection was made.

A subtle yet distinct feeling. Adonai tried calling out with his mind, "Hello?"

"Hello?" Ciela echoed back.

Adonai stumbled away from her in surprise. "Can you . . . can you understand me?"

"Yes."

He smiled to himself, and that smile soon devolved into laughter. "I did it. I did it! I freaking did it! I'm a freakin' genius!"

Ciela cocked her head as she watched him jump around and punch at the air in celebration.

"Ciela, can you really understand me?" He asked again.

"Yes, I can understand you."

Adonai punched the air one last time; he couldn't wipe the smile off his face. "You've been calling me Ciela, what is Ciela?"

The question caught Adonai off guard. "Oh, I guess I kind of gave you a name. Do you not like it?"

"No, I like it. Bringer of food, what is your name?"

Adonai laughed. "Bringer of food, is that what you call me? That's funny. My name is Adonai."

"Adonai," she repeated.

As they talked, their bond deepened, and they gained a better understanding of each other. They spent hours talking, and soon, the sun began to set, painting the sky a beautiful mixture of orange, yellow, and pink.

"It's getting late, I should be heading home," Adonai said regretfully. Then he had another idea. "Ciela, would you like to come with me to my home?"

Chaver was sitting with Dahlia at their usual table in the corner of the inn's common room.

"Don't you think you're drinking a little too much?" Dahlia said, concerned.

"Naw, it's fine. I've only had . . . well . . . I lost count. But that don't mean I've had too much. In fact, I don't think I've had nearly enough."

Dahlia sighed as Chaver gulped down the rest of his mug. "Well, at least you're good at holding your liquor."

As they sat talking, a commotion began to stir up outside. People started running back and forth, and then someone burst in through the inn's doors and started yelling, "Dire hawk! There's a Dire hawk!"

Chaver stood up so fast, it knocked his chair over. He and Dahlia ran over to the front window and tried to look up into the sky. There was little light left, the sun being nearly set, so it was hard to see.

"What is a Dire hawk doing in the valley?" Chaver asked. "I know they live in the mountains, but don't they hunt in the plains? You don't think it's hunting now, do ya?"

"I don't know, Chaver," Dahlia answered.

By now, the streets were deserted, everyone crowding into the closest buildings.

"I haven't heard its call," someone said. "Don't they usually screech when they're hunting? Maybe it's fine, it's probably not hunting—"

Then it screeched. There was some cursing among the group in the inn. "Guess that theory's gone."

"What do we do now?" someone asked in a worried voice.

Chaver's parents were trying to calm everyone down. A couple of his younger siblings were crying because of the panic. Everyone was huddled together, looking out the windows trying to catch a glimpse of the hawk.

"Where is it?" somebody asked. Someone else shushed him. "Be quiet."

"Be quiet?" a man started. "What do ya mean be quiet, it ain't gonna hear us in here." Then the Dire hawk landed right in the middle of the street, right in front of the inn. "Crap!" Chaver blurted out, startled, ducking down to hide from the window.

Everyone began to panic. But then they each gradually began to notice the figure sitting atop the Dire hawk's back.

"Good Celestials . . . is that Adonai!" Chaver shouted. "Holy crap, it is Adonai!" He was the first one to burst through the doors and come running outside. "Adonai, you crazy shmuck! You nearly gave half the town a heart attack!" Chaver shouted as he ran over.

Adonai hopped down from Ciela's back with a grin. "I'd be lying if I said I didn't intentionally cause a commotion."

Dahlia followed Chaver out of the inn, and then gradually more people began to leak outside into the streets. Before long, a large crowd was gathered around Ciela.

"Is this what you've been doing up in the mountains all this time? Taming a Dire hawk? You really are a crazy shmuck!" Chaver exclaimed.

"She's pretty, ain't she?" Adonai said proudly.

"You could say that, but if you ask me, she looks more terrifying than anything else."

Ciela shuffled uncomfortably, bothered by all of the sudden attention. People were slowly approaching, trying to get a closer look. Adonai noticed this and set a soothing hand on her neck, ruffling her feathers.

"It's fine. They mean you no harm," he told her.

For a while, he showed her off to all the townsfolk, even allowing people to come up and touch her. This only lasted a short while, though, as it was dark out. So finally, Adonai took Ciela over to the stable beside the inn. When they entered the stable, all the horses panicked and shrunk away to the corners of their stalls, trying to get as far away from the Dire hawk as possible. Adonai felt a little bad, but they would come to get used to her presence.

He led Ciela into one of the stalls at the very back of the stable, with lots of hay strewn across the ground.

"This is a bed for you. You can sleep here. This way, we can be closer," Adonai told her.

"I liked my nest up on top of the mountain," Ciela commented.

"Wasn't your nest just made of snow? There's still lots of snow down here. We can fill your stall up with it so that it resembles your nest. But for now, it's late, so just sleep on the hay for tonight."

"Alright." Though Ciela grumbled about it, Adonai could tell that she was also somewhat excited about her new home. After she got settled in, he himself went home to get some sleep—he was tired.

Chapter 22

Adonai sat near the edge of a snowy cliff. He was meditating. A bright white aura glowed around his body. The air swirled around him, and pieces of rock, metal, and wood hovered with it, along with a small flame and a bead of water. His breathing was slow and steady. Very slow. A whole hour passed between each breath. Every day, he had been slowly working on perfecting the use of all six elements. By doing this, his mana and control had soared by leaps and bounds. The cliff he was meditating on was on Glacier Mountain. Glacier Mountain was located in the Glacier Mountain range along the east side of Glacier Valley. Aside from the Glacier Mountains, there was the Northern Mountain range; along the western side of the valley lay the Upper Jaw Mountains, and in the south lay the Lower Jaw Mountains. All of this made up the Dire Mountain range, where each mountain was massive and every peak reached high above the clouds. Those high peaks used to be unreachable, but ever since Adonai had returned from his bonding ritual, there wasn't a single peak he had yet to summit. And together with Ciela, they had nearly explored the entirety of the Dire Mountains.

The only place left unexplored was the Northern Ridge, a massive cliff that lay just beyond the Dire Mountains. It was this cliff that separated the Northern Mist from the rest of the world. A place that was seen as a bad omen, a place that should never be visited.

As Adonai meditated, Ciela nudged him with her beak. "How much longer do you plan to sit there? It's nearly been two days."

He broke his concentration and opened his eyes. "Sorry, Ciela, I lose track of time," he said as he climbed to his feet and dusted the snow off his pants.

"Are we going back home now?" Ciela asked, her big black eyes piercing into Adonai; they were full of curiosity, they always were.

"No, not yet. There's a place I want to go to before we return," he told her as he picked up one of her feathers from the ground and placed it in his pack.

"A place?"

"Yes, there's one more place we haven't been to yet."

"A place we haven't been to yet... Wait, you don't mean—" A bit of fear began to creep into Ciela's curious eyes.

Adonai nodded. "Yeah, I want to go to the Northern Ridge—"

"No. You can't. The Northern Ridge is a bad place. A very bad place. It's not a place we should explore. Please, don't go there."

"It is indeed a bad place," Aeolian pitched in. Most of the other bonds agreed as well. The only one who shared Adonai's interest in visiting the Northern Ridge was Arson.

"Relax, relax. It'll be fine," he assured them. "It's not as if I'm even going near the Northern Mist, so there's nothing to be worried about."

"Still..." Ciela was worried.

Adonai ruffled her feathers. "Don't worry, let's get going," he said as he hopped on her back. With a powerful flap of her wings, Ciela took off.

The Northern Ridge was a desolate place. There was a stretch of barren ground between the forests of the Dire Mountains and the edge of the Ridge. Not even the animals roamed the barren land. It was understood by every living creature that the Northern Mist was a place not to be trifled with. However, despite the lack of life, this land was brimming with mana, the foundation of all life. Adonai and Ciela flew along the side of the Ridge, looking out over the rocky fields.

"There's nothing to see here. We should be leaving," Ciela insisted.

"No, not yet. Let's keep going." For some reason, Adonai had a feeling that he should keep exploring the Ridge. He wasn't sure why; after all, it was just like Ciela said, there was nothing to see here. But still, he continued. And then they came across an opening.

"Ciela, land there," Adonai said, pointing to the cave.

She was hesitant. "Are you sure? I don't think we should go there."

"Just land."

She obeyed, and they landed on the ground just before the opening in the Ridge. It was like a crack. A great, big crack that went up almost the entirety of the wall. Adonai climbed down from Ciela's back and began to approach the crack, stopping just outside the entrance. It was dark in there.

"Please, Master," Ciela begged. "Don't go in there." His bonds were saying the same thing.

Even Arson was hesitant about entering the crack. Adonai was hesitant as well. This was a dangerous place, he could tell. But for some reason, he couldn't pull himself away from it. He couldn't resist the feeling that he needed to go in there. For a long time, he stood outside the opening, gazing into the darkness.

"We should be going; daylight is fading," Ciela pleaded. The sun would be setting behind the mountains soon.

"No." Adonai was determined. He took a step forward and then another. There was nothing that was stopping him. Ciela watched helplessly as he entered the crack.

Once inside, he ignited a small flame to provide light. The cave was dark and damp. Adonai had been in other caves as he explored the mountains. Something he noticed about those caves was that there was always a smell of feces. A sign of life. But there was no smell of feces here. There was no sign of life. His bonds were all urging him to turn back; he ignored them. When Adonai reached the end of the tunnel, what he found was not a wall of rock, but another opening. And that opening was covered by a wall of thick, white mist. At this moment, Adonai became one of the few people in history to ever stand before the Northern Mist. An ominous presence leaked from the Mist and the mana was dense here.

"We should turn back," Brine insisted, the other bonds agreeing with him. Still, Adonai remained where he stood, just an arm's length away from the white wall. He felt something deep within him urging him to go forward and enter the Mist. He felt that strange shard urging him. For a second, that feeling almost overcame him. But then, Adonai broke contact with the Mist and turned away. A feeling of relief washed over him as he left, but there was also a hint of regret. It was dark outside when he emerged from the crack.

Ciela happily welcomed him. "Let's never return to this place," she said. Adonai didn't say anything; he just climbed atop her back and they flew back home in silence.

Chapter 23

Adonai lay on the grass in the field just outside his family's house. He tossed a rock up into the air, and it began to swish around as if it were swimming through the air, doing loopty-loops and figure eights before once again returning to his hand. Then he would toss it up again and repeat the process. He had gotten pretty good at manipulating earth, so playing around with a rock like this was nothing. As he lay there playing with the rock, he kept finding himself thinking about the Northern Mist. It had been a few days now since his encounter with the Mist in the crack, and over these past few days, he couldn't stop thinking about it—the ominous feeling he got just from looking at the Mist and the strange shard urging him to enter it. Even now, while he was far away at home, he still felt that strange shard urging him to return to the crack and go to the Mist. Sometimes, he felt like listening to that urge... sometimes. But it was best to never even go near that crack again, much less the Northern Mist. After all, it was common knowledge that the Northern Mist was not a place to be taken lightly. But still, he couldn't shake the urge to return.

"Adonai!" Maybel called out as she ran up to him with a big smile. She stopped a short way away from him and watched as he manipulated the rock in wonder. "Wow."

Adonai sat up and let the rock fall to his hand. "Would you like to try?" he asked her with a smile.

"Can I?" she asked excitedly.

"Of course, come here, I'll help you." He set the rock in her hands. "Okay, now concentrate on the stone. Focus, feel the mana flowing through the stone."

"I'm focusing," she said with her eyes shut tight.

"Good, now throw it up." She did as he said and tossed the rock up into the air, and just like before, it began to swish around in the air, going in loops and figure eights.

"I'm doing it!" she cheered.

"Hold on, focus, you're not done yet." She focused again, staring intently at the rock, following its motions with her hand. After dancing about, the stone returned to Maybel's hands.

"I did it!" she giggled.

"Yes, you did," Adonai said, patting her on the head. "Let's do it again! Let's do it again!"

"Alright. Alright. Remember, you have to concentrate."

"Yup!" And she concentrated, she concentrated hard, as hard as she could. Then she tossed the rock back up into the air and again, it danced about. Of course, during all of this, it was really Adonai moving the rock through the air; whether or not Maybel was aware of this, he was unsure, but either way, she was happy and that made him happy. After playing with the rock for a while, Adin and Laor came over and watched the rock as it flew around in the air.

"You guys finished with your chores?" Adonai asked them.

"Yep, we just finished," Laor told him.

"That's good."

At this point, there weren't really all that many chores to do around the farm since Adonai was able to complete all of the hard work ridiculously fast. After a little while, Adin left and came back with two long wooden sticks that were meant to resemble dull spears.

"Is it alright if we do a little sparring?" Adin asked Adonai.

Adonai smiled. "Sure. Here, Maybel, we're done with the rock for now. Me and Adin are gonna have a spar, but you can watch us."

"Okay." She walked over and plopped down next to Laor. Adin and Adonai both took a spear and faced off against each other.

"You can do it, Adin!" Maybel cheered. Then she turned to Laor and whispered, "I don't think he can do it."

Adonai and Adin traded blows for a while. Adonai made sure to take it easy and did his best to give tips and help guide Adin. After a few rounds of fighting, Adin fell to the ground exhausted and bruised.

"I almost had ya," he panted.

Adonai laughed. "No, you didn't. Okay, Laor, are ya ready?"

"Yeah!" Laor jumped to his feet and then the two of them fought with each other.

It was a bit strange, Adonai's strength. It made him stick out like a sore thumb in his family. Neither his parents nor siblings had much talent for mana control or fighting. But for whatever reason, he possessed an extreme amount of talent. It didn't make much sense. He must have won some sort of lottery when he was born. After a while, their parents, Adon and Lily, came over and watched their kids spar. Adonai had a few more rounds with Adin and Laor before he stopped. Then Adin and Laor sparred against each other as he tried to coach them. It was a good time. As the sun set, they made a small fire and sat around it, enjoying each other's company.

Later that night, when Adonai was lying in bed, he found himself thinking about the Northern Mist again. It was at the point where the thought of it made him unable to sleep.

"You're thinking about it again, aren't you?" the wyrm bond, Ore, asked him.

"I know. I shouldn't be, but for some reason, I can't escape it," Adonai responded.

"You're not actually going to return there, are you?" Brine asked.

"You shouldn't," Aeolian told him. "It's best if you forget about it."

"But how am I supposed to forget? I don't know if I'll ever be able to forget..."

The night was long and silent. Adonai liked the silence, but right now, it felt as if it were choking him. He wanted something to distract his mind.

"Just go," Arson said suddenly.

"You fool! Don't say such things!" Brine shouted at him; the other bonds agreed.

But Arson resisted. "There must be a reason as to why you can't stop thinking about it. Just return to the Mist, you don't even have to enter it. Just revisit that place and maybe you'll be able to find why you can't escape it." Arson tended to be chaotic and rambunctious, but there seemed to be some sense to what he said this time.

The Northern Mist... "Maybe... just maybe I should go," Adonai said at last. His bonds still didn't like the idea of it, but this time, none of them tried to dissuade him. He got up from bed. It was still the middle of the night, but if he waited until morning, he might hesitate to leave after seeing his family. He didn't want that. So he got up and left in the middle of the night. He went to the stable and fetched Ciela.

"We're going back to the crack," he told her.

She began to get upset. "What! You want to go back to that place! But—"

"I know," Adonai interrupted her. "I know I shouldn't, but for some reason, I have to."

Ciela still didn't like the idea, just as the bonds didn't, but she could sense Adonai's determination. So reluctantly, Ciela allowed him on her back, and together, they flew to the Northern Ridge. The whole flight, Adonai felt sick. Anxiety filled his entire being. The short trip to the ridge felt incredibly long, while at the same time, it felt incredibly short. Ciela landed on the rocky earth before the giant crack in the Northern Ridge. "Are you really sure about this?" she asked as Adonai climbed down from her back. "No..."

Then he walked into the crack and disappeared from view without another word. The walk through the tunnel felt longer than it did the first time. Adonai's heart was practically beating out of his chest. Every step felt heavy. Every breath felt labored. Everything he had ever heard about the Northern Mist passed through his mind. A place not meant for the living. Some even considered it to be the land of the dead. There were supposedly all sorts of monsters. The Mist was thick and rendered anyone who entered blind. It even affected the mind, making you lose all reason and senses. In the past, many people had attempted to venture into the Northern Mist; of those people, only a very few made it back alive. And of those few that did make it back alive, none of them ever returned to the Mist. There had never been a case where someone had successfully explored the Northern Mist—never. And once again, Adonai found himself standing before that very Mist.

"If you enter now, there's no turning back," Weald said.

"You may die," Aeolian added.

For a long time, he stood there, staring into the Mist, and it almost felt as if the Mist was staring back. With one last deep breath, Adonai stepped forward and entered the Northern Mist.

Chapter 24

The Northern Mist was thick. That was the first thought Adonai had as he walked through it. He could only see maybe one or two meters ahead of himself. And the air was dense with mana, much denser than it was outside. As he walked, he recalled the story he had heard from Harold one night about his venture into the Northern Mist. How at first everything was fine, but after going deeper into the Mist, after reaching a certain point, that was when the true colors of the Northern Mist surfaced. Apparently, it would distort the senses and create confusion and panic. Those with a weak mind would succumb to madness, while those with a strong mind and enough perseverance would eventually regain control over their senses... well, somewhat regain control. But then again, that was all from a story told by an old man. Adonai wasn't sure whether he should believe in that story or not, but so far, it proved to be true because, just as Harold had said, at first, the Mist seemed safe. And if that part were true, then that must mean that eventually, he would also suffer the true viciousness of the Mist.

As Adonai walked, he took note of the land. It was barren, similar to the land surrounding the Northern Ridge. There was no sign of life anywhere, plant or animal. It was hard to say how long he had been walking—maybe an hour, maybe more. And then it hit. He had reached the true Northern Mist. And it was worse than he had imagined. His mind went blank, completely and utterly blank. A sudden chill filled his body. His senses weren't just disoriented; they were gone. Where was he? What direction had he come from? He spun around in circles, straining his eyes, trying to see something, anything. He saw nothing. He heard nothing. He felt nothing. He fell to the ground, or at least he thought he did. It felt as if he were going insane, as if the madness were consuming him. For a long time, Adonai sat there, in the Mist, alone. But he never stopped fighting. Eventually, he regained some of his senses. He tried to think, but every time he did, his head was met with a throbbing pain.

"Guys?" he called out, trying to speak with his bonds. "Guys, are you there? Hello?" There was no response. He couldn't make contact with his bonds. Another wave of pain washed over his body, and he went into another panic. And in that panic, he ran. He ran and ran and ran. First in one direction, then another, and then another. He ran back and forth, and every time he changed direction, it felt as if he were going the wrong way. Finally, he fell to the ground once again and cried. He cried until his eyes dried up. And then he just sat there, and time passed. How much time, it was hard to say. At some point, Adonai came to terms with his situation, and he discovered a newfound determination. He wasn't going to die here. He wouldn't allow that.

Getting up and running in a random direction would be useless. Instead, he became determined to regain his senses. No, he became determined to make his senses even stronger and sharper than before. The Northern Mist... a place where no man can tread... damn the Mists. He was going to conquer them. He took in a deep breath and began to meditate. He did his best to feel the mana within himself. With the distortion of the Mist, it was impossible to sense any mana, but he searched for it anyway. Trying to use his mind sent a wave of pain throughout his entire body, but he dove down deeper and deeper anyway, and then finally, he found it. Just a small wisp of mana, deep within his spirit. It was small, but it was something. So he built off of that. And gradually, the amount of mana he could sense grew and grew, until he regained control of his spirit.

"Guys? Can you hear me?"

"Master? Is that you? Yes, we can hear you," his bonds replied.

Adonai cried when he heard them. Finally, he was no longer alone. He continued to meditate, reaching out for the mana within himself. And eventually, he regained complete control over his body. His senses fully returned. It no longer pained him just to think. But this wasn't enough. Even though he regained complete control over his senses, he still had no idea how to find his way back home. The Mist was still thick, and he could still hardly see. So he continued his meditation, reaching outward to the mana that flowed around him. As he did, his pure white aura began to gradually form around him, and it continued to grow bigger and brighter. And then, something clicked. He could sense everything around him. He remembered the paths he had taken and knew where to go. It was as if he had gained a sixth sense. Confidently, he stood up and began to make his way back home.

It didn't take Adonai long to return to the tunnel he had entered from. For the first time in a long time, he stepped outside of the Northern Mist. And something had changed. He felt strong. Very, very strong. Because of his experience in the Mist, his mana had grown at an incredible pace. It almost made him want to laugh. To think that such a terrible situation would turn out like this. He conjured a bright flame and began to make his way through the dark tunnel. And then he finally returned to the outside world. The air felt amazing. He could see. He could see the snow on the ground, the sky, the trees, the mountains. He could see it all, and it was beautiful.

And there was Ciela. "Master!" she cried when she saw him and quickly flew over to him, knocking him over as she crashed into him. She had been waiting for him all this time. She continued to cry, "You're alive! You're really alive!"

Adonai laughed. "Yes, I am alive."

"I'm so glad you're back! You've been gone for so long!"

He pushed Ciela off of him and climbed back to his feet. "How long have I been gone?"

"Three months. You've been gone for three months. I thought you were dead."

Three months? That was longer than he had expected. He thought he had only been gone for maybe a week or two, but three months? His birthday had passed, he was fifteen now. What did everyone back home think?

"Let's quickly return to Never Thaw," he told Ciela.

"Yes, yes. Let's go home."

Adonai went straight to his family's farm. His brother and sister were the first to welcome him. They all cried as they hugged and reunited. His parents saw the Dire hawk from the fields and came running, and they joined the embrace with their children. Word of Adonai's return spread through the town like wildfire. There wasn't a single person who didn't come outside to welcome him home. As he was welcomed by friends and neighbors, the exhaustion finally caught up to him. He realized that he hadn't slept for over three months because he had been meditating the whole time. With the exhaustion suddenly catching up, he could barely stay awake where he stood.

Everything ended up being cut short, and Adonai retired to bed. He slept for two days.

Later on, Adonai sat down with his friends at their usual table at Chaver's family's inn.

"So where in the world have you been all this time?" Chaver asked.

Adonai grinned and leaned in close, whispering, "I went to the Northern Mist." Silence. His friends stared wide-eyed at him. Chaver muttered a curse.

"You... are you being for real?" Asher asked in a hushed voice.

Adonai nodded.

"You're a shmuck, ya know that? A freakin' shmuck," Chaver said and then added, "But since you already went, tell us what it was like."

Adonai smiled and shared the story with them. He told them about how he initially found the entrance and how the discovery of the Mist was gnawing away at him until he finally gave in and returned. He talked about the things the Mist did to his mind, how he was almost consumed by madness and then hopelessness. And then he told them about his sudden determination to make it out alive and about how he meditated and unlocked a sixth sense.

"Man, that's crazy," Chaver said when Adonai finished relaying the story. There wasn't really much to tell, but it was still captivating to his friends.

"Now I'll be ready for when I go back," Adonai said.

Chaver was drinking bourbon when Adonai said that, and he promptly spit it out all over the table.

"What did you just say?"

"That I'll be ready for when I go back," Adonai repeated.

Chaver nodded, taking it in, while Dahlia and Asher sat there dumbfounded.

Then Chaver slammed his hands on the table and shouted, "Are you a freakin' idiot!" The whole common room got quiet, and everyone looked over at their table in the corner.

"Ah, sorry, sorry, everyone, just ignore me," Chaver said.

His mother was staring daggers at him as he said it. As he sat down, he continued their conversation, "Do you really mean that? Are you really goin' back there?"

Adonai nodded. "Yeah."

"Why? Why would you go back there?" Dahlia asked.

"It'll be fine. Remember what I said? I gained a sixth sense. Think about it, I could be the first person to successfully explore the Northern Mist."

"But still, it's the Northern Mist."

"I know, I know. Perhaps I shouldn't go; in fact, I probably shouldn't. But now that I've been once and was able to safely get back home, I don't think I'll be able to resist the urge to go back."

"Well, as long as you're confident," Asher said at last.

"You're still a fool," Chaver muttered. The four of them spent the rest of the night enjoying each other's company.

Chapter 25

Adonai spent more than a week at home in Never Thaw. He spent his time playing with his younger brothers and sister. When he could, he would also spend time with his friends. Chaver was busy helping run the inn with his family, Dahlia was learning about plants and medicines, and Asher worked as a blacksmith. All his friends were pursuing some sort of path. However, Adonai... he wasn't entirely sure what path lay before him. He could probably go on to inherit his family's farm or something, but when he thought of the future, he could only think of one thing... the Northern Mist.

Ever since returning home, he constantly found himself yearning for the Mist. It was as if they were calling his name. And so finally, he answered that call. Ciela was still uneasy about Adonai leaving to go to the Northern Mist, but she believed in him and promised to wait for his return. Now, for the third time, Adonai found himself standing before the white wall of the Northern Mist in the depths of the crack. But unlike the previous times he had stood in this place, he did not feel afraid; instead, it was more like excitement. He had also come prepared this time, bringing along his spear and a pack filled with supplies. And so for the second time, he stepped forward and entered the Northern Mist. Just like last time, the Mist seemed harmless. Then once he reached the true Mist, its unrelenting attacks began, but this time, he had no trouble resisting the effects. He traveled north. For a long time, the land was barren.

After a while, Adonai stopped walking and broke out into a jog in order to cover ground more quickly. It was hard to say just how long he had been running, but he finally came across the first signs of life in the Northern Mist. He reached the Pale Mist Plains. The grass was tall and had a pale coloring. In the distance, he could sense herds of Pale bison and Mist elk grazing. Fox-like creatures called salphins weaved through the grass. The antlers of the Mist elk glowed vibrant colors that shone through the thick Mist. The environment in the Northern Mist was strange. Rather than feeding off of sunlight and nutrients in the soil, the plants thrived on the dense mana within the Mist.

Adonai stopped and knelt down next to a bush covered with

berries. The berries had a nearly transparent skin, and he could see the seeds within. He plucked one from the bush and contemplated eating it. But instead of eating it, he decided it would be better to take it back to Never Thaw and have Dahlia's family examine them first. With that thought in mind, Adonai picked lots of the berries and stored them in his pack. He also came across some star-shaped flowers that had milky white petals. He picked lots of those as well to bring back to Dahlia. He continued to take samples of various plants as he went.

For some reason, the Northern Mist actually seemed peaceful. That thought didn't last long because Adonai noticed something strange. He couldn't sense the bison, the elk, the salphins, or any of the other smaller animals. They were all gone. When did they all disappear? That was when Adonai heard the first click. He froze in place as he sensed a pack of animals approaching. Mist clickers. The clicking sounds continued. Click, click, click. It steadily grew louder. Click, click, click. The pack of Mist clickers split off into two separate groups. Adonai quickly backed away, trying to avoid being surrounded, but as he made his move, the Mist clickers broke out into a sprint. They were fast. The air was filled with the sound of their clicking. Click, click, click—it wouldn't stop. Adonai stopped backing up and stood his ground. If he wanted to explore the Northern Mist, he would have to be capable of defending himself against monsters like these. For what felt like ages, he stood there gripping his spear. The beasts circled around him. Then the first of the Mist clickers lunged out for him. He jumped to the side and it flew past him, claws flailing. The others weren't far behind. Two more Mist clickers lashed out and Adonai weaved between their attacks. The Mist clickers were vicious monsters. They were like giant lizards, nearly the size of a horse. They had no eyes; instead, they used echolocation to navigate and they had no teeth. Rather than teeth, they had long, serrated claws that they would use to tear and rip apart their prey, gulping down the shredded corpse. The Mist clickers continued to lunge at Adonai, coming at him from every angle. He stabbed one with his spear as he evaded the attacks, then ripped the spear out and stabbed another. When he went to stab a third, the wooden spear split in half as it sunk into its body. Another one of the monsters lunged at him and he rolled beneath it. As soon as it passed over him, two more were after him.

He evaded the first, but the second slashed his leg. Adonai raised his right hand and wooden tendrils burst up from the ground around him and wrapped around the nearby Mist clickers. Then he thrust his hands to both sides and sent out a powerful gust of wind in every direction, blowing the Mist clickers away. But they quickly recovered and came charging again. Adonai began punching at the air. With each punch, a concentrated blast of wind flew or a blazing fireball flew out of his fists. He raised one of his feet and stomped down, and the ground ruptured and cracked, creating uneven terrain, causing many of the approaching Mist clickers to stumble and fall. Blood was trickling down Adonai's leg from where the Mist clicker had slashed him earlier. Adonai had spent lots of time training himself in all kinds of ways, but he lacked combat experience, and that was catching up to him here. Some of his attacks, he put in too much mana, while in others, he didn't put in enough. He was getting tired and the Mist clickers showed no sign of relenting. They continued to lunge at him again and again and again. He did everything in his power to fend them off. Corpses were piling up around Adonai, while at the same time, his body was accumulating cuts and gashes.

Then something unexpected happened. There was a roar. A loud, terrible roar. A roar that struck fear into the very depths of Adonai's spirit. It was the most terrifying sound he had ever heard. It made his blood run cold and his hairs stand on end. He froze, unable to bring himself to move as a heavy pressure weighed down on him. And he wasn't the only one who froze in fear. The Mist clickers were also frozen in fear. As the roar faded, silence prevailed. Nothing stirred. Nothing except the beast that unleashed that terrible roar. Adonai could sense it. A large creature barreling toward him and the Mist clickers. A blood curdler. Adonai screamed at his body. Move! Move, please just move! But his body wouldn't respond. He kept pleading with himself, trying to get himself to move. The Mist clickers were the first to regain control of themselves and they began to flee in every direction. Move! Please move!

"Move!" Adonai shouted.

Finally, he regained control of himself and he fell to the ground. He quickly climbed back to his feet and ran as fast as he could. He heard the blood curdler's roar again as he fled and a chill ran down his spine, but he kept running. The blood curdler was more distant this time; it must have gone chasing after some of the Mist clickers. But even though he seemed safe, Adonai continued to run and run, until he couldn't sense the blood curdler or the Mist clickers anymore. When he finally stopped running, he collapsed to the ground, out of breath, his chest heaving.

"I think… I think I got away," he muttered to himself.

"Seems you did," Aeolian agreed.

"We should go back and fight it," Arson urged. He was ignored.

After catching his breath, Adonai climbed back to his feet, where he stood for a moment and thought.

"Are you going to leave?" Ore asked.

Adonai was tempted to, but… not yet. He didn't want to leave just yet. "No. I'm gonna keep going," he told his bonds.

"You're gonna keep going? Are you sure? What if we run into that beast again?" Aeolian asked, worriedly.

Adonai began to jog north. "Just a bit more, I just want to see a bit more and then I'll leave," he told his bonds.

Luckily, things went smoothly. Before long, he once again began to run into herds of Pale bison, Mist elk, and other animals, which was a good sign. Throughout this whole expedition in the Northern Mist, Adonai had been circulating mana constantly, maintaining an aura in order to sense his surroundings. It was exhausting, but that was alright. He was growing stronger by the second, he could feel it. And the deeper he pressed into the Northern Mist, the denser the mana seemed to grow.

As Adonai ran, a flying animal appeared and began to quickly speed toward him. He didn't think much of it until a lightning bolt suddenly shot down from the sky and nearly struck him. It left a small crater in the ground and sent chunks of earth flying into the air. If Adonai had been a second slower in his reaction, he would have been hit. Suddenly, the sky seemed to glow through the Mist. Lightning rained down. It was one lightning bolt after another. The ground rumbled and thunder roared. It was terrifying. But compared to the roar of the blood curdler, this thunder was nothing. Adonai dashed back and forth, dodging every lightning strike. It was as if the lightning was targeting him. That was when he realized that the animal he had sensed flying toward him earlier was circling around in the air above.

Adonai honed his senses on the animal and he realized something that made goosebumps rise all over his body. The mana presence of this animal was strong. Very, very strong. This animal... this animal was a mana beast. The lightning continued to rain down, and Adonai continued to evade it. He began to launch boulders into the air with his mind, and finally, one of the boulders struck the mana beast that had been attacking him. It came crashing down into the ground. The lightning stopped.

Adonai ran over to the animal, and as he got closer, he was able to make out the details of its body. It was a pegasus, a horse with wings. Adonai crouched down next to it. The pegasus's body was just ever so slightly rising and falling. It was still alive, but its life was quickly fading. He ran his hand across the pegasus's side. It was an elegant black color. There were six known mana beasts in the world of Oalm Catantan. It was believed that those were the only mana beasts. Yet right here, right in front of him, there was a seventh mana beast. A mana beast that controlled lightning.

He continued to examine the pegasus. "Does this mean there are more mana beasts in the Northern Mist unknown to the rest of the world? If there is a seventh, then couldn't there be even more?" Adonai said, thinking to himself aloud.

"It seems that way," Weald told him. "This is not something that can be taken lightly."

Adonai ran a hand through his hair. He was feeling so many emotions all at the same time. "Is this really real? I—I don't understand, how is it that no one has ever documented the existence of additional mana beasts?"

"It does make some sense; after all, you're the first to ever successfully explore the Northern Mist," Ore stated.

Adonai was still dumbfounded.

"Are you going to declare the existence of new mana beasts in the Northern Mist?" Terra asked.

Adonai was pacing back and forth. "I don't know... probably not. It would probably be best to leave this a secret."

"That would probably be best. Who knows how the world will

react upon hearing this news," Weald agreed.

Adonai crouched back down next to the pegasus. It was a beautiful animal; it was a shame it attacked him. After another minute or so, the slight rising and falling of the pegasus's chest stopped. It was dead. Adonai stood up and began to walk away, then he stopped.

"Wait a minute." He had an idea. "What if I formed a bond with the pegasus?"

"Is that possible?" Aeolian questioned.

"I don't know, but I've formed bonds with all of you. Since it's dead, its spirit no longer holds a body, so shouldn't it be possible to form a spirit bond with it? I'm gonna try," Adonai said that, but he wasn't really sure where to start.

The current bonds he had, he formed in the pantheon with the ritual prepared by Inuuk. Was it even possible to form a bond without the ritual? Adonai sighed; he was beginning to realize this was probably going to be far more difficult than he thought. Unsure of what to do, he decided to enter a meditative state and began to focus on feeling the mana flowing through the pegasus. He reached out, searching for its spirit. He dove into its body with his mind and shifted through the mana. It was strenuous work, but he kept pressing forward. Finally, he touched upon the pegasus's spirit.

He reached out as if to grab hold of it with his mind. Then he tried calling out to it, "Hello?" There was no response.

He focused harder and created a stronger connection and then called out again. Still no response. Now he was pouring as much energy into manipulating the mana as possible. He pressed against his limitations and then slightly, just slightly, broke past them. He surpassed his limitations and gained more control over the mana and gained a stronger connection with the pegasus's spirit, and he called out for a third time.

"Hello?" This time, there was a response. "Wha—what is this?"

Adonai conversed with it in a gentle manner. "My name is Adonai."

"Ad-o-nai? I don't understand. What is this?"

"This is death. You are dead," Adonai told it.

139

"Dead? I'm dead…"

"Yes, you are dead. I am Adonai, and I am trying to form a bond with you…" For a moment, the pegasus didn't respond, then it asked, "How did I die?" Adonai hesitated. "I… I killed you."

"Oh…"

"Are you not angry?"

"I… no… I don't know. I'm still very confused. What is this bond you spoke of?"

Adonai continued speaking in a gentle manner, "Forming a bond with me means joining your spirit with mine. You will become a part of me and you will continue to live through me." Again, the pegasus was silent.

"Will you form a bond with me?" Adonai asked again.

For a moment, there was silence again, and then it answered, "Yes, I will form a bond with you."

With that, Adonai attempted to begin the process. He forged a pathway out of mana between the pegasus's spirit and his own. Then he reached out and began to pull in the pegasus's spirit. He grabbed hold of it gently and slowly began to absorb it into his own spirit. It was strenuous work. It made his body and mind feel as if they were on fire, but he kept going. And then it was finished. Their spirits joined together and became one.

"From now on, your name will be Zolt," Adonai told the pegasus.

"Zolt… I will carry this name proudly," the pegasus responded.

Then Adonai woke up from his meditative state. He was exhausted. He lay back on the ground and groaned.

"Good work," his bonds told him.

This all was more than enough for his first expedition. It was time he went home. But first, he would take a nap, just a short one. He fell asleep in the middle of the field.

Chapter 26

William pulled his hood further over his face. It was the middle of the night, and he was in the outer section of the Imperium. It had been a few months now since he was attacked by the mysterious organization and the man who called himself the Second Descendant. Ever since that day, he had been moving carefully, almost never daring to leave his estate. They were watching him, he knew it. The reason he had finally managed to leave his home and come to the Imperium was because of trade tariffs that he needed to adjust. Normally, this could have been done by one of his subordinates, but instead, he had chosen to do it himself in order to finally make a move without arousing suspicions.

The streets of the Imperium's outer section were incredibly filthy. There were lots of people passed out, lying throughout the streets, some of them barely seemed alive. William moved quickly, snaking through one alley after another, making sure he wasn't being followed. Finally, he slipped into a thin alleyway hardly wide enough for him to walk through. He stepped over the body of a passed-out drunkard and then disappeared through a small doorway. The building was seemingly empty. It smelled of mold and piss. He went down a dark staircase and entered a dimly lit room. Seven people sat around an old table.

"About time you show up," a man by the name of Jared said bitterly.

"My apologies," William told them as he sat down. "I had to make sure that I wasn't followed."

The individuals who sat in the room with William were all trustworthy people he had come to know during his time serving as a Pillar. There was Dylan Ortal, a noble of Direland; James Ad, one of the Pillars of Wysteria; Finnick Kochav and Jared Ivor, nobles from Kaspian; Pabo Kling, a Pillar from Griffland; Sandra Lester, a Hyring Pillar; and Diana Grung, a Hyring noble. These people, along with William, were all powerful people of mortal birth. The reason William felt he could trust these people and the reason he had chosen them was because they all shared one main trait: they all feared the Telestials.

"So, are you going to tell us why you reached out out of nowhere and made us gather in such a disgusting place?" Jared demanded.

"Calm down, can't you tell why we're here just from who's gathered?" Finnick said, "Clearly this has to do with the Telestials."

"Well, I know that much," Jared grumbled.

"Thank you, Finnick," William said and then continued, "It's as Finnick said, I've gathered you all here because the thing we have all feared is finally coming to fruition. The Telestials are making their move." Everyone wore serious expressions and listened intently. "The first thing I want to bring up is that Yir'on, a fellow Pillar of mine, a friend of us all, is dead."

"Yir'on is dead?" Diana gasped.

"I thought he was only missing," Dylan commented.

"Officially he isn't even missing, but we have reason to believe he was killed."

"But who would have killed a man as powerful as Yir'on?" Sandra asked.

"While I'm not entirely sure," William told them, "I do have some idea. There seems to be a mysterious organization led by people who call themselves the Descendants. Henry was investigating Yir'on's death when he ran into them and sent me a message warning me of their existence. Not long after, Henry went missing. And then I as well was attacked by these… we'll call them… the black cloaks. They were powerful, definitely not a group of common criminals."

"So you're saying that the Telestials have formed this group, the black cloaks. And through this group, they are finally making a move to what… overthrow the government?" Finnick asked, trying to clarify.

William nodded, "That's what I believe."

"And what is it that you want us to do?" Jared asked.

"I was getting there. When Henry was conducting the investigation, he believed there was a connection between the Imperial Saints and Yir'on, so he personally investigated the Imperial Saints. Apparently, there seems to be a connection between the Saints and the black cloaks. I gathered you all here because I want to raid the Imperial Saints' southern church."

"Wait, wait, wait. You want us to raid the Saints?" Jared questioned.

"Isn't this a bit much? You said that you only believe there is a connection between the Saints and the black cloaks. What if we break into their church and find nothing? How will we explain that? We'll become criminals," Sandra added.

The others nodded in agreement.

"I know, I know," William told them, "It seems ridiculous. The Saints are renowned for helping those in need. But what else are we supposed to do? This is the only lead we have. And think about it, if the black cloaks really are a group created by the Telestials with the intention of overthrowing the government and subjugating the mortals like we think it is, then this is a conspiracy that runs deep, very deep. We can't just sit back and wait while they work in the shadows. We have to do something. We have to fight back somehow; and this is the first step."

For a moment, there was silence as everyone thought over what William just said.

Pabo was the first to speak up, "Let's make those darn Telestials bleed. I'm in for whatever."

Though his words were a bit rough, the others agreed with him— they needed to act. "When does this raid begin?" Jared asked.

William answered him, "Tomorrow night."

Chapter 27

"This is the place," William said in a hushed voice.

He and his companions stood together on a roof near the Imperial Saints' church. The church was built within a compound. Thick stone walls surrounded it and separated it from the rest of the city.

"Remember, if you come into contact with one of the Descendants, fall back, do not fight them alone," William reminded everyone.

Pabo rolled his eyes. "Yes, yes, we know, be careful around the scary men with marked masks."

Pabo was impatient; unlike the others, he was eager to spill blood, a little too eager. The eight of them were dressed in brown cloaks infused with mana to further hide their presence. Beneath their cloaks, each of them wore armor, also infused with mana. Rather than carrying a sword on their hip, they each carried interspatial rings and stored their swords inside, allowing them to call out the sword, making it materialize in their hand at any moment.

William gave the order. "Let's begin."

Pabo created a draft of wind from where they stood to the compound walls. With the draft of wind, they were each able to easily jump from the roof over the walls, landing silently on the ground beyond. Aside from the guards outside at the compound's entrance, there was no sign of any within the compound. Rather than continuing to speak out loud, a mana link was created, allowing the eight to communicate to each other through their minds.

"Everyone to your position. Let's be quick about this," William said through the mana link.

Everyone split up and moved around the building in silence. William and Pabo took the front entrance. The two stood on either side of the front doors. William held up three fingers and counted down. At zero, he and Pabo burst through the front entrance into the central chamber. There were a few Saints scattered throughout the hall silently worshiping the statue of Inuuk that was erected in the center. At the sound of them bursting through the doors, the Saints ceased their worshiping and turned to see what the commotion was. But before any of them had time to react, Pabo quickly dashed to each one and knocked them out with a single blow. Pabo was incredibly fast. William knew this, yet he was still stunned every time he witnessed his full speed. As the body of the last Saint slumped to the ground, Pabo turned and looked at William with a big grin on his face.

"You're enjoying yourself too much," William told him. Pabo just shrugged, and then William continued, "Quickly, we need to search the building for anything suspicious."

The two of them quickly darted around the room, looking into the hallway that branched off from the central chamber.

"Over here," Pabo called out. "There's a staircase leading down." William quickly arrived at his side. "Let's go."

The staircase spiraled down and was dark. The further down they went, the colder the air grew. The stairs ended in a hallway dimly lit by a few torches spaced too far apart. They walked down the hallway and found a thick steel door.

"This door is suspicious."

"It is," William agreed. They tried opening it; it was locked. "Step back," Pabo told William.

Then he struck the door and knocked it off its hinges. As soon as it burst open, a putrid smell hit their noses.

"By the Celestials . . ." Pabo gasped as they walked in.

Cages lined the room; each one was crammed with people. Some of the people weren't even alive, their bodies just left there to rot. The people started groaning and begging for help. Both William and Pabo were speechless.

"I . . . I can't believe what I'm seeing. What in the world is going on here?" William mouthed.

"What do we do?" Pabo asked, his easygoing expression now turning into a serious one. "We can't be hasty—" William started, but then he was cut off by a loud boom, followed by the shaking of the room.

William cursed. "It's starting. The black cloaks must be here. We need to help the others. After that, we can figure out what to do with the people here."

Pabo nodded in agreement, and the two of them sprinted out of the room. But when they went out into the hallway, there were three black cloaks blocking the way to the staircase. Their masks were blank, meaning none of them were Descendants. Without a word or a shred of hesitation, Pabo dashed forward, sword materializing in his hand, and slashed at the three enemies. Two of them barely managed to evade the attack; the one in the middle didn't and ended up losing his head. William summoned roots up from the ground, which reached out from the walls and floor and wrapped around one of the black cloaks. Pabo exchanged a few blows with the other black cloak before striking him down. William dashed forward and cut down the man he had ensnared with his roots. Then the two of them quickly made their way up the stairs to reunite with their companions.

Sandra Lester climbed up a wall on the back side of the church. There was an open window on the third floor, and she climbed in through it. A Saint was sleeping soundly on a bed in the corner of the room. Sandra silently made her way across the room and slipped out into the hallway. It seemed she was in the boarding section of the church where the Saints lived. She swiftly made her way through the hallway with silent feet. Then, as she turned a corner, she ran into one of the black cloaks. For a short moment, the two stood motionless and stared at each other.

"You're not supposed to be here," the black cloak told her as his sword materialized and an orange aura formed around him.

"And what about you?" Sandra asked as her own sword materialized, as well as her own brown aura. "You don't look like a Saint."

"You're right, I'm not a Saint. I'm more, so much more."

Then the black cloak dashed and swung his blade at Sandra's neck. She blocked the attack, and the two exchanged several blows before a bit of distance was reestablished between them. An orange flame ignited in the black cloak's free hand. Then he fired a fireball, which Sandra easily evaded.

"Seems I'm going to need a little more if I'm to handle a pest like you," the black cloak sneered.

His palm reignited, and this time, his arms and back also went up in flames. He launched a massive blast of fire that began to consume the entire hallway. Sandra used her mana to take control of the stone walls and ceiling and brought them tumbling down in an effort to crush the black cloak. A plume of smoke and dust puffed up into the air. The collapse had destroyed a small section of the church and made the whole building rumble, some of the Saints surely being caught up in it. At this point, the sound of battle had begun to ring out all throughout the compound.

The black cloak burst up from the rubble; he was angry. Sandra raised an arm, and chunks of stone floated up into the air. Then she threw her arm forward, and the stone surged toward the black cloak. In lightning-fast attacks, he cut down every approaching rock with his sword. But as the dust settled, he found Sandra dashing right for him. He barely managed to get his blade up in time to block the attack. They exchanged more blows, periodically stepping back to throw a fireball or send a chunk of stone flying. The fire that Sandra evaded splashed into the walls and began to spread across the building.

"I need to hurry this up," Sandra muttered to herself.

She mustered up all of her mana and put it into one powerful slash of her sword. The black cloak met her sword with his own, but when the blades collided, her sword cut through his own and then through his body. In one deft movement, she had cut him and his sword in half.

Dylan Ortal breathed heavily, and sweat dripped down his brow. He had faced his fair share of opponents throughout his life, and it was safe to say that this black cloak was the most powerful one of them all. The two of them were fighting out in the courtyard. Their battle had originated within the church, but after a powerful attack, Dylan was sent flying through the wall.

After taking their fight into the courtyard, the two had exchanged numerous attacks. Dylan attacked with the wood element, and the black cloak attacked with both the earth and fire elements. A thin layer of stone had formed a suit of armor around the black cloak; as he swung his sword, a flare of fire would lash out. Wooden tendrils would burst up from the ground, as well as sharp wooden spikes. The black cloak evaded them all. As they fought, the ground had turned into a mess, covered in holes and craters, and wooden extremities were sticking up everywhere. Their attacks went wild. With a powerful strike, Dylan struck the black cloak in the side, shattering his stone armor and making him cough up blood. Dylan tried to finish it there, but his enemy evaded. Dylan tried to continue his attacks, not giving the black cloak a moment to recover. Then a rock sailed through the air and struck Dylan in the face, sending him sprawling backward. Blood dripped down from a newly formed gash in his forehead as he staggered back to his feet. His vision was blurry, and his head throbbed. The black cloak had also recovered, and the two injured men once again faced off against each other. Dylan's green aura was fading, but so was the black cloak's. They readied their blades and then clashed again. They lacked the energy to utilize elemental attacks, so their fighting had become limited to their blades. Slowly, they both inflicted minor wounds on each other. Then finally, with a powerful thrust of his blade, Dylan drove his sword through the black cloak's abdomen.

Jared and Finnick were battling together against three other black cloaks. The two nobles from Kaspian fought with water elemental attacks while they were attacked with wood and air elemental attacks. Like Dylan, their fight had originated in the church, but as the intensity of the attacks increased, the nearby walls broke down and the two nobles were pushed back into the courtyard. Jared mustered up some mana and summoned a kraken tentacle. The tentacle burst up and then slammed down into the ground, crushing one of the black cloaks and splattering his blood across the ground. Now the fight was two versus two. But Jared and Finnick were still at a disadvantage. They both had suffered several injuries.

Then they felt the mana link with William reconnect, and William called out to them. "Jared! Finnick! The church is on fire! There are people in there whom we need to keep alive, as well as evidence! I need you to put the fire out!"

"We'd love to, but we're kinda in the middle of something," Jared replied, irritated. "Don't worry about that; Pabo is on his way."

Finnick clashed with one of the black cloaks when his sword was knocked away. The black cloak went in to deal the final blow. He raised his sword to strike Finnick down, but then a blur rushed past him. For a moment, the black cloak remained motionless, then his arms fell to his sides, and he dropped his sword as his head slowly slid off his shoulders. A short distance away, Pabo was standing with a big grin on his face. He swung his sword to the side, flinging most of the blood off his blade. The other black cloak, who was engaged in combat with Jared, only just noticed the arrival of his new foe, and then a blur flew past him. Just like his companion, his head was sent flying. Pabo licked the blood from his blade. He was enjoying himself a little too much. With their foes defeated, Jared and Finnick quickly ran back to the church and fired streams of water at the spreading fire.

James and Diana had been fighting on the fourth floor. When they had entered the building, they had been quickly noticed and confronted by one of the black cloaks. The two of them fought the one black cloak together. Though he was outnumbered, this black cloak easily fought back against the two of them. It was hard to distinguish the strength between the black cloaks. Their strange cloaks blocked out their presence entirely, making it impossible to gauge their mana. The only way to differentiate their strength was whether or not they were marked as one of the six Descendants. This black cloak wildly sent fire flying in every direction, constantly fighting with wide-range attacks with no consideration of his surroundings. James fought with the metal element. He created a maelstrom of metal that shredded the roof and walls but failed to eliminate the target. At the same time, Diana was launching chunks of stone. Without fail, this black cloak evaded and blocked every single attack. James stopped attacking with the metal shards and retracted it all, forming a rough suit of armor around himself. He charged in and fought the black cloak head-on. Their swords clashed violently, and all the while, all Diana could do was sit back helplessly and watch. This was a battle she wasn't capable of interfering in. This was a battle between a Pillar and someone else who possessed power equivalent to that of a Pillar. Diana couldn't even follow their movements. After hundreds of attacks, James landed a heavy blow across the black cloak. A few more strikes, and he landed another blow, and then another and another. The black cloak was covered in deep cuts, and he fell to his knees, and with one final attack, James cut him down.

All of these battles started and finished in a matter of minutes. William quickly gathered all his companions and they fled the scene together, leaving the rest to the Imperial Army, who had surely noticed the commotion by now. With this, the Imperial Army would discover the atrocities of the Imperial Saints and launch an investigation, hopefully leading to the discovery of the black cloaks.

It was still late at night when Captain Fluke arrived at the Imperial Saints' compound. There had been a big battle here, and it was very evident. Everyone in the city within a kilometer of the compound was up and buzzing, and it was a pain to hold them back and keep them away from the scene. Fluke walked with his men across the courtyard to the front of the church that had nearly been reduced to rubble. It made no sense; why would someone attack the Saints? Some of the other Imperial soldiers were helping escort injured and frightened Saints out from the building.

"What do you think this was all about?" Gin, the second-in-command, asked.

"I don't know," Captain Fluke said, "But what I do know is that we'll find the terrorists who attacked this place and bring them to justice, or I'll die trying."

"Well said, sir."

After a few minutes, some guards returned from the church with grievous expressions. "What's the matter?" Captain Fluke asked them as they walked out.

One of the soldiers turned toward him with a distant gaze. "You... you should see for yourself, Captain..."

"Can you show me the way?"

Reluctantly, the soldier turned around and guided Fluke to the staircase descending underground. Fluke thought he was prepared for whatever he was about to face; he thought wrong. He reached the hallway, and the horrible smell struck him like a brick.

"In here, sir," the soldier said.

Captain Fluke walked into the first room and was horrified by what he saw. He had to turn around and walk back out of the room to avoid puking.

"My Celestials... What... Why? I-I don't understand. What is all this?"

"We're not sure ourselves, sir," the soldier told him. "But there's more."

"More?"

"Yes, there's a lot more."

They went on to find several rooms filled with cages and people. All of the people being held were either elderly, sick, or afflicted in one way or another. They also found the sacrificial rooms where countless bodies had been burned. Fluke left and returned to the surface, where Gin was waiting.

"Gin, I need you to contact the higher-ups. Tell them to launch a full-scale investigation of the Imperial Saints. This isn't something the likes of us can handle."

Chapter 28

Adonai woke up. He sat up and stretched. After traveling so much, he had really come to appreciate the comfort of his own bed. It was nice being home. His family was eating breakfast when he walked out of his room.

"Good morning," his mother greeted him cheerfully.

"Good morning," Adonai replied.

As soon as he sat down to eat, Maybel was already tugging at his arm and singing, "Time to play, let's go playyy."

He didn't budge. "Sorry, May May, I have some things I need to take care of today."

"Nooooo, we have to go play, it's snowing outside!"

Adonai laughed. "It's always snowing."

She wasn't giving up. "Not like today. Today it's special snow. So we have to go out and play."

"Maybel, leave him alone; he said he has stuff to do today," Laor told her.

"Nooooo," she groaned, still pulling on Adonai's arm.

This went on during all of breakfast. When he was done eating, Adonai said goodbye and went off into town. The first place he stopped by was the blacksmith's. He found Asher there hammering away at a piece of metal, so focused that he didn't notice him walk in.

Adonai watched him for a few seconds, then shouted his name. "Asher!"

Startled, Asher stopped and spun around. When he saw his friend, he dropped what he was doing and his face lit up. "Adonai! What brings ya 'round here? I heard you returned just a couple of days ago."

"Yeah, I've been with my family. I came over here because I have an order to place."

"Aw, it ain't just to see an old friend?"

Adonai laughed. "Of course, it's nice to see an old friend. But I do have another reason for coming. I need a new spear, one made entirely of steel; a wooden spear with a steel tip won't cut it anymore."

Asher nodded. "I can do that. And since it's for a friend, I'll take care of it right away. But why do you need a new spear? What happened to the old one?"

Adonai grinned. "It broke while I was fighting some monsters in the Northern Mist."

Asher cursed. "The Northern Mist. Honestly, you're a psychopath... I'll never understand how you could go to the Northern Mist of your own free will. What were the monsters like? Now that you've told me this much, I gotta know everything."

Adonai laughed again and then told him about the Mist clickers, what they looked like and how they fought, and how the roar of something terrifying scared them all away. After he finished the story, he left and Asher got to work on the spear.

The next place Adonai was going to was the Greenfields' home, Dahlia's family.

Her mother, Gil, was the one to answer the door. "Adonai, what are you doing here?" she asked in surprise.

"I brought some things for your family. Is it alright if I come in?"

"Please do." She gestured him in.

Dahlia and her father, Charly, were sitting at the table looking over a book about plants. Dahlia was surprised to see Adonai when she looked up.

"What are you doing here?" she asked.

Adonai had a big grin on his face. "Your family likes researching plants, right?" he asked as he slid his pack off his shoulders and set it on the ground.

"Yes, we research plants," Charly replied.

Adonai still had a big grin on his face. "Well, I brought you all some stuff to work with." He opened his pack, exposing everything he had gathered. It was filled to the brim with all sorts of plants. Slowly, all their faces began to display excitement as they realized his pack was filled with plants they had never seen before.

"Bring that over here," Charly said.

Adonai brought the pack over and set it on the table, and they began to dig through it, pulling out the transparent berries, star flowers, grasses, and forbs.

"What is all of this? I've never seen anything like these!" Dahlia asked, amazed. But as she asked, she realized where they came from, and her smile faded. "You..."

"Yeah. I found them in the Northern Mist," Adonai told them.

They froze. The silence was loud.

"What do you mean you found these in the Northern Mist?" Charly asked.

"It's exactly as I said. I went into the Northern Mist, found these plants, gathered them, and then brought them back."

Dahlia's parents were dumbfounded, unsure of what to say.

"Have you... have you really been to the Northern Mist?" Gil asked.

Adonai nodded. "It's not the first time either."

Her parents still didn't know what to say. They wanted to scold him, to tell him to never go again, to tell all the other parents in the village. But they felt conflicted. This was an opportunity to explore the unknown.

"You're not going to go back, are you?" Gil asked.

"I am."

Silence again.

"Well... I suppose if it's you, it should be alright," Gil said at last.

"Did you know about this?" Charly asked Dahlia.

She nodded. Her father sighed. "How could you, as his friend, allow him to do this?"

"I know. I should have stopped him," Dahlia said quietly, then quickly added, "But he had already been there once and he told us he was confident in returning. So I thought it would be fine."

Charly sighed again. "It's like Gil said, maybe if it's you, maybe then it'll be fine."

"Thank you," Adonai said.

He really was thankful. He was afraid that they might make it known to everyone else what he was doing and then they would try to stop him from going.

"Just promise us you won't get hurt. We could never forgive ourselves if something happened to you since we've allowed this to continue," Gil told him sternly.

"Who else knows about this?" Charly asked.

"Chaver and Asher also know. Please don't tell anyone else. I don't know when, but I'll make it known eventually. But... just not yet."

"I see, so not even your family knows?"

Adonai nodded. "If they knew, they would do everything in their power to stop me."

"And why us?" Gil asked. "I can understand why you would tell your three closest friends, but why would you tell us about this?"

Adonai shrugged. "I needed somebody who could study the plants I brought back."

Charly sighed. "You really are a reckless one, ain't ya?"

After dropping the plants off at the Greenfields' house, Adonai returned home. He would stay in Never Thaw a little longer before returning to the Mist.

Chapter 29

The Crimson Woods is a forest that lay beyond the Pale Mist Plains. The forest was made up of strange trees, bleeding trees. The bleeding trees had what looked like white bark with a slight shade of pink; however, every single one of the trees was scorched, giving the bark more of a black color. Blood-red sap seeped through the bark and dripped down the trunks and branches, making it look as if the trees were bleeding. Though the trunks were scorched, the leaves remained untouched. The leaves had a vibrant red color, and glowing pink fruits hung from the branches: crimson peaches. The vibrant trees made these crimson woods a beautiful place. The transparent berries that grew in the plains also grew here in this forest. Adonai had begun to call them Ghost berries. And then the rest of the forest floor was covered in all other sorts of orange and yellow grasses and forbs.

Adonai carried with him the new steel spear Asher had forged for him. Asher was surprisingly good at what he did. The spear was a fine one. As Adonai continued further, the glowing crimson peaches were seemingly calling out to him. He wanted to eat one. He wanted to eat one so bad. They looked delicious. But he shouldn't eat one. Not until Dahlia and her family took a look at them to confirm if they were safe to eat or not. But . . . they really did look tasty. . . . Finally, Adonai gave up resisting the temptation and plucked one of the peaches. He turned it over in his hand, looking it over, and then he took a big bite. It was amazing. It had a soft flesh that was sweet like honey. He quickly devoured it and then plucked another one. As he ate them, he began to notice that there was a difference within himself. His mana. It felt as if it had become easier to control his mana. He leaned against one of the trees and eagerly ate two more fruits, and as he plucked a third, he noticed that a cute little salphin was slowly approaching him. Adonai watched as it slowly crept closer and closer. When it was only a meter or so away, he took the third peach and held it out for it.

"Here, do you want this?" he asked in a soothing voice.

Cautiously, the salphin continued to edge its way closer to him until it was right in front of his hand. Then it quickly snatched the fruit and began to scamper off.

"What a cute little guy," Adonai said, smiling as he watched it leave.

As it was running away with the peach, a swarm of bloodflies descended from the treetops and swarmed the salphin. Adonai watched in horror as they devoured the salphin in a matter of seconds, leaving behind nothing but bones. Then the swarm of bloodflies turned their attention toward him. They were approaching fast. In a panic, he raised a hand and shot out a stream of fire. As soon as the fire left his hand, everything around him went up in flames. Everything. It was a chain reaction. The entire forest burned like the surface of the sun. And then, after just a few seconds, the flames died out. Adonai had been protecting himself with mana, but the flames were so intense, he could still feel the heat.

"What just happened?" he asked himself after everything had died down. "That was incredible!" Arson cheered. "Do it again! Do it again!"

"Shut up, Arson."

"What happened?" Aeolian asked.

"I don't know, I only threw out a small flame to burn the bloodflies, and then suddenly everything went up in flames."

As Adonai looked around, he wandered over to one of the trees. The blood-like sap that had been dripping down the trunk was all burned away, and now new sap was slowly seeping out. This sap . . . could it really be the sap? Adonai lit a small flame just over his finger and then moved toward the sap. As it got close, the sap suddenly burst out in flames.

"The sap is flammable."

No wonder everything went up in flames. It was a shame, he didn't have anything to collect the sap with. Maybe the next time he came, he would bring some jars. After going a little further, Adonai came across a giant flower. It had strange bulbs that resembled the carcass of a dead animal in the center of four large petals. Curious, he walked over to the center of the flower to take a closer look. He crouched down and examined the bulbs. They really did resemble the corpse of an animal, which was strange. Then the petals of the flower suddenly snapped shut around him, trapping him inside.

"Oh, I see. The flower lures prey over with the bulbs and then devours it. Interesting," Adonai was talking to himself as he looked around. If it had been some other animal, it would probably die here. Unfortunately for the flower, its prey was Adonai. He took his spear and swung it in a wide arc, cutting straight through the thick petals, and then casually walked away. As Adonai continued to travel north, he came across some Mist elk and other smaller creatures. Every now and then, a swarm of bloodflies would attack. Fire was the easiest way to deal with them, but he was afraid of starting another chain reaction, so instead, he used a powerful gust of wind to simply blow the flies away . . . far, far away. At one point, a crimson boar charged at him. That boar was met with the tip of Adonai's spear. He then ate the boar out of spite. Eventually, his pack was filled to the brim with all kinds of plants just like last time, but he didn't stop there. He pressed on further, continuing to explore. And he didn't travel slowly. He began running. It was easy for him to move swiftly without rest for days and days on end.

Suddenly, a roar resounded throughout the woods. Adonai froze in his tracks. It was a familiar roar, one that he could never forget. A blood curdler's roar. The roar of death itself. It wasn't too far off. Crap. Move. He began to beg his legs to move. Please just please move. There was another roar, this time closer. Adonai began muttering curses and punching his legs. He had been training every day and still, the roar of a blood curdler practically crippled him. Anger began to boil up deep inside of him. Why? Why was he still so helpless? He hated that. He hated his weakness more than anything. But that rage was just what he needed. The anger allowed him to regain control of his legs, and he began to run. And he ran as fast as he could. In addition to Adonai's regular training, because of his new bond with Zolt, he had been practicing and experimenting with the lightning element. That effort paid off. Lightning flowed through his veins. It enhanced his nerves and brain, allowing him to think and react faster than ever before. And he used that now. He used it to run incredibly fast. Another roar resounded throughout the woods as he ran; this time, it was a little further away, a comforting thought.

"Turn around! Turn around and fight it!" Arson began shouting. He was ignored.

When Adonai finally put enough distance between himself and

the blood curdler, he let himself fall down to the ground. His legs felt weak. "By the Celestials . . ." he muttered to himself. "I never wanna hear one of those things again."

With that all over, Adonai decided this had been enough, and it was time for him to return home. He quickly made his way back to the crack and left the Northern Mist.

Chapter 30

William lay in his bed in his estate. He had just recently returned from the Imperium. Paranoia was setting in. He couldn't stop thinking about the black cloaks. The raid on the Imperial Saints was a success. They uncovered the secrets of the Saints and exposed them to the Imperial Army. An official investigation was launched, but before they could do anything, the remaining churches of the Imperial Saints were razed to the ground, leaving nothing behind, and all the people who served as Saints were slaughtered. The black cloaks must have thought that covering up their tracks would hide their existence. But just the fact that the Saints were mysteriously erased was evidence enough to show that there was a deeper conspiracy. The Keystone Urias had noticed this. The Imperium and all six nations were put on high alert. Imperial soldiers were deployed to nearly every town across the face of Oalm Catantan. Countless people were digging into the black cloaks trying to uncover who they were, but as far as William knew, they had yet to uncover anything. He was also trying to look into it, but he couldn't find anything. It was so frustrating. It was so obvious that there were Telestials plotting something sinister, yet there was no way to actually prove it.

William tossed and turned in bed, unable to sleep. He couldn't help but be afraid. He hadn't slept once since the raid. He couldn't bring himself to; he was afraid that if he shut his eyes even for a moment, they would catch him. He had tripled the guards at his compound, yet he still felt unsafe. William turned back over, and as he did, he caught a glimpse of something in the corner of his room near an opened window. When did he open a window? He shot up. He tried to summon his sword, but he wasn't wearing his interspatial ring. A person in a black cloak was standing in his room, staring at him.

"There's no need to be so alarmed," the black cloak said as he slowly stepped closer. "We know it was you, William."

"Who are you?" William demanded.

The black cloak ignored him. "We know it was you who attacked our Saints. Some of us... many of us would like you dead. But while we would like to kill you, it has been deemed to be an unnecessary action that will only draw unwanted attention. The fact that you alerted our existence to the Imperial Army really makes it difficult for us to move around as we please."

William stepped down from his bed and grabbed a nearby sword.

"Please don't try to kill me. That's completely unnecessary. As I said, we're not here tonight to kill you."

"Tell me. Who are you? Not just you, but your group. What are you after?"

"That's not something I can tell you. But in time, you will come to know. That is, of course, unless you decide to join us. That's really the best option. Just join us, and that will make things easier for everyone."

"Screw you and your cult," William hissed.

The black cloak continued talking, "Anyways, you may think you've dealt a blow to us... but in reality, you have done nothing of significance. Everything will continue as we have planned. Everything."

"What exactly is it you're here to say to me?"

"I guess I'm just trying to say that no matter what you do, our victory is inevitable. So just go on living your life. Do your duties as a Pillar. Have a family. Or do whatever it is you want to do, we don't really care. Because as I said, there is *nothing* you can do."

The black cloak turned and jumped through the open window. William ran over to the window and looked outside; the black cloak had already disappeared. He muttered a curse to himself. What was he supposed to do?

Chapter 31

It was the middle of winter when Adonai once again returned home to Never Thaw. The air was cold, and the ground was covered in snow. Oh, how Adonai loved the snow! The Northern Mist wasn't like the rest of the world. In the Mist, the weather never changed; there was no rain nor snow, nor any other sort of weather; all there was, was the thick, unrelenting fog. Even though it was further north than Never Thaw, the Mist wasn't particularly cold; it was strange. Spending so much time in the Northern Mist, Adonai had really come to appreciate the outside world. He could still sense things all around him within the Mist perfectly fine, but it wasn't the same as actually seeing with the eyes. The world was incredibly beautiful, it really was.

It had been a couple of days now since Adonai's return, and at the moment, he found himself walking through the village roads to Dahlia's home. He had his pack filled with all sorts of plants, and he was eager to see what they had learned about the plants he had already brought them. When he arrived, Gil warmly welcomed him in. Dahlia and her father were both excited to see him arrive.

"Let us see, let us see," Charly beamed as Adonai came over and set his bag on the table.

Immediately, he and Dahlia began to dig through the pack. The glowing peaches instantly caught their attention.

"This is incredible," Dahlia mouthed as she held one up.

"Crimson peaches," Adonai told them. "That's what I decided to call them."

"I've never seen a fruit glow like this," Charly said, amazed.

Adonai rubbed the back of his head and nervously told them, "I may or may not have already eaten some of them."

"You've already eaten some? You idiot! What would have happened if you got poisoned?" Dahlia scolded him.

"Yeah, I know, but I couldn't help it; they just looked so appetizing."

Dahlia sighed, "Well, since you seem to be okay, I'm guessing that means these are safe to eat."

"Yes, they're safe to eat. And they... well, just take a bite, you'll understand once you taste it," Adonai told them.

Dahlia and her parents proceeded to each take a bite out of a peach. "It tastes good," Charly said as he chewed, not thinking anything special of it.

"Just keep eating, you'll see why I think they're so amazing."

They kept eating, and slowly each of their faces lit up. "This... does this enhance mana?" Dahlia asked.

Adonai nodded his head, "It does. Pretty incredible, ain't it?"

"Incredible is an understatement," Charly said, "I've never heard of a raw food being capable of enhancing mana. Sure, there are ways to prepare food in a manner that allows it to enhance mana, but that takes a great deal of experience and effort. These... these are already capable of doing something only an experienced chef can prepare."

After tasting the peaches, they began to examine the other plants Adonai had brought back with him. Then Dahlia remembered, "Oh, we almost forgot! We've studied the other plants you brought to us previously, and they're incredible. Hold on just a second."

She ran off and came back holding an armful of jars and vials and began to hand them to Adonai. "None of these are quite as amazing as the crimson peaches, but they're still each incredible in their own way. To start, the clear berries you brought back, we've been calling them Ghost berries; anyways, they're safe to eat, and they slightly enhance the senses! Not as amazing as enhancing mana, but still incredible," Dahlia said excitedly and then continued, "This one here." She took one of the vials with a white liquid inside. "This is the nectar from the star flowers. It tastes bitter but gives you a burst of energy. And this..."

She continued on explaining what everything was and all the uses they had discovered for the plants while Adonai sat patiently and listened. There wasn't a single plant that didn't have some sort of medicinal use. The fact that they grew off of mana rather than normal sources was what gave them all such dramatic effects.

"Oh, by the way," Dahlia began after she finished explaining everything, "Chaver wanted to talk with you about something; I think it has to do with the Northern Mist, but I'm not sure. He just wanted me to tell you in case you hadn't already seen him."

"Got it, I'll head over there now." Adonai thanked them for their hard work and left.

He then went straight to the inn. Chaver got excited when he saw Adonai come in and asked his parents to be excused from work for a short while. The two of them sat down at their usual table in the corner.

"Are you really just going to drink water?" Chaver asked as they got their drinks.

"Yeah, I don't care much for alcohol," Adonai said plainly.

Chaver shook his head, "Such a shame, you're really missin' out." He took a swig from his mug.

"Dahlia told me you wanted to talk about something," Adonai mentioned.

"Yup, I did. Dahlia told me about the plants that you had brought back from the Northern Mist for her and her family."

"Yeah," Adonai nodded, listening.

"So I was thinking, since you want to explore the Northern Mist, and since you're bringin' back all this stuff for Dahlia to research, I was thinkin' that we make a business. Ya know, like selling stuff that you gather from the Northern Mist."

"I don't know..." Adonai said, unsure of the idea. "I don't really want to deal with a business."

"Ah, don't worry about that," Chaver told him, "I'll take care of managing everything; all you have to do is keep doing what you're doing. I mean, think about it, there's so much money to be made! Think about the things that we could do for this town!"

"I suppose that's true; it could help a lot of people around here," Adonai agreed and then asked, "But where do we even start?"

"That's exactly what I've been thinkin' about," Chaver said; his eyes were shining. He really was excited about this. "There's two main problems. First is we need a way to sell our products. Never Thaw is practically isolated from the rest of the world, so that will be difficult for us. And second, if we're to actually make this a business, we're going to need more stuff to sell, a lot more stuff. But as you are now, you can only gather so much."

"Okay, and I'm assuming you've already thought up a solution to these problems?" Adonai responded.

Chaver smiled, "I have. My thought was that we go to Plain City."

"Plain City? How will that help us?"

"You didn't let me finish. There's lots of merchants in Plain City. What we need to do is find someone trustworthy. A merchant with an already established business. With their help, we'd have a way of getting our product on the market. And the answer to our second problem is with something we buy from the Plain City market. An interspatial ring. We should be able to buy one in Plain City."

Adonai nodded, "That does sound like a good plan. But how are we supposed to get an interspatial ring? Interspatial rings are ridiculously expensive. And how are we sure we can find a trustworthy merchant to work with us?"

Chaver nodded, "You're not wrong. It probably won't be so easy. Interspatial rings are expensive, but we should be able to scrounge up enough money to buy a cheap one. As for finding a trustworthy merchant, we'll just have to hope we can find the right person."

Adonai took a drink of his water and set his glass down. "Alright, sounds like a plan. I'm in."

Chaver smiled and raised his mug, "Then, to a successful venture."

The following day, Chaver met Adonai at the stables where Ciela lived.

"Are you really sure we should both ride her?" Chaver asked nervously. "I mean, wouldn't it be better if I just rode a horse?"

"No. It'll be much faster if we both ride Ciela," Adonai told him.

Chaver cursed, "Alright, fine. But I ain't gonna like it."

Adonai brought Ciela out from the stall and strapped their things to her back. Then he climbed atop her and helped Chaver up. Then Ciela powerfully launched off the ground up into the air. Chaver screamed as he held onto Adonai for dear life. It was going to be a long trip.

Chapter 32

It was late when John walked into his favorite tavern. It was a smaller joint in the middle of Plain City that not many people visited, and that was what John liked about it.

"I'll have the usual," he told the barkeep as he sat down.

"Gotcha." The barkeep turned and began to mix up his drink.

It had been a while since he had a chance to sit down and relax. He was constantly working. After all, he had to work hard if he wanted to compete with the bigger merchant guilds. Unlike most merchants, John was one of the few who worked independently. The two major guilds in Plain City were the Plain Guild and the Direland Guild. The Direland Guild, in particular, gave John a lot of trouble. They were the largest guild in the nation and one of the largest guilds in the world. No matter what it was, the Direland Guild always seemed to have their hands in it, which made things particularly difficult for small merchants like John.

He was halfway finished with his drink when a group of three guys walked into the bar. They were also regulars at this tavern: Masos, Tohar, and Nov. John knew them well. Normally, they were the quiet type, but tonight, they walked into the bar talking excitedly.

"Did ya see the size of that thing's talons? They were huge!" Tohar exclaimed.

"No kiddin', I've heard of nobles who ride Dire hawks, but I ain't never seen one before," Nov added.

They sat down at a table near John, ordered some drinks, and then continued talking. John wasn't really the type to delve into other people's business, but their conversation had piqued his interest.

"Ya know the craziest part is the fact that the two riding the thing were both kids!" Masos told his friends, and they all agreed.

"Must be the children of some wealthy family."

"Probably Telestials."

"What do ya'll reckon them kids are doin' here?" Nov asked.

"Probably nothin' good. I've heard all kinds of stories about young Telestials being punks and making trouble," Tohar replied.

Masos nodded in agreement.

"Excuse me," John interrupted them. "What's all this talk about a Dire hawk?"

"Ya haven't heard?" Tohar asked and then continued, "Two kids just arrived by the north gate on the back of a Dire hawk. Was just a couple of hours ago; the whole city's been buzzing since. Everybody's talkin' about it."

"Interesting." John took out a couple of coins and tossed them on his table, more than enough to pay for his drink.

"I'll be leavin'!" he announced.

The barkeep waved him goodbye, and the other three guys went back to their conversation. John wasn't entirely sure what it was that he planned to do, but he found himself looking for those kids. Something about the situation just allured him. So he wandered through the streets to the northern side of town.

Rad led his little gang through the streets. Most people might refer to the four of them as nothing more than typical thugs, but they were more than that. Rad saw himself as a sort of... connoisseur, a connoisseur who helped keep the streets clean—yeah, that's what he was. His three buddies, Harel, Elihav, and Einav, walked behind him. They walked with purpose. Everyone stepped out of the way as they came through, paying respect to their greatness. There was word going around that a couple of kids arrived in the city on the back of a Dire hawk. And apparently, they were alone. Foolishness. Everyone knows that only the ultra-wealthy can keep Dire hawks as pets. So the fact that these kids arrived on one meant that they came from a wealthy family, and that meant they must have a lot of money on them. They were probably pretty strong for their age— all Telestials were—but that strength must have gone to their heads.

Because no matter how strong they were, in the end, they were still just kids. Wealthy kids. Rad was determined to find them quickly and... make sure their money was safe. After all, there were a lot of crooks in this city who might try and rob them. It was by Rad's good nature and kind heart that he decided to go out of his way to relieve these kids of their money.

When Rad reached the northern side of the city, he began to corner helpless civilians and press them to figure out if they knew where the two brats were. After confronting several people, Rad got up in the face of a scared elderly man.

"Oi, you, you know where them two brats are? The ones who arrived on the back of a Dire hawk."

The old man was too scared to reply properly, so Rad yelled, "I asked you if you knew where them two brats are! Are you gonna answer me, or am I gonna have to teach ya a lesson?"

That seemed to help the old man find his words.

"Ah, yes. I think I saw them go into an inn."

"Which one?"

"The... the Jin Jan Inn. It was the Jin Jan Inn."

Rad smiled. "Thank you very much, sir."

Then he pushed the old man out of his way and called out to his buddies, "Come on, I found out where them brats are."

His companions all smiled and joined him. A short while later, they burst through the front door of the Jin Jan Inn.

"Oi! Where's them brats with the Dire hawk!" Rad shouted.

Everyone was terrified. That is, everyone except for the two brats sitting in the far corner.

"I asked where them brats are!" Rad repeated.

A lady pointed with a shaky hand to the two kids who were in the corner, the two who showed no reaction. Rad stormed over to them and slammed a fist down on the table.

"Oi, when I asked for the brats with the Dire hawk, why didn't you punks answer me?"

It was a bit weird. Telestials had a certain air about them, but these two kids definitely weren't Telestials, as Rad had assumed they would be. In fact, they didn't even look wealthy. One of them was eating a roasted fowl completely unbothered. The other kid, the stronger-looking one, was eating some sort of soup. It was this kid who turned and spoke with him.

"Sorry, sir, we were enjoying our meal. Please forgive me for not answering you the first time. What is it that you want?"

Rad put on a big grin; his buddies were also grinning like idiots behind him, almost trying not to start laughing.

"Well, ya see, there's a lotta bad folks in this town," Rad started, "So us here, out of the kindness of our hearts, thought we'd come over and protect your money for ya. So why don't ya hand it on over? It'll be in good hands."

The boy took a napkin and wiped at his mouth before speaking again, "Thank you for your offer, but I think we'll be alright holdin' on to our money ourselves."

Rad's grin faded. He leaned over and got closer to the boy's face.

"Allow me to rephrase that. Give. Me. Your. Money. Now!"

Rad slammed the table again. The kid still seemed completely unafraid. No, he actually looked a bit annoyed. Was it just a farce? An attempt to bluff his way out of the situation? Rad looked over at the other boy, who was still eating his fowl completely unbothered, as if Rad and his gang weren't even there.

"Oi, were you dropped on your head?" Rad said to the boy. The boy still ignored him.

"You brat, answer when you're spoken to!" Rad screamed at him.

Finally, the boy looked up from his meal, looked at Rad, then turned to his friend and said, "Adonai, who are these guys?"

Adonai shrugged.

Rad was baffled. All his life, people feared him. All his life. But here were these two little brats who treated him like he wasn't worth the time of day. It made him furious. Rad pulled out a knife.

"Give me your money!" he screamed at them. "Give me your money now, or I'll kill ya both right here, right now!"

Elihav set a hand on Rad's shoulder. "Oi, maybe just calm down a little—"

Rad threw Elihav's hand off his shoulder and screamed, "Don't tell me to calm down!"

Then he turned back to the two brats. Adonai sighed deeply, and a little smile began to creep across Chaver's face.

"You guys should probably run, he's really annoyed now," Chaver said to the thugs.

Somehow, Rad found himself even more baffled than he already was... and even more angry. He turned back to Adonai with anger burning in his eyes. Rad squeezed his dagger until his knuckles turned white. He screamed a curse and swung the knife at Adonai's head. Adonai caught the blade with a bare hand and lowered it. The two of them locked eyes, and finally, Rad understood that these kids weren't bluffing. He tried to pull his knife back, but the kid's grip on it was firm. Sweat began to bead on Rad's forehead. Adonai's gaze alone made him feel as if there were a hundred daggers pointed at him. Then, Adonai slowly rose to his feet, his hand still on the dagger.

"Oi, let go," Rad said in a shaky voice.

Then Adonai threw a punch. An uppercut that landed directly on Rad's chin and sent him flying backward. Rad's companions took a moment to process what had just happened. Then they turned to Adonai with angry expressions.

"You dang brat! I'll kill ya!" Harel shouted.

Elihav and Einav both drew daggers and charged the kid. Throughout all of this, Chaver watched while munching on his food. It was always nice to have a good show during a meal.

Adonai slipped past the thugs' daggers and, in two swift motions, punched them both in the gut. Elihav and Einav both crumpled to the ground, coughing up blood. Only Harel remained standing. The entire inn had their eyes on this fight. Harel stood frozen, Adonai waited. Finally, Harel threw down his knife, turned, and ran away as fast as he could. Adonai sat back down and resumed eating his soup. Elihav and Einav climbed to their feet and stumbled over to Rad. They picked up their buddy and carried his unconscious body outside the inn.

John watched wide-eyed as a single kid easily took down a group of thugs. One of the thugs pushed his way past him and ran outside, and then the other three weren't far behind. What in the world did he just witness? In all his years, John had never seen a fight like that. He was almost too afraid to approach them, but finally, he worked up enough courage to walk over to the two kids.

"Excuse me, is it alright if I take up a bit of your time?" John asked.

Adonai looked at him with a bit of an annoyed expression, but then gestured for him to sit down at the table.

"Thank you," John said as he took a seat.

"What is it that you want? As you can see, we're in the middle of a meal." This time, it was Chaver who spoke.

"My apologies. My name is John. I'm a merchant here in Plain City, and I was beyond curious to see the two kids who arrived in town on the back of a Dire hawk."

Both of the boys' faces seemed to light up a little bit after hearing John say he was a merchant. Now they were actually interested in the conversation.

"My name's Chaver Rolfe, and that there is my good friend Adonai Alaric."

"A pleasure to meet you two," John said to them. "Might I ask what family you hail from?"

"What do you mean, what family do we hail from? Is that some sorta noble talk?" Chaver asked.

"So you're not nobles?"

"Not at all. The two of us are from a small town up north," Chaver told him.

"Really? Then may I ask how you acquired that Dire hawk? I really am curious," John asked.

"It was Adonai. He ran into it up in the mountains and tamed it himself. Her name is Ciela."

John's mouth dropped. He turned to look at Adonai, who was still casually eating his soup.

"You—you tamed a Dire hawk?"

"Yeah."

John was astounded. Now it was Chaver's turn to ask some questions.

"You said you're a merchant, right?"

"Yes, I'm actually the most successful unaffiliated merchant in Plain City," John told him proudly.

Chaver smiled real big.

"That's perfect! We actually came here looking for a merchant."

"Really? And why is that?" John asked, even more interested than before.

Chaver paused before answering and turned to look at Adonai.

"You think we can trust this guy?"

Adonai looked John over, then looked back to Chaver, "Yeah, I think we can trust him."

"I'm sorry, I'm not following," John said.

"It's alright, let's continue this talk somewhere more private," Chaver told him. They waited for Adonai to finish his soup, then Chaver got up and gestured for John to follow. They went up to their room and resumed the conversation there, and Chaver began to explain their situation.

"So we're looking for a merchant because we're looking to start a business. Ya see, Adonai... Adonai has been exploring the Northern Mist."

Yet again, John was dumbfounded.

"You've been to the Northern Mist? No, wait, you haven't just been, but you're actively exploring the Northern Mist?"

Adonai nodded, "Yeah."

John began to pace back and forth in the room, deep in thought, which the boys thought was a bit strange.

Chaver continued to explain, "You see, Adonai's been gathering stuff from the Northern Mist. Just plants so far. And each and every one of these plants is unique to the Mist and has some sort of incredible effect. We wanted to start selling the stuff Adonai gathers, but we have no way of getting it on the market since we live in a remote town in the far north."

John nodded as he followed along.

"I see, so you need an experienced merchant's help in order to sell your products. And that merchant is me? But wouldn't it be better for you guys to approach one of the major merchant guilds?"

"We thought about that, but we don't really trust them. We'd rather work with an individual like you. So, can you do it?" Chaver asked.

John smiled, "I can do it, I for sure can do it."

Now Chaver smiled as well, "Perfect. Oh, and there's one more thing. We need an interspatial ring. As things are now, all Adonai has is a little pack."

"I can definitely take care of that," John told them.

Chaver clasped his hands, "Perfect."

With that, the negotiations were complete, and John left for the night. He was all giddy as he walked back home, filled with excitement about this new venture. It wasn't the fact that this was a huge opportunity to make a lot of money, which was nice and all, but it wasn't John's main concern. Rather than the money, John was more interested in those boys and getting to work with them. This, this is what he had been looking for all his life. This was something that gave him a true sense of purpose, something that money never did.

Chapter 33

John met with Adonai and Chaver again the next day. He treated them to lunch at the inn they had been staying in. As they ate, he pulled out a box and slid it across the table to the two boys.

"What's this?" Chaver asked with a mouthful of food. John was smiling, "Open it, you'll see."

Adonai opened the box as Chaver continued to wolf down his food. There were two interspatial rings inside. Adonai picked one up and examined it in awe. He wasn't very familiar with things like this, but it looked expensive.

"Each of those holds two hundred kilograms," John told them.

Their eyes went wide. "Two hundred kilograms?" Adonai repeated. He didn't know much, but he knew enough to understand that these rings were on the valuable side, and there were two of them at that. "Why did you buy these? Me and Chaver could have bought ourselves a cheap one."

"Don't worry about that. Consider this an investment," John said happily.

Adonai set the ring back in the box. "Thank you. This is far more than we could have asked for."

"Eh, it could be better," Chaver joked.

Adonai punched him half-heartedly. "Shut up and say thank you, ya bloke."

Chaver grinned and lowered his head. "Thank you very much, good sir. We greatly appreciate your kindness."

John laughed; it was nice to see the two of them mess with each other like that.

"When do you plan to return to your home?" John asked.

Chaver finished his food and took over the conversation. "Now that we have the interspatial rings, we'll be leaving today."

"So soon?"

"Yeah, now that everything's been taken care of, neither of us really cares to stick around."

"I see. Then allow me to see you off," John told them.

After they finished their lunch, Adonai went and fetched Ciela from the stables. John marveled at her. She was a magnificent bird.

"Can I?" he asked, reaching out toward her.

"Yeah," Adonai nodded.

John ran his hand along the hawk's long feathers. They were smooth and soft.

"When are you planning on traveling north?" Chaver asked.

"I'll leave in a few days. I have some things I need to take care of before I depart," John told them.

"Sounds good."

Adonai climbed onto Ciela's back and then helped Chaver up. Just like before, Chaver held onto Adonai for dear life and screamed as Ciela launched into the air. John watched them soar into the sky and disappear into the distance.

After taking care of some personal matters, John sat waiting in his usual tavern. After a little while, a man dressed in fine clothes walked into the bar and sat down with him.

John greeted him, "James, it's nice to see ya."

"And you as well," James said as he pulled out a chair and sat down. "You said you had something important to talk about?"

John nodded. "I do, but we'll wait until the others arrive."

"Who else is coming?"

"Harry and Jane."

"Both Harry and Jane, huh? Seems you have something big planned considering the fact that you're gathering all four of us. What would make someone like you, who always insists on working alone, suddenly decide to work with others?" James asked.

"As I said, I'll tell you all about it once everyone's here. For now, why don't you order yourself a drink? I don't want to be the only one drinking."

"Alright, fine."

After a bit longer, Harry arrived. He was old with graying hair and a rough beard. Not long after his arrival, Jane walked in. She was a similar age to John and James, in their early thirties. She was one of the few female merchants in Plain City. All four of them sat around the table together.

"Alright, now that everyone's here," John started, "I'll get down to business. I recently stumbled upon the opportunity of a lifetime. No, it's better than that. This is an opportunity better than most men would even dream of. As you all have probably heard, two young boys arrived on the back of a Dire hawk yesterday near the north gate."

"Of course, word spreads fast 'round here," Harry mentioned. The others agreed.

"Well," John continued, "I had the opportunity to meet these two boys. Contrary to the rumors, they don't hail from a wealthy family. They're from the far north, a little town called Never Thaw. Their names are Adonai and Chaver, and that Dire hawk they traveled here on, that boy Adonai, he tamed it himself."

The others suddenly became very interested in the conversation. Harry leaned forward in his chair. "You ain't pullin' our legs now, are ya?" Harry demanded.

John shook his head. "Everything I'm telling you is the truth, and what I'm about to say is even crazier than the Dire hawk. Adonai... he's been exploring the Northern Mist."

Silence. None of them were sure what to say.

". . . No, there's not a chance," James mouthed in disbelief.

"The Northern Mist has never been successfully explored. And now you're trying to tell us that a mere boy is doing it all on his own?" Jane said.

"I know it's hard to believe, but it's true," John assured them.

"How can you be so sure? Did they have proof? How do we know we can trust these boys?" Harry pressed.

"Oh... right, proof..." John stumbled over his words. "Well, I didn't exactly get proof... but there was something about these kids. They were trustworthy, I promise!"

Harry shook his head. "You're crazy."

"I'm being serious!" John said, desperately trying to win them over. "That boy Adonai, I watched him take out four thugs single-handedly! And like I said, there's just something about him. I promise ya, he's the real deal. He carried that kind of atmosphere around him."

"Geez..." Jane sighed. She was trying to decide whether or not to get up and leave right then and there. "This... this is ridiculous... but... I suppose if it's you, John, then maybe, just maybe this is true."

The other two sat quietly, thinking it over.

"If Jane trusts you, then I'd have to as well," James added.

Then they all looked at Harry, who had yet to answer.

"Alright, I'm in. You are a trustworthy man," Harry grumbled.

"So say this is all true, what is it you want from us?" James asked.

John smiled, glad that he was able to win them over. "As I said, that boy's exploring the Northern Mist, but he's not just exploring. He's bringing back stuff. Plants unique to the Northern Mist. Those two boys are looking to sell the things Adonai brings out from the Northern Mist. So that's where we come in. They're way up north, their town is practically isolated. That's why they came here; they came looking to find a merchant who could help them get their products on the market. That's why I gathered all of you; this may start out small, but it has incredible potential. It's something that I won't be able to handle alone. What I want is for us to form our own guild. I want us to monopolize the Northern Mist. So what do ya say, are you guys in?"

There was silence again after John finished speaking. James, Harry, and Jane were all seriously thinking it over.

"Alright, I'm in," Jane said at last.

"Then I as well."

"And I," Harry added.

"Perfect, then it's settled. We'll band together and make this the most successful business this world has ever seen."

The four of them raised their glasses and had a toast. After that, they all immediately began their preparations for what was to come. Blue Glacier Guild became the name of their new guild. John and James would be going to Never Thaw to manage things there, while Harry and Jane were going to stay in Plain City and take care of the ships that would be used to transport the goods down the Dire River. And with that, everything was settled.

A couple of weeks later, John and James arrived at Never Thaw with a train of wagons. Chaver ran out to greet them.

"John! It's about time you're here!"

"Sorry, but we don't have Dire hawks to fly on like you punks," John said with a smile.

"Well, it's nice to finally have ya here. Who's this?" Chaver asked, extending a hand out to the other merchant.

"My name's James. I'll be working with you guys in this business." They shook hands. "The more help, the better. Come on, I'll show you guys around." Chaver led the way, and John and James followed him into Never Thaw. Never Thaw was vastly different from Plain City. It was hard to know where to begin. For one, there was snow... everywhere, absolutely everywhere. Apparently, it snowed year-round; that was something the two merchants would have to get used to. Aside from that, the town was far smaller than a city. There were no city walls nor guard towers, and everyone seemed to know each other. As they went through the town, Chaver greeted everyone they came across. After getting an idea of what Never Thaw was like, they went to sit down at Chaver's family's inn to have a drink.

"So where's Adonai?" John asked after they sat down.

"Yes, where is Adonai? I'd like to meet him," James added.

"Adonai left for the Northern Mist about a week ago," Chaver told them.

"Really? So it's actually true, he's really exploring the Northern Mist?" James said.

"He sure is. Word of it is going to get out here before long. We were originally keeping it a secret, but now that we're starting a business, word's bound to get out, and then everybody 'round here will know about it," Chaver explained.

"I see. Is that going to be a problem?" John asked.

Chaver shrugged. "It'll work itself out."

After that, they discussed what would be happening moving forward. The first things they needed to take care of were expanding the town. They would need a headquarters for the new guild, as well as lodging for all of James's and John's workers. When they had time, Chaver brought them to Dahlia's house to show them all the products they had already made. And with that, the beginning of a new era for Never Thaw began. A small town that would soon bloom into a bustling metropolis.

Chapter 34

Adonai munched on a crimson peach as he walked. Now that he had two interspatial rings, he didn't have to carry a pack and he didn't have to carry his spear, a convenience he never thought he would have. Now, whenever he wanted to use his spear, all he had to do was think of it and then it would materialize in his hand. Gathering things also became much easier; all he had to do was pick up a plant and imagine himself storing it in the ring, and then it would dissolve into a sort of wisp that would flow into the ring. It was incredible, honestly.

He finished half of the peach he was eating and then tossed the rest to the ground. A nearby salphin scampered out from the bushes and snatched the rest of the fruit. Adonai walked through the Northern Mist with confidence now. His strength had grown tremendously since his first visit to the Mist. A few days ago, a pack of Mist clickers attacked him. The Mist clickers were dangerous hunters that attacked with strategy. After surrounding their prey, they would take turns leaping in and swiping at the prey with their claws and then leap back out of the way so that another could leap in, taking its place, and the process would repeat. This allowed for an unrelenting, continuous attack that came from all sides.

In his first encounter with the Mist clickers, Adonai had struggled. But not this time. He nimbly slipped past each and every attack and then countered with an attack of his own. He varied his attacks, sometimes striking with his spear, crushing bones with his bare hands, or launching some sort of elemental attack. He tried to utilize every element, further increasing his abilities. Before long, Adonai had found himself surrounded by the corpses of the Mist clickers. It had been easier than expected. After the battle, he harvested them, taking their claws, bones, and hides and storing them in the interspatial rings. The only problem with staying and fighting all those Mist clickers was that now Adonai was exhausted. He had used up a lot of mana in that fight. And in addition to all that fighting, the last time he slept was... well, it was a long time ago, a very long time. But he should be fine to keep going; at least that was what he was telling himself.

He stepped over a fallen branch. That was when he sensed it. A beast, a monster. A very dangerous monster. A blood curdler. It wasn't far away. It was nearby, curled up on the ground asleep. This was the closest Adonai had been to one. It was massive. More than three meters tall. Its entire body was covered in thick bone plating with blood-red skin showing through the gaps of the plating, making it look like its body was covered in war paint. It had a long tail with a club on the end, two horns that protruded from the sides of its head, four legs that all ended with murderous claws, and a mouth full of razor-sharp teeth. Adonai slowly took a step back and a branch snapped beneath his foot. He had gotten careless. The blood curdler's eyes suddenly flickered open and its gaze went straight to him.

"Move. Please move," he said to himself, but he couldn't. He felt frozen as he watched the blood curdler uncurl and climb to its feet while making a low grumbling noise. The two of them stood facing off against each other. And then the blood curdler raised its head and roared. Adonai went pale. He had grown so much, yet when he stood before the blood curdler's roar, it still invoked complete and utter terror throughout his entire being. His bonds were screaming at him to run. He was screaming at himself to run. But his legs wouldn't listen. The blood curdler charged. With every step, the ground seemed to rumble. It knocked aside every tree in its path as it ran. Move... move, move, move! Adonai rolled to the side, just barely evading the blood curdler's charge. He muttered a curse to himself as the blood curdler quickly stopped and turned around. It was surprisingly agile. Adonai quickly scrambled to his feet and took off running in the opposite direction. He was in too much of a panic to properly utilize his mana. His senses dulled, and suddenly it was as if he were running blind. He tripped over a tree root, and as he fell, his head slammed into the ground. His ears began ringing, and then, through the ringing, another roar resounded through the woods. Adonai tried scrambling back to his feet, and as he did, the blood curdler slammed into him. Its horns tore into his chest and then his body was sent flying. He crashed into a tree with such force that the tree exploded into splinters. Pain. Adonai lay on the ground with a pool of blood forming around his body. He closed his eyes.

Perhaps this was the end. He found himself thinking about his parents, his family, his friends. Maybel, Adin, Laor. Chaver, Asher, Dahlia. His home. The people around him. Emilio... Emilio, who had died protecting their lives. The Dire bear attack... Emilio... the other guards... they all died... died fighting the bear. The bear that he could have defeated. It was his fault that they died that day. If only he had chosen to fight... to fight... to fight? Fight. Fight back. He could still fight back. He could fight back right here and right now!

Adonai's eyes burst open and he shot up from the ground. He was overflowing with mana. His senses didn't just return, they were sharper than ever. The blood curdler was right before him with gaping jaws. Adonai slipped to the side just as its jaws snapped shut. Then, with lightning flowing through his veins, he punched the beast with all his force. The bone plating along the side of its body cracked and it went flying, crashing through a tree. It climbed back to its feet and shook the hit off. Adonai stood tall, his white aura shining brightly around him.

Impending doom. At this time, those were the only words that could be used to describe him. He became the impending doom that now stood before the blood curdler, what was once an apex predator. It raised its head and roared its terrible roar. But in the midst of its roar, Adonai dashed toward it and struck it in the throat. Once again, it was knocked back several meters. Adonai called his spear and it formed in his hand. Then he dashed again and closed the distance between them in a fraction of a second. The incredible bone plate armor that the blood curdler boasted was pierced as Adonai drove his spear deep inside its chest. The beast swiped at him with its claws, clinging on to life. He ducked beneath the claws and landed another blow on the chin of the blood curdler, stunning it. And he didn't stop. He showered punch after punch upon the beast until its face had been turned to mush. In a last attempt, it lashed out, slashing with its claws over and over again. But every time, the claws were evaded. Then Adonai grabbed hold of his spear and ripped it out from the beast's chest. He lifted it up high and then drove it into the blood curdler's head. The blood curdler fell to the ground, dead. With the fight over, Adonai began to calm down from his adrenaline rush. Exhaustion waved over him. He tried to stay on his feet, but it was too much. He collapsed and slipped out of consciousness.

Chapter 35

"Adonai... Adonai... Adonai, get up. Get up. You need to get up." Adonai's eyes slowly opened.

"About time you wake up," Arson quipped.

Adonai sat up. His body was sore, but his mind felt refreshed. "What happened?"

"You don't remember? You nearly died."

His senses were slowly returning. He noticed the corpse of the blood curdler next to him, and suddenly, he remembered. He had fought and killed a blood curdler.

"How long have I been asleep?"

"Two days."

Adonai muttered a curse. It was a miracle he hadn't been attacked by anything during the time he was unconscious. He climbed to his feet and stretched. His body ached, but he seemed to be okay. He had several broken bones all throughout his body, and his chest had been maimed pretty badly, but none of it was something he couldn't manage. After examining his body, he then went over and examined the blood curdler's body. Looking at its lifeless body now, it didn't seem all that scary. He pulled his spear out from the skull and wiped the blood off. Then he proceeded to take out a knife and collect some of the bone plating and horns. There was a lot of it, far too much to store in the interspatial rings, but he still collected a good bit of it.

"What now? Are you going to return home?" Weald asked as Adonai stored the knife back in the ring.

"We should continue to explore," Aeolian insisted.

They hadn't been in the Northern Mist that long; going home now would cut the trip short.

"Let's go burn something!" Arson exclaimed. He was ignored.

Adonai reexamined his wounds. They had already begun to heal. It shouldn't be a problem if he were to continue his journey.

"Let's keep going," Adonai said at last. Just as before, he traveled north. Beyond the Crimson Woods lay the Ravaged Lands, or that's what Adonai called them anyways. The ground was bare, hard, and rocky. Deep cracks and crevasses snaked back and forth across the ground, and tall pillars of rock stuck up like trees in a forest. Most of the plant life consisted of moss and fungi, along with a few weeds that sprouted up here or there. Occasionally, a little grag, a small rodent, would scamper across the ground from one crevasse to the next. Aside from all that, there wasn't much to see here in this place. But then, after traveling for a while, Adonai stumbled across a cave that led into the depths of the ravaged lands. He stopped at the edge of the cave. He could sense a presence from the depths... A strong presence. A presence that filled Adonai with both excitement and fear. It was the presence of a mana beast.

"Should I go?" Adonai asked his bonds.

"Why are you asking that when you've already made up your mind?" Aeolian pointed out.

Adonai grinned, "You guys know me so well."

For a moment, he stayed there on the edge of the cave staring into the abyss. Even his bonds were stirring with excitement within him. They had come to love the thrill of battle, and Adonai was no different. He descended down into the cave. It led deeper and deeper until he arrived in a large chamber with a large pool of water in one of the corners. Glowing blue veins ran along the walls. In the center of the chamber was a cluster of boulders. That was where the presence of the mana beast was coming from, but there was no sign of it.

Adonai walked further into the chamber, trying to hone his senses. Then the cave began to shake. The cluster of boulders shifted and moved around. It was the boulders; the boulders were the mana beast. It was a golem. It climbed to its feet and made a low grumbling noise. It was huge. Adonai called his spear and then launched it at the golem. It pierced into its rock body, but it was nowhere near enough to defeat it. He tried to call his spear back, but it was stuck in the golem's body. Then he tried directly manipulating the golem's body, but the golem had enough control over itself to prevent him or anything else from directly manipulating its body. Then something strange happened. Adonai began to slowly float up into the air. It was as if his body no longer had any weight. And then suddenly, his body grew incredibly heavy, and he was slammed into the ground hard enough to make the rock floor crack. Adonai groaned, and as he tried to climb to his feet, he was once again lifted up into the air and then slammed back into the ground. The golem was manipulating gravity, removing it and then amplifying it. Again, Adonai felt himself being lifted up into the air, but he resisted and managed to keep himself on the ground. Then the gravity increased dramatically again. He remained standing. His body grew heavier and heavier. So heavy that the ground beneath his feet began to snap and crack. But even then, he remained on his feet. Still, the gravity continued to increase. Adonai yelled as he launched a nearby boulder with his mana. It crashed into the golem and exploded on impact, staggering the golem. Adonai took this opportunity to dash forward and strike the golem's body with an open palm. The stone body cracked. He struck it again. It cracked. And then he struck it again and again; each time, new cracks formed in the golem's body. Then the golem slapped Adonai with one of its massive hands and sent him flying into the cave wall. And then he felt the gravity increase again and pull him into the ground. Now he was lying down with his face buried in the ground. He pressed his hands against the ground and tried to push up. The ground cracked beneath his hands. Slowly, he raised his body, but at the same time, the gravity continued to increase. It was battle. Adonai continued to push against the ground with all his might, and slowly, he climbed to his knees, then to his feet. Sweat was dripping down his brow, and his muscles ached. Adonai took one step. Then another. Each step shaking the cave. And then Adonai smiled to himself. This golem was strong... but not strong enough. He punched at the air in the direction of the golem. The force from the punch carried forward and slammed into the golem, sending it flying back into the wall. Its control over the gravity faded, and with his newfound freedom, Adonai dashed forward and dealt a flurry of blows that completely shattered the golem's head. It was over. Adonai let himself fall to the ground, breathing heavily. He was exhausted... but for some reason, he couldn't wipe this smile off his face.

"Did-did you guys see that?" he asked his bonds.

"Of course we saw it, we see everything you see," Brine said bluntly. "It was incredible, Master," Aeolian complimented him.

"You should have used more fire," Arson said sadly. He was just the same as always.

His bonds continued to talk on and on about the battle. They had all become good friends.

Then Adonai remembered. "I need to form a bond with the golem." He immediately got up and entered a meditative state and found the golem's spirit. This time, he was going to do things a little differently than before, like with Zolt. He reached out and took hold of the spirit and began to absorb it into his own. Surprisingly, the golem's spirit put up no resistance. It was strenuous work, but it was easier than the first time. Finally, the golem's spirit integrated into Adonai's body, where it dwelt with the other spirit bonds.

"What is this?" the golem asked.

"I've formed a spirit bond with you," Adonai told it and then proceeded to explain what that was to it.

When he finished, the golem just said, "Okay."

"Do you have a name?" Adonai asked.

"No."

"Do you want one?"

"Okay."

Adonai thought about it for a moment and then suggested, "Goh. How does Goh sound?"

"Okay."

That was it. That was all it said. It just said "okay." The golem didn't care about the situation or anything else for that matter. It made Adonai chuckle. After the fight and after forming a bond with Goh, he got up and went to examine the blue veins that covered the cave walls. It was some sort of metal ore. A powerful ore.

"What is this?" he asked as he ran his hand along the stone wall.

"I'm not sure. But it looks like some sort of powerful metal," Ore told him. "Is it adamantium?"

"No, adamantium has a slight purple hue to it. This is different." It wasn't Direite either. This was a new metal. One that had never been seen before.

"Celestite," Adonai whispered. "That's what we'll call this, celestite, named after the Celestials."

"It's a good name," Aeolian told him.

Adonai examined the metal a little longer; he wanted to gather some but wasn't sure how. After thinking it over for a second, he simply punched the cave wall as hard as he could. It shattered, and chunks of stone flew off. He proceeded to punch the cave wall again and again until he had collected enough celestite to fill up the rest of the room in his interspatial rings. Then Adonai began his journey back home.

Chapter 36

Silas descended down the stony steps. The air was damp, and the walls were moist. The stairs went down and down and down. It was almost ridiculous how deep this went, but it was necessary; secrecy was of utmost importance. He finally reached the bottom of the stairs. There was a steel door reinforced with adamantium, further ensuring the secrecy of their meeting. Silas pushed open the door and entered the dimly lit room. There were five individuals already seated around a table. Each of them was dressed in the same attire as Silas: black cloaks, black masks, each mask marked in red with the numerals one through six. This was a gathering of the six Descendants. Silas himself was the Fifth Descendant. He pulled out a chair and took a seat with the others. He was the last to arrive, yet he was still fifteen minutes early.

"Fifth, welcome," the First greeted him.

"It seems the newly appointed Second is here," Silas responded.

The Second raised his hand to greet the arrival of the Fifth. These six individuals, though they worked together as leaders, none of them knew each other's real name, nor what they looked like, nor what they sounded like, nor anything else. When they put on the black cloak and mask, they became entirely new people.

The First began the meeting, "I believe we all know why we're here today."

"Of course," the Fourth began, "Our cleansing site was destroyed and exposed to the rest of the world."

"Because of that, we had to remove the other sites and dispose of the puppets. A true shame," the Sixth added.

"A shame indeed," the First agreed, "But it's nothing but a trifling matter. Those cleansing sites were of no significance to the plan He has prepared for us. They were simply there to satisfy our own desires."

"Do we know who it was that attacked our cleansing site?" Silas asked.

"We're not entirely sure. What we do know is that it was a team of eight highly skilled individuals. Those eight being led by William Hart," the First told him.

"William Hart . . ." the Third repeated, "He's the one who killed the previous Second, wasn't he? Why is he still alive?"

"He's still alive because he's powerful," the Sixth remarked.

And then Silas added, "We're in a difficult position as of right now. Because our cleansing sites were exposed, the Keystone, Urias, has become aware of our existence. The entire empire is on high alert. Attacking William would surely bring attention. And in addition to that, it's not necessary to kill William. Sure, he knows of our existence, but aside from knowing the fact that we exist, he knows nothing else. No matter how hard he tries, he cannot do anything of any significance. Our victory is already inevitable."

"Well put," the First said, "It's just as Silas says, as of now, there's no reason to kill William Hart. When the time does come, He will take care of William himself."

"Then what about the others?" the Third asked.

"We don't know who they are yet, but we will find them. When the time comes, they will be forced to either join us or die," the Fourth explained.

"Do we know how long until He is ready?" the Sixth asked.

"Soon," the First answered, "Soon, He will be ready. He just needs a little bit more time to recover his strength. And once He does, we can finally cleanse this filthy world. But until then, we must lay low. We must wait until the day arrives where we can finally show ourselves."

Chapter 37

Never Thaw was in the midst of changing when Adonai returned. The establishment of the Blue Glacier Guild had been completed. A headquarters had been constructed for the guild. The new headquarters was a large building with exceedingly fine craftsmanship, making it stand out amongst the rest of the town. Lodging had also been built for the many workers John and James brought along, and a laboratory was built for Dahlia and her family to process the goods brought from the Northern Mist. With all of that, the town had grown considerably. Adonai had mixed feelings about the growth of the town, but the money from the business would benefit everyone, so he willingly went along with it.

As before, he spent the first day after his return at home with his family. His parents, Adon and Lily, were out working in the field when he arrived on Ciela's back.

"Adonai!" his mother called out as she and his father ran to him and tightly embraced him.

"How long has it been?" Adonai asked. It was nearly impossible to keep track of time in the Northern Mist.

"It's been more than a month," Adon told him.

"I can't believe you've been going to the Northern Mist. You're going to be the death of your mother with how much you worry me," Lily scolded him with teary eyes.

"Sorry, I was going to tell you, but it just wasn't the right time."

"As if there would ever be a right time. Come, come, let's go inside," Lily told him. They walked to the house together.

"Adonai!" his siblings cried out in unison when they saw him coming back with their parents. They all ran to him together, and once again, he found himself in a tight embrace.

"Let's go inside," Adonai told them. "I want to sit down."

He let his tired body fall onto a chair. When word got out about the Northern Mist business, Adonai's family, particularly his parents, were nearly overwhelmed with concern for their child. But by the time they found out, Adonai had already returned to the Northern Mist, and they never had the chance to stop him. Chaver had to assure them that everything would be okay, and eventually, his parents somewhat calmed down, yet their anxiety for their son remained.

"So, are you going to tell us about this Northern Mist business you've recklessly gotten yourself involved in?" Lily demanded.

Adonai smiled sheepishly. "Yeah, sorry about that." He then went on to explain how he discovered the entrance to the Northern Mist and how it was seemingly calling out to him. His family sat around him, listening intently as he talked about his adventures in the Northern Mist. He spent hours telling them about the Pale Mist Plains, Crimson Woods, and Ravaged Lands, as well as all the diverse creatures he had encountered. As the sun set, he found himself still sharing his stories around candlelight. It was late at night when he and his family finally retired to bed. Before he fell asleep, Adonai offered up a prayer to Celestial Inuuk. Then he had one of the best night's rest of his life.

The next day, Adonai stopped by the new laboratory to drop off all the plants and things he had collected from the Mist. As he was leaving, he ran into John and James. John's face lit up when he saw Adonai.

"Adonai! You're back. It's good to see you alive and well." They shook hands, then John introduced James. "This is James, a partner of mine." Adonai shook hands with him as well.

"It's an honor to meet the great Adonai Alaric," James praised him.

"I don't know about great..." Adonai replied.

"No need to be humble, your achievements are incredible. Even more so because of your age; it's crazy to think that the first person to successfully explore the Northern Mist is just a boy."

"We were just on our way to the inn for breakfast. Would you like to join us?" John asked.

"No, I actually had some business to take care of," Adonai declined.

"Very well, then, we'll be going."

"Ah, wait," Adonai called after them. "Could you actually get me another interspatial ring? I feel like I can gather a lot more than what I'm currently gathering. I just don't have anywhere to store it."

"I'll get it taken care of," John said with a smile. After that, they parted ways and Adonai left for the blacksmith.

Asher was hammering away at a plowshare, shaping it the way he had been taught by his father. He was always working on something like this, something boring. When he first became a blacksmith, Asher had dreamed of forging swords and armors that would be renowned across all of Oalm Catantan. However, these dreams faded as he worked on nothing but common tools and items. As he was hammering, the door to the smith opened behind him. He turned around to see his friend.

"Adonai!" he exclaimed and immediately dropped what he was doing. "It's good to see ya! But what brings ya over here?"

"Nothing much, I just came by to see a good friend," Adonai replied.

"C'mon, if you wanted to see me, you wouldn't have come while I was in the middle of work. So what do ya need? Another spear? Armor? I'm happy to make anything you need."

"You're keen. Yeah, I did come by because I had something to request. It's a hefty request though, are ya sure you can handle it?"

"You kidding me? Whatever it is you need, I'll get it done."

Adonai smiled. "That's what I expected to hear from ya. Let's go sit down. I've got something to show ya." The two of them stepped away from the forge and sat down.

"So what have ya got for me?" Asher asked. Adonai had one of his interspatial rings with him, and he pulled out a chunk of the Celestite he had found in that cave and set it on the table.

Asher's eyes grew wide. "What is this?"

"Celestite," Adonai said proudly. "I found it in a cave in the Northern Mist."

Asher picked up the piece of ore and examined it in awe. "This… this is amazing. I've never seen anything like it. I've never worked with adamantium, but I have seen it. And I can tell you right now with full confidence that this celestite is of a far higher quality than adamantium. Something like this could make huge waves in the world."

"I thought the same thing," Adonai agreed. Then he leaned over the table closer and said, "The reason I came here with this is because I have something I need you to make."

Asher's mouth dropped. "You mean with this? The celestite? You want me to make something with it?"

"Yeah."

Now Asher was grinning from ear to ear; he couldn't hide his excitement, but then his excitement somewhat faded. "But me? Are you sure? I don't know if I'm the best person for this. There are plenty of blacksmiths with far more experience than me, wouldn't they do a better job?"

Adonai shrugged. "You're probably right, but how could I not give this opportunity to one of my best friends? That and I know I can trust you. That alone is more than enough of a reason to rely on you."

Asher's excitement began to return. "So what do ya want me to make?"

"A spear. Ten of them. And a suit of armor, a full suit of armor."

Asher rubbed at his chin where some stubble was growing. "That's a lot. And ten spears? Why do you want ten spears?"

Adonai smiled. "I have a reason for that. So, can you do it?"

Asher nodded, thinking it over. "Yeah… I can do it. But do you have enough of this stuff to make all that? After all, it is a lot."

"Oh, you don't need to worry about material. I have plenty." Adonai handed him the interspatial ring with all the celestite inside.

When Asher took it, his mouth dropped. "Why is there so much?"

"Because there was a lot to gather. And that's just what I could fit inside the ring. There was still a lot more left in the cave," Adonai told him.

"What do you plan to do with all the extra?" Asher asked.

Adonai shrugged. "I was just gonna give it to you, let you do what you want with it."

Asher's face lit up; for a second, Adonai thought he was gonna cry. "You're such a good friend, man. I don't even know what to say."

"Just make good use of it. You always dreamed of becoming a famous blacksmith; with this, you can forge the greatest swords and armors in the entire world. Everyone will know your name."

Asher had to wipe at his eyes and sit there quietly for a moment to allow himself to process everything. Then he got up and said, "Alright, let's get to work on your gear." They took measurements of Adonai's body to make the perfect armor and make the spears the perfect length.

"Anything specific you want to request?" Asher asked.

Adonai thought about it for a moment, then said, "Not really, just do what you feel is best. How long until you finish with all of this?"

"Uhh, geez. It could take me a while, especially since I'm working with a metal I've never worked with before... I don't know, maybe two or three months."

"Two or three months..." Adonai said, disappointed, then added, "Well, if that's how long it takes, I look forward to seeing what you make."

Asher smiled. "You should be, I won't disappoint."

Chapter 38

Adonai was up in the mountains with Ciela. He had spent a few weeks now at home in Never Thaw. Normally, he would be getting ready to leave again by now, but he had decided to wait until Asher was done with his spears and armor before returning to the Mist. Though he wanted to return to the Mist, Maybel, Laor, and Adin were all ecstatic that their big brother was home and was going to be staying longer than usual. And Adonai made sure to spend lots of time with them. He would go hunting with his brothers or sword fight with them, and he would play with his little sister. When he wasn't with his family, he was with his friends. He would assist Asher in the forge or assist Dahlia in the lab or sit down and talk with Chaver. They were all doing very well; each of his friends was benefiting from this new business. Chaver was helping manage everything as John's apprentice, and he was doing a good job. Everything with the business was going smoothly. They had sent their first wagon load full of things made from the Mist not that long ago. There was a lot—fruits, herbs, spices, extracts, hides, claws, bones, and teeth, and other products derived from the various things Adonai brought back from the Mist in that wagon load.

Once it all reached Plain City, it would be moved to cargo ships and sailed down to Dire City, where it would all be put up on the market for auction. Once that happened, news of merchandise exclusive to the Northern Mist being sold would spread like wildfire across all of Oalm Catantan. Once that happened, they would really have to buckle down and work hard. There was no chance of keeping up with demand, but they were going to try their best. So with all that, there was always something for Adonai to do. But even so, during all of this, he never once neglected his training. And through his training, he had grown tremendously physically, mentally, and spiritually. His shoulders had grown broader, and his muscles were bigger and more defined. He was slowly looking less and less like a boy and more and more like a man.

He continued to look out over the valley, admiring the beauty of the mountains, trees, and clouds. He had come up into the mountains this day for a specific reason. He had come here to try and summon one of his bonds. Summoning was an advanced practice that only the strongest were capable of performing. And even when a person was capable of summoning a bond, it was very strenuous. In most cases, it wasn't suitable for combat, as it was easier to just utilize the bond's powers directly yourself rather than summon it. That, and oftentimes, when a summon was used, it led to widespread destruction. For these reasons, summoning was usually avoided. But in the few rare cases where a powerful person was fighting in a remote place where collateral damage wasn't an issue, then in those cases, summons became a powerful tool.

Now, the question was, who was Adonai going to summon? He had eight bonds now: Aeolian, Terra, Ore, Brine, Arson, Weald, Zolt, and now Goh. As Adonai thought about it, his thoughts fell on Arson. Since his fire was white, he wondered if Arson would be a white phoenix. So he decided to summon Arson and began the process. He closed his eyes to concentrate better and breathed in and out deeply. He channeled his mana, focused on it, and felt it. He wasn't actually entirely sure how to summon a bond; he was just acting on instinct. He started by gathering a lot of mana to form a sort of pathway from his spirit to his body and then to the outside world. This pathway of mana would serve as the means for the bond to travel from his spirit to the outside world. Then he gathered and condensed mana at the end of the pathway. And he gathered a lot. Bringing in more and more and condensing it down even further. The more mana a person could gather and condense, the stronger their summon would be. Finally, Adonai finished gathering all the mana he could manage. Then he muttered one short phrase:

"Arson... come forth."

A bright light formed, and then the body of a phoenix materialized where he had been gathering the mana. It was a large, majestic white bird enveloped in a cape of fire. White fire. Sure enough, it was just like the fire Adonai utilized—white. He wished he had some answers; he wanted to know why his fire was white and what that meant.

"This is nice," Arson said, stepping side to side, testing his body. "We should go set something on fire."

"No," Adonai said firmly.

"But—"

"I said no."

Arson mumbled a curse, a few curses. After the summoning was complete, Adonai realized that it didn't feel particularly difficult to summon Arson. He wanted to push himself. So he decided to summon Aeolian as well.

He went through the same process, and when the process was complete, he muttered the same simple phrase as before:

"Aeolian... come forth."

Again, there was a bright light, and then the body of a griffin materialized. To Adonai's surprise, Aeolian had beautiful white feathers. Perhaps this was connected to Arson being white and the white fire that Adonai utilized. Aeolian was also larger than Ciela.

Looking at Aeolian's body, Adonai suggested, "Let's fly around for a bit." He climbed on the back of Aeolian, and they took off and flew around the peak of the mountain; Arson and Ciela followed. After doing this for a while, they landed back on the peak. And Adonai noticed again that he wasn't at his limit. He could do more. So for a third time, he went through the process, and this time, he summoned Ore. The large serpent-like body of a wyrm materialized.

And again, just like Arson and Aeolian, Ore was covered in white scales. Now Adonai was really intrigued. He wanted to see if the rest of his bonds would also be white; however, he was reaching his limit.

"I'm sorry, guys, I'm going to have to call you back."

There was some complaining as Adonai unsummoned his three bonds. Their bodies whisped away. Then he summoned the Dire bear, Weald. Weald had white fur. He unsummoned Weald and summoned Terra. She had white scales. He dismissed her and summoned one of Brine's tentacles. The tentacle burst up from the ground; it was also covered in white scales. Then he summoned Zolt and Goh. Zolt had white fur, and Goh was made of what looked like white marble. They were all white. Exhausted, Adonai undid all of his summons and sprawled out on the ground.

There were rare colors for each of the mana beasts. A rare phoenix was blue, a rare griffin was golden, a rare wyrm was silver, a rare hydra was black or gold, a rare Dire bear was silver or gold, and a rare kraken could be blue or gold. Usually, a rare coloring was associated with the summoner being a prodigy. But white... white was an unheard-of coloring. Was it because he was born with the mark of the prodigy? Adonai wondered. After all, that mark marked him as a prodigy of prodigies. Or maybe it had something to do with that strange glowing shard that appeared during his bonding ritual.

Adonai sighed. "Forget it," he finally muttered to himself.

He could worry about this some other time. For now, he was exhausted and ready to go home. He had really pushed himself by summoning all eight bonds, even if they weren't all simultaneously. Thankfully, he had Ciela to help him get back home; otherwise, he might have ended up having to stay and sleep on the mountain peak.

Soon, just like that, two and a half months had passed. Adonai once again found himself heading over to the blacksmith. Asher greeted him excitedly when he arrived.

"How's it gone?" Adonai asked.

"Well. Very well," Asher said with a big grin, eager to show his friend his work. "My dad was pissed that I had to stop helping him with work in order to make this stuff for you," Asher went on, "But he was also happy that I had this opportunity and encouraged me."

He led Adonai into his house, and they walked through into a storage room. Once there, Asher presented the ten spears and armor. They were magnificent. They were all a silvery metal with a hint of blue.

"What do ya think?" Asher asked haughtily.

"It's amazing," Adonai said, as he picked up one of the spears. It was surprisingly lightweight, much lighter than steel. Even more impressive was the fact that mana didn't just flow through the spear; mana was amplified through it. The spears had a smooth shaft and long, leaf-like heads with small wings. They were simple and elegant. Then there was the armor. Adonai set down the spear and lifted up the silvery-blue breastplate. The armor was subtly ornate, except for the helmet. What made the helmet stand out was a loop that started at the back of the base of the helm and rose up behind, completing just above the helm. This created a circle that seemed to hover behind the head and looked like a sideways halo. Asher noticed Adonai staring at the helmet.

"What do ya think? Ya know those old paintings of the Celestials, how they have those circles behind their heads that are supposed to be halos? I thought I'd create something that resembled that. I wanted to create something that would show greatness."

Adonai picked up the helmet and turned it over in his hands and muttered, "It's really cool."

"Alright, let's try it on," Asher said eagerly.

Adonai put on the suit of armor. It fit perfectly and didn't restrict his movements at all. "Now what about all these spears? Why did you ask for so many?" Asher asked.

Adonai smiled. "Here, I'll show ya." He used mana and lifted up all ten spears, then absorbed them into the interspatial ring he was wearing.

"Whoa, did you just pick up all ten at the same time?" Asher asked.

"Yeah, let's go outside," Adonai said, gesturing for Asher to follow him.

As they walked through the street to an open field, everyone they passed marveled at the armor Adonai was wearing. When they reached the open field, Adonai stopped and called out all ten spears. One appeared in his hand, the other nine hovered in the air around him. Asher watched his friend in awe as he maneuvered all ten spears through the air. They went back and forth as if they were swimming in water. The reason Adonai was able to control all ten like this so easily was because of how much his elemental powers had grown. Not only was his mana stronger, but he also learned to combine the effects of several elements together. And with his newest bond, Goh, he gained the ability to manipulate gravity, which he had found to be particularly useful. What he did was manipulate the gravity so that it didn't affect the spears, then he used his ability to control metal to move the spears, and his ability to control the wind to aid that ability to move the spears. With this combination, he was able to effortlessly move the spears around in the air, making them twirl around and do loopty-loops or dart back and forth. He didn't explain all that to Asher though; he thought it was more fun to leave his friend wondering.

After a while, Adonai called back all the spears and stored them in the ring, as well as the armor. With the ring, he was able to make both the spear and armor materialize and disappear at any moment. This was great because with this, he was able to instantly equip his armor at any given moment.

"So, what did ya think?" Adonai asked.

Asher shook his head. "You're crazy. I don't know what you did to be able to do that, but you're crazy for doin' it."

Adonai laughed. "Yeah, you're probably right, I just may be a bit crazy."

They started walking to the inn together to grab a drink to celebrate Asher's hard work. "So, I can really keep all that other celestite and do with it as I please?" Asher asked as they walked.

"Absolutely," Adonai responded, then added, "You know what, I just thought of something else."

"What is that?"

"I've been collecting the feathers that Ciela sheds for a while now. I wonder, do you think I could make a cape with 'em?"

Asher laughed. "You should; that would be awesome."

And that's exactly what Adonai did that night when he returned home.

Chapter 39

The Northern Mist was divided into several small biomes. The first biome after entering the Mist was the Barren Lands. This was a stretch of land that ran along the entirety of the Northern Ridge and, therefore, was always the first biome a person would come across when entering the Northern Mist. The crack, the entrance that Adonai had discovered, was on the far west side of the continent. After passing through the Barren Lands, the next biome was the Pale Mist Plains. North of the Plains was the Crimson Woods, and north of the Crimson Woods was the Ravaged Land. That was the extent of what Adonai had explored so far. East of the Pale Mist Plains lay the Mist Marsh—a thick swamp.

This was where Adonai was currently. This was his fourth expedition now. Traversing the Mist had become easy at this point. Gaining the ability to manipulate gravity made flying easy. So, rather than trudging through the thick mud and waist-high water, Adonai was able to hover just over the surface. Mist gators lurked nearby, just the tops of their heads poking out of the water. There were lots of Mist snakes with glowing patterns in their skin and pale herons that waded in the water, jabbing at small fish. The most interesting animal Adonai came across was the angler toads. Giant toads with an antenna that hung in front of their faces, and at the end of the antenna was a glowing bulb. Adonai watched a heron curiously approach one of these bulbs only to be quickly snatched up and gulped down by the toad.

Further into the Mist Marsh, the environment became dominated by massive willow trees that were almost as big as the Dire trees. Their giant roots sprawled out across the ground, making for tricky terrain.

Adonai froze. He felt a powerful presence. A presence that was becoming all too familiar. The presence of a mana beast... two of them. He called out his gear, and the silvery-blue armor materialized over his body. The ten spears materialized—one in his hand, the other nine hovering in the air around him. His white cape of Dire hawk feathers hung from his back. Normally, there was some anxiety when facing mana beasts, but this time, there was only excitement. Adonai was eager to test out his new gear. The two mana beasts grew closer, and then they appeared. Two giant snakes—basilisks. They moved swiftly.

Adonai watched as they circled around him so that he was surrounded by their lengthy bodies. He didn't attack though, not yet. He was waiting to see what the basilisks would do first. Then something strange happened. His heart stopped. Just for a moment, his heart stopped and a sharp pain filled his chest. Then it went away. He hunched over, gasping for air. The basilisks had struck his heart with nothing more than their gaze. A venomous gaze. The two mana beasts must have expected their combined gaze to be enough to kill him because they were surprised when Adonai quickly recovered. He hadn't expected something like that, so it caught him off guard. He smiled to himself behind the helmet; fighting mana beasts really was exciting. And then he began his attack. His spears zipped through the air, each one burying itself deep in the basilisks' bodies. The two snakes roared out in unison from the pain. But the spears themselves weren't enough to take down the mighty beasts. The basilisks both lashed out lightning fast, snapping their jaws at Adonai. He easily evaded the attacks. His spears dug down deeper into the basilisks with enough force to tear straight through the body, leaving behind a hole. Then the spears immediately turned around and attacked again. The basilisks could do nothing as the spears tore into them again and again, ripping their bodies apart. Adonai danced around as the basilisks continued to lash out at him. It didn't take long for the two mana beasts to succumb to their wounds. With a flick of his wrist, Adonai sent two spears hurtling toward each of the basilisk's heads, where the spears tore through their skulls.

"That was a bit much, wasn't it?" Brine commented as the mana beasts' lifeless bodies collapsed.

"No, no. It was perfectly reasonable. But you should have used more fire," Arson asserted. Adonai waved them off.

"Are you going to form bonds with them as well?" Aeolian asked.

"Yeah." Adonai crouched down next to one of the basilisks' bodies. He found its spirit and forcibly took control of it and formed a bond with it. Then he did the same with the other one. He named them Radio and Radia. Once again, Adonai found his power growing. With every bond, his affinity with mana increased, and with each new bond, he gained access to a new power. With the basilisks' bonds, he gained the ability to control venom, even going as far as being capable of inflicting his prey with venom with nothing more than a gaze, just as the basilisks had done to him. After resting for a moment, Adonai got up and continued on.

After continuing to travel through the swamps, giant spider webs began appearing. The webbing covered the ground and the trees, and the amount of webbing continued to increase more and more until absolutely everything was coated in spider webs—from the ground all the way to the tops of the giant willow trees. It was like an entire cave system had been formed entirely out of spider webs. Adonai didn't hesitate to continue forward, though. As he went, there were carcasses of all kinds of animals suspended in the webs. And that was when Adonai began to run into the dread spiders. Giant, hairy spiders. Some of them were half the size of him, while others were the size of horses. But they weren't difficult to deal with. Adonai was able to continue flying through the cave of spider webs casually; all he had to do was wave his hand, and a spear would come sailing through the air and kill whatever stood before him. As he continued, the spiders gradually began to grow larger and tougher. He didn't think much of it, though, and continued on without a second thought. But then the number of spiders appearing gradually began to decrease until there weren't any at all. It became quiet.

"This is strange," Terra commented. "There should still be spiders. Why have they stopped coming?"

Adonai shrugged. "I don't know."

"You don't think this is something you should be worried about?" Aeolian asked.

"I'm not really concerned about it," Adonai said casually.

As he continued flying, still there was no sign of any spiders, and still, he didn't think anything of it. What he was unaware of was that even though he wasn't directly touching the web, his mana still sent signals up the webs, and the spiders were very well aware of these signals. Soon, Adonai reached the heart of the giant web. It was like a giant chamber with tunnels that branched out in every direction. That was when he began to sense the dread spiders again. They had waited—waited until he reached the heart of their home, where they had him completely surrounded. And now, thousands of spiders were rushing right toward him. Adonai muttered a curse.

"I warned you to be more careful," Aeolian remarked.

"Yeah, yeah, whatever." After his easy fight with the basilisks, Adonai had become somewhat arrogant. He waited as the spiders grew closer and closer. And then he unleashed a massive wave of white flames that enveloped the entirety of the web cave and incinerated all the spiders. At least that was what Adonai had thought would happen. Instead, most of the spiders came bursting out from the flames. And now, there were thousands of flaming spiders rushing toward Adonai. He cursed sharply and instantly began his next attack. All ten of his spears went flying all around the chamber, tearing apart every bug they came in contact with. But it wasn't enough to deal with them all. Suddenly, one spider dropped from above and landed on Adonai's back. He quickly threw it off, and then more spiders began to drop from above. He attacked with bursts of wind, fire, and lightning. Each attack decimated the foe, but with every foe slain, two more took its place. Adonai went on and on fighting. How long... how long had he been fighting? It had to have been more than an hour by now—more than an hour of constantly attacking and utilizing mana. Adonai was starting to become tired. And still, the spiders came crawling. He fought and fought. Things were looking bleak. But for some reason... for some reason, he couldn't stop smiling. He could feel his power growing.

"Come! Keep coming! You can all come and it still won't be enough!" he shouted as he battled for hours on end, all the while pushing his limits and surpassing them. And gradually, the onslaught of spiders began to slow down until they completely stopped coming. He won. Adonai let out a sigh of relief as the last spider scampered away. He had slaughtered thousands and thousands of spiders.

"That's enough," Adonai said to himself. "Let's go home." That was the end of his fourth expedition.

Chapter 40

"Faster, faster!" Maybel squealed with excitement.

"Hold on tight," Adonai said.

Ciela flapped her wings with power, and Adonai created a gust of wind to help speed her up, and they shot through the air. They could see the whole valley from this height. It was beautiful. Ciela flew higher, and they passed through a billowy, white cloud, which made Maybel squeal with even more excitement. They circled the valley a few more times, and then Ciela dipped down and they returned home. Adonai helped Maybel down; her hair was all crazy from blowing in the wind, but she had the widest grin. It was hard to believe that a kid her size could grin that big. Adin and Laor were waiting for them where they landed.

"My turn! My turn!" Laor beamed.

Adin was trying on Adonai's celestite armor. It was all too big for his body, but since it was light, he didn't have a problem with the weight. Adonai walked over and helped fasten the loose-fitting armor around him. Then Adin picked up one of the celestite spears and jabbed at the air with it. Adonai watched him for a while, then turned to Laor, who was waiting eagerly, and said, "Alright, Laor, let's go."

Adonai helped him up onto Ciela's back and then climbed on himself. Laor wrapped his arms around Adonai's waist tightly, and Ciela exploded up off the ground and took off flying around the valley just like they had done with Maybel. Adonai had been home for a while now. He had already dropped off the three interspatial rings at the laboratory, and Dahlia's family had gotten straight to work with all of it. After that, he stopped by the blacksmith. Asher still had a lot of celestite left from when Adonai originally gave him some, and he was putting it to good use. So far, he had crafted a few swords; each of them was exceedingly fine.

The next day, Adonai sat down with Chaver at the inn and they shared a meal.

"So how has everything been going?" Adonai asked before taking a bite of food.

"Everything's going good. Actually, better than good. Word's gotten out that the Blue Glacier Guild is selling merchandise from the Northern Mist, and our demand has soared. Everything we sell ends up being auctioned off for a ridiculously high price." Chaver gulped down some ale and then continued, "And that's all just from the first batch of stuff. The next batch we send out will have even more stuff, including the swords Asher's made. We've already made a ton of money, and soon, we'll be making even more."

"That's good," Adonai said.

"Yeah," Chaver agreed. "We've been distributing most of the money among the town like you wanted. Everyone's benefiting greatly from this. It's all thanks to you, ya know? If it weren't for you, Never Thaw would still be a struggling town isolated from the world."

Adonai shrugged, then he moved on, "I noticed that the town's grown a bit more. Did John bring in more people?"

Chaver shook his head. "No, we didn't bring in any additional people. After our stuff hit the markets and word got out, people have been showing up and settling down here. John says that we should expect even more people to arrive. People go where the money is, and right now, that's Never Thaw. There will be other people as well. People who will want to come and explore the Northern Mist themselves."

Adonai looked skeptical. "That's not a good idea; in fact, that is a terrible idea."

Chaver nodded. "Yeah, but there isn't much we can do about it. Since you've been able to successfully explore the Northern Mist, there are going to be other people who think they can do the same."

Adonai sighed. "I really don't like the idea of all these strangers moving in."

"It is what it is," Chaver said, then he leaned in closer with a big grin on his face. "That aside, guess what? I got to hold hands with Dahlia the other day. Holding hands, I tell ya!" He leaned back in his chair, all proud of himself.

"That's the most impressive thing you've said all day," Adonai told him.

"I know, right? I could hardly believe it when it happened."

The two friends continued chatting, and later on in the night, Dahlia and Asher came and joined Adonai and Chaver, and they all talked together like old times. Adonai spent a few more days in Never Thaw. He spent most of his time going around town helping out in any way he could. He loved Never Thaw, he really did. Then, before long, he once again returned to the Northern Mist.

Chapter 41

East of the Crimson Woods and north of the Mist Marsh was the Pale Mist Woods. There was an abundance of berries, nuts, and herbs here, as well as plenty of Mist elk, Pale moose, Ghost bears, and all kinds of other smaller creatures. The Mist was also thicker here, and the mana was denser. Adonai had reverted back to hiking rather than flying. It was hard on the body to fly constantly, and while he wanted to continue growing, he also didn't want to overdo it. He had stopped through the Crimson Woods and Ravaged Lands before coming to the Pale Mist Woods in order to stock up on things unique to those regions, particularly celestite.

As Adonai pressed further into the woods, suddenly things didn't seem quite right. A bit of fear began to rise up in the back of his mind, as well as anxiety. It was strange. There was no reason for him to be afraid, but for some reason, there was a bit of fear lingering in his mind... and it was growing more intense. Then a wave of depression smashed into him. He felt sick. His body felt heavy. He couldn't keep his thoughts under control. Adonai found himself thinking about that night. The night when the Dire bear attacked. The night when Emilio died... And it was all his fault. If he had only chosen to fight that day, then he could have stopped the guards from dying. He could have... he could have... Why? Why didn't he fight? He hated himself for it. He cursed himself for it. It made him wish he could take Emilio's place. The depression was stronger now than it had ever been before. It made Adonai want to tear his skin off. It made him want to fall to the ground and give up on life. Why? Why was all of this happening? Why was he losing the will to live? This didn't make any sense. As Adonai wallowed in pain, he realized that there was an external force attacking his mind. He fought back against that force and pushed it out of his head, finally returning to his senses as the wave of depression receded. It was a mana beast. It was a warden, a giant owl-like bird. Adonai quickly located it and took off in its direction. Fast. Very, very fast. The warden tried to attack his mind again and alter his emotions, but it was useless now. Adonai was upon the warden in an instant. He tackled the beast to the ground and called forth a spear. He held the warden down by the neck. Anger was taking him over as he stared into the eyes of the warden, and then he began to shout at it.

"Why! Why did you make me remember those things! You wretched bird! You..." His voice trailed off as he choked back tears. Then he whispered something quietly to himself, "I didn't want to remember those things."

He raised his spear and plunged it through the mana beast's heart, killing it instantly. Adonai lowered his head and remained in that position for a while as he recomposed himself.

"Are you alright?" Aeolian asked.

Adonai wiped his nose. "Yeah... I'm fine." He stood up and looked down at the warden's body. He felt tired. Not physically tired, but mentally. He didn't feel like straining himself, but he needed to form a bond with the warden. So he crouched back down, entered his meditative state, and forced the warden's spirit into submission. With the bonding complete, Adonai was able to relax, and he gave the warden a name.

"Your name will be Warden."

After that short battle, Adonai went back to gathering forbs, nuts, and other things. He killed a few Mist elk and collected their glowing antlers, and gathered the hides from Ghost bears and Pale moose as well. He continued his hunting and gathering for a few days. Then Adonai sensed something strange. He quickly dashed toward it and was baffled by what he stumbled across. A tower. He found a tower. Why was there a tower out here in the middle of the Mist? And it was tall. Very tall. So tall that he couldn't sense the top. At the base of the tower were two massive and magnificent doors, which opened for him as he approached. There was no Mist inside the tower, and Adonai could see clearly. He was in a large, grand room filled with white and gold. The room was very large, so large that as Adonai looked around, he realized that he couldn't see any of the walls. He spun around in a circle. No walls. Even the doors he had entered through were gone, and now he stood in the middle of a room that seemed to have no end. And in the center of the room, a short way away from him, were thrones. Compelled, Adonai approached the thrones. It was indescribable how beautiful and magnificent these thrones were. There were six of them, and the two in the center were raised a little higher than the other four. He stepped up to one of the central thrones. It felt familiar. It felt as if it were his own, and it felt natural as he sat down on it. It felt as if he had been in this place his entire life. When he sat down on the throne, Adonai found himself no longer in that endless room. Instead, he was floating in the middle of the air, overlooking the tower he had just entered. There was only one word that could describe that tower... glorious. It was a place of glory. And it had no end. It reached up and up, higher and higher, and never ended. It was infinite. But even though it was infinite, Adonai somehow felt as if he were above it. He was looking down on the tower, and he could see it all. He tried to delve down deeper, but his mind became blurry. He tried to refocus on what was going on around him. He wanted to know more. He wanted to know what all of this was. Then his eyes opened.

He was lying down on the ground, surrounded by Mist. He sat up and rubbed his eyes. He was in the middle of the Northern Mist. Had he been asleep? And if so, when did he fall asleep?

Adonai felt that he had a strange and important dream, but he couldn't remember any of it no matter how hard he tried.

"Interesting..." The voice startled Adonai.

Something was speaking to him through a mana link. "Who is this?" he called out.

"There's no need to fear, I'm not going to hurt you." It was a mana beast. A nine-tailed fox. The fox jumped down from a rock and strutted over to Adonai, brushing up against his side.

"You're interesting," the fox said.

"You... are you the one who made me fall asleep?" Adonai asked.

"Who, me?"

"Yes, you, who else would I be talking to?"

"I don't know. But yes, I am the one who made you fall asleep."

"Why?"

"Because that's what I do. I make other creatures fall asleep, and then I feed off of their dreams," the fox explained, then added, "It's strange though. Your dream was delicious. The most delicious dream I've fed on by far. But for some reason, I can't remember what your dream was about."

"I don't remember what my dream was either, but I feel it was important."

"Indeed."

"Could you give me that dream again?" Adonai asked.

"It doesn't work like that. I can make you fall asleep and dream, but I have no control over what you dream."

Adonai was still confused; it felt like there was so much going on and he had so little time to process all of it.

"Dreams aside, why are you talking with me? Aren't you afraid I might try to kill you?" Adonai pressed.

The fox brushed up against him again. "About that, I've taken a liking to you."

"A liking to me?"

"Yes. Your dream was something special; that makes you something special. I can sense the other spirits dwelling within you. I want to join them."

"You want to form a bond with me?" Adonai asked in disbelief.

"If that is what you call it, then yes, I want to form a bond with you," the fox said. "You know that I'll have to kill you in order for your spirit to be bonded to mine?" The fox paused for a moment, then continued, "That's fine."

"Alright then."

The fox came and sat down before Adonai and lowered her head. She let down all her defenses, giving him full control over her body. This allowed him to kill her with nothing more than a snap of his fingers, and that was exactly what he did. He snapped his fingers, and the lifeless body of the fox fell to the ground. Then he formed a bond with her.

"From now on, your name will be Alora," Adonai said when the bonding was complete.

"Alora... I like it. I look forward to what else you will show me."

With that, Adonai gained his twelfth bond. Since most of the gathering he had done had been done in a dream, he got up and promptly began gathering and hunting again. Then, with his interspatial rings full, he set off for home.

Chapter 42

"So this is Never Thaw," Jack said as he and his gang arrived at the outskirts of the small town.

"It looks like crap," Rom sneered.

"We've just arrived and I already hate it here," Faith added as she looked out over the town.

"No kiddin', I hate the snow," Rom's twin, Rin, complained.

"Shut up," Jack barked at them. "This is gonna be the place that'll make us rich, so y'all better learn to like it. I don't wanna hear no more complainin'."

"I still hate the snow," Rin grumbled.

Jack shot him a dirty look, which was enough to shut him up. There were seven members in their group. Jack was the leader, then there were the twins, Rom and Rin, and then Faith, Ling, Han, and Jin. They had been living as bandits, robbing and killing as they pleased. But they had become interested in Never Thaw after hearing word that merchandise from the Northern Mist was coming from there. Jack had brought his group here with the intention of taking over the little town and monopolizing the trade for themselves.

As soon as the bandits entered the town, the people began keeping their distance from them. There was a certain air about them, an uneasy air that spelled trouble. As they walked through the streets looking for a place to set up their headquarters, Rom snatched an apple from a stand as he passed by.

The man running the stand called out to him in a kind voice, "Excuse me, sir, I think you forgot to pay for that." Rom took a bite of the apple, ignored him, and kept walking. However, there were two of Never Thaw's guards patrolling nearby. After seeing what happened, the guards confronted the bandits.

"Is there a problem over here?" one of the guards asked.

Rom smirked. "Yeah, there's a problem. That clod over there claims I never paid for this apple."

The other bandits snickered at their friend's remark.

"We saw you take that without paying," the guard responded. "Just pay for it, it's more than a fair price," the other guard added.

"I already said, I paid for this."

"Again, we saw you steal it," the guard repeated.

Rom's smirk turned into a frown. He tossed the apple aside and got up in the face of one of the guards. "You're startin' to piss me off."

The guard stepped backward and pointed his spear at Rom. "We don't take kindly to thieves around here. Pay the man what you owe him."

For a moment, Rom stood there sizing up the guards. "Seems I need to teach you your place." In a deft motion, Rom drew his sword and knocked aside the spear being pointed at him. Then he slashed off one of the guards' arms. He dropped his spear and cried out in pain. The other guard raised his spear and went to attack. Rom knocked aside his spear as well and stabbed the guard through the heart. The bandits laughed and snickered as they watched the guard's lifeless body fall to the ground. The nearby townsfolk went into a panic.

"You punks won't get away with this," the guard who had lost an arm said as he held onto his bloody stump.

"Shut up," Rom spat and then beheaded him.

In the middle of this, Han and Jin had turned around and begun to destroy the apple stand. Han was beating the apple seller while Jin smashed the fruit stand.

"Alright, that's enough. Let's go find a place to settle down," Jack told his men. Han hit the apple seller one last time and then dropped him. They left the scene without a care. The next place they were going to was the Rolfes' inn. As they walked away, the witnesses immediately ran away. Several people went to go gather the other guards. As the guards were being gathered, the group of bandits burst through the doors to the inn loudly.

"Get us a round of beers!" Jack shouted. The rough group plopped down at the nearest table and began talking loudly, making dirty jokes. Everyone else in the inn noticed the loud group but didn't pay them any mind. Gabi brought them a round of beers, and they immediately began to gulp them down. Chaver, Asher, and Dahlia were sitting at their usual table in the corner of the room.

Ling took notice of Dahlia and called out to her, "Oi, girly, why don't ya come over here? I'll treat ya nice, I promise."

Rin snickered. "You're a pervert as usual, Ling."

Ling just shrugged and then looked back over to the table where Dahlia was sitting. They had simply ignored him, which pissed him off. He got up and stormed over to their table.

"Oi, you really just gonna ignore me, you wench?"

Chaver stood up and got in his face, but before he could say anything, Ling smacked him aside. The common room went silent. Dahlia rushed to Chaver's side, and Asher shot up from his seat, making the chair fall back. Chaver's father, Eshel, also came to their aid and shouted at Ling, "Hey! I don't know who you are, but we don't stand for that kinda crap around here."

The other townsfolk in the common room were also standing now and had their attention focused on Ling, several of the men ready to fight. Ling spat a curse and then drew his sword.

"Seems this whole town is in need of a lesson!" He raised it, but before he could strike Eshel, the front doors burst open and the town's guards stormed into the room. They formed a wide circle around the group of bandits.

The captain of the guard, Ander, marched forward and declared, "You lot are under arrest for the murder of innocent lives. Surrender yourselves immediately or suffer the consequences."

For a moment, there was silence. The bandits all exchanged looks and then burst out laughing. Jack stood up and drew his sword. "Seems Ling was right, this whole town is indeed in need of a lesson." A red aura began to glow around Jack. The other bandits also stood up, drew their weapons, and formed their auras. All the bystanders quickly fled the scene or cowered in the corners of the room.

Ander readied his spear and ignited his green aura as well. "Seems you have chosen the consequences."

All the other guards also readied their weapons and formed their auras. It was a tense situation. Then a fight broke out as the two groups clashed. The bandits were outnumbered three to one, but they were each far stronger. Slowly, one by one, the guards began to fall as they were cut down.

Then Jack took a step back and shouted, "I've had enough of this!" He raised a hand and a bright light formed above him. Then the body of a phoenix materialized. With the summoning of a phoenix, the fight was over. The phoenix unleashed a wave of fire, and the entire inn burst into flames. The remaining bystanders barely managed to escape alive. But the guards, who were the main targets, all perished. Chaver and his family watched as their home and business, what was practically their lives, burned to the ground.

"You'll pay for this!" Chaver shouted at the bandits as they left the burning building. "Just you wait! Adonai will come, and then you'll pay! You'll all pay!"

Jack stepped up to Chaver and shoved him down. "We'll pay? No, I think you're mistaken. I don't know who this Adonai is, but I'll kill him just as I did the others." Then Jack turned and shouted for all to hear. "This town is under new management! You all best learn to fall in line! If ya don't, I'll have your head! Understood?" He spit on Chaver and then rejoined his men. "C'mon, now we gotta find a new place to stay," he told them.

Their sights fell upon the Guild headquarters. The bandits went and stormed the building and settled down there. They took John and James as hostages.

Jack took them into one of the rooms and interrogated them. "Where's the entrance to the Northern Mist?" he demanded.

"We don't know," John told them.

"Well, then, who does?"

"Nobody. Nobody except Adonai knows where the entrance is."

Jack cursed and then pressed further. "Then this Adonai, where is he?"

"He's gone. He's away in the Northern Mist."

Jack cursed again. "When will he be back?"

"We don't know."

Jack slapped John. "You're pissin' me off. We don't know, we don't know, you say. Seems ya know nothin'!" He slapped him again.

"Just you wait. Adonai will come and he'll kill all of you," James spat.

Jack slapped him hard enough to draw blood and then left the room. They left John and James tied up and shut them in the dark. Jack rejoined his companions at the headquarters' common room. They were playing cards at one of the tables.

"So what'd ya find out?" Rom asked when he saw Jack returning.

"Nothing. Those useless clods didn't know nothin'. Apparently, this person named Adonai is the only one who knows anything," Jack grumbled.

"Then where is he?" Rin asked.

"At this moment, he's in the Northern Mist."

"You think he's strong?" Faith asked and then continued, "If he's the first to explore the Northern Mist, don't ya think that means he's real strong? Are ya sure we can take him?"

"Yeah, we can take him," Jack answered. "What's probably going on is that this guy discovered a safe entrance into the Northern Mist; that's why he's able to explore that place safely. That wench is probably just as pathetic and weak as the rest of 'em."

The others chuckled. "Yeah, that makes sense," Rom agreed.

"So we just gotta wait for this Adonai person to get back, is that it?" Ling asked.

Jack nodded and then smiled. "Since we're stuck in this dump waitin', why don't we go have some fun?"

The others also smiled. "I like the sound of that," Han said.

The group of bandits got up and then split up. They went around town storming into people's houses, stealing food, alcohol, money, and any other sort of valuable thing. Anyone that tried to stand up to them was beaten to a bloody pulp. Then they returned to the Guild headquarters with all their loot to wait for Adonai to return.

Chapter 43

It was nearing summer when Adonai returned to Never Thaw. As he arrived in town on the back of Ciela, he immediately knew something was off when he saw that the inn was burned down. He landed near his family's home and ran inside. He let out a sigh of relief when he saw that they were all okay.

"Adonai!" Maybel cried, running up and jumping into his arms. "We were so scared," she mumbled.

Adonai wore a worried expression. "What's going on?"

"It's a group of bandits," Lily began to explain while holding back tears. "They showed up about a week ago and have been terrorizing everyone. They've burned down the inn and... they killed the town's guards. All of them. Then they went around stealing anything of value from everyone. And every day, they've taken a few people and dragged them out to the streets where they beat them. They're monsters."

Adonai's expression darkened as he listened. Then he turned around and was about to storm out of the house, but Lily caught his arm. "Wait, they're strong. Please, you can't fight them. Please." She had tears streaming down her face now. His siblings and father were also worried. Lily continued to beg, "Don't go. Please don't go. Just stay here, stay with us, stay safe. Please."

Adonai took a deep breath and then gently took his mother's hand. "You don't have to worry. There won't be a fight. To say that there would be a fight would imply that two sides clash against each other. But that won't be possible. Because no matter how hard they try, they'll never even get the chance to struggle." He turned around and stormed out of the house.

Ling finished off another bottle of wine and wiped his mouth. He was drunk. They were all drunk. "It's been more than a week," Ling complained, leaning back in his chair. "I'm gettin' sick of this."

"Shut up and suck it up," Rom barked.

"What do you think happened to that one cute girl we saw at the inn that first day?" Ling asked, talking to no one in particular, and then continued, "Ya think I should go find her?"

"Do whatever you want, ya freakin' pervert," Jin said, annoyed.

Ling smiled to himself. He was about to get up and go find her, but then a wave of silence washed over the bandits. Complete. Utter. Silence. They all froze. They couldn't hear anything. Anything at all. Not their own breathing, not even their own heartbeat. Sweat began to break out on Ling's forehead. What was this immense pressure? It was unlike anything any of them had ever felt before. They each slowly turned their attention to the building's front doors. This strange silence, this presence, was overwhelming. It felt like they sat there forever, frozen, staring at the doors in terror. And then the doors burst open, and a white aura surged into the room. A man in silvery blue armor with a cape of white feathers stood at the entrance. A bright white aura surrounded him.

The bandits quivered in fear as he slowly walked into the room with his overwhelming presence. Rom was the first to shake off the fear. He roared and charged at Adonai. With a wave of Adonai's hand, Rom was taken off his feet and sent flying to the side, where he crashed into the wall. The sound of his bones crunching could be heard throughout the whole room. With that, the rest of the bandits got a hold of themselves as well, and they all drew their swords.

"He's... he's alone! There's no need to fear him! Fight together!" Jack shouted.

All of them were blinded with fear. Their fight or flight was kicking in, but they had nowhere to flee. Their only option was to fight; they each understood this. Han and Jin charged together. They swung their swords only to make contact with nothing but air. In a lightning-fast attack, Adonai punched both of them in the abdomen, and they crumbled to the ground.

"Hold him off!" Jack shouted as he raised his hand and began to channel his mana in an attempt to summon a phoenix.

Still, Adonai was slowly advancing toward them. Rin, Ling, and Faith took defensive positions with their swords ready. But suddenly, the weight of their bodies became overwhelming as the gravity increased several times over. The three of them crumbled to the ground as well. Jack cursed, but he finished. The body of an orange phoenix materialized.

"Ha! It's over for you now, fool! Witness the power of my phoenix—"

Adonai flicked his fingers and a small white fireball instantly vaporized the pathetic phoenix.

Jack's face went pale. He slowly began to back away. "Don't— don't hurt me. I'm warning you—"

Adonai's presence grew even more intense, and Jack found himself once again frozen, unable to move or speak. All he could do was watch as Adonai slowly walked toward him until he was standing right over him. Adonai raised a hand and pressed a finger against Jack's forehead and uttered a single word, "Suffer."

Jack fell unconscious. In a fraction of a second, he underwent hours upon hours of torture. When he came to, he fell to his knees and began to cry. "Please, please spare me. I don't wanna die. Please."

For a moment, Adonai stood there before Jack, glaring at him. He wanted to kill him. He wanted to kill him so badly... but... he couldn't. He couldn't bring himself to kill any of them. Instead, he pushed Jack down. He raised one of his feet and then stomped down on Jack's right leg, completely crushing it. Then he did the same to the other leg. Jack cried out in pain. Adonai didn't care. He kicked Jack's face, making it fling backward and smack against the ground. Then he stomped down on both of Jack's arms, crushing his elbows. Jack howled out in pain again.

Adonai released the pressure from his presence and spoke to the other bandits. "Get up." They all slowly climbed to their feet. "Leave." They didn't make a sound. They silently turned and began to leave, and then Adonai stopped them. "You forgot something," he said, gesturing to Jack, who was sobbing helplessly on the ground.

Rin and Ling meekly walked over and picked up Jack's limp body together and dragged him away. Adonai followed them outside and went with them through the town to the southern entrance. The townsfolk of Never Thaw came out and cheered as the bandits were marched through town. At the southern entrance, Adonai said one last thing to the lowly clods, "Leave here. Leave here and never even think of returning."

Over the next month, Adonai and the rest of the town worked

together to repair the damage done to Never Thaw. They returned all the things the bandits had stolen and hoarded. Those who had been beaten and injured were tended to and given some balm Dahlia had made with Mist moss, helping them recover quickly. A funeral was held for all the guards who were slain. Everyone also helped out in reconstructing the inn, and before long, the construction was finished. Things had mostly recovered, but there was still a depressing atmosphere around Never Thaw. It wasn't Adonai's fault, but he couldn't help but blame himself. If only he had been there, then he could have stopped anyone from dying. If only he had been there... but he wasn't. And because of that, so many people lost their lives. And in the end, the bandits were left alive. He just couldn't bring himself to kill them; he didn't want to become a killer. Adonai sighed as he sat at a table with Chaver in the newly repaired inn.

"It's not your fault," Chaver told him. "It was out of your control, and in the end, you still saved the day. You're a hero, ya know?"

"I know... but I still feel so... depressed."

"Yeah, I get it. I hate myself for being weak and unable to do anything. But you can't let something like this get you down. It was out of your control."

Adonai sighed again. "Yeah..." He just couldn't stop beating himself up over it. "When are you going back to the Northern Mist?" Chaver asked.

Adonai had been wondering about that himself. He still felt the Mist calling his name. "I want to go, but... I'm scared to leave. What if something else happens while I'm gone?"

"Again, you're worrying too much. I know you want to go back, just go."

Adonai shook his head. For a bit, the two of them just sat together in silence, Chaver drinking his ale and Adonai drinking his water. Then Adonai had an idea, and for the first time in a long time, his face brightened just a little. "What if I left a summon here?"

"You can do that?" Chaver asked.

"I think so. I know I can summon my bonds. However, maintaining the summon while I'm gone might be a little difficult, but

I think I can do it. And one of my summons should be plenty strong enough to protect the town against the average thugs and criminals."

"It's a good idea," Chaver agreed.

Adonai hopped up from his seat. "Wait, are you going to do it now?"

"Yeah," he replied as he began to leave eagerly.

Chaver got up and quickly followed him out to the street. "So who are you gonna summon?"

"My phoenix bond, Arson."

"You named him Arson?"

"Yeah."

Adonai raised his hand and channeled his mana. Then he said the simple phrase, "Arson... come forth." There was a bright light, and then the body of a white phoenix materialized.

Chaver gasped at the sight of it. "It's white?"

"Yeah. Perfectly pure. The marking of a true prodigy. At least that's what I came to think of it," Adonai said, proud of himself.

Chaver nodded. "Seems that way to me."

Arson dropped down to the ground and examined his surroundings. His gaze settled on Chaver.

"Who is this?" Arson asked through the mana link.

"This is Chaver," Adonai told him out loud.

Chaver looked at him confused. "Are you talking to the phoenix?"

"Yeah," Adonai said casually.

"Does it talk back?"

"Yeah, but only I can hear it."

"Oh... okay."

At this point, a large crowd had stopped and gathered around them to get a look at the phoenix. Adonai crouched down and began to debrief Arson.

"Alright, I'm going to be going back to the Northern Mist pretty soon. I need you to stay here and protect these people."

"Do I get to burn anything?" Arson asked eagerly.

"No, you don't get to burn anything. Well, I guess if bad guys show up, you can burn them. But that's it. You only get to burn someone if they're trying to harm the town."

"Good enough for me, I hope bad people show up," Arson said excitedly.

Adonai turned to Chaver. "Listen, I need you to keep a close eye on Arson. He can be a little... unhinged."

"Unhinged?" Chaver repeated, then asked, "Is everything going to be alright? I mean his name is Arson."

"Yeah, everything will be fine," Adonai assured him. With Arson summoned and established as the protector of Never Thaw, Adonai was able to sleep soundly that night, and the next day, he departed for Northern Mist once again.

Chapter 44

Adonai wiped the blood from his silvery-blue spear, then recalled it to his ring. The large carcass of a blood curdler lay at his feet. The beast whose roar had once sent shivers down his spine and made his hairs stand on end was nothing to him anymore. The roars didn't even phase him. He harvested the valuable parts of the body and left the rest. He didn't need to worry about leaving behind most of the remains; something would come along and eat it. Aside from the blood curdler, Adonai also heard lots of Mist clickers during his travels through the Mist. However, at this point, the Mist clickers seemed to have started avoiding him. His aura had grown much stronger since his first time entering the Mist, so that probably had something to do with it. He would also occasionally run into some of the various mana beasts he had discovered. But he avoided fighting with them since he already had bonds for each species so far.

Aside from that, things just went the same as always. He would travel quickly while also taking his time to gather the various plants that existed within the Mist, as well as hunt the various animals. The Mist was a strange place, truly. During his expeditions, Adonai had come to discover that the deeper he went, the thicker the Mist grew, and the denser the mana became. With this, the effects that distorted the mind and senses also increased. Because of this, Adonai had to strengthen his body and mind with more and more mana. But this had in turn led to rapid growth. And it wasn't just the Mist and mana that grew as one ventured deeper into the Mist. The animals became far more dangerous, and the plants became more potent. It was strange the way it forced a person to gradually become stronger and stronger. It was almost as if the Mist was a training ground. Perhaps it was a training ground, a place left behind by the great Inuuk for the people of Oalm Catantan to inherit. But honestly, that was just foolish thinking. There was no way Inuuk would create a training ground like this. It was a place far too dangerous to be a training ground. But then the question remained: why did a place like the Northern Mist exist? Adonai shrugged it off and kept walking.

East of the Pale Mist Marsh lay the Pale Hills. The Pale Hills were a forested area, very similar to the Pale Mist Woods. It was the sixth different biome Adonai had come across now. However, there was something strange about these hills. The moment he had entered them, he felt as if something was watching him. For a moment, just a moment, he sensed something powerful nearby. Then it vanished. But the feeling of being watched never went away.

"We are being stalked," Aeolian commented.

"I know," Adonai replied as he continued to walk unbothered.

"Are you not going to do anything about it?" Zolt asked.

"For now, no."

"Why not?"

"Because I don't feel like it," Adonai said casually.

"Ah, a fine plan. As to be expected of our master," Ore joked.

Adonai ignored him and kept going, occasionally stopping to pick a plant. As he traveled, the feeling of being watched never went away. What made the situation even more weird was that he was clearly being watched from every angle . . . but Adonai could only sense a singular beast.

Suddenly, there was a loud shriek in the distance. Then another and another. Loud, high-pitched shrieks. Steadily, they grew more frequent and closer. Shriek after shriek. They were coming for Adonai. He called out his gear, and the silvery-blue celestite armor materialized around his body and the spears materialized in the air, hovering around him, his white cape draped down his back. It was a swarm of Mist shriekers that were approaching him. As they drew closer, he could sense them more clearly. They were large, bat-like creatures, and there were maybe a hundred of them. Adonai let himself float up into the air to meet them. They drew closer. Closer. Closer still. Their shrieks were ringing in his ears . . . but he didn't care. The Mist shriekers began to swarm him. His spears zipped through the air in every direction, tearing apart everything they touched. Corpses rained down around Adonai and crashed into the ground. In a matter of seconds, all the Mist shriekers were dead. He let himself fall back to the blood-stained ground. But the fight wasn't over. The thing that had been watching him all this time finally decided to show itself. Adonai smiled to himself. It had come out after he fought against the shriekers, thinking he would be vulnerable, exactly as he expected. Just a few meters away, the air seemed to tear and a sort of portal opened. A phantom, a large wolf-like beast, walked out, and the portal closed behind it. A mana beast. It was larger than a war horse. A low growl sounded from it. Adonai raised a hand, and with a flick of his hand, his spears ripped through the air toward the phantom. In an instant, its body disappeared and the spears crashed into nothing. At the same time, the beast reappeared behind Adonai. He just barely managed to jump out of the way as its jaws snapped shut. But as soon as he jumped away, the phantom had blinked behind him again. A large paw whacked the side of his head. He quickly recovered and pulled his spears toward him. The phantom blinked away again, and the spears hit nothing. Adonai immediately directed the spears toward his back, expecting the mana beast to teleport behind him again. It didn't. It appeared directly in front of him. He wasn't able to evade this time. The phantom's jaws snapped shut around his head, and it shook his body back and forth before letting go, causing him to be thrown to the side. Thankfully, the celestite armor was enough to protect him. After crashing into the ground, Adonai quickly recovered and got back on his feet. Again, the phantom blinked behind him and it tried to chomp down on him again. He jerked his head to the side, evading the jaws, and threw a fist that planted itself into the phantom's chin. He finally hit it. The phantom staggered and teleported a short distance away. Adonai wasn't giving it any time to recover. His spears came tearing through the air from every direction. The phantom disappeared again and reappeared further away. Adonai pushed off the ground with enough force to leave behind craters where his feet had been, and he dashed after the phantom with all his strength. He threw a haymaker but missed as the beast blinked a short distance away. He quickly planted his feet and dashed toward it again. This went on again and again. The phantom would teleport a short distance away, and Adonai would almost immediately dash toward it again. He had come to realize something. The distance the phantom teleported was getting shorter and shorter. It was getting tired. And it wasn't just Adonai that the beast had to evade. His spears were flying through the air all around them. This limited the places the phantom could safely blink to. And finally, Adonai caught it. He landed a heavy blow that staggered the phantom and then landed two more blows before it blinked away. With incredible speed, he was once again upon it and landed a few more blows. Again, it blinked away, and again Adonai was instantly upon it. He struck it, and one of his spears planted itself in the beast's side. And then another spear and another. The phantom howled out in pain and teleported one last time, just a couple of meters away, where it then collapsed to the ground. One of the spears ripped through the air and went straight through the phantom's skull. Adonai walked over and pulled his spear out of its head. It was a hard-fought battle. He didn't waste any time; he crouched down, concentrated, and found the phantom's spirit.

He smiled and muttered to himself, "You're mine."

He forcefully took control of the spirit and then, like many times before, he formed a bond with it. Forming bonds was becoming easier and easier. The name Adonai decided on was Phantom. Phantom was probably the strongest mana beast he had faced so far, and he was the most unique. Phantom possessed the ability to manipulate space. And now, Adonai possessed that ability.

After his battle with Phantom, Adonai took a day to rest and then resumed his journey. Northeast of the Pale Mist Hills was the Mist Mountains. It was jagged, rough terrain. However, the rough terrain was nice; it reminded Adonai of the mountains around his home, except there wasn't any snow. The Mist was heavy here, heavier than it had been anywhere else. There weren't many animals that lived in these mountains. Among the few that did, there were the pale rams, Mist moose, and Mist bears. There were also lots of rare and potent plants that Adonai was seeing for the first time. He picked a lot as he went.

After traveling through the mountains for a couple of days, he found himself hiking up a trail. There was a little stream running on his right-hand side. A Mist moose was grazing on the other side of the stream. Pine trees covered the mountains here and reached high up into the mist-covered sky. Adonai stopped to pick some misty mountain flowers next to a boulder and then continued on. The trail turned and began to head downwards. Halfway down, there was a Mist bear snacking on some berries.

Then Adonai hiked up a trail. A little stream ran beside him, and a Mist moose grazed on the other side. He stopped to pick some flowers next to a boulder. The trail began to go downwards and he passed a Mist bear and then continued on. He hiked up a trail, a little stream running beside him where a Mist moose grazed. He stopped to pick some flowers and then passed a Mist bear. Then Adonai hiked up a trail, there was a small stream running beside him and a Mist moose grazed on the other side. He stopped to pick some flowers next to a large boulder . . . He stopped to pick some flowers . . . Hadn't he already done this? Adonai stood up and looked around, everything looked familiar. Hadn't he already passed through here?

"What's going on?" he mumbled to himself. He continued on further down the path and passed a Mist bear. A Mist bear that he could have sworn he had already passed. Then the trail began to go upwards and there was a little stream. Adonai stopped. He had just been here. This was the same trail, the same stream, the same Mist moose.

"Do you guys sense anything weird?" he asked his bonds.

"What do you mean?" Weald asked.

"We've already been here, I don't know how, but I keep coming across the same place."

"Are you going in circles?" Aeolian asked.

"No. I'm definitely not. Something else is going on here."

"What are you suggesting?"

"I-I don't know. I don't know why, but I know that something is off. I just—" Wait. There was something pressing down on Adonai, he could feel it now. It was like a barrier. It was kind of similar to when he encountered Warden. Something was weighing on his mind, but this was a little different. It wasn't just mental, this was physical as well. He concentrated and probed this barrier with mana. It reacted. So he wasn't just imagining it. Something was going on. He used more mana and pressed against the barrier harder and harder, but it kept resisting. He channeled as much mana as he could muster and hit the barrier with everything he had, and the barrier shattered. Adonai escaped the small dimension he had been trapped in and was back in the real world. He reached out with his senses, and that was when he found it. A mana beast. It was a spector, a large black bird similar to a raven, except it had three eyes and four wings.

"I found you." He pressed against the ground with his feet and pushed off, dashing toward it and closing the distance between them in an instant. The spector tried to fly away, but he grabbed hold of it. It frantically thrashed around trying to break free. Adonai reached up with his other hand and broke its neck. The bird's body fell limp in his hands. He set the spector's body down and reached out to its spirit. Then he forcibly took control of it and formed a bond with it.

"How did you do it?" the spector demanded after the bond was formed, catching Adonai off guard.

Normally, when he forcibly formed a bond with a mana beast, it was too exhausted to speak through a mana link.

"You seem lively," Adonai said to it.

"How did you do it!" the spector repeated.

"Calm down, calm down. How did I do what?"

"How did you break out of my time loop?"

"Is that what that was? A time loop, interesting."

"Yes, that's what it was. I control time. So, tell me, how did you break free of the loop?"

Adonai shrugged. "I don't really know, I just happened to notice something was off and then used brute force to break free."

For a moment, the spector was silent; then it asked, "So what is this? What did you do to me?"

"Well, I killed you and then formed a bond with you."

"A bond?"

"Yes, a bond. You are now a part of me, an extension." The spector was silent as it contemplated what Adonai told it; then Adonai asked, "Would you like a name?"

The spector remained silent for a moment longer; then it said, "Yes." Adonai smiled. "Then your new name will be Spector."

Chapter 45

Ronin and his company of fifty strong finally arrived at the little town known as Never Thaw. They were a band of mercenaries who had come after hearing word that the Northern Mist was being explored through a new entrance. Ronin had high hopes for himself and his company. This was a big opportunity that had the potential to turn their lives around for the better. As they arrived at the outskirts of the little town, Chaver and Arson came out to meet the company. Ronin dismounted his horse and went over to greet the young man.

"Who are you and what do ya want!" Chaver shouted as Ronin approached. Ronin raised his arms halfway and showed his empty hands as a sign of goodwill.

"Me and my company have come here to explore the Northern Mist," Ronin told him, exchanging a glance at the burning white phoenix that stood beside the boy. He had never seen such a phoenix; it was beautiful yet at the same time, it was dangerous. And there was something off about it. There was a crazed look in the phoenix's eyes, it was almost as if it were urging Ronin to step out of line.

"Is this your summon?" Ronin asked.

Chaver studied Ronin with a careful eye and then shook his head, "No, this is the summon of my friend. If you try anything, he'll reduce ya to ashes," Chaver spoke coldly; he wasn't welcoming at all.

"I see," Ronin said with an awkward smile and then continued, "I can assure you I have no intention of stirring up trouble and I'll see to it that my men don't either."

Chaver's expression softened a little, but his suspicions remained, and the crazed look in the phoenix's eyes never faded. "Well, as long as you and your men have no ill intentions, there shouldn't be a problem. I'm sorry for the cold welcome."

"It's no problem," Ronin replied, thankful that the situation had deescalated. After that, the mercenary company made their way into the small town. Ronin followed Chaver and Arson into town.

"We only have a single inn in our town. We ain't got much room for all your companions," Chaver explained as they walked.

"That's fine. I'll have them set camp just outside of town," Ronin said with a smile and then asked, "So who's the leader of Never Thaw?"

"We haven't really got one," Chaver told him, "But I suppose if I had to pick someone, it would be Adonai Alaric. The whole town admires him, he's done a lot for everyone here. He's also the one who's been exploring the Northern Mist; that's where he is now." Chaver began rambling. "This white phoenix here is Adonai's summon. His name is Arson. Adonai left him here to watch over the town while he's away. We used to have a small force of guards who protected this place, but there was a recent incident. A small band of thugs showed up and wreaked havoc. They slaughtered all the guards and took control of the town. That's why I was so cautious welcoming you. Adonai had been in the Northern Mist when the thugs arrived, and it was he who drove them out after returning." Then Chaver went on rambling about other random things, his mind seemingly becoming distracted every time he began talking about something.

Ronin followed him to the inn and patiently listened the whole while. He wanted to build a good relationship with the people here in Never Thaw. When Chaver stopped talking to order a beer, Ronin asked him, "Do you know where I might find the entrance to the Northern Mist?"

Chaver shrugged. "I don't know, actually. Nobody aside from Adonai knows. And I'd suggest you don't go lookin' for it. Adonai is a special case, he ain't ordinary like you and me. He's told me all kinds of stories about his time there. It ain't a place to be trifled with."

"Thanks for the concern, but I and my men can handle ourselves. So, you really have no idea where the entrance is?"

Chaver sighed, "I don't know exactly where it is, but when Adonai leaves, he travels northeast and goes through a glacier pass. It's probably somewhere not far from there."

Ronin thanked him and after sharing a drink together, he left. He returned to where his company had set up camp just outside of town. He was welcomed by his two vice-captains, Grace and Rose, and his right-hand man, Garret. Grace and Rose were sisters who were from a fallen noble family. It wasn't quite clear how their family fell, but it was suspected that it was orchestrated by the Telestials. They had red hair and strong bodies, and Rose wore an eye patch. There wasn't much known about his right-hand man, Garret. Ronin found him in a bar one day and they had been together ever since. Garret didn't talk much; in fact, all you would ever hear from him was the occasional grunt. Ronin himself had grown up in Grimlore, the capital of Griffland. After attending Grimlore Academy, he traveled around a little. The six nations were generally at peace, but they had small battles on occasion. Fighting between noble families was also common. Noticing this during his travels, Ronin had decided to form a mercenary unit.

"So what did you find out?" Rose asked when Ronin returned to camp.

"The entrance is northeast of here."

"When do we depart?"

"We'll wait a few days, give the men some time to rest," Ronin said, and then quickly added, "These folks here in Never Thaw recently had some unwelcome visitors stir up trouble. Spread word and make sure that everyone behaves themselves."

"Understood." Rose and Grace immediately set out to carry his words while he and Garret sat down and had a drink.

A few days later, the mercenary camp was bustling early in the morning as they prepared to depart for the Northern Mist. It was early, before the crack of dawn. It had been nearly a week now since their arrival at Never Thaw. During that time, Ronin had sent out ten teams of five to search for the entrance to the Northern Mist. The moment they found it, they immediately began making preparations to leave. Ronin was anxious to hurry up and get to work; he was excited to see what the Northern Mist was like. But at the same time, he was also a little afraid. There were many terrible stories of the Northern Mist. However, a single person, this Adonai Alaric, had been exploring the Northern Mist all on his own. Ronin wasn't sure what Adonai was like, but if Adonai could do it alone, then surely he and his company could manage it together. That and this entrance must be different from the other entrances; otherwise, there was no way that Adonai could keep coming and going through the Northern Mist.

"You nervous?" Ronin asked Garret as they finished up their preparations.

Garret just grunted.

Ronin climbed atop his horse and shouted out to the company, "All right! Let's move out!"

The mercenaries set out. They rode into the mountains. "What do you think it'll be like?" Grace asked Ronin as they rode.

Ronin didn't answer for a moment as he thought it over; then finally, he shook his head. "I don't know. I really don't. All sorts of things probably await us. It'll probably be an environment with monsters unlike anything we've ever seen. But I'm prepared for the worst."

"That's a lame answer. That's so like you," Grace told him. "If you ask me, I think there'll be a forest of great big trees covered in golden leaves and strange creatures like deer with three heads and six legs, and talking flowers or birds that sing the sweetest melodies."

"That's ridiculous," Rose butted in. "If anything, it'll be a desolate land with giant cacti and living skeletons. A place where the sun never rises and the moons don't shine."

"Right, living skeletons," Grace said, mocking her sister. "What about you, Garret? What do you think it'll be like?" Garret grunted, and then Grace said, "Yeah, that sounds about right."

By nightfall, they arrived at the Northern Ridge and then the crack. "That's a big entrance," Ronin said upon seeing it.

"The Northern Mist lies beyond there," Rose added.

Ronin turned and shouted to the company, "We'll set camp here for the night!"

They set camp, and everyone got what little sleep they could manage to get. The company rose early again on the morrow. Ronin tightened his steel breastplate and fastened his sword to his hip. There was an eerie silence over the camp as everyone quietly got ready to enter the Northern Mist. Before long, preparations were complete, and Ronin was leading his company into the crack.

"Those of you who can cast fire, provide light!" Ronin instructed. Several flames were conjured and cast their light against the tunnel walls. The only sound as they traveled through the crack was the clopping of their horses' hooves. Nobody spoke. Then they reached the end. Ronin stopped the line as he stood before the white wall of Mist. He stared into it, and it stared back. Then he gave the order, "Forward!"

They marched into the Northern Mist. It was thick and hard to see, but aside from the lack of vision, it wasn't so bad. Maybe Adonai really did discover a safe entrance into the Northern Mist. They marched slowly.

"This isn't so bad," Grace said.

"Yeah," Rose agreed, "But I was expecting more than just a barren land."

"The environment must change the further we go. That must be where all the valuable stuff is that that man gathers," Grace told them.

Ronin's companions seemed to be easygoing. But Ronin felt otherwise. Something wasn't right. But he ignored his instincts and led his company further into the Mist. And then it happened. The effects of the Northern Mist came in full force all at once. Everyone, all fifty company members, entered a state of panic and distress. The horses were even worse. Ronin was thrown from the back of his horse, and he fell to the ground where he watched his horse frantically gallop away and disappear into the Mist. All the horses did this. Everyone was thrown and shaken to the ground, and the horses ran off in every direction. But there wasn't anyone who was worried about the horses. Everyone was going through their own fit of insanity. Their minds became foggy. No, it was worse than foggy. It hurt just to try to think. And their senses became distorted. Many people began hallucinating and ran off in random directions in panic. Ronin himself was rolling around on the ground, gripping his head. There were even a few people who drew their swords and took their own lives. For days on end, they all remained in their distressed state. But gradually, each of them began to get a grip and somewhat return to their senses.

"Everyone, gather close!" Ronin shouted, and the company did so. They gathered into a tight group. They did a count on the remaining members. There were already eleven missing or dead. "Does anyone remember the way?" Ronin asked.

But nobody could remember anything. So he took a deep breath. "Alright, everyone remain calm and follow me. I'll get us out of here," he said, but he wasn't so sure.

They began a blind march, moving in one direction, hoping to find safety. They were dead. That was what they were all thinking, but none of them wanted to say it. Instead, they all held onto this frail hope that Ronin would be able to lead them out. After marching for a long time, they arrived at the Pale Mist Plains. Ronin stopped the line when they arrived.

"There's grass," he said, almost in disbelief. Then he turned to his companions, "Did we cross a place like this when we entered?"

"I-I don't remember. I can't remember," Grace answered.

"Does anyone remember if this is the right way?" Ronin shouted to the company.

Everyone began murmuring among themselves. "I think this is the right way!" someone shouted out. Some agreed with him, others disagreed. They couldn't make a decision.

"We'll have a vote!" Ronin shouted. "Either we march on through the Plains, or we march on through the barren land! All those for marching through the Plains!" Several people shouted and called out voting for the Plains.

"And for the barren land!" Ronin shouted. Again, several people shouted out, but there weren't as many. "The Plains it is! Everyone stay close to one another! The closer, the better!"

Ronin led the company forward. Though there were many who thought the Plains were the wrong direction, none of them digressed. They all trusted Ronin and followed his orders. For a long time, they marched through the Plains. The grass was tall. They passed a group of Mist elks and could faintly see their antlers glowing in the distance, but they were all too afraid to investigate it.

"Are you sure this is the right way?" Rose asked as they marched.

"No. I don't know," Ronin told her.

"Should we turn around?"

"I… I don't know. Let's just stay the course a while longer, and then we'll change direction."

The only one who didn't seem bothered by the situation was

Garret. Garret didn't seem to have a care in the world. Then there was a click in the distance. It was far away. Then there was another click.

Ronin put up one of his arms and stopped his companions. "Did you guys hear?" he asked.

"Hear what?" Rose asked.

"Listen."

They all remained motionless. And then they heard it. A click. It was faint and far away. "What do we do?" Grace asked worriedly. There was another click. Then another. This time, the clicks were a little closer.

"Draw your weapons!" Ronin shouted. This didn't feel right. This... this was something dangerous. More clicks sounded. They were growing closer. Click, click, click. "Defensive positions!" Ronin shouted.

They all formed a tight circle. The clicks were still growing even closer. Click, click, click. Everyone was tensing up. Click, click, click. They gripped their swords tightly. Click, click, click. They strained their eyes, trying to see into the Mist. Click, click, click. Sweat trickled down Ronin's brow. Click, click, click. The clicking was louder than ever. Click, click, click. It was coming from every direction. Click, click, click. They were surrounded. Click, click, click. Louder. Click, click, click. The intensity grew. Click, click, click. The clicks rang in their ears. Click, click, click, click, click, click.

"Gaahh!" A Mist clicker leapt through the Mist and tackled one of the mercenaries and tore at him with its long, serrated claws. More men cried out as more Mist clickers leapt into the group. There was nothing they could do.

"This is it, lads! This is it! If we must die, let us die together!" Ronin shouted out.

They fought back. Slowly, they began to kill the Mist clickers. But there were so many. Ronin ducked as one of the beasts flew over his head. He spun around and drove his sword into its back, and then Rose finished it off. Garret cut down a Mist clicker, then another leapt at him. Garret caught it by the neck with his bare hand and threw it to the ground, where he stabbed it through the heart. Ronin cut down another Mist clicker. Then another one leapt at him and swiped him across the chest with its claws. Adrenaline was pumping through his veins; he felt no pain, nor did he notice the blood seeping down his chest. They all fought viciously. But they were no match. As the mercenaries died, they began to fall quicker and quicker as they were overrun by the beasts. Tears began to stream down Ronin's face. He couldn't help but cry. He was these men's leader. They looked up to him. They trusted him. And now, he had led them all to their deaths. It seemed this was the end. What a terrible way to end.

But then, a silence fell over the battlefield. A complete, an absolute, an utter silence. Everyone, everything froze as a heavy presence descended down upon the battlefield. A presence unlike anything Ronin had ever felt before. Even the Mist clickers had frozen in fear. And then they began to fall. Ronin couldn't see it, but he knew it was happening. Something was killing the Mist clickers at a remarkable pace. In a matter of seconds, dozens and dozens of monsters were slaughtered. The heavy presence over the field lifted, and for the first time, Ronin realized he had been holding his breath.

"Are you alright?" a man asked. He stepped through the Mist right before Ronin, extending a hand out to him.

"Who—who are you?" Ronin mouthed.

"Adonai. My name is Adonai Alaric."

Chapter 46

Ronin woke up lying down in a bed. His body was bandaged. He had deep wounds all over. His body hurt. But he was alive. After Adonai's arrival, he had guided everyone out of the Northern Mist to safety. In the end, only nineteen of the mercenaries survived. More than half were wiped out, and everyone that did survive was badly wounded. They were being treated by the kind people of Never Thaw now. Ronin began to cry as he lay there in bed. His body was in pain, but that wasn't why. He was crying because of the loss of his men, his friends, his family. There was a knock at the door, and then it slowly opened. The young savior, Adonai, walked into the room accompanied by Chaver.

"How are ya doing?" Chaver asked as he set a bowl of fruit down on a small table next to the bed.

Ronin looked down over his body, then looked back to them. "I guess I'm doing alright. I don't think I ever thanked you. You not only saved me but lots of my men as well. Thank you. Really, thank you, Adonai."

"Yeah, I'm just sorry I didn't arrive sooner."

"No, don't be; what you did for us was more than I could ask for. But is there a reason you've come here?"

"There is, actually," Chaver told him. "For one, we just wanted to check up on you; your injuries were pretty bad. But the other reason is because we wanted to ask you about what you plan to do moving forward."

"Moving forward . . ." Ronin muttered to himself. "I don't know. I don't know what I'm going to do. I don't even know how I'm going to face my companions again . . ."

"It's alright," Chaver assured him. "I'm sure they bear you no grudge." Ronin sighed. "I hope so. But why do you ask about my plans?"

The two friends exchanged a glance. "Well, the thing is . . . we wanted to recruit you."

"Recruit me?"

Chaver nodded his head. "You see, a while ago, the guards in our town were . . . well, they're not around anymore. So Adonai had the idea of asking you to ask your company to become the new guards of our town. If you don't want to, then it's no worry."

Ronin looked up to the ceiling and let out what was sort of a sigh of relief, and once again, he found himself crying. "Thank you. Truly, thank you. Not only do you save our lives, but you continue to show us grace."

"So, is that a yes?" Chaver asked.

"Yeah, that's a yes. I'll talk to my companions. We will happily serve this town." After talking a bit longer, trying to cheer Ronin up, Adonai and Chaver left.

"You want to go grab a drink?" Chaver asked.

"No," Adonai declined. "I'm actually going to go stop by the temple."

"Really? I get stopping by the temple every now and then, but why do you go so much?" Adonai shrugged. "I like to show my love for the Celestials."

"You're a religious nut," Chaver joked.

Adonai just shrugged again and left for the temple. He sat there in a meditative state for a long time. Not a meditative state that was intended to grow his strength, but a meditative state to worship the Celestials. While he was there, he also offered up many prayers. Prayers to Inuuk. He spent the rest of the day doing this and then returned home to his family.

Chapter 47

Adin took a deep breath and gripped the celestite spear tighter. He circulated his mana, as much as he could, then he drove his feet into the ground and dashed forward with all his might. Adonai blocked his attack. But Adin wasn't finished. He swung the spear around again and again and attacked as ferociously as he could. But every strike was met with Adonai's spear. Maybel and Laor cheered on the sidelines as their brothers battled. Finally, Adin couldn't go on any longer. He dropped his spear and fell to the ground, breathing heavily.

"I-I almost had you," Adin said between breaths.

Adonai came over and sat down with him and said, "Yeah, it was pretty close."

"You say that, but I have a feeling I wouldn't be able to beat you . . . ever."

"Naw, you just gotta keep practicing, you'll get there," Adonai encouraged him and then added, "Your mana has grown stronger, I can tell."

"Yeah, I've been training a lot but I'm still nowhere close to as strong as you were," Adin replied.

"That's alright, besides, you haven't even received your bond yet."

"Yeah, just one more year," Adin grinned.

"My turn!" Laor chimed, running over with one of the celestite spears in hand. He began tugging at Adonai's arm.

"Alright, alright, let me get up," Adonai told him. The two of them sparred for a while and Adin and Maybel watched. Adin and Laor continued to take turns fighting against Adonai throughout the day. Adonai stayed in Never Thaw for a few weeks. Once Ronin and his men recovered and took up the duty of guarding the town, he felt confident that he could leave the town in their hands. After saying goodbye to his family, Adonai set out for the Northern Mist.

Northeast of the Pale Mist Hills was the Bright Mist Jungle. The Mist was incredibly thick here, so thick that Adonai couldn't even see his hand in front of his face. And the pressure was immense too. He pressed his way through the thick foliage. Thick vines hung from the tree tops. There were glowing flowers and great, big bioluminescent mushrooms. There were also great, big carnivorous flowers with petals covered in thorns.

As Adonai walked, the vines and roots along the ground began to shift. Everything was moving as if the jungle had come to life. Then the giant carnivorous flowers rose up from their resting places. It was like a scene straight out of a nightmare. At least for most, that would have been a nightmare. Adonai began to slaughter the flowers. He didn't even need his gear. With just a swipe of his hand, he could launch a wind blade that cut through the stems of the flowers. But as he cut them down, they quickly regrew. This went on for a while. Adonai would cut down the flowers, then they would regrow and commence their attack again.

"What are you going to do? They keep regrowing," Aeolian commented.

"We should burn them!" Arson said excitedly. For once, he wasn't ignored.

"Burning them probably is the best option," Adonai agreed, "So why don't you do it yourself? Arson . . . come forth."

He raised his hand and then the body of a white phoenix materialized.

"Let them burn." Arson stretched his wings and unleashed a wave of white fire that consumed everything within a kilometer, leaving behind nothing but ashes.

"That was a bit much," Adonai commented.

"No, it wasn't nearly enough," Arson growled, eager to burn more things.

"Yeah, you're done, bud." Adonai undid the summoning and Arson's body faded away.

"So soon?" Arson complained.

"If I didn't, then you'd end up burning the whole jungle down."

"And what's wrong with that?" At this point, Arson was once again being ignored. After his short battle with the carnivorous flowers, Adonai continued to press further into the jungle. He came across more animals, like the twin-tailed panther and the orange Mist monkeys. A twin-tailed panther had tried to pounce on him from behind. He killed it without even turning around. Then the pack of Mist monkeys had surrounded him. There were roughly two hundred of them. Adonai called out his spears and they whisked around the jungle, ripping through all the monkeys in an instant. As he collected plants and hides and explored, Adonai stumbled across some strange tracks. He followed them deeper and deeper into the jungle and then stumbled across a strange monster. He stumbled across a volite. It stood on six legs, was covered in scales, and had a long whip-like tail. Each pair of legs was different from the others. The front legs ended in talons, the middle legs had sharp claws, and the back legs were thick and hairy. Adonai stopped and just watched the monster. The volite took notice of him and hissed. Then it charged him. He casually waved his hand and a blade of wind cut into the volite. The monster was cut deep and fell to the ground. A large pool of blood began to form around it.

"That was easy." Adonai turned away to continue gathering plants but then he sensed the monster twitch. He turned around. It was still alive. He watched as the wound quickly healed. As it climbed to its feet, he could sense something else about it. Something strange. It was subtle, but it was as if the monster's skin was changing.

By the time the volite was on its feet, it was completely healed. It charged at him again. And again, Adonai waved his hand and sliced the beast with a blade of wind. But this time, the wind didn't cut as deep and instead of falling, all it did was flinch. It continued its charge toward Adonai. He jumped back and this time, condensed mana to the tip of his finger and fired a concentrated bullet of wind. It struck the volite in the face and went directly through its brain. The beast died instantly and crumbled to the ground at Adonai's feet.

"What a strange creature," he whispered as he crouched down and began to closely examine the monster. He pressed his hand against its hide. It was tough, very tough, definitely hard enough to stop a wind blade. Which was strange because the first wind blade had nearly killed it. Did it really grow that much stronger in that short battle? Aside from that, it had a very unique hide. Adonai drew a knife and harvested the body before moving on deeper into the jungle.

Before long, he found two more volites. He could tell they were volites from the presence they carried, but anatomically, they were completely different. These two were eerily similar to the twin-tailed panther but were definitely different. They both had six eyes instead of two and they had sharp spines that rose up out of their backs. Adonai decided he was going to experiment a little with them. As expected, when he got close enough and they noticed him, they charged at him. He launched a large flame at them but kept the heat under control. The two volites writhed on the ground in pain as their fur burned away. But then, they quickly began to change. Their skin hardened. Adonai sent out another flame as they climbed to their feet; this time, the fire was a little stronger. They withstood the fire. The two beasts charged again. Adonai flew up into the air, easily evading their attacks. One of the volites ran up a nearby tree and lunged at him from the branches. He kicked it in the head, sending it flying away. However, the other volite was doing something strange. It remained on the ground. Its body was tensing up and it was clearly in pain. Then two wings sprung up from its back. It jumped up off the ground and began to fly. Adonai cursed as he evaded another attack. He pointed a hand at it and increased the gravity several times over, sending it crashing into the ground. At this point, the other volite he had kicked had come back running. Adonai took control of the surrounding jungle. The roots reached up from the ground and wrapped around the approaching volite's legs. Then the roots ripped off all four legs and the volite crashed into the ground. The volite with wings was coming again now as well. Adonai called out one of his spears and fired it. It went through the volite's head and body and out its rear. The dead beast crashed into the ground. Then Adonai turned his attention back to the volite that had its legs ripped off. Four new legs had already begun to quickly form. He watched as it completed its new legs and climbed to its feet. Then he immediately sent his spear flying through its head, killing it instantly. Adonai got up and just like last time, he walked over to the corpses and inspected the bodies.

"What are these beasts?" Weald asked.

"They seem to be changing in the midst of battle," Terra said. Adonai nodded, "They are. They're adapting. Evolving."

"But evolving at such a rapid pace . . ."

"I know, it's strange."

"If we run into any more of these, it would be best to kill them as quickly as possible."

"Yeah," Adonai agreed.

He harvested the two bodies and went further. In such a short span of time, he had run into three different volites. They weren't traveling in a pack, but there seemed to be a lot of them in this area. Further in the jungle, there was a large opening. And in the center of this opening was a massive mound.

"A nest," Adonai muttered to himself.

It was like an ant's nest. He stayed at the edge of the clearing, keeping his distance from the nest. He could sense them. The volites. He could sense a lot of them, teeming under the ground.

"Let's go fight them. Let's burn them all to ashes," Arson urged excitedly. He was ignored.

"What are you planning?" Aeolian asked.

Adonai remained motionless.

"I . . . I think I'm going to turn away here. I don't think it'd be a good idea to fight against a whole hive of these volites."

"Leaving would probably be best," Aeolian agreed.

"What about my idea?" Arson interjected. "What about burning them with fire?" He was ignored.

Adonai turned and left the clearing. After that, he spent a few more days going around the jungle, collecting mushrooms, flowers, and fruits. After that, he began his return home. And the trip back home went just like all the other trips in the past. Adonai swiftly flew through the Mist straight to the crack. It was all fine. There was nothing off . . . nothing.

Chapter 48

Adonai sat at the inn with Chaver. He was just finishing up telling him about the volites.

"So they really evolved in the middle of combat?" Chaver asked.

Adonai nodded his head, "Yeah, I've never seen anything like it. Honestly, it kind of scares me."

"Really? You, scared? Don't be ridiculous, I know very well you ain't scared of nothin'."

Adonai chuckled, "You're right, I suppose they ain't that scary. But I'll have to be careful if I encounter them again. I'll have to make sure to kill 'em as quickly as possible so that they don't end up evolving into unkillable beasts."

Chaver's mother stopped by and placed a bowl of soup in front of Adonai. "Here ya go," she said with a warm smile.

"Thank you, Miss Rolfe." He ate a spoonful and then told Chaver, "The town seems bigger."

Chaver took a swig of beer and said, "It is bigger. Lots of people have been showing up and settling down here lookin' to make better lives."

"Any of 'em causing any trouble?" Adonai asked.

Chaver shook his head. "Things have been peaceful. Ronin and his companions fully recovered a while ago, and they've been doing a good job watching over the town."

"That's good. I'm glad we were able to form a relationship with them."

"It is good," Chaver agreed; he finished his beer and set the mug aside.

"How's everything else? The business?" Adonai asked.

"It's mostly been good. Asher is the most famous blacksmith across the entire world now. Everything has been selling very well at super high prices. But . . . ." Chaver sighed. "We've been having trouble with pirates. It started just a few weeks ago. So far, we've already lost two ships worth of merchandise. Thankfully, our crews have been able to return home safely. Me and John and James aren't sure what to do—wait." A smile crept across Chaver's face. "What if you go with the next shipment? You can personally handle the pirates. It's perfect, there's nobody better for the job than you."

Adonai ate his soup as he listened. "I guess I can do that. A few pirates shouldn't be too difficult to handle."

"Yeah! That's my buddy, always coming through!" Chaver exclaimed. He leaned back in his chair in a more relaxed manner. "Man, this pirate thing had been eating away at me for weeks. To think that the solution was so obvious. Thank goodness, you're really saving my neck."

Adonai shrugged, "It ain't that big of a deal."

Chaver sat back up in his seat, "Don't downplay it. This whole business was built on your back. You're honestly the hero of this town."

"You praise me too much," Adonai said that, but he couldn't help but smile.

Chaver changed the subject, "It's almost your birthday, ain't it? Finally turnin' sixteen."

"Yup."

"You excited?"

"Not really."

Chaver laughed, "That's just like you. You never were one to celebrate. But I guess that's fine."

"Your birthday passed not that long ago, didn't it? Sorry I wasn't around for it," Adonai told him.

"Naw, don't worry about it. It was nothing special."

"Still, it's a shame I wasn't around . . . Ya know, I might start taking off more time from the Northern Mist. I've seen most of what it has to offer. It'd be nice to spend more time at home."

Chaver nodded, "I think that's a good idea. With the three interspatial rings, you're already bringing back more than enough,

Dahlia and her family have been struggling to process everything at your pace, so slowing down will actually do more good than harm."

"Well, that makes me feel better about it. I wasn't actually sure if I should slow down or not, but it seems slowing down is the right decision."

"Of course, knowing you, even though you'll supposedly be taking time off, you're still gonna work your rear off, aren't you?"

Adonai smiled, "I like helping out around town. That and I can't neglect my training."

Chaver shook his head, "You're a nut."

The two friends continued to talk late into the night. It made Adonai happy to be able to sit down and spend some time with his friend.

The following morning, Adonai rose early and went to fetch Ciela. The two of them took off together and headed toward Plain City. When they arrived at the north gate, Jane and Harry were there waiting.

"You must be Adonai," Jane said as he climbed down from Ciela's back.

"Yeah, that's me. Who might you two be?"

"I'm Jane and this is Harry. We formed the Blue Glacier Guild with John and James. We're the Plain City branch who oversee the shipments going out of Glacier Lake. Here, come with us."

"I see, it's nice to meet the both of you." Adonai followed them into the city.

"John had contacted us through a mana note informing us of your arrival. I know it might be rude but I must ask, are you really the one who's been exploring the Northern Mist? You look so young," Harry asked him.

Adonai nodded, "Yeah, I'm the one who's been exploring the Mist."

"Wow. It's hard to believe that after all this time, the person to finally conquer the Northern Mist is just a young man. How old are you?"

"I'm almost sixteen."

They walked through the city toward the harbor. And as they went, Harry continued to ask questions.

"Are the rumors of the Northern Mist true?"

"Some of them. Others, like the rumor that the Mist is where dead spirits go to rest, that's just nonsense," Adonai told him.

"Interesting. And what about you?"

"What do you mean?"

"Well, how did you become strong enough to explore the Northern Mist? From my understanding, you're just a farm boy from an isolated town. How did you come to be capable of exploring the Northern Mist all on your own?" Harry asked; Jane was also eager to hear what Adonai had to say.

But all he did was shrug and say, "I'm not entirely sure why I am the way I am. I just suppose I was born this way."

"You didn't have some sort of teacher or master?" Jane asked.

Adonai shook his head, "Aside from a few books I was lucky enough to get my hands on, everything I know, I taught myself."

The two merchants were in awe of this young man.

"You know, ever since we first started this business, I always wondered what made John take such a strong liking to you so quickly. But now that I've met you, I think I understand why John was so eager about this business," Jane said and Harry nodded in agreement.

"Let's stop here," Jane said, gesturing to a nearby small shop that overlooked the harbor. "We'll treat you to lunch."

They sat down near a window so that they could see out over the lake.

"That's one of our ships right there," Harry said, pointing out to one of the larger ships docked in the harbor. People were walking back and forth loading things into the ship.

"That's the ship you'll be leaving on later today," Jane told him. A waitress brought over several plates of food. A lot of it was food unfamiliar to Adonai, and so he dug in eagerly.

Jane continued talking, "We've arranged for a group of fifteen mercenaries to accompany you during the voyage. They may not be at your level, but they are strong and should provide you with strong support."

Adonai gulped down a mouthful of food, "That won't be necessary. I'll be able to handle the pirates all on my own."

Jane was unsure. "These pirates aren't weak. I don't know if you've heard, but they're capable of summoning an entire kraken."

That was rare. Though the mana beasts were all strong, there was still definitely a gap between their strength. And the one who stood at the top was the kraken. It was far larger and more powerful than the other mana beasts. However, because of this power difference, summoning an entire kraken was far more difficult than summoning one of the other mana beasts. Because of that, people with a kraken bond were incapable of summoning an entire kraken. They got around this by just summoning one or more tentacles at a time. In this case, the pirates were combining their mana together in order to fully summon a kraken. But that didn't bother Adonai.

"Summon a kraken or not, it won't be a problem."

Jane and Harry exchanged a glance. "If you say so. But we've already paid the mercenaries, so they'll be coming either way," Jane told him.

"That's fine," Adonai said casually as he continued to indulge in the delicious food before him. After the meal, Adonai went to board the ship with Ciela.

"Just, please be careful," Jane said one last time. "These pirates are dangerous. We know you're strong, but you're just a single person. There's only so much you can do alone."

Adonai just smiled. "Don't worry, everything will be alright." Then he departed with the ship down the Dire River.

After boarding the ship, the leader of the mercenary group, Ken, approached Adonai. "Are you that special individual they sent with us?"

"Yeah, my name's Adonai." He reached out to shake hands, but Ken didn't accept. "I don't know where they get off sending some brat on a mission like this. This ain't some joy ride, alright? It's gonna get dangerous. So when the fighting starts, just stay out of the way. You understand?"

Adonai just nodded his head. "Yes, sir, I understand."

The leader gave him a look and then walked away. Days later, they were still sailing south on the Dire River. Adonai stood at the bow with Ciela, watching as the ship rose and fell with each wave. This was his first time on a boat. The vast Dire River lay out before him. It was nearly too wide to be considered a river. A few clouds blew by in the breeze high up in the sky, and the sun shone down. There hadn't been much going on over the past few days. Adonai spent most of the time in the lower deck meditating or up in the air playing with Ciela. None of the mercenaries liked him. They all seemed to think that he was just some brat from a rich noble family who was playing hero. He just ignored them. Adonai was spaced out when the call was sounded.

"Pirates!" one of the sailors yelled. And sure enough, there was a pirate ship fast approaching.

"Everyone, to your battle stations!" the captain shouted. Everyone was rushing back and forth. Adonai just remained at the front of the ship and silently watched the approaching pirates. They drew closer and closer, and still, Adonai just watched.

Finally, he extended a hand forward and called, "Brine... come forth." The water, as if a storm had suddenly descended upon them, began to stir violently. Then the massive body of a white kraken emerged from the water. And it wasn't alone. Over, closer to the pirate's ship, a massive green kraken emerged from the water. Everyone on board the ship was shocked, especially the mercenary leader when Adonai summoned his kraken. The two krakens began to clash. And they clashed mightily. Giant tentacles rose and fell and wrapped around each other as the two gigantic beasts struggled to submit to the other. The ships rocked back and forth violently. Adonai smiled; he was going to have some fun with this. His silvery-blue armor materialized around him, and one of his spears materialized in his hand. He sprinted to the edge of the ship and launched himself up into the air toward the battling krakens.

Adonai called out as he fell, "Brine, catch me."

One of the giant white tentacles rose above the water for Adonai to land on. Then he dashed forward, using the tentacles as a path. He slipped and weaved past the thrashing tentacles as he ran for the head of the green kraken. One of the tentacles attempted to smash him. He swung his spear in a wide arc and slashed off the tentacle. Then he leapt forward and stabbed the kraken in one of its eyes. It cried out in pain. The kraken then slammed its face with one of its own tentacles in an attempt to crush Adonai. But he evaded and then continued to dart around the twisting tentacles, dealing a blow here or there. All the while, the two ships remained on opposite sides of the fight. Now that the pirates had been faced with an opposing kraken, they didn't know what to do. Finally, Adonai decided enough was enough. He hurled his spear with all his might at the green kraken, and it ripped a huge hole through its head. Then the body quickly dissipated as the summon was released. The pirates began to turn their ship around and flee, but Brine submerged and darted through the water, quickly cutting them off. Silence washed over the pirate's ship as Adonai flew over to them. He slowly descended down onto the deck.

His presence was so heavy, none of the pirates made a move. They just remained frozen wherever they stood.

"Who's the captain here?" Adonai asked.

"I-I am," a big, burly man with black hair said. "What's your name?"

"Quinn."

Adonai began walking toward him. Quinn took half a step back, then it felt as if something seized control of his body.

"Don't move away from me," Adonai told him, then asked, "Do you surrender?"

"Ye-yes."

"Do you hear that!" Adonai shouted, turning around. "Your captain surrendered! Any of you got a problem with that?" Silence. He received no answer. "I'll take that as a yes."

After a short while, the boat Adonai had come with arrived. Ken and a few of the other mercenaries boarded the pirate ship. As his men began to tie up the prisoners, Ken approached Adonai.

"Who... who the heck are you?" Ken asked in disbelief.

Adonai grinned real big at the change in attitude from the mercenary captain. "I am the first-born son of Adon, conqueror of the Northern Mist, prodigy of prodigies. I am Adonai Alaric."

After everything settled down, Adonai decided to leave the rest in the hands of the crew and mercenaries. He was done here and wanted to go home. So he hopped on Ciela's back, and they flew off.

Chapter 49

"Okay, guys, let's make this a festival he'll never forget!" Chaver shouted, and people cheered with him.

They had gathered outside next to the temple. The whole town of Never Thaw had come together to create a festival for Adonai's sixteenth birthday. It was going to be a surprise, since normally, Adonai would object to everyone doing so much for him. That was one of his flaws—he was great at helping others, but he was terrible at accepting their goodwill in return. People were out in the streets hanging lanterns and setting up other decorations. The band was practicing their music while people set up all sorts of stands with games and food.

"How long until he returns?" Dahlia asked Chaver as they walked through the streets checking out what everyone was doing.

"At this point, he should have already encountered and dealt with the pirates. So he should be back any moment."

"That's good." Dahlia took Chaver's hand and smiled, and they continued to walk around admiring the festival decorations. It was a wonderful night. Everyone was in high spirits. Everyone was happy. Was... screams. Screams tore through the air and rang through the streets. Terrible, terrible screams.

"What's going on?" Dahlia asked in a frightened voice.

"I don't know," Chaver said to her, also in a frightened voice.

"Should we go do something?" Dahlia asked. Chaver hesitated before answering. He wanted to go. He wanted to see what was happening and help. But he couldn't.

"No. Let's hurry back to the inn and find our families. It'll be safe there. Ronin and the guards will be able to take care of whatever is going on."

"Okay."

More screams rang out as they ran through the streets to the inn. They weren't sure why people were screaming, but it was clear that something terrible had just begun.

Ronin sprinted through the streets along with Garret to the source of the screams. It was coming from the north side of the town.

"We have to hurry, Garret!" Ronin shouted, as they ran with their swords in hand. Garret grunted in return.

The two reached the northern side of town, and they stopped dead in their tracks when they saw the beasts. Volites. Dozens of hideous and terrible volites. Several mangled bodies already lay strewn about the street, and many of the buildings had been broken into and ripped apart. Ronin cursed under his breath. He could tell just from looking at them that these were beasts he and his companions weren't capable of beating. Grace and Rose arrived at the scene just after Ronin and Garret. They all shared the same reaction. They were all afraid.

"Run," Ronin muttered.

"What?" Rose asked.

"I said run. Now! Go! Hurry and gather the people! We have to evacuate the town! Go, go now!"

"But what about you—"

"I said go! We don't have time for questions! Hurry up and go!"

Grace and Rose both turned and ran back into town. They had tears streaming down their faces. They understood all too well what the current situation was. They would have liked to have stayed and fought, but they also knew that even if they did stay and fight, the outcome wouldn't change. And someone had to evacuate the civilians. As for Ronin and Garret... those two were undoubtably going to die.

The volites lost interest in the bodies of their first victims and began to advance once again. Landerson, Mason, and Hert arrived to back up Ronin and Garret. They all took defensive stances as the volites curiously strolled toward them. Thankfully, the beasts seemed to be interested in all the lights and decorations; it was slowing them down. Then their attention turned toward the five guards who stood before them.

"Pray to Inuuk. Pray for his mercy, for today, we die," Ronin told his companions. And then he roared as he charged toward the volites.

The others followed his lead. Ronin cut down the first volite and swung at the next. It evaded his attack and leapt at him. He tried to jump out of the way, but it caught his leg with its claws and tore it open. He began to bleed profusely; he clambered back to his feet, and pain shot through his leg, but he ignored it. He thrust his sword into a volite's skull and it fell down dead. But as soon as that one was killed, another was upon him. It tackled him to the ground, making him drop his sword. He squirmed beneath, trying to break out. It pressed against his chest. He could feel his bones snapping beneath its weight, and he was left gasping for air. But he wasn't done. He wouldn't let it end like this. He pulled out a knife and stabbed the volite in the eye. It reared back in pain, then slammed one of its thick paws into Ronin's head, crushing his skull. Garret managed to cut down three, and the others each managed to kill one as well. But they noticed something strange. It continually became harder and harder to cut into the volites. They were evolving, and their skin was hardening. Finally, Garret raised his sword and slammed it down onto one of the volite's heads. The sword cut a few centimeters into its skin and stopped. The volite shook its head, making Garret's sword fly out of his hands. Garret punched it with all the strength he could muster. It staggered the beast, but then it returned with an attack of its own. With a swipe of its claws, Garret was ripped in half, and his entrails spilled out onto the ground. At the same time, Landerson, Mason, and Hert were fighting losing battles as well. Landerson was crushed and trampled, while Mason and Hert were eaten alive. Landerson could hear them screaming for help from where he lay, but he couldn't do anything as his own life was quickly fading away.

Chaver and Dahlia rushed into the inn, where a large group of people had already gathered; Asher was there as well.

"What's going on?" somebody asked.

"Why are they screaming?" another person added.

Everyone was talking at once. Chaver found his family; his mother was trying to soothe the younger kids who were crying.

"What's going on out there?" Eshel asked.

"I don't know. Me and Dahlia came here straightaway when we heard the screams," Chaver told him.

There were still more screams ringing throughout the streets, and the screams were growing closer.

"What are the guards doing?" Asher asked.

"I don't know, but they'll handle it, whatever is going on," Chaver told him, though he wasn't so sure himself.

He liked Ronin and the other mercenaries. They were kind people, and they were strong too, stronger than the previous guards; so surely everything would be alright, right? Chaver gripped Dahlia's hand tighter. The crowd of people that had gathered at the inn continued to talk loudly. Slowly, some of the people worked up the courage to go outside and see what was going on, while others chose to stay where they felt safe.

"I'm gonna go out there," Eshel said as he got up.

"Wait." Chaver stopped his dad and hugged him. "I love you, Dad."

"I love you too, Chaver." As Eshel turned away and walked toward the entrance, the doors burst open, and someone frantically ran inside screaming. "Run! Monsters! There are monsters! We all need to run!" The man then immediately turned around and ran back outside. Now everyone in the inn was in a panic.

There were those who wanted to run and others who thought it would be safer in the inn. In the end, it didn't matter what decision they made because the volites arrived. They burst through the door and windows and crashed into the inn's common room. Chaver, his family, his friends, and most of everyone else pressed back into the corner to try to get away. A few of the men stepped forward and attempted to fight. They used mana to make roots burst up from the ground and attack the volites, but the attacks had no effect. The men gave up the attack and backed away. The volites slowly crept across the room toward the frightened people. It was as if they were savoring this moment. Chaver, Dahlia, and Asher all embraced each other tightly.

"I love you, guys. I love you guys so much," Chaver said with his eyes shut tight. Tears were dripping down his cheeks. Tears were dripping down everyone's cheeks. Many of the people had begun offering up prayers to the Celestials. Chaver himself offered up a silent prayer to Inuuk. The volites drew closer and closer. Chaver could smell the stench of blood coming from them. And then they attacked. The volites leapt into the crowd and began to tear and rip everyone apart. A massacre.

"Mommy, I'm scared," Maybel cried.

"I know, I know, it's okay, it'll be okay." Lily soothed her. "Everything will be okay, Daddy will be right back and he'll protect us."

Adon had run into the town after hearing the screams tear through the night. Their farm was on the outskirts of the eastern side of town. They were far away from where the incident began, yet they could still hear the screams clear as day. Lily, Maybel, Adin, and Laor all cowered in the corner of their cellar. More and more screams sounded.

"Where's Daddy?" Maybel cried again.

"Daddy will be back soon," Lily assured her. But it was hard to calm your child when you yourself were crying.

"I want Daddy. I want big brother," Maybel wailed.

Should they get up and run, or should they stay? Lily didn't know. She didn't know what to do. She was just hoping, praying that her husband was safe and would come back soon. Once Adon was back, then he would know what to do and everything would be alright.

Maybel continued to quietly sob. "I want Daddy. I want big brother. I want Adonai."

"It's okay," Lily said again, "Daddy will be right back and so will big brother. Adonai's always there when we need help, isn't he? Don't worry, they'll both be here," she said that, but she knew Adonai wasn't going to come, and as for her husband... Lily offered up a prayer to Inuuk and her sons did the same. They all offered up prayers to Inuuk, begging for safety. How long had they been in this cellar? It had felt like an eternity. Suddenly, there was a crash above. A crash followed by thumping and stomping. Lily covered Maybel's mouth as she was about to cry out again and tried to soothe her. The thumping and banging above continued. Stomp. Stomp. Bang. There were multiple volites rummaging through their house above. Then there was a bang against the cellar door. They all held their breath. It banged again. Bang! And then again. Bang! There was a pause. Whatever it was, it was still standing at the cellar entrance. Then there was one last bang. A volite crashed through the doors and fell down the stairs into the cellar. It picked itself up and shook off the debris. It was a hideous one, even for volites. Its body was covered in rough scales and a mane of fur wrapped around its neck. It walked on two legs like a person and had four arms. Eyeballs covered it from head to toe. It opened its mouth and began to croak. And then the croaks began to shift into something else. It began to mimic the cries of Maybel. "I want Daddy! I want Daddy!" it screamed. "I want big brother! I want Adonai! Mommy, I'm scared!"

Maybel closed her eyes, covered her ears, and cried, "Make it stop, make it stop! Adonai! Adonai, save us!"

Then the volite chuckled. It laughed at them and then mimicked Lily's soft voice as it took half a step closer. "Don't worry, everything's going to be okay. Everything's going to be okay."

Lily pushed Maybel off her lap to the side and got up in front of the volite. She wasn't strong but she still possessed some power. She threw a hand up and roots burst up from the ground and began to wrap around the volite. The volite broke through them as if they weren't even there. Despair set in as Lily stood face to face with death. Maybel was sobbing. Adin was sobbing. Laor was sobbing. Lily stretched her arms out as if to create a barrier with her body and she closed her eyes as she braced for the inevitable. The volite grabbed her by the arms and then ripped them off. Lily began to scream as blood sprayed out from her shoulders, but her scream was cut short as the volite chomped down on her head and then ripped it off. More blood sprayed from her neck and splattered across the kids. The volite began mimicking Lily again as it slowly approached the crying children. "Don't worry, everything will be okay." And then it pounced.

Rose reached the southern end of Never Thaw with as many people as she could get to come with her. Back in the town, a lantern had been knocked over and it set fire to the buildings. Rose and the crowd watched the flames dance back and forth in the night sky. Their home... was no more.

"Keep running!" Rose shouted as the survivors quickly traveled down the road.

"Wait, my husband's still back there!" a woman cried out as she began to run back toward the town.

Rose stopped her and took her by the shoulders. "It's too late.

You have to run!"

"But—"

"Run!"

The woman reluctantly turned and ran with tears streaming down her face. That woman wasn't alone; everyone who had escaped had family that had been left behind. Rose continued to shout. "Keep running! All we can do now is save ourselves!"

Save themselves. Save themselves... What a pathetic thought. No... That wouldn't be happening. Nobody would be saved tonight; after all, He was ensuring that. Rose stayed and ushered as many people south as possible.

"Where do we go?" a man asked as he walked past.

"Plain City," Rose told him. "We have to go to Plain City. Hurry, make sure everyone knows that. We don't stop until we've reached the safety of that city."

Suddenly, there was a commotion at the front of the crowd. The people couldn't go any further. There was an invisible barrier. They tried to press through with all their might, but it was no use.

"We're trapped!" someone screamed.

People were panicking even more now. And then, as if things couldn't get any worse, the volites showed up. Rose cursed and began to run south into the crowd. "Run! Keep running!" she cried.

But the crowd wasn't moving. Everyone was bunching up in one place. "We can't! There's something stopping us!" someone cried out.

Rose cursed again and looked behind her. The volites were rapidly approaching. Screw it. She drew her sword and charged toward the monsters. She managed to take down the first one. But she was immediately overrun by the others. The people were still trying to get past the invisible barrier, but it availed nothing. Screams rang out as the volites slaughtered the remaining townsfolk. That night... nobody escaped. Nobody was saved. Nobody was spared. That was the end of Never Thaw.

Chapter 50

Adonai and Ciela soared through the air. The sky was clear and beautiful. Glacier Valley sprawled out before them, and the massive Dire Mountains towered above the forest floor. They were almost back to Never Thaw. Adonai looked forward to returning home. He always did. Never Thaw was perfect, he loved it there. He loved his family, his friends, and his neighbors; he loved it all. But for some reason, he had this uneasy feeling. A feeling that just wouldn't go away. He was anxious to return home.

When they finally reached the town, Adonai's heart sank. An inexplicable feeling of dread filled his entire being. It was destroyed. There wasn't a single building that hadn't been torn apart or burned down. And the most worrisome part were the beasts that crawled throughout the streets. Volites.

"Ciela, get us home... now." She sped up and dipped toward his family's farm. Why were there volites here? How? It didn't make any sense. Adonai jumped off Ciela's back before they even reached the ground and took off running. There was a gaping hole in the front of the house. He ran through it and frantically looked around, calling out for his family.

"Mom, Dad! Maybel! Adin! Laor!" he called for them all but received no response. The house was empty.

He ran back outside. Some of the volites had taken notice of him and were beginning to move closer. He ignored them. He ran to the cellar—the door was busted. When he reached the entrance, the stench of death hit his nostrils. Adonai muttered curses under his breath as he quickly descended the steps, afraid of what he might find. What he found at the bottom was a hideous volite gnawing on the bones of his family. Blood and entrails covered the walls. Adonai felt sick. He felt dizzy. It felt as if the world was coming to an end. But even more so than the pain, the fear, and the despair, what Adonai felt most of all... rage. Pure rage. His white aura began to emanate from his body.

The volite that had been gnawing on the bones stood up and looked down on Adonai. And then it called out to him in Maybel's voice. "Mommy... I'm scared. I want Adonai."

Hatred. Utter hatred spread through every fiber of Adonai's entire being. And then the silence came. The silence washed over everything, and a heavy presence accompanied it. The volite that had been mocking him froze. Its grin faded. Adonai walked past it as if it weren't even there. He walked past it to the corner of the room where most of the remains lay. He crouched down and gently set his hand on the bloody remains.

"May you rest in peace," he prayed. During this time, the volite had been frozen in fear. But as Adonai prayed, it mustered up its courage and turned around to face him. There was only one thing running through the volite's mind at this time. It needed to kill this boy. It needed to kill him now or else it would die. But then another wave of pressure washed over the volite, a wave far heavier than the first, and it once again froze. Adonai finished his prayer. He stood up and slowly turned around to face the monster. And he glared. He glared at the beast with all his hatred. The volite fell to its knees. Blood began to trickle from its nostrils and eyes, and its body began to shake. Adonai walked until he stood right before it, where he stopped and looked down on it.

And as he looked it in the eye, he muttered a single word that carried a world of hatred, "Perish."

The volite's eyes rolled to the back of its head, and its body began to convulse violently before it burst into white flames. The volite began to scream, but the scream was cut short as its body exploded. Nothing remained of the monster. It had been wiped away into oblivion. For a moment, Adonai just stood there staring. It felt as if a void had opened up in his heart. But this wasn't the time for mourning. He needed to check on the rest of the town. Yeah. The rest of the town. Surely there was still someone alive. He ran up the steps of the cellar and back outside. There were many volites approaching him, but he ignored them and flew into town.

"Someone. Someone still has to be alive," he muttered to himself over and over again. Everything smelled of death. "Someone." The streets were filled with blood and carnage.

"Just one person." More and more volites were taking notice of him as he flew around. "Be alive." He went to the inn, the blacksmith, the lab, and the Guild headquarters. There was nothing but death. The last place he went to was the temple in the center of town. There had to be someone. Just one. Just one person had to have survived. But there was no one.

Adonai let himself fall to his knees. There was no hope. There was no one alive. They were all dead. So many feelings welled up inside of him. Feelings more intense than he had ever felt before. He tried taking deep breaths. He tried to stay calm. But he couldn't. The pain, the despair, the rage, it all overwhelmed him. His aura grew brighter and brighter. Adonai looked up to the sky and screamed a scream of anguish. And with the scream, he unleashed all his mana. An explosion of pure mana burst out from his body in every direction. Everything in the immediate vicinity was completely destroyed. The temple and nearby volites were blown away, and all that was left was a large crater in the ground. Adonai floated up into the air, consumed by his rage. And once again came the silence. The silence fell over the entire valley. A complete and utter silence where nothing could be heard. For a moment, nothing moved, no animals stirred, no breeze passed by, no time wore on. Then the sky darkened and the silence faded as the sound of thunder resounded throughout the entire valley. A tremendous storm formed around Adonai. The wind swirled like a raging tornado, and lightning rained down from the sky. Time, space, and gravity were all distorted. Adonai's bonds called out to him. They tried to get him to regain control over himself. But he could not hear them. Ciela could do nothing but watch from afar. The ground ruptured and split open, and lava bubbled up to the surface. Many of the volites were quickly swept away and killed by the storm. But as the storm raged on, there were also many volites that survived. And those volites began to evolve. They grew stronger and stronger. Finally, Adonai had far exceeded his limits. The storm ceased, and he fell from the sky and crashed into the ground. He was completely unconscious. With the storm receded, the volites were quick to take action, and they came running toward him. But Ciela was faster. She swooped down and scooped Adonai up with her talons, then quickly flew away, leaving the volites behind. She didn't know what to do, so she took him to the closest safe place she could think of and headed south to Plain City.

Chapter 51

Lily cowered in the corner of the cellar with Maybel in her arms. Adin and Laor were right next to her. They were all crying the same thing.

"Adonai! Adonai, save us! Please save us, Adonai!" Volites burst into the cellar. His family cried even louder. "Save us, Adonai!" Then the volites pounced.

Adonai's eyes shot open. He woke up in an unfamiliar bed in an unfamiliar room. His entire body ached, and his mind felt fuzzy.

"You're awake!" a nurse exclaimed when she saw him open his eyes. She had been sitting nearby, watching over him.

"What—what's going on?" Adonai asked her.

"We were wondering the same thing. Stay here. I'll be right back." The nurse hurried out of the room and closed the door behind her.

Adonai stared up at the ceiling; it strained his mind to try to think, but he tried anyway. And then it all returned to him. He quickly sat up in bed despite the pain and started muttering curses. The volites. Never Thaw. There were volites in Never Thaw. He needed to warn everyone. He ignored the pain pulsating throughout his body and stood up, which made him feel dizzy. Then the door opened again. Jane and Harry rushed into the room with the nurse who had been there earlier. They looked worried.

"Thank goodness, you're awake!" Jane exclaimed. Adonai tried to speak, but they talked over him.

"Sit down, sit down. You need to sit down," she said, gently guiding him back to the bed.

"No—no, you don't . . . you don't understand; we have to—" Adonai struggled to get the words out.

"Slow down. Just sit," Jane said in a soothing voice as he sat back down on the bed.

Adonai kept trying to tell them about the volites, but he was struggling to express himself.

"Take it easy, just take it easy."

Adonai took a deep breath and calmed down a little bit. "How did I get here?" he asked.

Jane began to explain, "Your Dire hawk arrived in the middle of the night with you in her talons. She screeched incredibly loud over and over again as soon as she arrived, garnering as much attention as possible. The guards rushed to you and found you on the verge of death. After that, you were immediately taken here to this monastery to receive healing. I and Harry rushed here when we learned it was you who had suddenly shown up. We were wondering—"

Adonai interrupted her. "Monsters. There are monsters in Never Thaw."

"Huh?"

"Monsters have attacked Never Thaw," he repeated.

"I see . . . it'll be okay," Jane told him. "After seeing you arrive in that condition, we reached out to John and James through a mana note. When they didn't respond, we sent a mercenary group north to check on the town—"

"It's too late. Everyone is already dead. Everything is gone. Everything is lost," Adonai said in a quiet voice. Jane and Harry were taken aback. Adonai went on, "When did they leave, the mercenaries?"

"That was four days ago," Harry told him.

He muttered a curse. "They're dead. They're all dead. Those aren't monsters ordinary men can handle."

"You can't be sure of that. Surely it's possible that they live—"

"No. I know what those monsters are like. We have to contact the Imperial Army. Only the Imperial soldiers can resolve this."

Jane and Harry exchanged a look; their faces were paling as they began to realize the severity of the situation. "Okay. We'll contact the Imperial Army," Jane said.

Adonai nodded. "Good," he said softly. He was tired. His body hurt.

"You need to lie back down. Your body hasn't fully recovered," the nurse told him. He didn't want to, but he couldn't help it. He lay back down and quickly slipped back to sleep.

Further north, the mercenary company recruited by Jane and Harry was nearly at Never Thaw. Captain Lee rode his horse, leading the way, and his vice-captain, Paul, rode right beside him. It was colder than they liked, and there was a layer of snow on the ground despite it not quite being winter yet. Lee wondered how anyone could want to live in such a cold place.

"What do you think we'll find?" Paul asked as they rode.

Lee shrugged. "Probably not much. All we're doing is checking on a small town after they failed to respond to a mana note. Chances are we'll show up, everything will be fine, and then we'll just end up turning around and marching right back to Plain City."

"It's such a lousy mission," Paul complained.

"It is boring, but it's easy money," Lee told him.

Paul groaned. "I suppose you're right, but it still sucks."

Finally, they arrived at the small town of Never Thaw, or at least what should have been the small town of Never Thaw. As they arrived, a feeling of dread began to stir within them.

Paul muttered a curse. "What happened here . . ."

Lee was too astonished to say anything. Everything was completely destroyed. It looked like an extraordinary natural disaster had swept through here. They slowly rode into the mess on what was once a road. The stench of death filled the air, almost to the point where it was unbearable. Everything was trashed. Where buildings had once stood, there now lay piles of rubble, and the ground was uneven and cracked as if there had been an earthquake. The streets were soaked in blood. Decomposing corpses of both humans and monsters alike littered the town.

"Everyone, watch yourselves!" Lee shouted out to his company. There was a massive crater in the center of the town.

"It doesn't look like anything is alive here," Paul commented. "What do you think happened?"

"Haven't got a clue. The only possibility I can think of is that there was a natural disaster, but . . . it must have been one heck of a natural disaster to cause this much damage," Lee said as he hopped down from his horse and went over to examine one of the monster corpses.

It was unlike anything he had ever seen or even heard of. And the fact that it was here puzzled him even further. The monsters here would explain why the town was destroyed, but even the monsters were dead.

"What are you thinking?" Paul asked as he walked over to Lee's side. Lee shook his head. "I'm not sure. I just can't make sense of all of this."

"I was thinking the same thing," Paul responded.

A nervous atmosphere had descended upon the mercenary company. The men were beginning to grow uneasy. Paul was about to ask Lee another question when a scream tore through the air. It was the scream of a little girl crying for help. Lee quickly shot up to his feet.

"It's a survivor!" he shouted as he swung back onto his horse. "Paul, Reeman, York, and Keith, come with me!"

He spurred his horse and took off in the direction of the voice; his men quickly followed behind. The scream was coming from the north side of the town. They rode swiftly as the little girl continued to scream out.

"Help! Help! Please, somebody help me!"

"It's coming from the woods!" Lee shouted as they reached the edge of town. They rode into the forest without hesitation. And then the screaming stopped.

"She's somewhere close! Keep your eyes peeled!" Lee shouted. They went a little deeper into the woods and kept looking. Then they heard the little girl giggling. Lee didn't know why, but an indescribable fear began to well up inside of him. The giggling continued; it was coming from up in the trees. Then more girls began giggling. Lee and his men were completely surrounded. Then the giggling abruptly stopped, and for a moment, there was silence. Then a beast dropped down from above and landed before them. Its body changed from a green color to a red color. It had been blending in. It looked humanoid, but it was covered in scales, and horns protruded from its head. Then more volites dropped down from the trees around them. They were all hideous and possessed a humanoid form, but they were most definitely not human. The horses were spooked, but the mercenaries managed to keep control over them. Lee drew his sword, as did the others. The first volite cocked its head as it stared at them with its beady eyes. Then it opened its mouth and screamed a terrible scream and charged. Lee raised his sword and brought it down upon the approaching beast, but it caught the blade and ripped it out of Lee's grasp. Then the volite smacked the horse, breaking its jaw, and it reached over and pulled Lee off the horse and threw him. The volite killed the horse, then turned its attention back to Lee. Lee cursed and leapt for his sword, which was lying in the snow a short distance away. He got the blade. The volite lunged for him as he swung around blindly and slashed it. He cut it across the abdomen, and it staggered backward. This was it. There was hope. But then the volite smiled. Lee's heart sank as the wound he had just inflicted quickly healed right before his eyes. Then the volite charged again; it got a hold of Lee and began to rip him apart as he screamed in agony. Paul, Reeman, York, and Keith didn't fare any better. In just a short moment, they were all brutally killed.

Back where the rest of the company was, they remained near the crater in the center of the town, waiting for their leader and comrades to return.

"It's taking them a while," Fickle said to Riley.

She just shrugged. "You're worrying too much. It's a little kid; she's probably hiding out of fear and won't come out, so they have to search for her."

"Yeah, you're probably right," Fickle agreed, but as he sat atop his horse, he thought he saw something move out of the corner of his eye.

"Hey, did you see that?"

"See what?" Riley asked.

"Something moved over there," Fickle said, pointing to one of the nearby destroyed buildings.

Riley looked for a moment, and when she didn't see anything, she said, "Your eyes are playing tricks on you, you're just nervous."

". . . Yeah . . . you're probably right . . ."

As they continued to wait, they heard a shriek come from one of the buildings. Then there was another shriek and then another. And then there was shrieking coming from all over the town.

Fickle cursed and shouted, "Defensive positions!" The mercenaries all drew their swords and backed up into a tight circle. The horses were becoming uneasy. And then the volites began to emerge. They had been hiding in the rubble and buildings. They came out in all sorts of shapes and sizes. Each of them different from the rest, yet just as equally ugly. The volites began to charge. They were fast and wild. The mercenaries didn't last long. Their attacks did nothing to the monsters, and so they were quickly overrun. Men cried out as they witnessed their friends being torn apart right next to them, only to be silenced a second later by another volite. In only a matter of minutes, the entire company was wiped out.

Chapter 52

Adonai lay in bed. A heavy depression gnawed away at him. A tray of untouched food sat on a table beside the bed. Even though his stomach grumbled, he didn't feel like eating. He couldn't bring himself to get up or do anything; all he could do was wallow in his sorrow. Why?

Why were there volites in Never Thaw? He just couldn't get it. The only answer he could come up with was that they must have followed him out. But if they were following him, he should have been able to sense them, and he never sensed any, so there was no way they followed him. Maybe he just let his guard down. He definitely didn't do anything wrong, but the more he thought about it, the more his memories became distorted, and he gradually came to believe that he really did do something wrong. And because of him, his family . . . He choked back tears. His family and home and friends and everything, it was all gone. And it was all his fault. It was all because of his own selfish desire to explore the Northern Mist. If he had never stepped foot in the Mist, then none of this would have ever happened. But he did step foot in the Mist. He did cause all of this. It wasn't the volites that killed everyone he loved; it was him. He was the reason they were dead. He was the one who killed them. And he wasn't even there in their time of need. Perhaps he could have saved them if he had stayed in the town, or even just left behind one of his bonds. But he didn't stay, and he didn't summon one of his bonds. Instead, he was far away. And because he was far away, everyone died; so again, it was all his fault. Adonai wiped at his eyes and nose and muttered a curse under his breath. Maybe . . . maybe he should just die. Wouldn't that be better? What was the point of living anyway? He no longer had any reason to stay. He had no path laid out before him. There was nowhere he wanted to go and there was nothing he wanted to do.

As he wallowed in his own self-pity, a little girl appeared at the doorway. She was maybe eight years old. When Adonai noticed her and looked over at her, she hid herself behind the wall and then poked her head out to peek at him. For a moment, the two just stared at each other. Adonai didn't really feel like talking. He just wanted to be alone. He just wanted to disappear. But for some reason, this little girl wouldn't leave. Finally, he just decided to ignore her and turned over on his side and stared at the wall. After he looked away, he could sense her slowly creeping into his room. After she was about a meter into the room, he turned back around. She took a step back when she saw him looking at her again, but she didn't leave. She was eyeing the tray of food beside his bed. Among the food, there was an apple tart. Adonai looked to the apple tart and then back to the girl. He sat up, and when he did, she took another step back.

He looked back to the tray of food. "You can have it if you want it."

She was hesitant, but after a moment, she slowly crept closer and closer until she was within arm's reach of the food, where she paused.

"Go on," Adonai told her.

She reached out and grabbed the tart and then quickly pulled it close to her body, as if somebody were going to take it. He thought that would be that and she would leave after taking the tart, but instead, she stood there motionless.

"You look sad," she said at last. Adonai was taken aback. He didn't know how to react, nor what to say, but he felt some tears welling up. He fought them back. When he didn't say anything, the little girl looked down at the tart, then back up to him, and then she hesitantly held the tart out for him while she trained her eyes on the ground.

"Here. This will make you feel better."

Adonai couldn't help but crack just a slight smile. "That's okay, you eat it," he told her.

She brought it back to herself, but she was still hesitant. He forced himself to smile and then said again, "It's okay, it's yours." He could see a hint of joy in her eyes when she heard that and began to shyly nibble on the tart.

"My name's Adonai. What's your name?"

"My name is Mary," she said and then walked over and happily plopped down on the bed next to Adonai. What a strange little girl. She sort of reminded him of Maybel. It hurt, but at the same time, it brought a sense of comfort.

"Why are you sad?" Mary asked.

Adonai hesitated before answering. "I . . . I lost my family."

"Oh . . . that is sad." She took another bite of the apple tart. "I lost my family too," she told him. "My Mommy and Daddy got sick, but I don't remember what happened to them after that. Now I live here with the bald guys." The bald guys being the monks who ran the monastery they were staying in. "Are you gonna live here too?" Mary asked.

Adonai didn't answer; he didn't know what to say.

"I think you should live here," she told him. "That way, you can be my big brother."

Adonai couldn't help but crack another smile and chuckle softly. "Big brother . . . Yeah, I guess I could live here."

"Yay!" she beamed. She quickly finished the last of the tart and began to tug at Adonai's arm. "Come with me, come with me. I'll show you around."

He smiled and got up to follow her. She guided him throughout the monastery, telling him what each area was.

"This is where the bald guys sleep, this is where the bald guys eat, this is where the bald guys pray." Lastly, she took him outside to the garden. "And this is where the bald guys grow plants. This is my favorite place." She was very proud of herself for showing Adonai around. She brought him over to an apple tree and sat down in the shade. "This is my favorite spot," she told him.

Adonai smiled. "Yes, this is a very nice place." They sat together and watched the clouds up in the sky.

"Do you think you'll ever see your family again?" Mary asked.

Adonai waited a moment before he answered. "Yeah. I'll see them again. Their spirits have returned to the Celestials in the center of Celestia. Your parents are there too."

"Really?"

"Yeah, and one day, we'll get to see them again when we reunite with the Celestials."

Mary smiled real big. "You're a good big brother." They spent the rest of that afternoon sitting in the shade of the apple tree.

Chapter 53

Silas was in his office, looking out the window over the open fields and manors of the inner section of the Imperium. The sky was cloudy, a lousy day. He was one of the six Pillars in the Imperium. In the distance was the wall that separated the wonderful inner section from the disgusting middle section. He looked on with disdain. Many of the residents of the inner section were Telestials, as it should be. But there were also many mortals in the inner section as well. He hated that. He hated mortals, those lousy inferior beings who think they deserve to live with Telestials as equals; it was disgusting. Silas himself was a pure Telestial; there weren't many like him. Someone knocked on the office door.

"Come in," Silas called.

Philip opened the door and walked in; he was one of the captains who served under Silas. "Sir, we've received an urgent request."

"An urgent request? What is it?"

"Here." Philip handed Silas a slip of paper, and Silas read it.

"So a little village in the northwest was attacked by monsters from the Northern Mist, and they request the help of the Imperial Army. Interesting, this is that little village that has been selling merchandise from the Northern Mist, isn't it? Bunch of pathetic mortals overstepping their bounds; serves them right."

"Indeed," Philip agreed.

Silas read over the note again. "Why should we send aid?" he asked.

"Well, there is the issue of the monsters traveling to other cities and regions. It poses a serious problem," Philip told him.

Silas sighed, "I know that. But who cares if a few more mortals get killed off? If anything, that's a good thing."

"I agree, but it's not a matter we can dismiss. If we neglect this call for help, we will get in trouble with the Keystone."

Silas sighed again. Stupid mortals... But then a smile slowly spread across his face. He had an idea. An idea to get rid of a thorn that had been in his side for far too long. "Philip, send an order to Dire City. The Pillar William Hart is to lead an extermination team that will eliminate these monsters in the north."

Philip was puzzled. "Why would we send William Hart, sir?"

Silas was still grinning. "How can you not see it? This is the perfect opportunity to get rid of that wretched man. We'll order him to go north and kill off the monsters in Never Thaw. And when those monsters are eliminated," Silas's smile grew even bigger, "we'll order him to continue the expedition into the Northern Mist to find the source of these monsters and eliminate them for good."

Now Philip was smiling as well. "I see, we send him on a suicide mission."

"Yes, a suicide mission. It will be wonderful. And to make sure he's taken care of, I need you and a few of your lieutenants to accompany the extermination team. Just in case William survives the Northern Mist, you'll be there to make sure he doesn't."

"A wonderful plan, sir. When do I depart?"

"Immediately. Gather whichever men you want with you, it doesn't matter to me, and head to Plain City. That's where we'll gather the team. The sooner William dies, the better," Silas told him.

"Understood." Philip dismissed himself and closed the door behind him as he left.

Silas walked back over to the window and smiled to himself. Suddenly, this lousy day seemed a little brighter. The day he had been waiting for his whole life was fast approaching. Soon, their leader will finally return, and when that happens, they can finally create the world they've always deserved. What a wonderful thought.

William was in his office when he received the message. He was ordered to go north to eliminate a group of dangerous monsters. But that part wasn't what concerned him. What concerned him was that he was also instructed to lead the extermination team into the Northern Mist to completely remove the threat. That just didn't sit right with him. There was no reason to take the expedition into the Northern

Mist. It was both far too dangerous and unnecessary. For some reason, William couldn't help but suspect that the black cloaks were involved in this order. Ever since the raid on the Imperial Saints' church, he had been laying low. Even though the Imperial Army was now on the lookout for the black cloaks, William still didn't feel safe venturing outside of his mansion. He had been doing everything he could to try to dig up who these black cloaks might be, but he could find nothing. And that scared him.

"Go fetch Hebron and Dathan," William told the soldier who had brought him the message.

"Understood." The soldier left, and a short while later, Hebron and Dathan arrived.

Hebron and Dathan were William's last two remaining captains. They both knew nothing of the black cloaks. After being betrayed by Benjamin, William lost his trust in his other captains. The only one he felt he could trust was Henry, but Henry was gone.

"We've received orders to go north to exterminate a threat," William told the two captains. "I've chosen to bring the both of you. Go gather your lieutenants and meet me in the courtyard; we are to depart immediately."

The two captains left, and William was once again alone in his office. He sighed deeply. There was something else going on with this mission, he could feel it. He just didn't know what that was. A short while later, he met with his team down in the courtyard. The full team consisted of William, Hebron, Dathan, Raphael, Samson, Shaphan, Kohath, and Philemon. They were all suited up in their armor and green cloaks of the Direland military. With all of them ready to leave, they set out, and William led the group north.

"Adonaiiiiii," Mary sang. "Helloooooooo, I'mmmmm talkingggg toooo youuuuuuu." Adonai cracked his eyes open and smiled. "What are you doing?" Mary asked.

"I was meditating," he told her.

"Meditating? What's that?"

"It's a way to grow more in tune with the mana of the world."

"Wooow," Mary said enthusiastically.

"You don't understand, do you?"

"Nope. Not one bit." Mary said it so proudly that it made Adonai laugh.

Over the past few weeks, his depression continued to gnaw away at him. Every night, he had nightmares of his family being slaughtered by volites. The only thing that got him out of bed was Mary's constant pestering. They spent every day together and had become the best of friends. They would sit for hours under the apple tree, and Adonai would tell her all kinds of stories. Sometimes, they went flying on Ciela's back around the city; Mary loved that. They would also sneak food out of the kitchen. Adonai didn't really care for the food, but it made Mary really excited to sneak around and steal delicious treats. He even introduced her to his bonds. Not just the few he had admitted to having, but all of them. She was the only one to know that he possessed fourteen different bonds.

Adonai patted the ground next to him. "Come here, I'll show you how to meditate."

"Okay," she said happily and sat down next to him.

"Alright, now close your eyes. And no peeking," he told her, and she giggled. "There are two parts to every living being," Adonai began to explain. "Every being has a body and a spirit. Your spirit dwells deep within your body. Start by reaching down deep within, find your spirit. Take deep breaths, in and out, slowly."

She listened surprisingly well and did her best to do as Adonai instructed. "Am I doing it right?" she whispered.

"Yes, now no talking, ya punk." She giggled and then quieted down. He watched over her as she did her best to meditate. She was still really young and didn't really grasp the concept, so Adonai decided to help out a bit. He set his hand against her back and poured some of his mana into her to make her feel like she was accomplishing something.

"We should teach her how to use fire," Arson suggested. He was ignored.

While Mary attempted to meditate and Adonai watched over her, a monk walked out into the garden, accompanied by a man in a green cloak with a Pillar's insignia. "Is this the boy?" William asked.

"Yes, this is him," the monk replied.

"What's going on?" Adonai asked.

"My name is William Hart. I'm one of the four Pillars of Direland, and I'm here to lead the team that will exterminate the monsters in the north. I understand that you're both the one who has been exploring the Northern Mist as well as the sole survivor from Never Thaw."

Adonai stood up and stepped away from Mary. "Yes, that's me, my name is Adonai Alaric."

Mary broke her concentration and looked up at them. "What's going on?" she asked.

Adonai turned around and crouched down to talk to her soothingly. "Don't worry, I just have to talk with this man for a bit." Then he turned to face William again.

"Adonai, the reason I've come is because I want to recruit you into the extermination team."

"Me? Why do you need me?"

"We have need of your experience with the monsters as well as the Northern Mist. I was hoping you could serve as our guide. We'll make sure to protect you."

"You want me as a guide? I . . . wait . . . Did you say you need help with the Northern Mist? Why would you need my help with the Northern Mist? The monsters aren't in the Mist, they're in Never Thaw."

William shifted. "Well, that's the thing. I've been ordered to lead the team into the Northern Mist after removing the monsters from the town. We are to uproot this monster problem for good."

Adonai frowned. "That is a terrible, terrible idea. There is no reason for any of us to go into the Northern Mist. Absolutely not."

"It's an order from the Imperium. I have no choice. Even if you don't guide us, we will still have to go," William told him.

Adonai muttered a curse. He was a bit frustrated, but he understood; besides, he really did want to go. He wanted to avenge the deaths of his loved ones. He wanted to go and squash the volites beneath his feet. "Alright then, I'll serve as your guide. But I'm going to need your full cooperation as well as everyone else's. If any of you ignore me, then it's not my problem when you end up dead."

"I understand."

"Then I guess I'll go with you."

William smiled. "Very good. Come with me."

Adonai began to leave with William, but Mary tugged at his sleeve. "Is big brother going to leave?" She wore a worried expression.

Adonai stopped and knelt down so he was at eye level with Mary. "Yeah, big brother has to leave for a bit. But don't worry, I'll come back."

"You promise?"

"I promise."

They interlocked pinkies, and then Adonai left with William. They went to the northern side of the city and met up with the rest of the extermination team.

The team was gathered at a tavern. The team was made up of two groups with the addition of Adonai. There was William's group, which consisted of the two captains and five lieutenants, and then there was Philip's group, which also consisted of eight. The members of Philip's group were Edna, Luke, Triton, Rachel, Naiad, Huck, and Nivi. Everyone in Philip's group were Telestials, whereas the members of William's group were ordinary mortals. Adonai could tell that there was a bit of tension between the two groups as soon as he arrived. The mortals resented the Telestials, and the Telestials resented the mortals. Everyone there was dressed in their respective cloaks. William's group was wearing the green cloak of Direland, and Philip's group was wearing the silver cloak of the Imperium.

"Everyone, this is Adonai," William told them as they joined the team at the tavern. "He is the one who has been exploring the Northern Mist and is also from the town where the monsters attacked. He is going to serve as our guide."

"Are you kidding me? Look at him. He's just a boy, he'll only get in the way," Philip complained.

"What do you mean he'll get in the way? If he's the one who's been exploring the Northern Mist, he's more than qualified to come along with us," Raphael snapped.

"Strong or not, he's still a child," Triton declared.

"Enough!" William barked. "He is coming with us. None of you are to discuss the matter any further."

Philip grumbled something incoherent, then returned to the conversation he had been having with his friends.

"Welcome to the team," Raphael said, throwing an arm around Adonai's shoulder. "We're glad to have ya," Hebron added.

"Oi! Bar keep!" Raphael shouted. "Get my boy here a beer—"

"That's okay," Adonai stopped him. "I don't drink."

Raphael was taken aback, as if he had just heard the most ridiculous thing in his life. "Ya don't drink?"

"No."

". . . Alright, whatever." After meeting the team, Adonai left for the night. The following morning, he arrived at the northern gate at the brink of dawn with the other extermination team members. It was time to begin the expedition.

Chapter 54

Adonai and Ciela were flying low to the ground as they led the extermination team north. William and Philip rode right behind them. They had been traveling for a while now, and the sun was setting.

"Let's stop here for the night," Adonai said to William, who then turned and repeated it, "Halt! We're stopping here for the night!"

Everyone climbed off their horses and began to set up camp. The two groups made separate fires and sat away from each other. Adonai also made his own fire and sat by himself. Memories began to flood his mind as the flames danced before him. He remembered the time when he was returning to Never Thaw after receiving his bond, when a Dire bear had attacked and he chose to run away rather than help and fight. Emilio died because of him. Even more so, he remembered the carnage he found upon returning home from fighting the pirates—finding everyone dead. And it was all his fault. If he had never gone to the Mist, then the volites would have never come after him and attacked Never Thaw. He hated it. He hated the volites, himself, the world, and he hated the Celestials for allowing such a thing to happen. Despite the heat from the fire, it was still cold. The ground was covered in snow. Adonai used to love the cold. It reminded him of home, of Never Thaw, his friends, and family. The cold still reminded him of those same things, and that was precisely why he hated the cold now. All it did was bring back unpleasant memories and remind him of his own failures. As he sat there wallowing in his pain, William, Raphael, and Philemon came over and sat down with him.

"We thought you could use some company," William said as he sat down on a log. Adonai didn't say anything. William continued talking, "How long till we arrive at the town?"

"Less than a day," Adonai told him.

"Are you nervous?" Raphael asked.

"No."

There was a moment of silence. The three soldiers could tell Adonai was in a bad place and were determined to bring him out of it.

"What was the name of this town again?" Philemon asked.

"Never Thaw," Adonai told him, his eyes never leaving the fire.

"You were the one exploring the Northern Mist, right? You must be pretty strong," Raphael commented.

"Not strong enough . . ." Adonai said in a quiet voice.

William could tell that this wasn't working, so he changed the subject.

"These monsters that we're about to fight, what are they like?"

Adonai broke out of his slump a bit and began to talk.

"They're terrible, horrible monsters. I've fought plenty of them now. They're all disgusting. They may seem weak at first, but if given the opportunity, they'll quickly evolve and become stronger."

"They evolve that fast? Like in the middle of a fight?" Raphael asked.

Adonai nodded, "They evolve almost instantly and adapt to any situation. When we fight them, we'll have to finish off each one as quickly as possible. Otherwise, we might not win."

"I see. . . . We'll have to make sure everyone is aware of that before we fight them tomorrow," William said.

"What's the Northern Mist like?" Philemon asked.

"Dangerous. I don't understand why the Imperium would order us to continue the mission into the Mist."

"Well, yeah, but that wasn't exactly what I was talking about. I mean, you're the one who had been exploring the Northern Mist, right? I wanted to hear about it. What kind of stories do you have?" Adonai's mood began to shift some more. At least, this was taking his mind off of worse things. He went on to tell them about some of the adventures he had and what the Mist was like. The three soldiers listened intently the entire time. After a while, they began to share some of their stories as well. They all talked late into the night before retiring to bed. That night, Adonai had nightmares again.

The extermination team rose early in the morning. They mounted their horses, Adonai mounted his Dire hawk, and they advanced toward Never Thaw. Adonai's heart was pounding, and it intensified the closer they got. Feelings of rage and hatred were building up within him. He was eager to fight.

"We're here," Adonai said as they arrived at the outskirts of the small town.

"I'll take the lead from here," William told him and then shouted, "Ready yourselves!"

Armor materialized around each of the soldiers as they called it out from their interspatial rings, and their swords materialized in their hands. Adonai did the same; his silvery-blue armor formed around his body and one of the spears in his hand, while the rest hovered nearby. Several of the extermination team members became distracted for a moment when they saw Adonai's armor; then they quickly refocused.

William continued shouting, "Summon your bonds! Hold nothing back!" Dozens of mana beasts materialized and an aura formed around each soldier. Adonai summoned three of his own bonds: Arson, Ore, and Aeolian. They advanced a bit more and then stopped again, but the volites still remained hidden.

"Wake them up," William told Philip.

Philip grinned, "With pleasure." He raised an arm and formed a massive fireball. Then he launched the fireball into the town, and there was a large explosion that made the ground shake.

That was enough to drive them out. The volites all began to emerge. At this point, all of the remaining volites were highly evolved and powerful. Each one was unique. There were volites with antlers and horns; some were large, some were very, very large, and others were small. They had all sorts of other characteristics, like hard exoskeletons or fur or scales or bare skin, or some sort of combination. The one thing they all had in common was the fact that they were hideous. Absolutely disgusting to look at. After the fireball Philip launched, the volites were swarming from their hiding places.

William raised his sword and pointed it at the encroaching horde and said in an even tone, "Kill them."

The extermination team charged with their summons at their sides. The two forces clashed against each other. It was a viscous battle. Fires erupted, the ground quaked, bullets of water rained down, and all sorts of elemental attacks were used. It was more chaotic than anything

Adonai had ever experienced. He chose to limit the elements he used to just the three he had chosen. He didn't want to expose all of his power in front of all these people. Arson flapped his wings and unleashed a wave of white fire. Aeolian flapped his wings and unleashed powerful and sharp gusts of wind. Ore's body was covered in metal, and he thrashed around in the center of the battlefield. Adonai was flying around on Ciela's back, raining down spears. But the battle was raging on longer than it should have. The volites were growing stronger. Slowly, one by one, the summons were killed and their bodies dissipated. But nobody backed down. They fought on, and soon, they began to push the volites back. They cut them down one after another. Finally, they closed around the last one, and it quickly succumbed to their blades. The battle was over, and the dust began to settle.

That was when they noticed the others. There were still several other volites that had remained at the edge of the rubble. These volites were strange; they didn't join the fight, and instead, they stayed back and observed the battle. And unlike the other volites that resembled beasts and monsters, these volites had humanoid forms. And there was something else about them. Something very worrisome. These remaining volites . . . they possessed auras. They had evolved to the point where they had learned how to use mana. And all of the extermination team members noticed this. Adonai launched one of the spears at one of them. It easily swatted the spear aside. For a moment, the two opposing forces watched each other, waiting for someone to make a move. Then the volites turned and ran.

"After them!" William shouted.

Adonai and Ciela took off and left everyone behind as they chased the volites through the town. He fired his spears, and they managed to hit one of the slower volites and pierce through its back. It stumbled to the ground and writhed in pain. Adonai left it there and continued on after the others. His spears soared through the air. He hit another one of the fleeing volites. Then another. Each one he hit stumbled to the ground, unable to continue running, and the rest of the extermination team, who was lagging behind, would finish them off. The volites were fleeing north. Things became more difficult when the monsters left the town and reached the tree line. Adonai lost sight of them as they sprinted into the forest. He did his best to continue following them, but they were evolving and going faster and faster. At last, Adonai lost them. He turned around, and he and Ciela flew back and reunited with the rest of the extermination team. There were eight that had managed to get away. He had followed them as far as Glacier Pass. Though he lost them, he had a good feeling about where they were headed. They were running back to the Mist.

Chapter 55

Adonai and the extermination team arrived at the crack, the entrance to the Northern Mist. They had followed the tracks of the fleeing volites, and sure enough, they had fled back to the Mist. They stopped for the day and set camp just outside the crack. That night, Adonai sat around a fire with William and his subordinates. He was feeling a bit better now, particularly because he didn't have a chance to sit and ruminate about the things he had come to lose.

"What a battle!" Samson exclaimed as he took a swig of wine. Kohath offered some wine to Adonai, who turned it down.

"You were great out there," Raphael told Adonai.

"Indeed," Philemon agreed. "I saw you out there, flying above the battlefield, raining down those spears of yours. I had expected you to be strong, knowing that you were the one who had been exploring the Northern Mist, but I was still surprised. Heck, you're probably stronger than me."

Normally, Adonai would've grinned slightly, but right now he couldn't muster it.

"Fighting aside, that armor of yours is quite incredible. It's made of pure celestite, isn't it? Mind if we have a look?" Raphael asked.

Adonai nodded. He pulled the suit of armor out of his interspatial ring and showed everyone around the fire. Hebron took hold of the helmet and whistled, "This is incredible. I've never seen anything like it. Who made it?"

Adonai hesitated before answering, "My friend made it. His name was Asher. All of the celestite equipment we made was forged by him."

"Oh . . . and he's . . . he's not with us anymore, is he?" Adonai nodded.

"He's with the Celestials now."

William patted Adonai on the shoulder. "You're right, he might not be here with us, but he's in a better place. All of them are."

They ate roasted elk that a few of the team members had hunted down when camp was being set. It had been a while since Adonai had last had a proper meal, so it tasted amazing.

"So we leave for the Northern Mist tomorrow," Kohath said. "You guys nervous?"

Shaphan laughed at him. "Nervous? Not the least bit. Come tomorrow, and we'll be the second group to ever successfully venture into the Northern Mist."

"How are you so sure that we'll be successful?"

"How could I not? After all, we have the first group to ever successfully explore the Northern Mist right here with us. We got Adonai. Ain't that right, Adonai?"

The others agreed, but Adonai grew a bit serious. "I'll be doing my best, but don't expect everyone to return alive."

For a moment, it was quiet around the fire again before Dathan broke the silence.

"Welp, it is what it is!" he exclaimed before gulping down some more wine. After that, the conversation changed to a less serious tone, with everyone joking around; even Adonai was able to have some good laughs.

Come morning, the camp was taken down and everyone prepared themselves to enter the Northern Mist. Adonai had his silvery-blue armor on and held his helmet at his hip. He stood at the front of the crack, facing the rest of the extermination team.

"When we enter, the Mist will seem normal and safe. That's a trap. Once we've reached a certain point, the effects of the Mist will set in. You'll lose your senses, your ability to think, your mind. It is of utmost importance that we stick close together and do not panic. It will take some time for everyone to grow accustomed to the Mist. We will wait in one place until that happens. Is that understood?"

"Yes, sir!" the team said in unison.

Now that they were entering the Mist, Adonai had taken over as the leader of the extermination team. It was weird— all of these highly trained, incredibly powerful individuals were willingly at his command.

"Let's move out!" Adonai shouted as he turned and led the team into the crack. They left the horses behind with Ciela, as the animals would only be a hindrance in the Mist. When they reached the end of the tunnel and arrived at the wall of thick, white mist, Adonai continued forward without a second thought. William and Philip were right behind him, but they both stopped before passing through the white wall. Adonai turned around to see what was keeping them. He could understand their hesitation. The Mist was seen as a forbidden place, a place no man should ever attempt to enter.

William took a deep breath and entered, and Philip followed, along with the rest of the team. They marched in two lines, every man staying close to the person in front of them. After a while, Adonai stopped the line.

"This is it!" he announced. "This is where the real Mist begins!"

The team slowly pressed further until they all had reached the true Mist. The effects set in just as Adonai had said they would. There wasn't a single one of them who wasn't down on their knees, struggling with themselves.

"Deep breaths! Focus on regaining control of your mind! Get your thoughts straight!" Adonai instructed. Several of the team members were groaning or shouting in pain. They stayed there for hours. Finally, everyone seemed to get a grip. They regained their sanity, but their senses were still greatly distorted.

"Expand your auras! Use the mana around you to sense your surroundings!" Adonai told them.

But for some reason, they just couldn't seem to grasp the concept.

"Use your sixth sense!"

"We're trying!" Philip shouted in anger, frustrated that he couldn't use it like he normally could.

"Adonai, this just doesn't seem to be working. I can't use my sixth sense either," William told him.

"It's already been three days. We might be practically blind, but we can still fight. Just guide us already," Philip insisted.

"Alright," Adonai reluctantly agreed. He didn't understand why they couldn't do it. He didn't understand that they simply lacked the talent. "Stay close and stay on guard!" he shouted as they resumed their march.

Days passed by. Weeks. Adonai had to guide them slowly. He did his best to avoid the monsters, particularly the mana beasts. He went as far as taking the team on detours to avoid the occasional mana beast.

"Do you even know where you're going?" Philip demanded as they marched.

"Yes," Adonai told him.

"How? We've been wandering this place for weeks now. Do you even know where to find the volites?" Philip asked, irritated.

"Yes, I've been to the nest. I know where they are."

"Are ya sure? Cause it seems to me like we've been going in circles."

"It only seems that way because you can't use your sixth sense. You would think a soldier of your caliber would be capable of that much, but apparently not," Adonai said to him bluntly, which made Philip even angrier.

"Boy, you best watch that tongue of yours or you'll lose it."

"Philip, that's enough," William asserted.

After that, Philip didn't say anything more and just followed along. Suddenly, a loud roar rippled through the air. An absolutely terrifying roar. The roar of a blood curdler. Everyone in the line began to panic somewhat.

"What was that!" someone shouted. Someone else threw up.

"It's fine! It's fine!" Adonai shouted at them. "It's just a blood curdler!" Then there was another roar, this time from the other direction. There were two of them. Adonai's heart dropped when he heard a third roar. And then a fourth. And then a fifth. After five roars, everyone was in a state of panic. Adonai muttered a string of curses. Five blood curdlers. Why was there five?

"We're surrounded!" Philip shouted.

Even William was afraid, but he kept his composure. "What do we do, Adonai?" he asked.

Adonai muttered another curse. "Our large group must have attracted them. If it was one or two, it wouldn't be a problem. But five..."

"Then what does that mean?" William asked. One of the blood curdlers roared again; this time, it was closer.

"It means a lot of us are going to die," Adonai told him. He was doing his best trying to figure out what to do. He had to do something. Something. If only they could properly use their senses, then five blood curdlers wouldn't be a problem at all. Another roar tore through the air. The blood curdlers were all growing closer. Adonai kept thinking harder and harder. And then he had an idea. What if he shared his aura with the others? Lent them power that would help them use their sixth sense. Aura sharing was incredibly difficult, and doing so with this many people should be impossible. But he had to try. At this point, everyone had gathered into a tight circle.

"Adonai, it would be great if you did something!" Philip shouted.

"I'm working on it!" Adonai shouted back. He channeled his mana. Expanded his aura. And then, he injected it into each of the team members. And suddenly, it was as if their eyes were opened for the first time. William smiled to himself. With their senses recovered, everyone quickly regained their composure. They were ready to fight. More roars tore through the air, louder and closer than ever. The first of the blood curdlers charged into the group. Everyone was able to evade the attack and then quickly counterattacked. But the other blood curdlers weren't far behind. They lashed out at the extermination team members. Everyone scattered to avoid the attacks. Adonai whisked his spears around and sank them deep into the sides of the monsters. One after another, the extermination team members drove their swords into the blood curdlers' hides. Fireballs and boulders were tossed along with other elemental attacks. And one by one, the blood curdlers fell. When it was down to just the last one, Adonai leapt at it and slammed his spear down into the skull of the blood curdler. That was it. All five were dead. None of the team members were injured. A perfect battle.

"Let's keep going!" Adonai shouted after everyone had a moment to recuperate. Now that they could sense their surroundings with the aid of Adonai's mana, the marching speed picked up tremendously. He led them deeper into the Mist. "Just a little longer. A little longer, and then we'll arrive at the nest."

Chapter 56

Adonai stopped at the edge of the clearing. The extermination team had finally reached their destination. The volite nest lay right before them.

"We're here," Adonai told the others.

William nodded. "You can sense them, right?"

"Yeah, I can sense them." There were hundreds, thousands of volites teeming beneath the surface. "Let's go," Adonai said as he began to walk forward, but William grabbed his arm and stopped him.

"Wait, you've done well enough thus far. Let us take the lead from here." Adonai pulled away. "I can still fight."

"I know you can still fight, and I won't stop you from fighting. But you don't have to take the lead anymore. You're still just a kid, you shouldn't be risking your life on the front lines. Just stand back and provide support from behind."

Adonai only nodded and took a step back. He wasn't a leader, he knew that. But during the time when he had been guiding the extermination team, it had felt like he really was a leader. He liked that. He liked the feeling of having a purpose.

William turned around to face the rest of the team and began speaking. "This is it. We've come all this way for this very moment. The volite nest lies right before us. These monsters evolve as the battle goes on. We must not give them that chance. Let us finish this and go home."

As they marched across the clearing to the nest, the ground began to rumble.

"They're coming," Philip muttered.

"Formations!" William shouted. Everyone had their weapons drawn. Adonai stood at the back of the group with his spears. The cries of the volites grew louder and louder. And then the beasts began to pour out from the nest and charge toward the extermination team. Thousands of them. But these volites were all weak. They were all completely unevolved, it was like they were seeing the volites' true form for the first time. They were almost as large as a horse, and they had insect-like bodies. The team cut them down by the dozens. With every swing of his sword, William was able to cut down a dozen volites all at once. Adonai remained at the back, his spears flying through the air and impaling every monster that crossed their path. This one-sided slaughter went on and on. The corpses piled up and up, and the ground was soaked in blood. Hundreds died. Thousands died. And then they stopped coming. Adonai and the extermination team stood on a mountain of corpses. All the volites were dead. Or at least the weak ones were. Because what emerged from the nest next were humanoid volites that had auras encompassing their bodies. They were the volites that had escaped the battle in Never Thaw. There were eight of them in all.

"Be ready," William told everyone. "These ones are different."

The volites approached slowly as they looked over the carnage that was strewn about their home. Adonai gripped his spear tighter. The two groups stood facing off against each other. One of the volites, the largest of the eight, which was covered in thick purple skin, muttered something.

"What?" William called out to it after he failed to hear it.

"Kill you... I'm going to kill you," the volite repeated in a raspy voice.

William raised his sword so it was pointing at the monster. "Then do it. Kill me."

The volite gave out a war cry and was soon followed by the others, and then they charged. The two forces clashed. These volites were actually capable of fighting the extermination team. The purple volite had lunged for William. He slashed it with his sword, and it fell backwards down the hill of corpses. But then it got back up.

"Kill. Must kill," the volite continued to mutter to itself. It roared again, and its aura flared as it came barreling toward William. He swung his sword for it again, but it dodged this time and punched him in the ribs. The hit hurt, but it wasn't nearly enough to cause any serious harm. The volite continued to throw lightning-fast punches, and William continued to cut with his sword. The two weaved and danced around each other's attacks. The same was happening throughout the rest of the battlefield. The volites and extermination team members were locked in a heated battle. Adonai flew around and looked for opportunities to smite the volites down with his spears. One by one, he found these opportunities, and one of the spears would blindside the targeted volite. And as each volite fell, the easier the battle became. And just like that, there was only one volite left. The team surrounded it.

It was bloody and beaten; it coughed up some blood and then said, "You'll die for this. You'll all die for this—"

"Shut up," Philip said as he blasted its head off with a fireball. A few of the men had been slightly injured— a few cuts, bruises, and broken bones. Nothing serious.

"Let's keep going," William told the team, though he didn't really need to. They could all sense it. There were still more volites down below ground. And these ones were far more powerful than the ones they had fought so far. They climbed down the mountain of corpses and ventured into the depths of the volite nest. Adonai took up the rear while William and Philip took the lead. The nest was made up of several tunnels that branched out in all directions. But because they could sense the remaining volites, they knew which paths to take. And since all the weak volites had already rushed out to fight them, there was nothing to slow them down. The extermination team arrived in a large chamber, a very large chamber. The other end of the chamber branched out into five different tunnels.

"I'm sure you can all sense that," William said.

"Of course," Philip answered.

A powerful mana was overflowing from each of the five tunnels, the five guardians of the Queen.

"It looks like we split up into five groups," William began. "The first group will comprise of me, Raphael, Hebron—"

"Wait," Philip cut him off. "I'm sure you've noticed, the mana coming from the middle tunnel is stronger than the others. Since we're the strongest, the both of us should take the middle tunnel together."

William didn't like the idea of grouping up with Philip, but he had to agree with what he said. "Very well. Then the third group who will be taking care of the middle tunnel will be me, Philip, Raphael, and Edna." William then went on to organize the other four groups. The first group consisted of Hebron, Philemon, Shaphan, and Adonai. The second group consisted of Dathan, Samson, and Kohath. The fourth group was Luke, Triton, and Rachel. And the last group was Naiad, Huck, and Nivi. With all the groups formed, they were ready.

"Let's finish this," William said as he turned around to face the tunnels.

Chapter 57

Adonai walked at the back of the group while Hebron led it. They had been walking down the first tunnel for a while now, and the presence of the volite was growing stronger. None of them talked to each other; they were all on edge. A high-pitched bugling echoed through the cave. Hebron raised a hand, signaling the group to stop. They all entered fighting stances as the volite approached them. The volite had a humanoid figure and the head of an elk with large antlers. Hard scales covered its muscular body. The volite stopped a short distance away.

"We'll attack together—" Philemon began, but his words were cut off.

Blood splattered across Adonai's face, and Philemon's now headless body fell to the ground. Adonai's eyes went wide. He frantically spun around to face the volite. In an instant, it had dashed past them, smiting off Philemon's head as it passed. They had been taken off guard. This volite was fast, very fast. The volite slowly turned around to face the group. All at once, everyone attacked. Wooden tendrils burst up from the ground as well as the tunnel walls and ceiling. Adonai sent all his spears speeding toward the volite. The volite danced around as it evaded and blocked the attacks. Shaphan continued to send wooden tendrils chasing after the volite as Hebron engaged with his sword. Adonai snapped his fingers, and his spears burst into white flames. As the volite continued to defend itself against the onslaught, it began to evolve. Two more arms suddenly popped out from the volite's side, so that it had four, and its movements were speeding up. A wooden tendril pulled at the volite's leg, and Hebron slashed it with his sword. It tore out from the wooden shackles, and as it furiously threw punches at Hebron, one of Adonai's spears landed and pierced through the back of the volite. It cried out in pain as the burning spear dug deeper into its flesh. It ripped the spear out and tossed it aside, while at the same time swatting away other spears. A giant wooden tendril shot up from the ground and smacked the volite, sending it staggering to the side. Another one of Adonai's spears planted itself in the volite's body. Four more spears quickly followed. Hebron ran in to deal the final blow, but as he swung down, the volite caught his sword and then punched him in the stomach, sending him flying back. For a moment, the battle came to a pause. Shaphan helped Hebron to his feet. The volite was bloody; there were five spears sticking out of its back and chest. The volite ripped out one of the spears that had been in its chest and tossed it aside. It snorted as it glared at its enemies. Adonai was the first to make another move. He sent his spears flying toward the volite, and it jumped out of the way. Again, an intense battle resumed as Hebron and Shaphan attacked in unison. An exchange of attacks was made at an incredible pace, and blows were landed on both the extermination team and the monster. As they battled, the volite reached out and managed to grab hold of one of Shaphan's arms and rip it off. Shaphan gritted his teeth and went on fighting as if it never happened. The volite was being harmed faster than it could evolve. And finally, they gained the edge over it. One blow after another was landed. The volite was cut, bashed, and beaten. Hebron dealt the final blow, cutting off the volite's head with his sword. The headless body staggered backward and then fell to the ground. Adonai wiped the sweat from his brow. They were all out of breath. Shaphan sealed his wound as they all made their way over to where Philemon's corpse lay. Hebron muttered a curse. Adonai offered a silent prayer to Inuuk.

"We should keep going," Hebron said at last. "I'm sure you two can sense it . . . there's another one further down. Our job isn't finished yet."

Dathan led Samson and Kohath through the second tunnel. "It should be here soon," Dathan said. Suddenly, a powerful gust of wind surged through the tunnel. The three of them shielded their faces with their arms. Even with their feet firmly planted, they couldn't stop the wind from slowly pushing them back. And then, after just a few seconds, the wind died down, and the volite appeared. It also had a humanoid form. Its body was covered in feathers and a thick aura, and two extremely large wings sprouted from its back. It walked on a pair of talons and had two long arms. It watched the group with its wide yellow eyes.

Dathan cracked his neck and tightened his grip on his sword. "Let's get this over with."

He charged forward with impeccable speed. Wooden tendrils burst out from the tunnel and attacked the volite. The volite jumped backward and unleashed another powerful gust of wind with a single flap of its wings. Dathan stomped on the ground, and a wooden wall rose up in front of him and blocked the wind. When the gust died down, he kicked the wooden wall he had created, and it went flying at the volite. The volite smacked it aside, and with another powerful flap of its wings, it came barreling forward with its talons raised. Dathan leapt out of the way, but the volite continued on past him. It began to attack Kohath with rapid attacks. Kohath launched fireballs, and Samson called forth great wooden tendrils to attack. Kohath's sword clashed with the volite's claws, and sparks flew in the air. Dozens of attacks were made in a matter of seconds. Dathan came running to assist Kohath, who was slowly being driven back. Dathan was too late. The volite slashed Kohath across the chest with its talons. He fell to the ground, and a pool of blood quickly began to form around him. Samson cursed and charged. The volite darted away, avoiding his attack, but as soon as it had done that, Dathan was flying toward it. It evaded Dathan, but then Samson was flying toward it again. A game of cat and mouse started as the volite darted back and forth around the tunnel, and Dathan and Samson chased it. They darted back and forth and back and forth. Finally, Dathan crashed into the volite and tackled it to the ground. He stabbed one of its wings with his sword. As it cried out in pain, Samson landed right beside it and drove his sword into the volite's chest. As it squirmed around, wooden tendrils rose up from the ground around it, and then they fell upon the volite, swallowing it into the ground. Dathan ran to Kohath's side, who was bleeding out on the ground. His breathing was growing shallower and shallower.

"Hold on, Kohath, just hold on. We'll get you outta here," Dathan said as he choked back tears.

Kohath coughed up some blood. "It's alright. Don't worry about me—"

"No, we can still save you."

"No . . . you can't. But it's alright, I've lived a good life." Kohath shut his eyes, and his shallow breathing came to a stop.

"Kohath? Kohath! Kohath!" Dathan shook his body, trying to wake him up. He was in hysterics. Kohath had served under him for years and years. They were close friends. And now that friend was dead.

"He's moved on," Samson said, trying to comfort Dathan. "We

need to move on as well. Our job here isn't finished."

Dathan wiped his tears away and stood up. He didn't say anything more; he just walked silently in the direction of the powerful presence he felt.

William, Raphael, Philip, and Edna walked through the third tunnel. The presence coming from this tunnel had been the strongest. But even though this tunnel seemed the most dangerous, William didn't quite understand why Philip insisted they should go together. Neither of them liked the other. There was one possibility that came to mind . . . But that seemed ridiculous. The volite groaned loudly as they approached. This one was strange. It was like a giant ball of flesh that hovered in the air with hundreds of tentacles draping down from its body. There were dozens of eyes spread all across the volite's grotesque body.

"This will be fun," Raphael said with a smirk.

"No. No, I don't think it will," William replied.

The volite attacked, its slimy tentacles thrashing around. William and the others blocked the attacks with their swords. Philip fired a beam of fire that burned through dozens of tentacles. Wooden tendrils were also bursting up from the ground, entangling the volite. Edna launched shards of ice. Still, the tentacles continued to attack relentlessly. Every time William cut down one of the tentacles, another would take its place. Philip continued to blast it with fire. One of the tentacles slammed into Raphael's side, sending him crashing into the tunnel wall and breaking several of his ribs. At last, William had had enough; he dashed forward, and with a single swipe of his blade, he cut down dozens of tentacles. He landed on the giant ball of flesh and plunged his sword into it. The volite squealed in pain and began to thrash around more violently. William pushed his sword in deeper. Then Philip landed on the volite next to him. Philip pressed both hands against the volite, and a stream of fire erupted from them.

"Cover me!" Philip shouted as he continued to blast the volite.

Dozens and dozens of tentacles were flying toward them. William took his sword and cut down every tentacle in a lightning-fast chain of attacks. Philip soon burned a massive hole all the way through the volite's body. It crashed into the ground, where it squirmed around briefly before it finally went motionless.

"That wasn't too bad—" Raphael began. His sentence stopped when a blade went through his back and out his chest. "Wha-what . . . Why . . . is there a sword in me?"

William watched Raphael's body fall to the ground as Edna pulled her sword out from his back. Then William was stabbed in the back as well.

"Sorry to do this to ya," Philip snarled, "But we've been wanting to get rid of you for a long time. At least some of us. Most of 'em wanted to recruit you, bring you over to our side. But I disagree with that. I'd rather you just die."

He pulled his sword out of him. But when he did, William didn't fall to the ground. He stayed standing on his feet. And then he slowly turned around to look Philip in the eye as blood seeped from the large wound in his abdomen.

"If you'd rather I just die, then you should have killed me properly," William said coldly.

Philip's smirk didn't go away, though. He blasted William, engulfing his body in fire. But as William burned, he still remained on his feet, unmoving. "Did you really think this much would kill a Pillar?"

Now Philip wasn't smiling. He went to stab William again, but William caught the blade and pushed him back. Edna charged at William from behind. Without even turning around, he swung his sword and slashed off Edna's head. Philip climbed back to his feet. The fire that had engulfed William went out. His body was covered in burns, yet he seemed completely unfazed. Philip dashed at him. Their swords collided and clashed against each other over and over again. Philip was giving it his all. But William . . . William wasn't even trying. Philip jumped back, putting some distance between them; he was breathing heavily.

"Do you really think you can hold out in that state? Just give in. Just die," Philip told him.

"If I'm going to die, then why don't you tell me about the black cloaks. What is it you're after?" William asked, and Philip groaned.

"Oh come on. You already know what it is we're after. And you also already know who most of us are. Honestly . . ." A wide smile spread across Philip's face. "That's what makes you so amusing. You know this war is coming, but there's absolutely nothing you can do about it. Nothing!"

William charged, and their swords clashed again. "Tell me! Tell me everything you know!" he shouted.

Philip was still grinning. Wooden tendrils burst up through the volite's body they were fighting on and wrapped around Philip's ankles. William knocked Philip's sword out of his hand and then cut his head off. Philip's body fell to the ground and turned to ash. William muttered some curses. He looked to where Edna had died; her body had also turned to ash. Black cloaks, both of them. He sealed his wound. It hurt, but he would be fine. What he needed to do right now was keep going. The mission wasn't finished.

The fourth group consisted of Triton, Rachel, and Luke. Triton led the way down the tunnel.

"How do you think the others are faring?" Luke asked his companions.

"They're probably fine," Rachel replied.

"What about Philip? Do you think he succeeded?"

There was a pause before Rachel answered, "It's hard to say; that William is a Pillar, he's strong."

"Yeah, but he's just a mortal."

"True," Rachel agreed and then said, "That William is probably dead."

"What should we do if he survives?" Luke asked.

Rachel shrugged. "He'll probably be weakened, we'll just have to finish him off."

"Stop," Triton said abruptly. "It's here." A figure had appeared in the tunnel, and shortly after, the volite came into full view. It was hideous. It had a humanoid body covered in thick gray fur. It had the head of a snake, the tail of a scorpion, and hooves for its feet. The sound of its hooves clacking against the ground echoed through the tunnel. The three Telestials drew their swords.

"That thing's ugly," Rachel commented. They spread out and waited as the volite came closer and closer until it was only several meters away, where it began to emit an aura. The volite hissed and dashed toward Triton, who was in the middle. He evaded its claws as it swiped at him. Then it struck with its tail and hit Triton in the shoulder. Searing pain instantly shot through his entire body. Before the volite could harm him any further, Luke came flying in and kicked it. The kick knocked the volite off its feet and toward Rachel, who proceeded to grab it and slam it into the ground. She began beating it ferociously while she sat on top of it. Luke dashed and cut off the volite's tail before it could attack Rachel. Luke then joined in on the beating by kicking the volite in the head as Rachel punched it. Triton stumbled over, fighting through the pain, and also began to kick the volite. They beat it. And beat it. And beat it. The volite stood no chance. Finally, it stopped struggling. That was when Rachel stopped punching. Luke and Triton stopped kicking shortly after. Its body had been turned into a bloody pulp. Triton spat on its corpse.

"That's enough for this bugger. Let's move on, I can sense another." The others grunted in agreement. He and Rachel began to walk away; Luke got in one last kick and then joined them.

"Hopefully, the next one will put up more of a fight," Rachel griped.

Naiad, Huck, and Nivi took the last tunnel.

"This thing's emitting a strong aura," Nivi said to the others as they walked.

"Eh, it ain't that strong," Naiad said. She lied; it was a strong aura, and she was honestly a little scared.

"My back is itching to fight," Huck complained.

"That's just your rash," Nivi told him.

"Oh yeah, I forgot about that," Huck said, embarrassed. Huck wasn't very smart.

A howl echoed through the tunnel. The volite leapt out from the darkness and landed before them. It was like a giant monkey, but it had two heads and two tails. The volite was holding a club and seemed to dance around when it saw them. "New prey, new prey," it sang to itself, clapping its hands. Huck clapped along but stopped when Naiad glared at him. Suddenly, the volite's happy mood seemed to vanish, and its aura flared. It slammed its fists on the ground and roared. Then it charged. Naiad launched shards of ice, and Nivi launched shards of metal. Huck stepped forward to confront the volite head-on. The volite used its thick forearms to block the shards and then bashed Huck with the club, sending him flying into the wall. It continued its charge toward Naiad. She rolled out of the way as it bashed the ground with its club. Then it continued to swing and swing. Naiad nimbly ducked and evaded every attack. Nivi was still launching shards of metal. Blood dripped from where all the shards had struck the volite, but it seemed unfazed by them.

The volite raised its club to swing at Naiad again, but Huck tackled it, making it drop its club. His body was covered in armor made of rock. He got in a few punches before the volite threw him off. Nivi stabbed one of its heads with her sword. But that didn't kill it; instead, the volite became enraged. It swung its arm in a wide arc. Nivi jumped back in time to dodge the volite's attack. Naiad didn't. The strike hit her and completely destroyed her body, splattering her against the wall. Huck chucked a boulder that burst apart when it slammed into the volite, making it stagger. Nivi launched another metal shard that hit the volite in one of its eyes. It roared out in pain and blindly charged at her. As she ran away, Huck stomped on the ground, and a series of rock spikes burst up from the ground at the volite. It crashed into the spikes and wailed out in pain. Nivi dashed toward it and smote off the remaining head, killing it.

After the battle, Huck wandered over to where Naiad had been killed. There was nothing that even came close to resembling a body.

"Naiad?" Huck asked while sadly staring at the gore.

"Naiad's gone," Nivi told him and then continued, "Let's keep going. We're not done." Huck wiped at his nose, grunted, and followed her.

Chapter 58

The five tunnels all led to the final and largest chamber of the nest. Luke, Triton, and Rachel were the first to arrive. They wished they weren't. What they had stumbled upon was the Queen's chamber. Eggs covered the ground and walls. The Queen was curled up in the back of the room. She was big. Very big. She uncurled as the three extermination team members arrived in the room. She had thirteen serpent-like heads and stood on six thick legs, each of them ending with vicious claws, and she had a long thick tail. Her body was covered in black scales. A red aura formed around the Queen and filled the entire chamber. Triton muttered a curse.

"How are we supposed to win against that?" Luke said to himself.

The Queen made a low growling noise as her heads lifted up and scanned the room, her gaze falling upon the three Telestials. None of them moved.

"Intruders . . ." The voice caught them all off guard. The Queen was speaking to them through a mana link.

"Be ready!" Triton shouted as the heads all reared back. Their mouths opened and a fire began to rise up in the back of their throats.

"Perish," the Volite Queen uttered.

The heads all unleashed a torrent of fire that engulfed the entire room. All Triton and the others could do was shield their bodies with as much mana as they could muster. The fire raged for several seconds before dying down.

"You guys still alive?" Rachel shouted.

"Yeah . . . let's kill this wretched beast," Luke responded as he shook the soot off his body. Then he pushed off the ground and launched himself at the Queen. As the heads snapped at him, he spun around in a circle while swinging his sword. The slash extended past the blade and cut into everything in the path of the swing, the Queen as well as the chamber walls all around. But the attack didn't do nearly enough damage. As soon as Luke landed, he darted backwards away from the Queen just in time to avoid being crushed by one of her legs. Though she was big, she was agile. Luke returned to Triton and

Rachel's side where they observed the reaction of the Queen. After a few seconds, her wounds began to quickly heal. The Queen paid no heed to her eggs when she trampled them as she charged at the three. They evaded her relentless attacks while looking for openings to attack.

Adonai was walking with Hebron and Shaphan when the tunnel began to rumble violently.

"We need to hurry," Hebron said and then he broke out into a sprint.

Adonai and Shaphan followed right behind. None of them mentioned it, but the presence coming from the end of the tunnel was far stronger than the Volite they had just faced. When they arrived at the chamber, they found Triton, Luke, and Rachel in a fierce battle with the Queen. At the same time, Huck and Nivi also arrived. They all had the same reaction, a reaction of dread. One of the heads snapped shut on Triton in mid-air and then another one of the heads quickly bit down on the other half of his body, and he was ripped apart.

"Shaphan, help me tie it down!" Hebron shouted as he threw up his arms.

Giant wooden tendrils shot up from the ground and latched onto the Queen and pulled her down. She thrashed around trying to break out of the restraints. When she couldn't, she unleashed another torrent of flames that once again engulfed the entire room. Everyone managed to shield themselves from the heat, that is, everyone except Rachel. She was already running out of stamina and didn't have the strength to shield herself against the fire, and the flames consumed her. When the fire died down, Hebron immediately dashed at the Queen, and with a powerful swing, he cut off one of the heads. But as the fight went on, the head quickly regenerated and it was the same with the other wounds. And most of the elemental attacks did nothing to pierce the thick black scales. Hebron jumped away from the fight when Dathan's group arrived.

"How's the fight looking?" Dathan asked.

"Bleak," Hebron responded. "Everything we try isn't working. It just regenerates the moment we harm it."

"My spears are doing nothing," Adonai added.

"Constant attacks to wear it down aren't going to work. If we're going to kill this thing, we've gotta hit it with a powerful attack strong enough to take it down in one blow," Hebron told them.

"Where's William's group? The only one capable of delivering a blow like that is either William or Philip," Dathan responded.

"Is there no one else?" Samson asked.

Hebron turned and looked at Adonai. "Can you?"

"I can try—" Adonai responded.

"Shield yourselves!" Hebron suddenly shouted. The Queen unleashed another powerful wave of fire. Huck screamed out as the fire devoured him.

"Just keep it distracted," Adonai told them when the fire died down. They nodded and charged into battle. Adonai took one of his spears and began to fill it with as much mana as he could. He imbued it with lightning, fire, poison, and space distortion, and all of that was amplified by the celestite. He was using so much mana that his body began to convulse slightly and blood seeped from his nose, but even then, he kept on pouring in mana. Then he threw the spear with every ounce of strength he could muster. The spear made contact with one of the heads and completely obliterated it. The spear continued through two more of the heads and then into the body, blowing a massive hole through the body. The Queen wailed out in pain and collapsed to the ground. Everyone stopped. The heart and organs were exposed from the hole made by the spear and the entrails were spilling out. The heart wasn't beating. It seemed dead. Adonai's chest heaved as he struggled to breathe. He had put everything into that one attack. But he did it. The Queen was dead. Hebron and Dathan arrived at his side.

Hebron set a hand on his shoulder. "You alright?"

"Yeah-yeah, I think I'm fine," Adonai stuttered.

But then it beat. The heart. It began to beat again. Adonai sank to the ground as he watched the wounds begin to close up.

"Hurry! Finish it off!" Hebron shouted. They all charged. That was what the Queen wanted. Her own bones shot out of her skin as long, thin spikes. It caught them all off guard; they barely managed to evade the attack. Most of them. Samson and Nivi were both impaled. The bones retracted and the Queen climbed back to her feet as her wounds continued to heal. Giant wooden tendrils shot up from the ground and grabbed hold of the Volite Queen, but she broke out of them. This entire time, she hadn't just been healing, she had been steadily growing stronger. Adonai's heart sank even further as he watched the heads rear back yet again. He didn't have the strength to shield himself. The fire would consume him this time. The others were unaware of this. They wouldn't be helping him. Adonai closed his eyes and prepared for the end. But as the Queen unleashed the fire, a barrier was formed around him. He opened his eyes and saw William standing there next to him.

"William . . . you're finally here. It's all left up to you. Everyone is worn out. We can't finish this," Adonai said to him.

William smiled. "That's alright. I'll show you what it means to be a Pillar." The fire died down. William planted his feet and exploded off the ground. The Queen saw him and her heads lashed out at him. With a single swing of his sword, he cut down every head that was before him. And then with an unbelievably fast chain of attacks, he cut the Queen into chunks. She crashed into the ground, dead. Adonai watched with wide eyes. He had thought his strength was far superior to everyone else's. But he was wrong. With this, he realized that there wasn't just a massive gap between those who were average and those who were strong, but that there was an even larger gap between the strong and the strongest.

William walked back over to Adonai and helped him to his feet. "Let's go home," he said with a smile, and Adonai also cracked half a smile. They had done it. They defeated the Queen.

Chapter 59

"Adonai, Adonai," Mary chimed, pulling him along, "I've been practicing my meditation. Come look, come look."

Adonai couldn't help but smile. "Alright, alright, I'm coming."

They went out to the garden to their favorite spot below the apple tree. They had only recently returned to Plain City. The extermination team's mission had been a success, but it came with a heavy price. Of the seventeen that ventured out into the Mist, only six came back alive: Adonai, William, Hebron, Dathan, Shaphan, and Luke. With the expedition over, Adonai returned to the monastery in Plain City.

"Alright, let's see it," Adonai told Mary.

She sat down, squeezed her eyes shut, and began to take deep breaths. Slowly, the mana within her began to stir and grow. It was subtle, but it was something. She peeked one of her eyes open. "Am I doing it?"

Adonai chuckled and praised her. "Yeah, you're doing great." She grinned real big and closed her eye again. Adonai lay down next to her and looked up at the sky. There were a few clouds slowly blowing by. As he gazed up, deep feelings welled up inside of him. He was happy being here with Mary, but . . . there was still a feeling of . . . emptiness. It was hard to describe, really. As he lay there with his new sister, William wandered into the garden.

"Mind if I sit here?" William asked.

Adonai nodded. "Go ahead."

They sat in silence for a moment before Adonai spoke up. "So, what are you still doing here in Plain City?"

"Just wrapping up a few things. I leave tomorrow."

"I see . . ."

William cleared his throat. "There was actually something I wanted to talk to you about."

"Yeah? What'd you want to talk about?" Adonai asked.

"I was curious about you. You're a talented individual, more talented than anyone I've ever seen. You have the potential to see a bright future. I wanted to offer that future to you . . . I want you to become one of my captains."

Mary started listening to their conversation when she heard that.

"You want me to become one of your captains?" Adonai asked.

William nodded. "Yes, of course, you can't become a captain right away. You'll have to graduate from an academy first. But once you've done that, you can work for me as a captain. Of course, just being a captain won't be your limit. Chances are you'll become a Pillar one day, maybe even a Cornerstone."

Adonai sat quietly as he thought it over, then he looked over at Mary, who looked worried. "I appreciate the offer . . . but I can't leave Mary behind." For a moment, they all sat there in silence.

"What if you don't have to leave her?" William started.

"What do you mean?" Adonai asked.

"What if I became her guardian and yours too? You'll need a benefactor to get into a good academy anyways, so I was already planning on taking you under my wing. It's no problem to give Mary a home as well," William said.

Mary's face lit up, and she got excited. "You mean we're gonna become a family?" she beamed.

William nodded, and Adonai smiled slightly. "Yeah, we're gonna become a family."

www.ingramcontent.com/pod-product-compliance
Lightning Source LLC
Chambersburg PA
CBHW070550260626
47161CB00002B/562